SOUTH BY JAVA HEAD

"Excitements come and go at breathless speed charged with superhuman courage, skill and stamina." THE TIMES

"Gripping. The action is fast and furious. Alistair MacLean is an outstanding writer of descriptive prose." BIRMINGHAM MAIL

ALISTAIR MACLEAN

South
by Java Head

Collins

FONTANA BOOKS

First published 1958
First issued in Fontana Books 1961
Fifteenth Impression June 1970

TO IAN

© *Alistair MacLean 1958*
Printed in Great Britain
Collins Clear-Type Press
London and Glasgow

bides its time beyond the horizon. It was the silence that comes upon men when they have not slept for a long, long time, and they are very tired. But, above all, it was the silence that comes with waiting. That kind of waiting where a man's nerves are stretched out on a rack, and every hour more of waiting is another turn of the rack, and if the waiting doesn't end soon the rack will turn too far and the nerves tear and sunder with the strain—but if the waiting does end then that will be even worse for it will be the end not only of the waiting, it will almost certainly be the end of everything.

The men of the *Viroma* had been waiting for a long time now. Or perhaps not such a long time—it was only a week since the *Viroma*, with a false funnel, dummy ventilators, the newly painted name of *Resistencia* and flying the flag of the Argentine republic, had rounded the Northern tip of Sumatra and steamed into the Malacca Straits in broad daylight. But a week has seven days, every day twenty-four hours and every hour sixty minutes. Even a minute can be a long time when you are waiting for something which must inevitably happen, when you know that the laws of chance are operating more and more inexorably against you, that the end cannot be much longer delayed. Even a minute can be a long, long time when the first bomb or the first torpedo may be only seconds away, and you have ten thousand, four hundred tons of fuel oil and high octane gasoline beneath your feet . . .

The telephone above the flag locker shrilled jarringly, insistently, cutting knife-like through the leaden silence on the bridge. Vannier, slight, brown-haired, an officer of only ten weeks standing, was nearest to it. He whirled round, startled, knocked over the binoculars on the locker-top behind him, and fumbled the receiver off its hook. Even through the tan the red flush could be seen creeping up through neck and face.

" Bridge here. What is it?" The voice was meant to be crisp, authoritative. It didn't quite come off. He listened for a few moments, said thank you, hung up and turned round to find Nicolson standing beside him.

" Another distress signal," he said quickly. Nicolson's cold blue eyes always made him feel flustered. " Up north somewhere."

" Up north somewhere." Nicolson repeated the words, his tone almost conversationaal, but carrying an undertone that made Vannier squirm. " What position? What ship?" There was a sharp edge to Nicolson's voice now.

"I—I don't know. I didn't ask."

Nicolson looked at him for a long second, turned away, reached down the phone and began to crank the generator handle. Captain Findhorn beckoned to Vannier and waited until the boy had walked hesitantly across to his corner of the bridge.

"You should have asked, you know," the captain said pleasantly. "Why didn't you?"

"I didn't think it necessary, sir." Vannier was uncomfortable, on the defensive. "It's our fourth call to-day. You—you ignored the others, so I——"

"True enough," Findhorn agreed. "It's a question of priorities, boy. I'm not going to risk a valuable ship, a priceless cargo and the lives of fifty men on the off-chance of picking up a couple of survivors from an inter-island steamer. But this might have been a troopship, or a cruiser. I know it's not, but it might have been. And it might have been in a position where we could have given some help without sticking our necks out too far. All improbable 'ifs' and 'mights', but we must know where she is and what she is before we make a decision." Findhorn smiled and touched the gold-braided epaulettes on his shoulders. "You know what these are for?"

"You make the decisions," Vannier said stiffly. "I'm sorry, sir."

"Forget it, boy. But one thing you might remember—to call Mr. Nicolson 'sir' once in a while. It's—ah—expected."

Vannier flushed and turned away. "Sorry again, sir. I don't usually forget. I'm—well, I think I'm just a little bit tired and edgy, sir."

"We all are," Findhorn said quietly. "And not a little bit, either. But Mr. Nicolson isn't—he never is." He raised his voice. "Well, Mr. Nicolson?"

Nicolson hung up the receiver and turned round.

"Vessel bombed, burning, possibly sinking," he said briefly. "0.45 N, 104.24 E. That makes it the Southern entrance to the Rhio channel. Name of the vessel uncertain. Walters says the message came through very fast, very clear at first, but quickly deteriorated into crazy nonsense. He thinks the operator was seriously injured and finally collapsed over his table and key, for he finished up with a continuous send—it's still coming through. Name of the ship, as far as Walters could make out, was the *Kenny Danke*.

"Never heard of it. Strange he didn't send his international call-sign. Nothing big, anyway. Mean anything to you?"

" Not a thing, sir." Nicolson shook his head, turned to Vannier. " Look it up in the Register anyway, please. Then look through the K's. Obviously the wrong name." He paused for a moment, the cold blue eyes remote, distant, then turned again to Vannier. " Look up the *Kerry Dancer*. I think it must be that."

Vannier riffled through the pages. Findhorn looked at his chief officer, eyebrows raised a fraction.

Nicolson shrugged. " A fair chance, sir, and it makes sense. N and R are very close in Morse. So are C and K. A sick man could easily trade them—even a trained man. If he was sick enough."

" You're right, sir." Vannier smoothed out a page of the directory. " The *Kerry Dancer*, 540 tons, *is* listed here. Clyde, 1922. Sulaimiya Trading Company——"

" I know them," Findhorn interrupted. " An Arab company, Chinese backed, sailing out of Macassar. They've seven or eight of these small steamers. Twenty years ago they had only a couple of dhows—that was about the time they gave up legitimate trading as a bad business and went in for the fancy stuff—guns, opium, pearls, diamonds, and little of that legally come by. Plus a fair amount of piracy on the side."

" No tears over the *Kerry Dancer*?"

" No tears over the *Kerry Dancer*, Mr. Nicolson. Course 130 and hold it there." Captain Findhorn moved through the screen door on to the port wing of the door. The incident was closed.

" Captain!"

Findhorn halted, turned round unhurriedly and looked curiously at Evans. Evans was the duty quartermaster, dark, wiry, thin-faced and with tobacco stained teeth. His hands rested lightly on the wheel, and he was looking straight ahead.

" Something on your mind, Evans?"

" Yes, sir. The *Kerry Dancer* was lying in the roads last night." Evans glanced at him for a moment then stared ahead again. " A Blue Ensign boat, sir."

" What!" Findhorn was jerked out of his normal equanimity. " A Government ship? You saw her?"

" I didn't see her, sir. The bo-sun did—I think. Anyway, I heard him talking about it last night—just after you'd come back from shore."

" Are you quite certain, man? He said that?"

" No mistake, sir." The high-pitched Welsh voice was very definite.

" Get the bo'sun up here at once!" Findhorn ordered. He went over to his chair, sat down, easy and relaxed, and thought back to the night just gone. He remembered his surprise—and relief—when he had gone over the side and found the bo'sun and carpenter manning the motor lifeboat that was to take him ashore, his surprise and relief when he had seen the butts of a couple of short Lee Enfields protruding beneath a piece of canvas thrown carelessly over them. He had said nothing about these. He remembered the distant sound of guns, the pall of smoke lying over Singapore from the last bombing raid —one could set a watch by the appearance of Japanese bombers over Singapore every morning—the weird, unnatural hush that had lain over city and roads. The roads themselves had been empty, deserted as he'd never known them, and he couldn't remember seeing the *Kerry Dancer* or any other ship flying the Blue Ensign as they went in. It had been too dark and he had had too much on his mind. And he had had even more to worry about on the way out. He had learnt that the oil islands of Poko Bukum, Pulo Sambo and Pulo Sebarok had been fired, or were to be fired—he had been unable to find out or even see for himself, the pall of smoke obscured everything. The last of the naval units had pulled out and there was no one to take his fuel oil. Nor his aviation spirit—the Catalinas were gone, and the only Brewster Buffaloes and Wildebeeste torpedo bombers that remained were charred skeletons on the Selengar Airfield. 10,400 tons of explosive fuel, trapped in the harbour of Singapore and——

" McKinnon, sir. You sent for me." Twenty years that hadn't missed out a sea or port in the world worth looking at had turned McKinnon from a raw, shy, unknowing Lewis boy to a byword among the sixty odd ships of the British Arabian Company for toughness, shrewdness and unvarying competence—but they hadn't altered a single inflexion in his slow, soft-spoken Highland voice, " About the *Kerry Dancer*?"

Findhorn nodded, said nothing, just continued looking at the dark, stocky figure before him. A commodore, he thought dryly, inconsequentially, has his privileges. The best first mate *and* the best bo'sun in the company . . .

" I saw her lifeboat yesterday evening, sir," McKinnon said quietly. " She left before us—with a full complement of passengers." He looked speculatively at the captain. " A hospital ship, Captain."

Findhorn climbed down off his chair and stood in front of

McKinnon, without moving, The two men were of a height, eye to eye. No one else moved. It was as if each one feared to break the sudden, utter stillness that had fallen on the bridge. The *Viroma* wandered one degree off course, then two, then three, and Evans made no move to correct it.

"A hospital ship," Findhorn repeated tonelessly. "A hospital ship, Bo'sun? She's only a little inter-island tramp—500 tons or so."

"That's right. But she's been commandeered, sir. I was talking to some of the wounded soldiers while Ferris and myself were at the jetty, waiting for you. Her captain's been given the option of losing his ship or sailing her to Darwin. There's a company of soldiers aboard to see that he does."

"Go on."

"That's all there is, sir. They filled up the second boatload before you came back—most of the cases were walking wounded but there were a few on stretchers. I believe there are five or six nurses, none British, and a little boy."

"Women, children and sick men and they stick them aboard one of the Sulaimiya Company's floating death-traps—and the whole archipelago swarming with Jap aircraft." Findhorn swore, quietly, savagely. "I wonder what mutton-headed genius in Singapore thought that one up."

"I don't know, sir," McKinnon said woodenly.

Findhorn looked at him sharply, then looked away again. "The question was purely rhetorical, McKinnon," he said coldly. His voice dropped almost an octave and he went on quietly, musingly, speaking to no one in particular, a man thinking aloud and not liking his thoughts at all.

"If we go north, the chances of our getting as far as Rhio and back again are less than remote: they do not exist. Let us not deceive ourselves about that. It may be a trap—it probably is: the *Kerry Dancer* left before us and she should have been through Rhio six hours ago. If it's not a trap, the probability is that the *Kerry Dancer* is at this moment sinking, or has sunk. Even if she is still afloat, fire will have forced passengers and crew to abandon ship. If they're just swimming around—most of them wounded men—there'll be mighty few of them left in the six or seven hours it would take us to get there."

Findhorn paused for some moments, lit a cigarette in defiance of the company's and his own regulations, and went on in the same flat monotone.

" They may have taken to their boats, if they had any boats left after bombs, machine-guns and fire had all had a go at them. Within a few hours all the survivors can land on any one of a score of islands. What chance have we got of finding the right island in total darkness in the middle of a storm—assuming that we were crazy enough—suicidal enough—to move into the Rhio Straits and throw away all the sea-room we must have in the middle of a typhoon?" He grunted in irritation as spiralling smoke laced his tired eyes—Captain Findhorn hadn't left the bridge all night—gazed down with mild surprise, as if seeing it for the first time, at the cigarette clipped between his fingers, dropped it and ground it out with the heel of his white canvas shoe. He stared down at the crushed stub for long seconds after it had gone out, then looked up, his gaze travelling slowly round the four men in the wheelhouse. The gaze meant nothing—Findhorn would never have included the quartermaster, bo'sun or the fourth officer in his counsels. " I can see no justification whatsoever for jeopardising the ship, the cargo and our lives on a wild goose chase."

No one said anything, no one moved. The silence was back again, heavy, foreboding, impenetrable. The air was still, and very airless—the approaching storm, perhaps. Nicolson was leaning against the flag locker, hooded eyes looking down at his hands clasped before him: the others were looking at the captain, and not blinking: the *Viroma* had now slewed yet further off course, ten, perhaps twelve degrees, and still swinging steadily.

Captain Findhorn's wandering gaze finally settled on Nicolson. The remoteness had gone from the captain's eyes now, when he looked at his first mate.

" Well, Mr. Nicolson?" he asked.

" You're perfectly right, sir, of course." Nicolson looked up, gazed out the window at the foremast swaying slowly, gently, under the lift of the deepening swell. " A thousand to one that it's a trap, or, if it isn't, ship, crew and passengers will all be gone by now—one way or another." He looked gravely at the quartermaster, at the compass, then back at Findhorn again. " But as I see we're already ten degrees off course and still slewing to starboard, we might as well save trouble and just keep on going round to starboard. The course would be about 320, sir."

" Thank you, Mr. Nicolson." Findhorn let his breath escape

44

in a long, almost inaudible sigh. He crossed over towards Nicolson, his cigarette case open. "For this once only, to hell with the rules. Mr. Vannier, you have the *Kerry Dancer's* position. A course for the quartermaster, if you please."

Slowly, steadily, the big tanker swung round, struck off to the north-west back in the direction of Singapore, into the heart of the gathering storm.

*   *   *

A thousand to one were the odds that Nicolson would have offered and the captain would have backed him in that and gone even further—and they would both have been wrong. There was no trap, the *Kerry Dancer* was still afloat and she hadn't been abandoned—not entirely.

Still afloat, at 2 o'clock on that sultry, breathless mid-February afternoon in 1942, but not looking as if she would be afloat much longer. She was deep in the water, down by the head and listing over so heavily to starboard that the well-deck guardrail was dipping into the sea, now lost in it, now showing clear as the long, low swell surged up the sloping deck and receded, like waves breaking on a beach.

The for-ard mast was gone, broken off about six feet above the deck; a dark, gaping hole, still smouldering, showed where the funnel had been, and the bridge was unrecognisable, a scrapyard shambles of buckled steel plates and fractured angle-irons, outlined in crazy, surrealist silhouette against a brazen sky. The fo'c'sle—the crew's quarters just for'ard of the well-deck—looked as if it had been opened up by a gigantic can-opener, the scuttles on the ship's side had disappeared completely and there was no trace of anchors, windlass or for'ard derrick winch; all this fo'c'sle damage the result, obviously, of a bomb that had penetrated the thin steel deck plating and failed to explode until it was deep inside the ship. No one there at the time could have known anything about it, for the lethal blast would have been far faster than realisation. Abaft the well-deck, the wood-lined accommodation quarters on the main and upper decks had been completely burnt out, gutted as far as the after well, sky and sea clearly visible through the gaunt and twisted framework.

It was impossible that human beings could have survived the bludgeoning, the consuming, metal-melting white heat that had reduced the *Kerry Dancer* to the charred, dead wreck drifting imperceptibly south-westwards towards the Abang Straits and faraway Sumatra. And, indeed, there was no life to be seen on what was left of the decks of the *Kerry Dancer*, no life to be seen any where, above or below. A deserted, silent skeleton, a dead hulk adrift on the China Sea. . . . But there were twenty-three people still alive in the after-castle of the *Kerry Dancer*.

Twenty-three people, but some of them had not much longer to live. These were the wounded soldiers, the stretcher cases that had been close enough to death already before the ship had pulled out from Singapore, and the concussive impact of the bombs and the gasping heat of the fires that had stopped short at the break of the after well-deck had destroyed what feeble resources and hold of life were left to most of them, and tipped the scales against recovery. There might have been hope for them, some slender hope, had they been brought out of that panting suffocation while there was yet time and lowered to the rafts and boats. But there had been no time. Within seconds of the first bomb falling, someone outside had sledge-hammered tight the eight clips that secured the only door—the water-tight door—that gave access to the upper deck.

Through this smoke-blackened door a man cried out from time to time, a cry not of pain but of anguished memory lacerating a darkening mind; there were whimpers, too, from other badly wounded men, again not moans of pain; the Eurasian nursing sister had with her all the drugs and sedatives she required, not pain but just the feeble, aimless murmur of dying men. Now and again a woman's voice could be heard, soothing, consoling, the soft sound of it punctuated from time to time by the deep angry rumble of a man. But mostly it was just the husky undertones of sick men and, very occasionally, the quivering indrawn breaths, the lost and lonely wailing of a little child.

*   *   *

Twilight, the brief tropical twilight, and the sea was milky white from horizon to horizon. Not close at hand—there it was green and white, great steep-sided walls of green, broken-topped and parallel-streaked with the wind-blown spume, waves that collapsed in a boiling, seething cauldron of rushing phosphorescence and foamed whitely across the low, wide decks of the *Viroma*, burying hatch-covers, pipe-lines and valves, burying, at times, even the catwalks, the gangways that stretched fore-and-aft eight feet above the deck. But further away from the ship, as far as the eye could see in the darkening night, there was nothing but the eerie, glistening whiteness of wind-flattened wave-tops and driving spray.

The *Viroma*, her big single screw thrusting under maximum power, lurched and staggered northwards through the storm. North-west should have been her course, but the fifty-knot wind that had hit her on the starboard beam, almost without warning and with the typical typhoon impact of a tidal wave moving at express speed, had pushed her far off course to the south and west close in to Sebanga. She was far round into the sea now, corkscrewing violently and pitching steeply, monotonously, as the big, quartering seas bore down on her starboard bow and passed over and below her. She shuddered every time her bows crashed into a trough, then quivered and strained throughout every inch of her 460 foot length when the bows lifted and fought their way clear of the press of cascading white water. The *Viroma* was taking punishment, severe punishment—but that was what she had been built for.

Up on the starboard wing of the bridge, muffled in oilskins, crouched down behind the negligible shelter of the canvas dodger, and with his eyes screwed almost shut against the lash of the driving rain, Captain Findhorn peered out into the gathering dusk. He didn't look worried, his chubby face was as composed, as impassive as ever, but he was worried, badly, and not about the storm. The wild staggering of the *Viroma*, the explosive, shuddering impact of plummeting bows burying themselves to the hawse-pipes in a massive head sea, would have been a terrifying experience for any landsman: Captain Findhorn barely noticed it. A deep-laden tanker has a remarkably low centre of gravity with corresponding stability—which doesn't make it roll any less but what matters is not the extent of the roll but whether or not a ship will recover from a roll, and a tanker always does: its system of water-tight cross bulkheads gives it enormous strength: and with the tiny access hatches securely battened down, the smooth, unbroken sweep of steel decks makes it the nearest thing afloat to a submarine. Where wind and weather are concerned, a tanker is virtually indestructible. Captain Findhorn knew that only too well, and he had sailed tankers through typhoons far worse than this, and not only across the rim, where he was now, but through the heart. Captain Findhorn was not worried about the *Viroma*.

Nor was he worried about himself. Captain Findhorn had

nothing left to worry about—literally: he had a great deal to look back upon, but nothing to look forward to. The senior captain of the British-Arabian Tanker Company, neither the sea nor his employers had anything more to offer him than two more years of command, retirement, and a sufficient pension. He had nowhere to go when he retired: his home for the past eight years, a modest bungalow off the Bukit Timor road, just outside the town of Singapore, had been destroyed by bombs in mid-January. His twin sons, who had always maintained that anyone who went to sea for a livelihood wanted his head examined, had joined the R.A.F. at the outbreak of war, and died in their Hurricanes, one over Flanders, one over the English Channel. His wife, Ellen, had survived the second son for only a few weeks. Cardiac failure, the doctor had said, which was a neat enough medical equivalent for a broken heart. Captain Findhorn had nothing to worry about, just nothing in the world—as far as he himself was concerned.

But selfishness had no root, no hold in Captain Findhorn's nature, and the emptiness of all that lay ahead had not robbed him of his concern for those for whom life still held much. He thought of the men under his command, men not like himself but men with parents and children, wives and sweethearts, and he wondered what moral justification, if any, he had had for risking the life of non-combatants in turning back towards the enemy. He wondered, too, about the oil beneath his feet again, about his justification, if any, for hazarding a priceless cargo so desperately needed by his country—the thought of the loss to his company he dismissed with the mental equivalent of an indifferent shrug. Lastly, and most deeply of all, he thought about his chief officer of the past three years, John Nicolson.

He did not know and he did not understand John Nicolson. Some woman might, some day, but he doubted whether any man ever would. Nicolson was a man with two personalities, neither of them in any way directly connected with his professional duties, or the manner of the performance of them, which was exceptional: next in line for command in the Anglo-Arabian fleet, Nicolson was regarded by Captain Findhorn as the finest officer he had had serve under him in his thirty-three years as master: unvaryingly competent when competence was called for, brilliant when competence was not enough, John Nicolson never made a mistake. His efficiency was almost inhuman. Inhuman, Findhorn thought, that was it, that was the other side of his character. Nicolson normally was courteous, considerate, even humorously affable: and then some strange sea-change would come over him and he became aloof, remote, cold—and above all ruthless.

There had to be a link, a meeting point between the two Nicolsons, something that triggered off the transition from one personality to another. What it was Captain Findhorn did not know. He did not even know the nature of the slender bond between Nicolson and himself, he was not close to Nicolson, but he believed he was closer than anyone he knew. It could have been the fact that they were both widowers, but it was not that. It should have been that, for the parallels were striking—both wives had lived in Singapore, Nicolson's on her first and his on her second five-year tour of duty in the Far East: both had died within a week of each other, and within a hundred yards of each other. Mrs. Findhorn had died at home grieving: Caroline Nicolson had died in a high-speed car smash almost outside the white-painted gates of Captain Findhorn's bungalow, victim of a drunken maniac who had escaped without as much as a single scratch.

Captain Findhorn straightened up, tightened the towel round his neck, wiped some salt from his eyes and lips and glanced at Nicolson, farther out on the wing of the bridge. He was quite upright, seeking no shelter behind the venturi dodger, hands resting lightly on the side of the bridge, the intense blue eyes slowly quartering the dusk-blurred horizon, his face impassive, indifferent. Wind and rain, the crippling heat of the Persian Gulf or the bitter sleet storms of the Scheldt in January were all the same to John Nicolson. He was immune to them, he remained always indifferent, impassive. It was impossible to tell what he was thinking.

The wind was backing now, slowly, very slowly, and as steadily increasing in strength, the brief tropical twilight was almost over, but the seas were as milky-white as ever, stretching away into the gloom. Findhorn could see their gleaming phosphorescence off to port and starboard, curving in a great heaving horseshoe round the stern, but he could see nothing for-ard. The *Viroma* was now thrusting north dead in the eye of the gale-force wind, and the heavy driving rain, strangely cold after the heat of the day, was sweeping almost horizontally fore and aft across the decks and the bridge, numbing his face with a thousand little lances, filling his eyes with pain and tears. Even with eyes screwed tight to the narrowest slits, the rain still stung and blinded: they were blind men groping in a blind world and the end of the world was where they stood.

Captain Findhorn shook his head impatiently, an impatience compounded equally of anxiety and exasperation, and called to Nicolson. There was no sign that he had been heard. Findhorn cupped his hands to his mouth and called again, realised that what little of his voice was not being swept away by the wind was being drowned by the crash of the plunging bows and the thin high whine in the halyards and rigging. He moved across to where Nicolson stood, tapped him on the shoulder, jerked his head towards the wheelhouse and made for there himself. Nicolson followed him. As soon as he was inside Findhorn waited for a convenient trough in the sea, eased forward the sliding door with the downward pitch of the ship, and secured it. The change from driving rain, wind and the roaring of the sea to dryness, warmth and an almost miraculous quiet was so abrupt, so complete, that it took mind and body seconds to accustom themselves to the change.

Findhorn towelled his head dry, moved across to the port for-ard window and peered through the Clear View Screen— a circular, inset plate or glass band-driven at high speed by an electric motor. Under normal conditions of wind and rain centrifugal force is enough to keep the screen clear and provide reasonable visibility. There was nothing normal about the conditions that night and the worn driving belt, for which they had no spare, was slipping badly. Findhorn grunted in disgust and turned away.

" Well, Mr. Nicolson, what do you make of it?"

" The same as you, sir." He wore no hat and the blond hair was plastered over head and forehead. " Can't see a thing ahead."

" That wasn't what I meant."

" I know." Nicolson smiled, braced himself against a sudden, vicious pitch, against the jarring shock that shook the windows of the wheelhouse. " This is the first time we've been safe in the past week."

Findhorn nodded. " You're probably right. Not even a maniac would come out looking for us on a night like this. Valuable hours of safety, Johnny," he murmured quietly, " and we would be better employed putting even more valuable miles between ourselves and brother Jap."

Nicolson looked at him, looked away again. It was impossible to tell what he was thinking, but Findhorn knew something at least of what he must be thinking, and swore quietly to himself. He was making it as easy as possible—Nicolson had only to agree with him.

" The chances of there being any survivors around are remote," Findhorn went on. " Look at the night. Our chances of picking anybody up are even more remote. Again, look at the night—and as you say yourself we can't see a damn' thing ahead. And the chances of piling ourselves up on a reef—or even a fair-sized island—are pretty high." He looked out a side window at the driving fury of the rain and the low, scudding cloud. " We haven't a hope of a star-sight while this lot lasts."

" Our chances *are* pretty thin," Nicolson agreed. He lit a cigarette, automatically returned the spent match to its box, watched the blue smoke eddying lazily in the soft light of the binnacle, then looked up at Findhorn. " How much do you give for the chances of any survivors on the *Kerry Dancer*, sir?"

Findhorn looked into the ice-cold blue of the eyes, looked away again, said nothing.

" If they took to the boats before the weather broke down, they'll be on an island now," Nicolson went on quietly. " There are dozens of them around. If they took to the boats later, they're gone long ago—a dozen of these coasters couldn't muster one regulation lifeboat between them. If there are any survivors we can save, they'll still be on the *Kerry Dancer*. A needle in a haystack, I know, but a bigger needle than a raft or a baulk of wood."

Captain Findhorn cleared his throat. " I appreciate all this, Mr. Nicolson——"

" She'll be drifting more or less due south," Nicolson interrupted. He looked up from the chart on the table. " Two knots, maybe three. Heading for the Merodong Straits—bound to pile up later to-night. We could come round to port a bit, still give Mesana Island a good offing and have a quick looksee."

" You're assuming an awful lot," Findhorn said slowly.

" I know. I'm assuming that she wasn't sunk hours ago." Nicolson smiled briefly, or maybe it was only a grimace, it was very dark in the wheelhouse now. " Perhaps I'm feeling fey to-night, sir. Perhaps it's my Scandinavian ancestry coming out . . . An hour and a half should get us there. Even in this head sea, not more than two."

" All right, damn you!" Findhorn said irritably. " Two hours, and then we turn back." He glanced at the luminous figures on his wrist-watch. " Six twenty-five now. The deadline is eight-thirty." He spoke briefly to the helmsman, turned

51

and followed Nicolson, who was holding the screen door open for him against the wild lurching of the *Viroma*. Outside the howling wind was a rushing, irresistible wall that pinned them helplessly, for seconds on end, against the after end of the bridge, fighting for their breath: the rain was no longer rain but a deluge, driving horizontally, sleet-cold, razor edged, that seemed to lay exposed foreheads and cheeks open to the bone: the wind in the rigging was no longer a whine but an ululating scream, climbing off the register, hurtful to the ear. The *Viroma* was moving in on the heart of the typhoon.

CHAPTER FOUR

Two HOURS, Captain Findhorn had given them, two hours at the outside limit, but it might as well have been two minutes or two days, for all the hope that remained. Everyone knew that, knew that it was just a gesture, maybe to their own consciences, maybe to the memory of a few wounded soldiers, a handful of nurses and a radio operator who had leaned over his transmitting key and died. But still only a hopeless gesture . . .

They found the *Kerry Dancer* at twenty-seven minutes past eight, three minutes before the deadline. They found her, primarily, because Nicolson's predictions had been uncannily correct, the *Kerry Dancer* was almost exactly where he had guessed they would find her and a long, jagged fork of lightning had, for a brief, dazzling moment, illumined the gaunt, burnt-out scarecrow as brightly as the noonday sun. Even then they would never have found her had not the hurricane force of the wind dropped away to the merest whisper, and the blinding rain vanished as suddenly as if someone had turned off a gigantic tap in the heavens.

That there was no miracle about the almost instantaneous transition from the clamour of the storm to this incredible quiet Captain Findhorn was grimly aware. Always, at the heart of a typhoon, lies this oasis of peace. This breathless, brooding hush was no stranger to him—but on the two or three previous occasions he had had plenty of sea room, could turn where he wished when the going became too bad. But not this time. To the north, to the west and to the south-west their escape route was blocked off by islands of the archipelago.

They couldn't have entered the heart of the typhoon at a worse time.

And they couldn't have done it at a better time. If anyone lived on the *Kerry Dancer* conditions for rescue would never be more favourable than this. If anyone lived—and from what they could see of her in the light of their canal searchlights and the port signalling lamp as they bore slowly down on her, it seemed unlikely. More, it seemed impossible. In the harsh glare of the searchlights she seemed more forlorn, more abandoned than ever, so deep now by the head that the for'ard well deck had vanished, and the fo'c'sle, like some lonely rock, now awash, now buried deep as the big seas rolled it under— the wind had gone, the rain had gone, but the seas were almost as high as ever, and even more confused.

Captain Findhorn gazed out silently at the *Kerry Dancer*, his eyes bleak. Caught in a cone of light, broached to and broadside on to the waves, she was rolling sluggishly in the troughs, her centre of gravity pulled right down by the weight of hundreds of tons of water. Dead, he thought to himself, dead if ever a ship was dead but she just won't go. Dead, and that's her ghost, he thought inconsequentially, and ghost-like she seemed, eerie and foreboding with the searchlights shining through the twisted rectangular gaps in her burnt-out upperworks. She reminded him vaguely, tantalisingly, of something, then all of a sudden he had it—the Death Ship of the Ancient Mariner, with the red, barred sun shining through the skeleton of her timbers. No deader than this one here, he thought grimly. Nothing could have been emptier of life than this. . . . He became aware that the chief officer was standing just behind his shoulder.

"Well, there she is, Johnny," he murmured. "Candidate-elect for the Sargasso Sea, or wherever dead ships go. It's been a nice trip. Let's be getting back."

"Yes, sir." Nicolson didn't seem to have heard him. "Permission to take a boat across, sir."

"No." Findhorn's refusal was flat, emphatic. "We've seen all we want to see."

"We've come back a long way for this." There was no particular inflection in Nicolson's voice. "Vannier, the bo'sun, Ferris, myself and a couple of others. We could make it."

"Maybe you could." Bracing himself against the heavy rolling of the *Viroma*, Findhorn made his way to the outer edge of the port wing and stared down at the sea. Even in the lee of the ship, there were still ten or fifteen feet between

53

troughs and wavecrests, the short, steep seas confused and treacherous. "And maybe you couldn't. I don't propose to risk anyone's life just to find that out."

Nicolson said nothing. Seconds passed, then Findhorn turned to him again, the faintest edge of irritation in his voice. "Well, what's the matter. Still feeling—what do you call it? —fey? Is that it?" He flung out an impatient arm in the direction of the *Kerry Dancer*. "Damn it all, man, she's obviously abandoned. Burnt-out and hammered till she looks like a floating colander. Do you honestly think there would be any survivors after she had been through that little lot? And even if there were, they're bound to see our lights. Why aren't they all dancing about the upper deck—if there's any deck left—waving their shirts above their heads? Can you tell me that?" Captain Findhorn was being heavily sarcastic.

"No idea, sir, though I should imagine a badly-wounded soldier—McKinnon said there were a few stretcher cases aboard—would find it difficult, far too difficult, even to get out of bed and take his shirt off, far less wave it all over the upper deck," Nicolson said dryly. "A favour, sir. Switch our search-lights off and on, a few 12-pounder ack-ack shots, half-a-dozen rockets. If there's anyone left alive, that'll attract their attention."

Findhorn considered for a moment, then nodded his head. "It's the least I can do, and I don't suppose there's a Jap within fifty miles. Go ahead, Mr. Nicolson."

But the flicking on and off of the searchlights, the flat, sharp crack of the 12-pounder echoing emptily over the sea had no effect, just no effect at all. The *Kerry Dancer* looked even more lifeless than before, a floating, burnt-out skeleton, deeper than ever in the water, the fo'c'sle only awash now in the deepest troughs. And then came the rockets, seven or eight of them, dazzling white in the pitchy darkness, curving away in shallow arcs to the west; one of them landed on the poop of the *Kerry Dancer*, lay there for long seconds bathing the heaving deck in a fierce white glare, then sputtering to extinction. And still nothing moved aboard the *Kerry Dancer*, no sign of life at all.

"Well, that's it." Captain Findhorn sounded a little weary: even with no hope in the first place he was still disappointed, more than he would have cared to admit. "Satisfied, Mr. Nicolson?"

"Captain, sir!" It was Vannier speaking before Nicolson

could answer, his voice high-pitched, excited. " Over there, sir. Look!"

Findhorn had steadied himself on the handrail and had his night glasses to his eyes before Vannier had finished talking. For a few seconds he stood motionless, then he swore softly, lowered his glasses and turned to Nicolson. Nicolson forestalled him.

" I can see it, sir. Breakers. Less than a mile south of the *Kerry Dancer*—she'll pile up there in twenty minutes, half an hour. Metsana, it must be—it's not just a reef."

" Metsana it is," Findhorn growled. " Good God, I never dreamed we were so close! That settles it. Cut the lights. Full ahead, hard a starboard and keep her 090—biggest possible offing in the shortest possible time. We're about due to move out of the eye of the typhoon any minute now and heaven only knows how the wind is going to break—what the devil!"

Nicolson's hand was on his upper arm, the lean fingers digging hard into his flesh. His left arm was stretched out, finger pointing towards the stern of the sinking ship.

" I saw a light just now—just after ours went out." His voice was very quiet, almost hushed. " A very faint light—a candle, or maybe even a match. The porthole nearest the well-deck."

Findhorn looked at him, stared out at the dark, tenebrous silhouette of the steamer, then shook his head.

" I'm afraid not, Mr. Nicolson. Some optical trick, nothing else. The retina can hold some queer after-images, or maybe it was just the scuttle reflecting the dying glow from one of our——"

" I don't make mistakes of that kind," Nicolson interrupted flatly.

A few seconds passed, seconds of complete silence, then Findhorn spoke again: " Anybody else see that light?" The voice was calm, impersonal enough, the faint edge of anger just showing through.

Again the silence, longer this time, then Findhorn turned abruptly on his heel. " Full ahead, quartermaster, and—Mr. Nicolson! What are you doing?"

Nicolson replaced the phone he had been using without any sign of haste. " Just asking for a little light on the subject," he murmured laconically. He turned his back to the captain and gazed out over the sea.

Findhorn's mouth tightened; he took a few quick steps forward but slowed up suddenly as the port light switched on, wavered uncertainly, then settled on the aftercastle of the *Kerry Dancer*. More slowly still the captain came alongside Nicolson, shoulder to shoulder, both hands reaching up for the dodger rail to steady himself: but seeking balance alone could not have accounted for the strength of his grip on the rail, a grip that tightened and tightened until the straining knuckles were burnished ivory in the washback of light from the beam pinned on the *Kerry Dancer*.

The *Kerry Dancer* was barely three hundred yards away now, and there could be no doubt about it, none at all. Everybody saw it, clearly—the narrow scuttle swinging in, then the long, bare arm stretching out and frantically waving a white towel or sheet, an arm that withdrew suddenly, thrust out a flaming bundle either of paper or rags, held on to it until the flames began to lick and twist around the wrist, then dropped it hissing and smoking, into the sea.

Captain Findhorn sighed, a long, heavy sigh, and unclamped his aching fingers from the dodger rail. His shoulders sagged, the tired, dispirited droop of a man no longer young, a man who has been carrying too heavy a burden for too long a time. Beneath the dark tan his face was almost drained of colour.

"I'm sorry, my boy." It was only a whisper; he spoke without turning round, his head shaking slowly from side to side. "Thank God you saw it in time."

No one heard him, for he was talking only to himself. Nicolson was already gone, sliding on his forearms down the teak ladder rails without his feet touching one step, before the captain had started speaking. And even before he was finished Nicolson had knocked off the gripes' release links on the port lifeboat, and was already easing off the handbrake, shouting for the bo'sun to muster the emergency crew at the double.

*   *   *

Fireman's axe in one hand, a heavy, rubber-sheathed torch in the other, Nicolson made his way quickly along the fore and aft passage through the *Kerry Dancer's* gutted midships superstructure. The steel deck beneath his feet had been buckled and twisted into fantastic shapes by the intense heat, and pieces of charred wood were still smouldering in sheltered corners. Once or twice the heavy, jerky rolling of the ship threw him against the walls of the passage and the fierce heat

56

struck at him even through the canvas gloves on his outflung hands: that the metal should still be so hot after hours of gale force winds and torrential rain gave him a very vivid idea of the tremendous heat that must have been generated by the fire. He wondered, vaguely, what sort of cargo she had been carrying: probably contraband of some sort.

Two-thirds of the way along the passage, on the right hand side, he noticed a door, still intact, still locked. He leaned back and smashed at the lock, straight-legged, with the sole of his shoe: the door gave half an inch, but held. He swung his axe viciously against the lock, kicked the door open with his foot, pressed the button of his torch and stepped over the coaming. Two charred, shapeless bundles lay on the floor at his feet. They might have been human beings once, they might not. The stench was evil, intolerable, striking at his wrinkling nostrils like a physical blow. Nicolson was back in the passage within three seconds, hooking the door shut with the blade of the axe. Vannier was standing there now, the big red fire extinguisher under his arm, and Nicolson knew that even in those brief moments Vannier had had time to look inside. His eyes were wide and sick, his face like paper.

Nicolson turned abruptly, continued down the passage, Vannier behind him, followed by the bo-sun with a sledge and Ferris with a crowbar. He kicked open two more doors, shone his torch inside. Empty. He came to the break of the after well-deck, and here he could see better, for all the lights of the *Viroma* were trained there. Quickly he looked round for a ladder or companionway, as quickly found it—a few charred sticks of wood lying on the steel deck eight feet below. A wooden companionway, completely destroyed by the fire. Nicolson turned swiftly to the carpenter.

" Ferris, get back to the boat and tell Ames and Docherty to work it aft as far as the well deck here. I don't care how they do it, or how much damage is done to the boat—we can't get sick and wounded men up here. Leave your crowbar."

Nicolson had swung down on his hands and dropped lightly to the deck below before he had finished speaking. In ten paces he had crossed the deck, rung the haft of his axe hard against the steel door of the aftercastle.

" Anyone inside there?" he shouted.

For two or three seconds there was complete silence, then there came a confused, excited babble of voices, all calling to him at once. Nicolson turned quickly to McKinnon, saw his own smile reflected in the wide grin on the bo'sun's face, step-

57

ped back a pace and played his torch over the steel door. One clip was hanging loose, swinging pendulum-like with the heavy, water-logged rolling of the *Kerry Dancer*, the other seven jammed hard in position.

The seven-pound sledge-hammer was a toy in McKinnon's hands. He struck seven times in all, once for each clip, the metallic clangs reverberating hollowly throughout the sinking ship. And then the door had swung open of its own accord and they were inside.

Nicolson flashed his torch over the back of the steel door and his mouth tightened: only one clip, the one that had been hanging loose, was continued through the door—the rest just ended in smooth rivet heads. And then he was facing aft again, the beam circling slowly round the aftercastle.

It was dark and cold, a dank, dripping dungeon of a place with no covering at all on the slippery steel deckplates, and barely enough headroom for a tall man to stand upright. Three-tiered metal bunks, innocent of either mattresses or blankets, were ranged round both sides, and about a foot or so above each bunk a heavy iron ring was welded to the bulkheads. A long, narrow table ran fore and aft the length of the compartment, with wooden stools on either side.

There were maybe twenty people in the room, Nicolson estimated; some sitting on the bottom bunks, one or two standing, hanging on to the uprights of the bunks to brace themselves, but most of them still lying down. Soldiers they were, those who were lying on the bunks, and some of them looked as if they would never get up again: Nicolson had seen too many dead men, the waxen cheek, the empty lustreless eye, the boneless relaxation that inhabits a shapeless bundle of clothes. There were also a few nurses in khaki skirts and belted tunics, and two or three civilians. Everyone, even the dusky skinned nurses, seemed white and strained and sick. The *Kerry Dancer* must have lain in the troughs since early afternoon, rolling wickedly, continuously, for endless hours.

" Who's in charge here?" Nicolson's voice beat back at him hollowly from the iron walls of the aftercastle.

" I think he is. Rather, I think he thinks he is." Slim, short, very erect, with silver hair drawn back in a tight bun beneath a liberally be-skewered straw hat, the elderly lady by Nicolson's side still had the fire of authority in the washed-out blue of her eyes. There was disgust in them now, too, as she pointed down at the man huddled over a half-empty whisky bottle on the table. " But he's drunk, of course."

"Drunk, madam? Did I hear you say I was drunk?" Here was one man who wasn't pale and sick, Nicolson realised: face, neck, even the ears were burnt brick in colour, a dramatic background for the snow-white hair and bristling white eyebrows. "You have the effrontery to—to——" He rose spluttering to his feet, hands pulling down the jacket of his white linen suit. "By heaven, madam, if you were a man——"

"I know," Nicolson interrupted. "You'd horsewhip her within an inch of her life. Shut up and sit down." He turned to the woman again. "What is your name, please?"

"Miss Plenderleith. Constance Plenderleith."

"The ship is sinking, Miss Plenderleith," Nicolson said rapidly. "She's lower by the head every minute. We'll be on the rocks in about half an hour, and the typhoon is going to hit us again any moment." Two or three torches were on now, and he looked round the silent half-circle of faces. "We must hurry. Most of you look like death, and I'm quite sure you feel that way, but we must hurry. We have a lifeboat waiting on the port side, not thirty feet away. Miss Plenderleith, how many can't walk that far?"

"Ask Miss Drachmann. She's the sister in charge." Miss Plenderleith's quite different tone left no doubt that she thoroughly approved of Miss Drachmann.

"Miss Drachmann?" Nicolson asked expectantly.

A girl in a faraway corner turned to look at him. Her face was in shadow. "Only two, I'm afraid, sir." Beneath the overtones of strain, the voice was soft and low and musical.

"You're afraid?"

"All the other stretcher cases died this evening," she said quietly. "Five of them, sir. They were very sick—and the weather was very bad." Her voice was not quite steady.

"Five of them," Nicolson repeated. He shook his head slowly, wonderingly.

"Yes, sir." Her arm tightened around the child standing on the seat beside her, while her free hand pulled a blanket more tightly round him. "And this little one is just very hungry and very tired." Gently she tried to remove a grubby thumb from his mouth, but he resisted her efforts and continued to inspect Nicolson with a certain grave detachment.

"He'll feed and sleep well to-night," Nicolson promised. "Right, all those who can, walk into the boat. Fittest first— you can help steady the boat and guide the wounded into it. How many arm or leg wounds, apart from the stretcher cases, nurse?"

59

" Five, sir."

" No need to call me ' sir '. You five wait till there's someone down there to help you." He tapped the whisky-drinker on the shoulder. " You lead the way."

" Me?" He was outraged. " I'm in charge here, sir—the captain, in effect, and a captain is always last to——"

" Lead the way," Nicolson repeated patiently.

" Tell him who you are, Foster," Miss Plenderleith suggested acidly.

" I certainly shall." He was on his feet now, a black gladstone bag in one hand, the half-empty bottle in the other. " Farnholme is the name, sir. Brigadier Foster Farnholme." He bowed ironically. " At your service, sir."

" Delighted to hear it." Nicolson smiled coldly. " On your way." Behind him, Miss Plenderleith's low chuckle of amusement came unnaturally loud in the sudden silence.

" By God, you shall pay for this, you insolent young——" He broke off hurriedly and took a step backwards as Nicolson advanced on him. " Dammit all, sir," he spluttered. " The traditions of the sea. Women and children first."

" I know. Then we'll all line up on the deck and die like little gentlemen while the band plays us under. I won't tell you again, Farnholme."

" Brigadier Farnholme to you—you——"

" You'll get a seventeen gun salute as you go aboard," Nicolson promised. His stiff-armed push sent Farnholme, still clutching his bag, reeling back into the arms of the expectant bo'sun. McKinnon had him outside in less than four seconds.

Nicolson's torch probed round the aftercastle and came to rest on a cloaked figure sitting huddled on a bunk.

" How about you?" Nicolson asked. " You hurt?"

" Allah is good to those who love Allah." The voice was deep, almost sepulchral, the dark eyes deepset above an eagle nose. He stood up, tall, dignified, pulling his black cap tightly over his head. " I am unhurt."

" Good. You next, then." Nicolson swivelled the torch round, picked out a corporal and two soldiers. " How do you boys feel?"

" Ach, we're fine." The thin, dark corporal withdrew his puzzled, suspicious stare from the doorway through which Farnholme had just vanished and grinned at Nicolson. It was a grin that belied the bloodshot eyes, the yellow, fever-ridden face. " Britain's hardy sons. We're just in splendid form."

"You're a liar," Nicolson said pleasantly. "But thanks very much. Off you go. Mr. Vannier, will you see them into the boat, please? Have them jump every time the lifeboat rides up near the well-deck—it should come within a couple of feet. And a bowline round each person—just in case. The bo'sun will give you a hand."

He waited until the broad, retreating back of the cloaked man had vanished through the door, then looked curiously at the little lady by his side. "Who's the boy friend, Miss Plenderleith?"

"He's a Muslim priest, from Borneo." She pursed her lips in disapproval. "I spent four years in Borneo once. Every river bandit I ever heard of was a Muslim."

"He should have a wealthy congregation," Nicolson murmured. "Right, Miss Plenderleith, you next, then the nurses. Perhaps you wouldn't mind staying a bit longer, Miss Drachmann? You can see to it that we don't do too much damage to your stretcher cases when we start carrying them out."

He turned without waiting for a reply and hurried through the door on the heels of the last of the nurses. On the well-deck he stood blinking for a few seconds, unaccustomed eyes adjusting themselves to the fierce glare of light from the *Viroma* that threw everything into harsh relief, a merciless whiteness broken by black, impenetrable blocks of shadow. The *Viroma* couldn't be more than a hundred and fifty yards away: with seas like these, Captain Findhorn was gambling, and gambling high.

Less than ten minutes had elapsed since they had come on board, but the *Kerry Dancer* was already appreciably lower in the water; the seas were beginning to break over the starboard side of the after well-deck. The lifeboat was on the port side, one moment plunging a dozen feet down into the depths of a trough, the next riding up almost to the level of the well-deck rail, the men in the boat screwing shut their eyes and averting their heads as they were caught in the glare of the searchlights. Even as Nicolson watched, the corporal released his grip on the rail, stepped into the lifeboat, was grabbed by Docherty and Ames and dropped from sight like a stone. Already McKinnon had swung one of the nurses over the rail and was holding her in readiness for the next upward surge of the boat.

Nicolson stepped to the rail, switched on his torch and peered down over the side. The lifeboat was down in the

61

trough, smashed jarringly into the side of the *Kerry Dancer*, despite all the crew could do to fend her off, as opposing seas flung the lifeboat and ship together: the two upper planks of the lifeboat were stove in and broken, but the gunwale of tough American elm still held. Fore and aft Farnholme and the Muslim priest clung desperately to the ropes that held them alongside, doing their best to keep the boat in position and to ease it against the shocks of the sea and the hull of the *Kerry Dancer*: as far as Nicolson could judge in the confusion and near darkness, their best was surprisingly good.

" Sir! " Vannier was by his side, his voice agitated, his arm pointing out into the darkness. " We're almost on the rocks!"

Nicolson straightened up and stared along the line of the pointing arm. The sheet-lightning was still playing around the horizon, but even in the intervals of darkness there was no difficulty in seeing it—a long, irregular line of seething white, blooming and fading, creaming and dying as the heavy seas broke over the outlying rocks of the coastline. Two hundred yards away now, Nicolson estimated, two fifty at the most, the *Kerry Dancer* had been drifting south at almost twice the speed he'd estimated. For a moment he stood there immobile, racing mind calculating his chances, then he staggered and almost fell as the *Kerry Dancer* struck heavily, with a grinding, tearing screech of metal, on an underground reef, the decks canting far over on the port side. Nicolson caught a glimpse of McKinnon, feet wide braced on the deck, an arm crooked tightly round the nurse outside the rail, bared teeth white and deepset eyes screwed almost shut as he twisted round and stared into the searchlight, and he knew that McKinnon was thinking the same thing as himself.

" Vannier! " Nicolson's voice was quick, urgent. " Get the Aldis out of the boat. Signal the captain to stand well off, tell him it's shoal ground, with rocks, and we're fast. Ferris—take the bo'sun's place. Heave 'em in any old how. We're pinned for'ard and if she slews round head into the sea we'll never get anybody off. Right, McKinnon, come with me."

He was back inside the aftercastle in five seconds, McKinnon close behind him. He swept his torch once, quickly, round the metal bunks. Eight left in all—the five walking wounded, Miss Drachmann and the two seriously injured men lying stretched out at full length on the lowest bunks. One was breathing stertorously through his open mouth, moaning and twisting from side to side in deep-drugged sleep. The other lay very still, his breathing so shallow as to be almost imperceptible, his face a waxen ivory: only the slow, aimless wandering of pain-filled eyes showed that he was still alive.

"Right, you five." Nicolson gestured at the soldiers. "Outside as fast as you can. What the hell do you think you're doing?" He reached out, tore a knapsack from the hands of a soldier who was struggling to slip his arms through the straps, flung it into a corner. "You'll be lucky to get out of this with your life, far less your damn' luggage. Hurry up and get outside."

Four of the soldiers, urged on by McKinnon, stumbled quickly through the door. The fifth—a pale-faced boy of about twenty—had made no move to rise from his seat. His eyes were wide, his mouth working continuously and his hands were clasped tightly in front of him. Nicolson bent over him. "Did you hear what I said?" he asked softly.

"He's my pal." He didn't look at Nicolson, gestured to one of the bunks behind him. "He's my best friend. I'm staying with him."

"My God!" Nicolson murmured. "What a time for heroics." He raised his voice, nodded to the door. "Get going."

The boy swore at him, softly, continuously but broke off as a dull booming sound echoed and vibrated throughout the ship, the noise accompanied by a sharp, sickening lurch even farther to port.

"Water-tight bulkhead abaft the engine-room gone, I'm thinking, sir." McKinnon's soft-spoken Highland voice was calm, almost conversational.

"And she's filling up aft," Nicolson nodded. He wasted no further time. He stooped over the soldier, twisted his left hand in his shirt, jerked him savagely to his feet, then stiffened in sudden surprise as the nurse threw herself forward and caught his free right arm in both her hands. She was tall, taller than he had thought, her hair brushed his eyes and he could smell the faint fragrance of sandalwood. What caught and held his almost shocked attention, however, was her eyes —or, rather, her eye, for the beam from McKinnon's torch lit up only the right hand side of her face. It was an eye of a colour and an intensity that he had seen only once before—in his own mirror. A clear Arctic blue, it was very Arctic right then, and hostile.

"Wait! Don't hit him—there are other ways, you know."

63

The voice was still the same, soft, well-modulated, but the earlier respect had given way to something edged with near-contempt. "You do not understand. He is not well." She turned away from Nicolson and touched the boy lightly on the shoulder. "Come on, Alex. You must go, you know. I'll look after your friend—you know I will. Please, Alex."

The boy stirred uncertainly and looked over his shoulder at the man lying in the bunk behind him. The girl caught his hand, smiled at him and urged him gently to his feet. He muttered something, hesitated, then stumbled past Nicolson out on to the well-deck.

"Congratulations." Nicolson nodded towards the open door. "You next, Miss Drachmann."

"No." She shook her head. "You heard me promise him—and you asked me to stay behind a little time ago."

"That was then, not now," Nicolson said impatiently. "We've no time to fool around with stretchers now—not with a slippery deck canted over at twenty degrees. Surely you can see that."

She stood irresolute a moment, then nodded without speaking and turned round to grope in the shadowed darkness of a bunk behind her.

Nicolson said roughly, "Hurry up. Never mind your precious belongings. You heard what I said to that soldier."

"Not my belongings," she said quietly. She turned round and pulled a wrap more tightly round the sleeping child in her arms. "But very precious to someone, I'm sure."

Nicolson stared at the child for a moment, then shook his head slightly. "Call me what you like, Miss Drachmann. I just plain forgot. And you can call that what you like—'criminal negligence' will do for a start."

"Our lives are all with you." The tone was no longer hostile. "You cannot think of everything." She walked past him along the sharply sloping deck, propping herself against the line of bunks with her free hand. Again the faint smell of the sandalwood drifted past him, a scent so faint that it was just a fleeting memory lost in the dank airlessness of the aftercastle. Near the door she slipped and almost fell, and McKinnon put out his hand to help her. She took it without any hesitation, and they went out on deck together.

Within a minute both the seriously injured men had been brought out on deck, Nicolson carrying the one and McKinnon the other. The *Kerry Dancer*, already settling deep by the stern, was still pinned fast for'ard, working jerkily round with

CHAPTER ONE

CHOKING, DENSE, impenetrable, the black smoke lay pall-like over the dying city. Every building, every office-block and house, the intact and the bomb-shattered alike, was invested by it, swathed in the dark anonymity of its gently swirling cocoon. Every street, every alley, every dock-side basin was full of it, drowned by it. It lay everywhere, sulphurous and evil, scarcely moving in the soft airs of the tropical night.

Earlier in the evening, when the smoke had come only from the burning buildings in the city, there had been wide, irregular gaps overhead and the stars had shone in the empty sky. But a slight change of wind had obliterated these gaps had brought with it the rolling, blinding oil-smoke from ruptured fuel tanks outside the city. Where the smoke came from, no one knew. Perhaps from the Kallang airport, perhaps from the power station, perhaps clear across the island from the naval base in the north, perhaps from the oil islands, from Pulo Sambo and Pulo Sebarok, four or five miles away. No one knew. All one could know was what one saw, and the blackness of that midnight was almost complete. There was hardly any light now even from the burning buildings, for these were burnt out and utterly destroyed, the last embers, the last tiny flames flickering to extinction, like the life of Singapore itself.

A dying city, and already the silence of death seemed to have enveloped it. Every now and then a shell would whistle eerily overhead, to splash harmlessly into the water or to erupt in a brief roar of sound and flash of light as it smashed into a building. But the sound and the light, extinguished and smothered in an instant by the all-enveloping smoke, had a peculiarly evanescent quality, seemed a natural, an integral part of the strangeness and the remote unreality of the night and left the silence even deeper and more intense than it had been before. Now and again, out beyond Fort Canning and Pearls Hill, beyond the north-west limits of the city, came the irregular crackle of rifle and machine-gun fire, but that, too, was distant and unreal, a far-off echo in a dream. Everything that night had the same dream-like quality, shadowy and unsubstantial: even those few who still moved slowly through the rubble-strewn and almost deserted streets of Singapore were like the aimless wanderers of a dream, hesitant, listless and unsure, stumbling blindly through the swirling banks of smoke, little figures lost and hopelessly groping through the fog of a nightmare.

*   *   *

Moving slowly, uncertainly through the darkened streets, the small group of soldiers, perhaps two dozen in all, made their way down towards the waterfront like very old, very tired men. They looked like old men, they walked with the faltering steps and the bowed head and shoulders of old men, but they weren't old men, the eldest of them was not more than thirty: but they were tired, terribly tired, tired to that point of uncaring exhaustion when nothing matters any more and it is easier to keep stumbling along than it is to stop. Tired and sick, wounded and ravaged by disease, their every action was now unthinking, automatic, their conscious minds had all but ceased to function. But complete mental and physical exhaustion carries with it its own blessing, its own drug and anodyne, and the dull, lack-lustre eyes staring emptily down at the ground beneath their trudging feet showed this beyond all doubt: whatever sufferings of the body they still endured, they had at least stopped remembering.

For the moment, at least, they no longer remembered the waking nightmare of the past two months, the privations, the hunger, the thirst, the wounds, the sickness and the fear as the Japanese had driven them down the endless length of the Malayan peninsula, over the now destroyed Johore causeway into the illusory safety of the island of Singapore. They no longer remembered their vanished comrades, the screams as some unsuspecting sentry was butchered in the hostile dark of the jungle, the diabolical yells of the Japanese as they overran hastily prepared defensive positions in that black hour before dawn. They no longer remembered these desperate, suicidal counter-attacks that achieved nothing but a few square yards of land bitterly, uselessly re-won for only a moment of time, afforded them nothing but the sight of the horribly maimed and tortured bodies of their captured friends and the civilians who had been just that little bit too slow in co-operating with the enemy. They no longer remembered their anger and bewilderment and despair as the last of the Brewster fighters and, latterly, the Hurricanes, had been driven from the skies, leaving them completely at the mercy of

6

the Japanese air force. Even their utter disbelief at the news, five days ago, of the landing of the Japanese troops on the island itself, their bitterness as the carefully nurtured legend, the myth of the impregnability of Singapore, collapsed before their eyes—these, too, had vanished from their memories. They no longer remembered. They were too dazed and sick and wounded and weak to remember. But one day, soon, if they lived, they would remember, and then none of them would ever be the same again. But meantime they just trudged wearily on, eyes down, heads down, not looking where they were going, not caring where they would arrive.

But one man looked and one man cared. He walked along slowly at the head of the double column of men, flicking a torch on and off as he picked a clear way through the debris that littered the street and checked their direction of progress from time to time. He was a small, slightly-built man, the only one in the company who wore a kilt, and a balmoral on his head. Where the kilt had come from only Corporal Fraser knew: he certainly hadn't been wearing it during the retreat south through Malaya.

Corporal Fraser was as tired as any of the others. His eyes, too, were red-rimmed and bloodshot, and his face grey and wasted with what might have been malaria or dysentery or both. He walked with his left shoulder far higher than the other, hunched up near his ear, as if he suffered from some physical deformity, but it was no deformity, just a rough gauze pad and bandage that a medical orderly had hurriedly stuffed under his shirt earlier in the day in a token attempt to staunch the bleeding from an ugly shrapnel wound. In his right hand he carried a Bren gun, and its weight of twenty-three pounds was almost more than his weakened body could carry: it had the effect of pulling down his right arm and dragging his left shoulder upwards, even nearer his ear.

The one-sided hunch, the balmoral askew on his head, the kilt flapping loosely about his wasted legs, made the little man appear grotesque and ridiculous. But there was nothing grotesque and ridiculous about Corporal Fraser. A Cairngorms shepherd to whom privations and gruelling exertions were of the very stuff of existence, he had yet to tap the last reserves of his will-power and endurance. Corporal Fraser was still very much a going concern as a soldier—the very best type of soldier. Duty and responsibility weighed heavily with him, his own pain and weakness didn't exist, his thoughts were only for the men who stumbled along behind, following

7

him blindly. Two hours ago, the officer commanding their confused and disorganised company on the northern city limits had ordered Fraser to lead all the walking wounded, and those whom they could carry, out of the firing-line and back to some place of relative safety and quiet. Only a token gesture, the officer had known, and Fraser had known it also, for the last defences were caving in and Singapore was finished. Before the next day was through, every single man on Singapore island would be dead, wounded or prisoner. But orders were orders and Corporal Fraser trudged resolutely on, heading down for the Kallang creek.

Every now and then, when he came to a clear stretch of street, he stepped to one side and let his men file slowly past him. It was doubtful whether any of them as much as saw him, either the very ill men on the stretchers, or the less ill but still sick and wounded men who carried them. And every time Corporal Fraser would have to wait for the last of the party, a tall thin youngster whose head swayed loosely from side to side as he muttered to himself continuously in a rambling and incoherent voice. The young soldier suffered from neither malaria nor dysentery, nor had he been wounded in any way, but he was the sickest of them all. Every time Fraser would seize his arm and hustle him on to catch up with the main party, the boy quickened his pace without protesting, just looked at Corporal Fraser out of incurious eyes that were empty of all recognition: and every time Fraser would look at him hesitantly, shake his head then hurry forwards again until he reached the head of the column.

*   *   *

In a winding, smoke-filled alley, a little boy cried in the darkness. He was only a very little boy, perhaps two and a half years old. He had blue eyes, blond hair and a fair skin all streaked with dirt and tears. He was clad only in a thin shirt and khaki-coloured haltered shorts: his feet were bare, and he was shivering all the time.

He cried and cried, a lost, anguished wailing in the night, but there was no one there to hear or heed. And no one could have heard him who was more than a few yards away, for he cried very softly, short muffled sobs punctuated by long, quivering indrawn breaths. From time to time he rubbed his eyes with the knuckles of small and grubby fists, as little children will when they are tired or weeping: and with the backs of his hands he tried to rub the pain away, from the black

8

every pounding wave that smashed along its starboard length, the bows coming slowly, inexorably, head on to the seas. A minute at the most, Nicolson estimated, and the lifeboat would have lost the last of its shelter and would be exposed, head on, to the heavy combers shorter and steeper than ever as they raced in over the shoaling seabed. Already the lifeboat, now plunging, now rolling in short, vicious arcs, was corkscrewing almost uncontrollably in the quartering seas, shipping gallons of water at a time over the port gunwale. Not even a minute left, Nicolson felt sure. He jumped over the rail, waited for the bo'sun to hand him the first of the two injured men. Seconds only, just seconds, and any more embarkation would be quite impossible—the lifeboat would have to cast off to save itself. Seconds, and the devil of it was that they had to work with sick men, maybe even dying men, in almost total darkness: the *Kerry Dancer* was so far round now that her superstructure completely blocked off the searchlights of the *Viroma*.

Nicolson, leaning inboard against the slope of the deck, took the first man from McKinnon, waited until the bo'sun had hooked his fingers in his belt, twisted round and leaned far out as the lifeboat came surging up out of the darkness into the thin beam of Vannier's torch. Docherty and Ames, each securely anchored by a couple of soldiers sitting on the side benches, rode up almost level with Nicolson—with the stern of the *Kerry Dancer* settling in the water the lifeboat was now riding comparatively higher—caught the wounded man neatly at the first attempt, had him lowered to the thwarts just as the lifeboat dropped from sight and fell heavily into the next trough in a welter of spray and phosphorescent foam. Only six or seven seconds later the other wounded man had joined his companion in the bottom of the boat. Inevitably their handling had been hurried, rough, and must have been agonising, but neither man had uttered even a whimper.

Nicolson called to Miss Drachmann, but she pushed forward two of the walking wounded: they jumped together, landed safely in the boat. One more soldier to come: even with all speed it was going to be touch and go, Nicolson thought grimly—the *Kerry Dancer* was far round into the sea already.

But the last soldier didn't come. In the darkness Nicolson couldn't see him, but he could hear his voice, high-pitched and fearful, at least fifteen feet away. He could hear the nurse talking too, urgency in the soft, persuasive voice, but her arguments didn't seem to be getting her anywhere.

"What the hell's the matter there?" Nicolson shouted savagely.

There was a confused murmur of voices, and then the girl called, "Just a minute, please."

Nicolson twisted round, looked for'ard along the port side of the *Kerry Dancer*, then flung up a forearm in instinctive defence as the searchlights of the *Viroma* cleared the slowly swinging superstructure of the *Kerry Dancer* and struck at his dark-accustomed eyes. The *Kerry Dancer* was right round now, heading straight into the seas, and the lifeboat with all protection gone. He could see the first of the steep-walled, spume-veined waves racing smoothly, silently, down the listing side of the ship, the next not far behind. How big they were Nicolson couldn't tell: the searchlights, paralleling the surface of the sea, high-lit the broken white of the wave-tops but left the troughs in impenetrable blackness. But they were big enough, too big and too steep: half-a-dozen of these and the lifeboat would fill right up and overturn. At the very least they would flood the engine air intake, and then the results would be just as disastrous.

Nicolson wheeled round, vaulted over the rail, shouted at Vannier and Ferris to get into the lifeboat, called to McKinnon to cast off aft, and half-ran, half-stumbled up the heeling, slippery deck to where the girl and the soldier stood half-way between the aftercastle screen door and the ladder leading to the poop-deck above.

He wasted no time on ceremony but caught the girl by the shoulders, twisted her round and propelled her none too gently towards the ship's side, turned round again, grabbed the soldier and started to drag him across the deck. The boy resisted and, as Nicolson sought for a better grip, struck out viciously, catching Nicolson squarely between the eyes. Nicolson stumbled and half fell on the wet, sloping deck, got to his feet again like a cat and jumped towards the soldier, then swore, softly, bitterly, as his swinging arm was caught and held from behind. Before he could free it the soldier had turned and flung himself up the poop ladder, his studded soles scrabbling frantically on the metal steps.

"You fool!" Nicolson said quietly. "You crazy little fool!" Roughly he freed his arm, made to speak again, saw the bo'sun, in sharp silhouette against the glare of the searchlight, beckoning frantically from where he stood outside the well-deck rail. Nicolson waited no longer. He turned the nurse round, hustled her across the deck, swung her across the

66

rail. McKinnon caught her arm, stared down at the lifeboat two-thirds lost in the shrouded gloom of a trough and waited for his chance to jump. Just for a moment he looked round and Nicolson could tell from the anger and exasperation on his face that he knew what had happened. -

" Do you need me, sir?"

" No." Nicolson shook his head decisively. " The lifeboat's more important." He stared down at the boat as she came surging up sluggishly into the light, water from a high, breaking wave-crest cascading into her bows. " My God, McKinnon, she's filling right up already! Get her away from here as fast as you can! I'll cast off for'ard."

" Aye, aye, sir." Mckinnon nodded matter-of-fact acknowledgment, judged his time perfectly, stepped off the side on to the mast thwart, taking the girl with him: ready hands caught and steadied them as the boat dropped down again into the darkness of a trough. A second later the for'ard rope went snaking down into the lifeboat, Nicolson bending over the rail and staring down after it.

" Everything all right, bo'sun?" he called.

" Aye, no bother, sir. I'm going under the stern, in the lee."

Nicolson turned away without waiting to see what happened. The chances of a water-logged lifeboat broaching to in the initial moments of getting under way in those heavy seas were no better than even, but if McKinnon said everything was under control then everything was: and if he said he would heave to under the stern, he would be waiting there. Nicolson shared Captain Findhorn's implicit faith in McKinnon's initiative, reliability and outstanding seamanship.

He reached the top of the poop-deck ladder and stood there with his hand on the rail, looking slowly round him. Ahead was the superstructure, and in the distance, beyond it and on either side of it, stretched the long, lean shadow of the tanker, a dark smudge on the water, half-seen, half-imagined behind the white brilliance of its searchlights. But the lights, Nicolson suddenly realised, weren't nearly as brilliant or intense as they had been, even ten minutes earlier. For a fleeting moment he thought that the *Viroma* must be standing out to sea, working her way clear of the shoal water, then almost instantly realised, from the size and unaltered fore-and-aft position of the vague silhouette, that it hadn't moved at all. The ship hadn't changed, the searchlights hadn't changed—but the beams from the searchlights were no longer the same, they seemed to have lost their power, to be swallowed up, dissipated in the blackness of the sea. And there was something else, too—the sea *was* black, a darkness unrelieved by the slightest patch of white, by even one breaking whitecap on a wave: and then all of a sudden Nicolson had it—oil.

There could be no doubt about it—the sea between the two ships was covered in a wide, thick film of oil. The *Viroma* must have been pumping it overboard for the past five minutes or so—hundreds of gallons of it, enough to draw the teeth of all but the wildest storm. Captain Findhorn must have seen the *Kerry Dancer* swinging head on to the sea and quickly realised the danger of the lifeboat being swamped by inboard breaking seas. Nicolson smiled to himself, an empty smile, and turned away. Admitted the oil all but guaranteed the safety of the lifeboat, he still didn't relish the prospect of having his eyes burnt, ears, nostrils and mouth clogged, and being fouled from head to foot when he went overboard in just a few seconds—he and young Alex, the soldier.

Nicolson walked easily aft across the poop-deck towards the stern. The soldier was standing there, pressed against the taffrail in a stiff, unnatural fashion, his back to it and his hands grasping the stanchions on either side. Nicolson went close up to him, saw the wide, fixed eyes, the trembling of a body that has been tensed far too long; a leap into the water with young Alex, Nicolson thought dryly, was an invitation to suicide, either by drowning or strangulation—terror lent inhuman strength and a grip that eased only with death. Nicolson sighed, looked over the taffrail and switched on the torch in his hand. McKinnon was exactly where he had said he would be, hove to in the lee of the stern, and not fifteen feet away.

The torch snapped off and quietly, without haste, Nicolson turned away from the rail and stood in front of the young soldier. Alex hadn't moved, his breath came in short, shallow gasps. Nicolson transferred the torch to his left hand, lined it up, snapped it on, caught a brief glimpse of a white, strained face, bloodless lips drawn back over bared teeth and staring eyes that screwed tight shut as the light struck at them, then hit him once, accurately and very hard, under the corner of the jawbone. He caught the boy before he had started falling, heaved him over the taffrail, slid across himself, stood there for a second, sharply limned in a cone of light from a torch new lit in the boat—McKinnon had prudently bided his time until he had heard the sharp thud of the blow—crooked an

68

smoke constantly laced a smarting path across the tear-filled eyes.

The little boy cried because he was very, very tired, and it was hours past his normal bedtime. He cried because he was hungry and thirsty and shaking with the cold—even a tropical night can be cold. He cried because he was confused and afraid, because he did not know where his home was or where his mother was— he had been with his old *amah*, his Malayan nurse, at a nearby bazaar a fortnight previously and had been too young and unknowing to appreciate the significance of the bombed and burnt-out rubble that awaited their return—and he and his mother had been due to sail out on the *Wakefield*, the last big ship from Singapore, on the same night of that 29th January . . . But he cried, most of all, because he was alone.

His old nurse, Anna, was half-sitting, half-lying on a pile of rubble beside him, like one lost in sleep. She had been wandering with him for hours through the darkened streets, carrying him in her arms for the last hour or two, when she had suddenly placed him on the ground, clasped both hands above her heart and sunk to the ground, saying that she must rest. For half an hour now she had been there, motionless, her head resting far over on one shoulder, her eyes wide and unblinking. Once or twice, earlier, the little boy had stooped to touch her, but only once or twice: now he kept away, afraid, afraid to look and afraid to touch, vaguely knowing, without knowing why, that the old nurse's rest would be for a long, long time.

He was afraid to go and afraid to stay, and then he stole another glance, through latticed fingers, at the old woman and he was suddenly more afraid to stay than go. He moved off down the alley, not looking where he was going, stumbling and falling over loose bricks and stones, picking himself up and running on again, all the time sobbing and shivering in the cool night. Near the end of the alley a tall, emaciated figure wearing a tattered straw hat eased himself off the shafts of his rickshaw and reached out to stop the child. The man meant no harm. A sick man himself—most of the consumption-ridden rickshaw coolies of Singapore usually died after five years—he could still feel pity for others, especially little children. But all the little boy saw was a tall menacing figure reaching down out of the gloom: his fear changed to terror, he eluded the outstretched hands and ran out through the mouth of the alley into the deserted street and the darkness beyond. The man made no further movement, just wrapped his night blanket more tightly around himself and leaned back again against the shafts of his rickshaw.

*   *   *

Like the little boy, two of the nurses were sobbing quietly as they stumbled along. They were passing by the only building still burning in the business quarter of the town, and they kept their heads averted from the flames, but even so it was possible to see the smooth broad-boned faces and upcurving eyes of their lowered faces. Both were Chinese, people who do not lightly give way to emotion: but both were very young, and both had been sitting very close to the explosion when the shell had blown their Red Cross truck into the ditch near the southern exit of the Bukit Timor road. They were badly shocked, and still very sick and dazed.

Two of the others were Malays. One was young, as young as the two Chinese nurses, and the other was well past middle age. The young one's great, sooty eyes were wide with fear, and she kept glancing nervously over her shoulder as they hurried along. The face of the elderly one was a mask of almost complete indifference. From time to time she tried to protest at the speed with which they were being hurried along, but she was incapable of making herself understood: she, too, had been sitting very close to the blast of the explosion, and the shock had blocked her speech centres, probably only temporarily, although it was too soon to say yet. Once or twice she reached up a hand to try to stop the nurse in the lead, the one who was setting the pace, but the other just removed her hand, gently but firmly enough, and hurried on again.

The fifth nurse, the one in the lead, was tall, slender and in her middle twenties. She had lost her cap when the explosion had blown her over the tail-board of the truck, and the thick, blue-black hair kept falling down over her eyes. From time to time she swept it back with an impatient gesture, and it was then that one could see that she was neither Malayan nor Chinese—not with those startlingly blue eyes. Eurasian, perhaps, but still definitely not European. In the flickering yellow light it was impossible to see her complexion, the colour of her skin, which was streaked with mud and dust anyway. Even under the caked dust, it was possible to see some kind of long scratch on her left cheek.

She was the leader of the party and she was lost. She knew Singapore, and knew it well, but in the enveloping smoke and

arm round the young soldier's waist and jumped. They hit the water within five feet of the boat, vanished almost silently beneath the oil-bound sea, surfaced, were caught at once by waiting hands and dragged inside the lifeboat, Nicolson cursing and coughing, trying to clear gummed-up eyes, nose and ears, the young soldier lying motionless along the starboard side bench, Vannier and Miss Drachmann working over him with strips torn from Vannier's shirt.

The passage back to the *Viroma* was not dangerous, just very brief and very rough indeed, with almost all the passengers so seasick and so weak that they had to be helped out of the boat when they finally came alongside the tanker. Within fifteen minutes of his jump into the water with the young soldier Nicolson had the lifeboat safely heaved home on her housing on the patent gravity davits, the last of the gripes in position and had turned for a final look at the *Kerry Dancer*. But there was no sign of her anywhere, she had vanished as if she had never been; she had filled up, slid off the reef and gone to the bottom. For a moment or two Nicolson stood staring out over the dark waters, then turned to the ladder at his side and climbed slowly up to the bridge.

CHAPTER FIVE

HALF AN hour later the *Viroma* was rolling steadily to the south-west under maximum power, the long, low blur of Metsana falling away off the starboard quarter and vanishing into the gloom. Strangely, the typhoon still held off, the hurricane winds had not returned. It could only be that they were moving with the track of the storm: but they had to move out, to break through it sometime.

Nicolson, showered, violently scrubbed and almost free from oil, was standing by the screen window on the bridge, talking quietly to the second mate when Captain Findhorn joined them. He tapped Nicolson lightly on the shoulder.

" A word with you in my cabin, if you please, Mr. Nicolson. You'll be all right, Mr. Barrett?"

" Yes, sir, of course. I'll call you if anything happens?" It was half-question, half-statement, and thoroughly typical of Barrett. A good many years older than Nicolson, stolid and unimaginative, Barrett was reliable enough but had no taste at all for responsibility, which was why he was still only a second officer.

"Do that." Findhorn led the way through the chartroom to his day cabin—it was on the same deck as the bridge—closed the door, checked that the blackout scuttles were shut, switched on the light and waved Nicolson to a settee. He stooped to open a cupboard, and when he stood up he had a couple of glasses and an unopened bottle of Standfast in his hand. He broke the seal, poured three fingers into each glass, and pushed one across to Nicolson.

"Help yourself to water, Johnny. Lord only knows you've earned it—and a few hours' sleep. Just as soon as you leave here."

"Delighted," Nicolson murmured. "Just as soon as you wake up, I'll be off to my bunk. You didn't leave the bridge all last night. Remember?"

"All right, all right." Findhorn held up a hand in mock defence. "We'll argue later." He drank some whisky, then looked thoughtfully at Nicolson over the rim of his glass. "Well, Johnny, what did you make of her?"

"The *Kerry Dancer*?"

Findhorn nodded, waiting.

"A slaver," Nicolson said quietly. "Remember that Arabian steamer the Navy stopped off Ras al Hadd last year?"

"Yes, I remember."

"Identical, as near as makes no difference. Steel doors all over the shop, main and upper decks. Most of them could only be opened from one side. Eight-inch scuttles—where there were scuttles. Ring-bolts beside every bunk. Based on the islands, I suppose, and no lack of trade up round Amoy and Macao."

"The twentieth century, eh?" Findhorn said softly. "Buying and selling in human lives."

"Yes," Nicolson said dryly. "But at least they keep 'em alive. Wait till they catch up with the civilised nations of the west and start on the wholesale stuff—poison gas, concentration camps, the bombing of open cities and what have you. Give 'em time. They're only amateurs yet."

"Cynicism, young man, cynicism." Findhorn shook his head reprovingly. "Anyway, what you say about the *Kerry Dancer* bears out Brigadier Farnholme's statements."

"So you've been talking to his Lordship." Nicolson grinned. "Court-martialling me at dawn to-morrow?"

"What's that?"

"He didn't approve of me," Nicolson explained. "He wasn't backward about saying so either."

"Must have changed his mind." Findhorn refilled their glasses. "'Able young man that, very able, but—ah—impetuous.' Something like that. Very pukka, the *Tuan Besar* to the life."

Nicolson nodded. "I can just see him stuffed to the ears, stewed to the gills and snoring his head off in an arm-chair in the Bengal Club. But he's a curious bird. Did a good job with a rope in the lifeboat. How phoney do you reckon he is?"

"Not much." Findhorn considered for a moment. "A little, but not much. A retired army officer for a certainty. Probably upped himself a little bit in rank after his retirement."

"And what the hell's a man like that doing aboard the *Kerry Dancer*?" Nicolson asked curiously.

"All sorts of people are finding themselves with all sorts of strange bed-fellows these days," Findhorn replied. "And you're wrong about the Bengal Club, Johnny. He didn't come from Singapore. He's some sort of business man in Borneo— he was a bit vague about the business—and he joined the *Kerry Dancer* in Banjermasin, along with a few other Europeans who found the Japanese making things a little too hot for them. She was supposed to be sailing for Bali, and they hoped to find another ship there that would take them to Darwin. But apparently Siran—that's the name of the captain, and a thorough-going bad lot according to old Farnholme—got radio orders from his bosses in Macassar to proceed to Kota Bharu. Farnholme bribed him to go to Singapore, and he agreed. Why, heaven only knows, with the Japs more or less knocking at the gates, but there's always opportunity for sufficiently unscrupulous men to exploit a situation such as exists there just now. Or maybe they expected to make a quick fortune by charging the earth for passages out of Singapore. What they didn't expect, obviously, was what happened —that the Army should commandeer the *Kerry Dancer*."

"Yes, the army," Nicolson murmured. "I wonder what happened to the soldiers—McKinnon says there were at least two dozen—who went aboard to see that the *Kerry Dancer* did go straight to Darwin, and no funny tricks?"

"I wonder." Findhorn was tight-lipped. "Farnholme says they were quartered in the fo'c'sle."

" With one of these clever little doors that you can only open from one side, maybe?"

" Maybe. Did you see it?"

Nicolson shook his head. " The whole fo'c'sle was practically under water by the time we went aboard. I shouldn't be surprised. But it could have been jammed by bomb burst." He swallowed some more of the whisky and grimaced in distaste, not at the drink but at his thoughts. " A pleasant little alternative, drowning or cremation. I should like to meet Captain Siran some day. I suspect a great number of other people would too . . . How are the rest of our passengers? They got anything to add?"

Findhorn shook his head. " Nothing. Too sick, too tired, too shocked or they just don't know anything."

" All sorted out, washed up and bedded down for the night, I suppose?"

" More or less. I've got them all over the ship. All the soldiers are together, aft—the two really sick boys in the hospital, the other eight in the smoke-room and the two spare engineers' cabins on the port side. Farnholme and the priest are together in the engineers' office."

Nicolson grinned. " That should be worth seeing—the British Raj breathing the same air as the dusky heathen!"

" You'd be surprised," Findhorn grunted. " They have a settee each there, a table between them and a bottle of whisky, almost full, on the table. They're getting along very well indeed."

" He had a half bottle when I saw him last," Nicolson said thoughtfully. " I wonder——"

" Probably drank it without coming up for air once. He's lugging around a great big gladstone bag and if you ask me it's full of nothing but whisky bottles."

" And the rest?"

" The what? Oh, yes. The little old lady's in Walter's room—he's taken a mattress into his radio room. The senior nurse, the one that seems to be in charge——"

" Miss Drachmann?"

" That's her. She and the child are in the apprentices' cabin. And Vannier and the Fifth engineer have doubled up with Barrett and the fourth engineer—two nurses in Vannier's cabin and the last of them in the Fifth's."

" All accounted for." Nicolson sighed, lit a cigarette and watched the blue smoke drift lazily up to the ceiling. " I only hope they haven't exchanged the frying pan for the fire. We having another go at the Carimata Straits, sir?"

"Why not? Where else can we——"

He broke off as Nicolson stretched out for the ringing telephone and put it to his ear.

"Yes, captain's cabin . . . Oh, it's you, Willy . . . Yes, he's here. Hang on a minute." Nicolson rose easily to his feet, vacating his seat for the captain. "The second engineer, sir."

Findhorn talked for perhaps half a minute, mostly in monosyllabic grunts. Nicolson wondered idly what Willoughby had wanted. He had sounded almost bored but then nobody had ever seen Willoughby excited about anything. Ernest Willoughby never found anything in life worth getting excited about. A crazy, dreaming old coot—he was the oldest man in the ship—with a passion for literature matched only by his utter contempt for engines and the means whereby he earned his livelihood, he was the most honest man, and the most completely unselfish, that Nicolson had ever met. Willoughby himself took no pride in this, and was probably unaware of it: he was a man who had little, but wanted nothing at all. With him Nicolson had little in common, superficially at any rate: but, almost as if by the attraction of opposites, he had formed the greatest liking and admiration for the old engineer, and Willoughby, unmarried and with only a threadbare bed-sitting-room in the company club in Singapore, had spent a good few evenings in his home. Caroline, he remembered, had thought the world of old Willy and had usually made a point of seeing that the best meals and the longest, coolest drinks were always waiting for the old engineer. Nicolson stared down at his glass, and his mouth twisted in bitter memory . . . Suddenly he became aware that Captain Findhorn was on his feet, looking down at him with a peculiar expression on his face.

"What's the matter, Johnny? You feel all right?"

"Just wandering, sir." Nicolson smiled and waved a hand at the whisky bottle. "A great help, this, when you're taking a walk around in your mind."

"Help yourself: take another walk round." Findhorn picked up his hat and turned for the door. "Wait here for me, will you? I have to go below."

Two minutes after the captain had gone the phone rang again. It was Findhorn speaking, asking Nicolson to come below to the dining-saloon. He gave no reason. On his way below Nicolson met the fourth officer coming out of the wireless operator's cabin. Vannier was looking neither happy nor pleased. Nicolson looked at him, an eyebrow raised in interrogation, and Vannier glanced back at the wireless operator's door, his expression a nice mixture of indignation and apprehension.

" That old battleaxe in there is in full cry, sir." He kept his voice low.

" The what?"

" Miss Plenderleith," Vannier explained. " She's in Walter's cabin. I was just dropping off to sleep when she started hammering on the bulkhead between us, and when I ignored that she went out to the passage and started calling." Vannier paused, then went on feelingly: " She has a very loud voice, sir."

" What did she want?"

" The captain." Vannier shook his head incredulously. " ' Young man, I want to see the captain. At once. Tell him to come here.' Then she pushed me out the door. What will I do, sir?"

" Exactly what she asks, of course." Nicolson grinned. " I want to be there when you tell him. He's below in the saloon."

They dropped down one deck and went into the dining-saloon together. It was a big room, with two fore-and-aft tables with seating for twenty. But it was almost empty now: there were only three people there and they were all standing.

The captain and the second engineer stood side by side, facing aft, giving easily with the rolling of the ship. Findhorn, immaculately correct in uniform as always, was smiling. So was Willoughby, but there all resemblance between the two men ended. Tall, stooped, with a brown, wrinkled face and a thick, unkempt shock of grey hair, Willoughby was a tailor's nightmare. He wore a white shirt—what had originally been a white shirt—unpressed, buttonless and frayed at the collar and half-sleeves, a pair of khaki duck trousers, wrinkled like an elephant's legs and far too short for him, diamond-patterned plaid socks and unlaced canvas shoes. He hadn't had a shave that day, he probably hadn't had a shave that week.

Half-standing, half-leaning against the buffet table, the girl was facing them, hands gripping the edge of the table to steady herself. Nicolson and Vannier could see only her profile as they went in, but they could see that she, too, was smiling, the righthand corner of her mouth curving up and dimpling the olive-tinted peach of her cheek. She had a straight nose, very finely chiselled, a wide smooth forehead, and long, silky hair gathered in a deep roll round her neck, hair black with that intense blackness that reflects blue under the strong sun and gleams like a raven's wing. With her hair, complexion and rather high cheekbones, she was a typical Eurasian beauty: but after a long, long look—and all men would always give Miss Drachmann a long, long look—she was neither typical nor Eurasian: the face was not broad enough, the features were too delicate and those incredible eyes spoke only of the far north of Europe. They were as Nicolson had first seen them in the harsh light of his torch aboard the *Kerry Dancer*—an intense, startling blue, very clear, very compelling, the most remarkable features in a remarkable face. And round and beneath these eyes, just then, were the faint, blue smudges of exhaustion.

She had got rid of her hat and belted bush-jacket, Nicolson saw. She wore only her stained khaki skirt and a clean white shirt, several sizes too large for her, with the sleeves rolled far up the slender arms. Vannier's shirt, Nicolson felt sure. He had sat beside her all the way back in the lifeboat, talking in a low voice and most solicitous for her welfare. Nicolson smiled to himself, sought back in his memory for the days when he too had been an impressionable young Raleigh with a cloak always ready to hand, a knight-errant for any lady in distress. But he couldn't remember the days: there probably hadn't been any.

Nicolson ushered Vannier into the room ahead of him—Findhorn's reactions to Miss Plenderleith's request would be worth watching—closed the door softly behind him, turned round and checked himself just in time to stop from bumping into Vannier, who had halted suddenly and was standing motionless, rigid, not three feet from the door, his clenched fists by his side.

All three had fallen silent and turned to the door as Nicolson and Vannier had come in. Vannier had no eyes for Findhorn and Willoughby—he was staring at the nurse, his eyes widening, his lips parting in shock. Miss Drachmann had turned so that the lamplight fell full on the left hand side of her face, and that side of her face was not pretty. A great, long, jagged scar, still raw and livid and puckering up the cheek where it had been roughly, clumsily stitched, ran the whole length of her face from the hairline of the temple to the corner of the soft, round chin. Near the top, just above the cheekbone, it was half an inch wide. On anyone's face it would have looked ghastly: on the smooth loveliness of hers it had

75

the unreality of a caricature, the shocking impact of the most impious blasphemy.

She looked at Vannier in silence for a few seconds, then she smiled. It wasn't much of a smile, but it was enough to dimple one cheek and to whiten the scar on the other, at the corner of the mouth and behind the eye. She reached up her left hand and touched her cheek lightly.

" I'm afraid it's really not very nice, is it?" she asked. There was neither reproach nor condemnation in her voice: it was apologetic, rather, and touched with a queer kind of pity, but the pity was not for herself.

Vannier said nothing. His face had turned a shade paler, but when she spoke the colour returned and began to flood all over his neck and face. He looked away—one could almost see the sheer physical effort it cost him to pull his eyes off that hideous scar—and opened his mouth to speak. But he said nothing ; perhaps there was nothing he could say.

Nicolson walked quickly past him, nodded to Willoughby and stopped in front of the girl. Captain Findhorn was watching him closely, but Nicolson was unaware of it.

" Good evening, Miss Drachmann." His tone was cool but friendly. " All your patients nice and comfortable?" If you want banal remarks, he thought, Nicolson's your man.

" Yes, thank you, sir."

" Don't call me ' sir '," he said irritably. " I've told you that once already." He lifted his hand and gently touched the scarred cheek. She didn't flinch, there was no movement at all but for a momentary widening of the blue eyes in the expressionless face. " Our little yellow brothers, I take it?" His voice was as gentle as his hand.

" Yes," she nodded. " I was caught near Kota Bharu."

" A bayonet?"

" Yes."

" One of these notched, ceremonial bayonets, wasn't it?" He looked closely at the scar, saw the narrow deep incision on the chin and the rough tear beneath the temple. " And you were lying on the ground at the time?"

" You are very clever," she said slowly.

" How did you get away?" Nicolson asked curiously.

" A big man came into the room—a bungalow we were using as a field hospital. A very big man with red hair—he said he was an Argyll, some word like that. He took the bayonet away from the man who had stabbed me. He asked

76

me to look away, and when I turned back the Japanese soldier was lying on the floor, dead."

"Hooray for the Argylls," Nicolson murmured. "Who stitched it up for you?"

"The same man: he said he wasn't very good."

"There was room for improvement," Nicolson admitted. "There still is."

"It's horrible!" Her voice rose sharply on the last word. "I know it's horrible." She looked down at the floor for some seconds, then looked up at Nicolson again and tried to smile. It wasn't a very happy smile. "It's hardly an improvement, is it?"

"It all depends." Nicolson jerked a thumb at the second engineer. "On Willy here it would look good: he's just an old sourpuss anyway. But you're a woman." He paused for a moment, looked at her consideringly and went on in a quiet voice: "You're more than good-looking, I suppose—Miss Drachmann, you're beautiful, and on you it looks bloody awful, if you'll excuse my saying so. You'll have to go to England," he finished abruptly.

"England?" The high cheekbones were stained with colour. "I don't understand."

"Yes, England. I am pretty sure that there are no plastic surgeons in this part of the world who are skilled enough. But there are two or three men in England—I don't think there are any more—who could repair that scar and leave you with a hairline so fine that even a dancing partner wouldn't notice it." Nicolson waved a deprecating hand. "A little bit of powder and the old war-paint, naturally."

She looked at him in silence, her clear blue eyes empty of expression, then said in a quiet, flat voice: "You forget that I am a nurse myself. I am afraid I don't believe you."

"'Nothing is so firmly believed as what we least know'," Willoughby intoned.

"What? What did you say?" The girl looked startled.

"Pay no attention to him, Miss Drachmann." Captain Findhorn took a step towards her, smiling. "Mr. Willoughby would have us think that he is always ready with apt quotations, but Mr. Nicolson and I know better—he makes them up as he goes along."

"'Be thou chaste as ice, as pure as snow, thou shalt not escape calumny'." Willoughby shook his head sadly.

"Thou shalt not," Findhorn agreed. "But he's right, Miss

Drachmann, in that you shouldn't be quite so ready with your disbelief. Mr. Nicolson knows what he's talking about. Only three men in England, he said—and one of them is his uncle." He waved his hand in a gesture of dismissal. "But I didn't bring you here to discuss surgery or to give me the pleasure of refereeing a slanging match. Mr. Nicolson, we appear to have run out of——"

He broke off abruptly, fists clenching tightly by his sides, as the klaxon above his head blared into sudden, urgent life, drowning his words as the raucous clangour, a harsh, discordant, shocking sound in a confined space, filled the dining-cabin. Two longs and a short, two longs and a short—the emergency action stations call. Nicolson was first out of the room, Findhorn only a pace behind him.

To the north and east thunder rumbled dully along the distant horizon, sheet-lightning flickered intermittently all round the Rhio straits, on the inner vortex of the typhoon, and, overhead, the half-seen clouds were beginning to pile up, rampart upon rampart, the first huge, tentative raindrops spattering on the wheelhouse top of the *Viroma*, so heavily, so slowly, that each single one could be heard and counted. But to the south and west there was no rain, no thunder, just an occasional flash of lightning over the islands, half-seen, half-imagined, far off and feeble flickers that left the darkness more impenetrable than before.

But not quite impenetrable. For the fifth time in two minutes the watchers on the bridge of the *Viroma*, elbows braced against the wind-dodger and night-glasses held hard and motionless against their straining eyes, caught the same signal winking out of the darkness to the south-west—a series of flashes, about a half-dozen in all, very weak and not lasting more than ten seconds altogether.

"Starboard 25 this time," Nicolson murmured, "and opening. I would say it's stationary in the water, sir."

"As near as makes no difference." Findhorn lowered his binoculars, rubbed aching eyes with the back of his hand, and raised the glasses again, waiting. "Let's hear you thinking aloud, Mr. Nicolson."

Nicolson grinned in the darkness. Findhorn might have been sitting in the front parlour of his bungalow at home instead of where he was, in the eye of a typhoon, not knowing which way it would break, with a million pounds and fifty lives in his hand and a new, unknown danger looming up in the darkness.

"Anything to oblige, sir." He lowered his own binoculars and stared out thoughtfully into the darkness. "It might be a lighthouse, buoy or beacon, but it's not: there are none hereabouts, and none I know of anywhere that have that sequence. It might be wreckers—the gentlemen of Romney, Rye and Penzance had nothing on the lads out here—but it's not: the nearest island is at least six miles to the south-west and that light's not more than two miles off."

Findhorn walked to the wheelhouse door, called for half speed, then came back beside Nicolson. "Go on," he said.

"It might be a Jap warship—destroyer, or something, but again it's not: only suicide cases like ourselves sit out in the middle of a typhoon instead of running for shelter—and, besides, any sensible destroyer commander would sit quiet until he could give us the benefit of his searchlights at minimum range."

Findhorn nodded. "My own way of thinking exactly. Anything you think it might be? Look, there he goes again!"

"Yes, and still nearer. He's stationary, all right . . . Could be a sub, hears us as something big on his hydrophones, not sure of our course and speed and wants us to answer and give him a line of sight for his tin fish."

"You don't sound very convinced."

"I'm not convinced one way or the other, sir. I'm just not worried. On a night like this any sub will be jumping so much that it couldn't hit the *Queen Mary* at a hundred feet."

"I agree. It's probably what would be obvious to anyone without our suspicious minds. Someone's adrift—open boat or raft—and needs help, badly. But no chances. Get on the intercom to all guns, tell them to line up on that light and keep their fingers on their triggers. And get Vannier to come up here. Ring down for dead slow."

"Aye, aye, sir." Nicolson went inside the wheelhouse and Findhorn again raised his night glasses to his eyes, then grunted in irritation as someone jogged his elbow. He lowered his glasses, half-turned and knew who it was before the man spoke. Even in the open air the fumes of whisky were almost overpowering.

"What the devil's happening, Captain?" Farnholme was irate, peevish. "What's all the fuss about? That damn' great klaxon of yours just about blasted my ears off."

" I'm sorry about that, Brigadier." Findhorn's tone was even polite and disinterested. " Our emergency signal. We've sighted a suspicious light. It may be trouble." His voice changed, subtly. " And I'm afraid I'll have to ask you to leave. No one is allowed on the bridge without permission. I'm sorry."

" What?" Farnholme's tone was that of a man being asked to comprehend the incomprehensible. " Surely you can't expect that to apply to me?"

" I do. I'm sorry." The rain was beginning to fall now, faster and faster, the big fat drops drumming so heavily on his shoulders that he could feel the weight of them through his oilskins: yet another soaking was inevitable, and he didn't relish the prospect. " You will have to go below, Brigadier."

Farnholme, strangely, did not protest. He did not even speak, but turned abruptly on his heel and vanished into the darkness. Findhorn felt almost certain that he hadn't gone below, but was standing in the darkness at the back of the wheelhouse. Not that it mattered: there was plenty of room on the bridge, it was just that Findhorn didn't want anyone hanging over his shoulder when he had to move fast and make fast decisions.

Even as Findhorn lifted his glasses the light came on again, nearer, this time, much nearer, but fainter: the battery in that torch was dying, but it was more than strong enough to let them see the message being flashed: not the steady series of flashes of the last few times, but an unmistakable S.O.S., three shorts, three longs, three shorts, the universal distress signal at sea.

" You sent for me, sir?"

Findhorn lowered his glasses and looked round. " Ah, it's you, Vannier. Sorry to drag you out into this damned deluge, but I want a fast hand on the signal lamp. See that signal just now?"

" Yes, sir. Someone in trouble, I take it?"

" I hope so," Findhorn said grimly. " Get the Aldis out, ask him who he is." He looked round as the screen door opened. " Mr. Nicolson?"

" Yes, sir. Ready as we can be, sir. Everybody lined up with their guns, and everybody so damned edgy after the last few days that I'm only afraid that someone may fire too soon. And I've got the bo'sun rigging up a couple of floodlamps, starboard side, number three tank, and a couple of A.B.s—all we can spare from the guns—getting a scrambling net out over the side."

"Thank you, Mr. Nicolson. You think of everything. How about the weather?"

"Wet," Nicolson said morosely. He pulled the towel more tightly round his neck, listened to the clack of the Aldis trigger and watched the beam lancing its way whitely through the sheeting rain. "Wet and stormy—going to be very soon. What's happening and where it's going to hit us I haven't a clue. I think Buys Ballot's law and the book on tropical storms are about as useful to us here as a match in hell."

"You're not the only one," Findhorn confessed. "We've been an hour and fifteen minutes now in the centre of this storm. I was in one, about ten years ago, for twenty-five minutes, and I thought that was a record." He shook his head slowly, scattering raindrops. "It's crazy. We're six months too early—or too late—for a real hurricane. Anyway, it's not bad enough for that, not for a real force twelve job. But it's far out of season and a complete freak in these waters at any season, and that must be throwing the book of rules out of kilter. I'm certain that we're at the point of recurvature of the storm, and I'm almost certain that it will break north-east, but whether we'll find ourselves in the dangerous quadrant or——" He broke off abruptly and stared at the tiny pinpoint of yellowing light winking mistily through the pouring rain. "Something about sinking. What else does he say, Walters?"

"'Van Effen, sinking'. That's all, sir—at least I think it was that. Bad morse. The *Van Effen*."

"Oh, lord, my lucky night." Again Findhorn shook his head. "Another *Kerry Dancer*. The *Van Effen*. Who ever heard of the *Van Effen*? You, Mr. Nicolson?"

"Never." Nicolson turned and shouted through the screen door. "Are you there, Second?"

"Sir?" The voice came from the darkness, only feet away.

"The Register, quickly. The *Van Effen*. Two words, Dutch. Fast as you can."

"Van Effen? Did I hear someone say 'Van Effen'?" There was no mistaking the clipped Sandhurst drawl, this time with an overtone of excitement in it. Farnholme's tall shadow detached itself from the gloom at the back of the wheelhouse.

"That's right. Know any ship by that name?"

"It's not a ship, man—it's a friend of mine, Van Effen, a

81

Dutchman. He was on the *Kerry Dancer*—joined her with me at Banjermasin. He must have got away on her boat after we'd been set on fire—there *was* only one boat, as far as I can remember." Farnholme had pushed his way through the screen door now and was out on the wing of the bridge, peering excitedly over the canvas dodger, oblivious to the rain thumping down on his unprotected back. " Pick him up, man, pick him up!"

" How do we know it's not a trap?" The captain's relaxed, matter-of-fact voice came like a cold douche after Farnholme's impatient vehemence. " Maybe it is this man, Van Effen, maybe it isn't. Even if it is, how do we know that we can trust him?"

" How do you know?" Farnholme's tone was that of a man with a tight hold, a very tight hold on himself. " Listen. I've just been talking to that young man in there, Vannier or whatever his name is——"

" Get to the point, please," Findhorn interrupted coldly. " That boat— if it is a boat—is only a couple of hundred yards away now."

" Will you listen?" Farnholme almost shouted the words, then went on more quietly. " Why do you think I'm standing here alive? Why do you think these nurses are alive, these wounded soldiers you took off the *Kerry Dancer* only an hour ago? Why do you think all of us you picked up, with the exception of Miss Plenderleith and the priest, are alive? For one reason only—when the captain of the *Kerry Dancer* was scuttling out of Singapore to save his own skin a man stuck a pistol in his back and forced him to return to Singapore. That man was Van Effen, and he's out in that boat now: we all owe our lives to Van Effen, Captain Findhorn."

" Thank you, Brigadier." Findhorn was calm, unhurried as ever. " Mr. Nicolson, the searchlight. Have the bo'sun switch on the two floods when I give the word. Slow astern."

The searchlight beam stabbed out through the darkness and lit up a heavy, rolling sea churned milky white by the torrential rain. For a moment or two the searchlight stayed stationary, the almost solid curtain of rain sheeting palely through its beam, then started to probe forward and almost immediately picked it up—a lifeboat very close to hand, riding on its sea-anchor and plunging violently up and down as it rode the short, steep seas that swept down upon it. But the waves in the heart of a tropical storm have little set pattern, and every so often a twisting cross sea would curve over and break inboard. There were seven or eight men in the boat, stooping and straightening, stooping and straightening as they baled for their lives—a losing struggle, for she was already deep in the water, settling by the minute. One man alone seemed indifferent: he was sitting in the sternsheets, facing the tanker, a forearm across his eyes to ward off the glare of the searchlight. Just above the forearm something white gleamed in the light, a cap, perhaps, but at that distance it was difficult to be sure.

Nicolson dropped down the bridge ladder, ran quickly past the lifeboat, down another ladder to the fore and aft gangway, along to a third ladder that led down to the top of number three tank, and picked his way surely round valves and over the maze of discharge lines, gas lines and steam smothering pipes until he came to the starboard side: Farnholme followed close behind all the way. Just as Nicolson put his hands on the guardrail and leaned out and over, the two floodlights switched on together.

Twelve thousand tons and only a single screw, but Findhorn was handling the big ship, even in those heavy seas, like a destroyer. The lifeboat was less than forty yards away now, already caught in the pool of light from the floods, and coming closer every moment, and the men in the boat, safely into the lee of the *Viroma*, had stopped baling and were twisted round in their seats, staring up at the men on deck, and making ready to jump for the scrambling net. Nicolson looked closely at the man in the sternsheets: he could see now that it was no cap that the man was wearing on his head but a rough bandage, stained and saturated with blood: and then he saw something else, too, the stiff and unnatural position of the right arm.

Nicolson turned to Farnholme and pointed to the man in the sternsheets. "That your friend sitting at the back there?"

"That's Van Effen all right," Farnholme said with satisfaction "What did I tell you?"

"You were right." Nilcolson paused, then went on: "He seems to have a one-track mind in some things."

"Meaning what?"

"Meaning that he's still got a gun in his hand. He's got it lined up on his pals in front, and he hasn't taken his eyes off them once while I've been watching."

Farnholme stared, then whistled softly. "You're dead right, he has."

"Why?"

"I don't know, I really can't guess at all. But you can take it from me, Mr. Nicolson, that if my friend Van Effen thinks it necessary to have a gun on them, then he has an excellent reason for it."

* * *

Van Effen had. Leaning against a bulkhead in the dining-saloon, a large whisky in his hand and the water pooling from his soaking clothes on to the corticene at his feet, he told it all quickly, concisely and convincingly. Their lifeboat had been fitted with an engine, had carried them quickly clear of the *Kerry Dancer* after she had gone on fire and they had managed to reach the shelter of a small island miles away to the south just as the storm broke. They had pulled the boat up on to the shingle on the lee side, huddling there for hours until the wind had suddenly dropped: it was shortly afterwards that they had seen the rockets going up to the north-west.

" Those were ours," Findhorn nodded. " So you decided to make a break for us?"

" I did." A wintry smile touched the Dutchman's steady brown eyes as he gestured towards the group of men, dark-eyed and swarthy-skinned, standing huddled in one corner. " Siran and his little friends weren't keen. They're not exactly pro-Allied and they knew there weren't any Jap ships in these waters. Besides, for all we knew these were distress rockets from a sinking ship." Van Effen downed the rest of his whisky at a gulp and laid the glass carefully on the table beside him. " But I had the gun."

" So I saw." It was Nicolson speaking. " And then?"

" We took off, towards the north-west. We ran into a long stretch of confused water, not too rough, and made good time. Then heavy seas hit us and flooded the engine. We just had to sit there and I thought we were finished till I saw your phosphorescence—you can see it a long way off on a night as black as this. If the rain had come five minutes earlier we would never have seen you. But we did, and I had my torch."

" And your gun," Findhorn finished. He looked at Van Effen for a long time, his eyes speculative and cold. " It's a great pity you didn't use it earlier, Mr. Van Effen."

The Dutchman smiled wryly. " It is not difficult to follow your meaning, Captain." He reached up, grimaced, tore the blood-stained strip of linen from his head: a deep gash, purple-bruised round the edges, ran from the corner of his forehead to his ear. " How do you think I got this?"

"It's not pretty," Nicolson admitted. "Siran?"

"One of his men. The *Kerry Dancer* was on fire, the boat—it was the only boat—was out on the falls and Siran here and all that were left of his crew were ready to pile into it."

"Just their sweet little selves," Nicolson interrupted grimly.

"Just their sweet little selves," Van Effen acknowledged. "I had Siran by the throat, bent back over the rail, going to force him to go through the ship. That was a mistake—I should have used my gun. I didn't know then that all his men were—what is the phrase?—tarred with the same brush. It must have been a belaying pin. I woke up in the bottom of the boat."

"You what?" Findhorn was incredulous.

"I know." Van Effen smiled, a little tiredly. "It doesn't make any kind of sense at all, does it? They should have left me to fry. But there I was—not only alive, but with my head all nicely tied up. Curious, is it not, Captain?"

"Curious is hardly the word." Findhorn's voice was flat, without inflection. "You are telling the truth, Mr. Van Effen? A silly question, I suppose—whether you are or not, you'd still say 'yes'."

"He is, Captain Findhorn." Farnholme's voice sounded oddly confident and, for that moment, not at all like the voice of Brigadier Farnholme. "I am perfectly certain of that."

"You are?" Findhorn turned to look at him, as had everyone, caught by something peculiar in Farnholme's tone. "What makes you so sure, Brigadier?"

Farnholme waved a deprecating hand, like a man who finds himself being taken more seriously than he intended. "After all, I know Van Effen better than anybody here. And his story *has* to be true: if it weren't true, he wouldn't be here now. Something of an Irishism, gentlemen, but perhaps you follow?"

Findhorn nodded thoughtfully but made no comment. There was silence for some time in the dining-saloon, a silence broken only by the distant crash of bows in a trough in the seas, the indefinable creaking noises a ship makes when it works with the waves in heavy weather, and the shuffling of the feet of the crew of the *Kerry Dancer*. Then Findhorn looked at his watch and turned to Nicolson.

"The bridge for us, Mr. Nicolson, I suggest: from the feel of things we're running into the heavy stuff again. For Captain

Siran and his crew, an armed guard for the remainder of the night, I think." Findhorn's eyes were as bleak and cold as his voice. " But there's one little point I'd like to clear up first."

He walked unhurriedly towards the crew of the *Kerry Dancer*, balancing himself easily against the heavy rolling of the ship, then halted as Van Effen stretched out his hand.

" I'd watch them if I were you," the Dutchman said quietly. " Half of them carry more than one knife and they're not slow with them."

" You have a gun." Findhorn put out his hand and took the automatic which Van Effen had stuck in his waistband. " May I?" He glanced down at the weapon, saw that the safety catch was still on. " A Colt .38."

" You know guns, yes?"

" A little." Soft-footed, Findhorn walked across to the nearest man in the group in the corner. He was tall, broad-shouldered, with a brown, smooth, expressionless face: he looked as if he had got out of the habit of using expressions a long time ago. He wore a hairline moustache, black side-burns that reached three inches below his ears, and he had black, empty eyes. " You are Siran?" Findhorn asked, almost indifferently.

" Captain Siran. At your service." The insolence lay in the faint emphasis on the ' captain,' the millimetric inclination of the head. The face remained quite expressionless.

" Formalities bore me." Findhorn was looking at him with sudden interest. " You are English, aren't you?"

" Perhaps." This time the lips curled, less in a smile than in a token of lazy contempt, perfectly done. " Anglo-Saxon, shall we say?"

" It doesn't matter. You are the captain—were the captain—of the *Kerry Dancer*. You abandoned your ship—and abandoned all the people that you left behind to die, locked behind steel doors. Maybe they drowned, maybe they were burnt to death: it doesn't make any difference now. *You* left them to die."

" Such melodramatics!" Siran lazily patted a yawn to extinction, a masterpiece of weary insolence. " You forget the traditions of the sea. We did all in our power for those unfortunates."

Findhorn nodded slowly and turned away, looking over Siran's six companions. None of them seemed at all happy, but one—a thin-faced man with a cast in one eye—was especially nervous and apprehensive. He shuffled his feet constantly and his hands and fingers seemed to have an independent life of their own. Findhorn walked across and stood in front of him.

"Do you speak English?"

There was no answer, just a furrowing of brows, the raising of shoulders and outspread palms in the universal gesture of incomprehension.

"You picked well, Captain Findhorn," Van Effen drawled slowly. "He speaks English almost as well as you do."

Findhorn brought the automatic up quickly, placed it against the man's mouth and pushed, none too lightly. The man gave way and Findhorn followed. The second step backward brought the man against the bulkhead, palms of his outstretched hands pressing hard against the wall, his one good eye staring down in terror at the gun that touched his teeth.

"Who hammered shut all the clips on the poop-deck door?" Findhorn asked softly. "I'll give you five seconds." He pressed more heavily on the gun and the sudden click of the safety catch snicking off was unnaturally loud in the strained silence. "One, two——"

"I did, I did!" His mouth was working and he was almost gibbering with fear. "I closed the door."

"On whose orders?"

"The captain. He said that——"

"Who shut the fo'c'sle door?"

"Yussif. But Yussif died——"

"On whose orders?" Findhorn asked relentlessly.

"Captain Siran's orders." The man was looking at Siran now, sick fear in his eye. "I'll die for this."

"Probably," Findhorn said carelessly. He pushed the gun into his pocket and walked across to Siran. "Interesting little talk, wasn't it, Captain Siran?"

"The man's a fool," Siran said contemptuously. "Any terrified man will say anything with a gun in his face."

"There were British soldiers—probably your own countrymen—in the fo'c'sle. A score, maybe two dozen, I don't know, but you couldn't have them cluttering up your getaway in the only boat."

"I don't know what you're talking about." Siran's brown face was still the same, still without expression. But his voice was wary now, the calculated insolence gone.

"And there were over twenty people in the aftercastle."

87

Siran might not have spoken for all the attention Findhorn paid to him. "Wounded men, dying men, women—and one little child."

This time Siran said nothing. The smooth face was impassive as ever, but his eyes had narrowed, just perceptibly. When he spoke, however, his voice still held its insolent indifference.

"And just what do you hope to achieve by all this stupid rigmarole, Captain Findhorn?"

"I hope for nothing." Findhorn's lined face was grim, the faded eyes bleak and relentless. "It's not a question of hope, Siran, but of certainty—the certainty of your conviction for murder. In the morning we shall take independent statements from all the members of your own crew and have them signed in the presence of neutral witnesses from my crew. I shall make it my personal responsibility to see to it that you arrive in Australia safely and in good health." Findhorn picked up his hat and prepared to leave. "You will have a fair trial, Captain Siran, but it shouldn't last long, and the penalty for murder, of course, is known to us all."

For the first time, Siran's mask of impassivity cracked and the faintest shadow of fear touched the dark eyes, but Findhorn wasn't there to see it. He was already gone, climbing up the companionway to the shrieking bridge of the *Viroma*.

CHAPTER SIX

DAWN, A cloudless, windless dawn with a lightening eastern sky mother-of-pearl in its opalescent beauty, found the *Viroma* far to the south-eastwards of the Rhio channel, twenty miles due north of the Rifleman Rock and almost half-way towards the Carimata Straits. The big tanker was travelling under full power, a wisp of hazed blue drifting aft from its funnel, the after-decks shaking in teeth-rattling vibration as Carradale, the chief engineer, pushed the big engine to its limit, and then a little beyond.

The typhoon of that long night was gone, the great winds had vanished as if they had never been. But for the salt-stained decks and upperworks and the long, heaving swell that would not die away for many hours yet, it might all have been a dream. But it had been no dream while it had lasted: a nightmare, perhaps, but no dream, not with Captain Findhorn driving the lurching, staggering tanker through the great quartering seas and cyclonic winds for hour upon endless hour, with no thought for the grievous punishment the *Viroma* was taking, with no thought for the comfort and welfare of passengers and crew, with no thought for anything but to put as many miles as possible between himself and Singapore before the day broke and the enemy could see them again.

The delicately-hued pastel shades to the east faded and whitened and vanished, all in a matter of minutes, and the big blurred silhouette of the sun climbed swiftly above the horizon, stretching out a broad, shimmering band of dazzling white across the sea, between itself and the *Viroma*. Not quite an unbroken band, however: something lay in the water, miles away, a big fishing-boat perhaps, or a small coaster, hull down, black as midnight against the rising sun and steaming steadily east, soon diminished to a little black speck in the distance and then nothing at all. Captain Findhorn, on the bridge with Barrett, watched and wondered until it was gone. Perhaps it had seen them, perhaps not. Perhaps it was Japanese, or pro-Japanese, perhaps not. Perhaps it carried a radio, perhaps it didn't. There was nothing they could do about it anyway.

The sun, as it always does in the open sea, seemed to rise straight up into the sky. By half-past seven it was already hot, hot enough to dry out the rain and sea-soaked decks and upperworks of the *Viroma*, hot enough for Findhorn to hang up his oilskins and move far out on to the wing of the bridge to bask in its heat and draw in great lungfuls of the fresh morning air—it wouldn't, he knew, be fresh much longer. Findhorn himself felt fresh enough, if a little tired in his bones: about half-way through the middle watch, when the teeth of the typhoon had lost their edge, Nicolson had persuaded him to go to his cabin and he had slept like a dead man for over three hours.

" Good morning, sir. Quite a change this, isn't it?" Nicolson's soft voice, directly behind him, jerked Findhorn out of his reverie. He turned round.

" Morning, Johnny. What are you doing up at this unearthly hour?" Nicolson, Findhorn knew, couldn't have had much more than a couple of hours' sleep, but he had the rested look of a man with at least eight solid hours behind him. Not for the first time Findhorn had to remind himself that, where durability and resilience were concerned, John Nicolson was a man apart.

" Unearthly hour?" Nicolson glanced at his watch. " It's

almost eight o'clock." He grinned. "Conscience and the calls of duty, sir. I've just been making a quick round of our non-paying guests."

"No complaints?" Findhorn asked humorously.

"I gather that most of them were a bit under the weather during the night, but otherwise no complaints."

"And those who might have know a damn' sight better than to make them," Findhorn nodded. "How are the sick nurses?"

"The two Chinese girls and the elderly ones are much better. A couple of them were down in the hospital and smoke-room when I was there, changing bandages. All five of the soldiers there were in fine form and hungry as hunters."

"An excellent sign," Findhorn interrupted dryly. "How about the two boys in the hospital?"

"Holding their own, the nurses say. I think that they suffer a good deal of pain, which is more than our worthy Brigadier and his pal are doing. You can hear 'em snoring twenty feet away and the engineers' office smells like a distillery."

"And Miss Plenderleith?"

"Taking her constitutional, of course. From one end of the fore and aft gangway to the other. The English cherish the delusion that they are a nautical race: Miss Plenderleith is enjoying herself thoroughly. And then there are three soldiers in the dining-saloon—Corporal Fraser and his two men. They've got a chair apiece, and they're all sitting very comfortably with their .303's and Brens cradled in their hands. I think they're praying for Siran or one of his men to take an extra deep breath so that they can have a cast-iron excuse for shooting a lot of big holes through them. Siran and his pals know exactly how these boys are feeling about them; they're only taking very small breaths indeed and blinking one eye at a time."

"I tend to share your confidence in the guards." Findhorn looked sideways at his chief officer, a quizzical expression on his face. "And how is our worthy Captain Siran looking this morning? A trifle worse of the wear, you would say?"

"Not he. Anyone can see that he's slept the deep, un-troubled sleep of a man with the conscience of a new-born child." Nicolson stared out to sea for a few moments, then said quietly: "I'd appreciate the opportunity of giving the hangman any assistance he may require."

"You'd probably be one of the last in a long queue," Find-horn said grimly. "I don't want to sound melodramatic,

Johnny, but I think the man's an inhuman fiend and should be shot down the same way as you'd destroy a mad dog."

" It'll probably come to that one of these days." Nicolson shook his head. " Mad or not, he's queer enough."

" Meaning?"

" He's English, or three parts English, I'll bet my last penny. He's come up through one of the big public schools, and it's an odds-on guess that he's had a damn' sight more education than I ever had. What's a man like that doing in charge of a miniature hell-ship like the *Kerry Dancer*?"

Findhorn shrugged. " Lord knows. I could give you a dozen explanations, all different and with only one thing in common—they'd all be wrong. You'll find half the dead-beats and black sheep of the world within a couple of hundred miles of Singapore—but he wouldn't come in either category, so that still doesn't answer your question. Frankly, I'm at a loss." Findhorn drummed his fingers on the dodger rail. " He baffles me, but, by Harry, he's not the only one!"

" Van Effen? Our worthy Brigadier?"

" Among others." Findhorn shook his head. " Our passengers are a strange bunch, but not half as strange as the way they act. Take the Brigadier and this Muslim priest. They're thick as thieves. Unusual, you might say?"

" Incredible. The doors of the Bengal and Singapore Clubs would be for ever shut against him. Not done, in capital letters." Nicolson grinned. " Think of the shock and the fearful mortality rate if it were known—in the upper military circles, I mean: all the best bars in the East littered with apoplectic cases, sundowners still clutched in their stiffening hands. Brigadier Farnholme is carrying a fearful responsibility."

Findhorn smiled faintly. " And you still think he's not a phoney?"

" No, sir—neither do you. Colonel Blimp, Grade A—then he does or says something off-beat, completely out of character. He just doesn't classify easily. Inconsiderate of him, very."

" Very," Findhorn murmured dryly. " Then there's his other pal, Van Effen. Why the devil should Siran show such tender concern for his health?"

" It's difficult," Nicolson admitted. " Especially when Van Effen didn't show much concern for his, what with threatening to blow holes in his spine and trying to throttle him. But I'm inclined to believe Van Effen. I like him."

" I believe him, too. But Farnholme just doesn't believe him —he *knows* Van Effen is telling the truth—and when I ask him why he backwaters at high speed and advances piffling reasons that wouldn't convince a five year old." Findhorn sighed wearily. " Just about as puerile and unconvincing as the reasons Miss Plenderleith gave me for wanting to see me when I went to her cabin just after you and Siran had finished your —ah—discussion."

" So you went after all?" Nicolson smiled. " I'm sorry I missed that."

" You knew?"

" Vannier told me. I practically had to drag him to the saloon to get him to give you her message. What did she say?"

" First of all she denied having sent for me at all, then gave me some nonsense about when would we arrive in port and could she send a cable to her sister in England, just something fabricated on the spur of the moment, obviously. She's worried about something and I think she was going to tell me what it was, then changed her mind." Captain Findhorn shrugged his shoulders, dismissing the problem. " Did you know that Miss Plenderleith came from Borneo too? She's been headmistress in a girls' school there and hung on to the last minute."

" I know. We had a long conversation on the catwalk this morning. Called me ' young man ' all the time and made me wonder whether I had washed behind the ears." Nicolson looked speculatively at the captain. " Just to add to your worries, I'll tell you something else you don't know. Miss Plenderleith had a visitor, a gentleman friend, in her cabin last night."

" What! Did she tell you this?"

" Good lord, no. Walters told me. He was just stretching out on his settee after coming off watch last night when he heard a knock on Miss Plenderleith's door—pretty soft, but he heard it: his settee in the wireless office is right up against the bulkhead of his cabin. Walters says he was curious enough to listen at the communicating door, but it was shut tight and he couldn't hear much, it was all very whispery and conspiratorial. But one of the voices was very deep, a man's murmur for certain. He was there almost ten minutes, then he left."

" Midnight assignations in Miss Plenderleith's cabin!" Findhorn still hadn't recovered from his astonishment. " I would have thought she would have screamed her head off."

"Not her!" Nicolson grinned and shook his head positively. "She's a pillar of respectability, all right, but any midnight visitor would have been hauled in, lectured over the old girl's wagging forefinger and sent on his way a chastened man, bent on leading a better life. But this was no lecture, I gather, but a very hush-hush discussion."

"Walters any idea who it was?"

"None at all—just that it was a man's voice and that he himself was too damn' tired and sleepy to worry about it anyway."

"Yes. Maybe he has the right idea at that." Findhorn took off his cap and mopped his dark head with a handkerchief: only eight o'clock, but already the sun was beginning to burn. "We've more to do than worry about them anyway. I just can't figure them out. They're a strange bunch—each one I talk to seems queerer than the last."

"Including Miss Drachmann?" Nicolson suggested.

"Good heavens, no! I'd trade the bunch of them for that girl." Findhorn replaced his cap and shook his head slowly, his eyes distant. "A shocking case, Johnny—what a ghastly mess those diabolical little butchers made of her face." His eyes came into focus again, and he looked sharply at Nicolson. "How much of what you told her last night was true?"

"About what the surgeons could do for her, you mean?"

"Yes."

"Not much. I don't know a great deal, but that scar will have stretched and set long before anyone can do anything about it. They can still do something, of course—but they're not miracle workers: none of them claims to be."

"Then damn it all, mister, you'd no right to give her the impression they are." Findhorn was as near anger as his phlegmatic nature would allow. "My God, think of the dis-illusionment!"

"Eat, drink and be merry," Nicolson quoted softly. "Do you think you'll ever see England again, sir?"

Findhorn looked at him for a long moment, craggy brows drawn deep over his eyes, then nodded in slow understanding and turned away. "Funny how we keep thinking in terms of peace and normality," he murmured. "Sorry, boy, sorry. Yet I've been thinking about nothing else since the sun came up. Young Peter, the nurses, everyone—mostly the child and that girl, I don't know why." He was silent for a few moments, eyes quartering the cloudless horizon, then added with only apparent inconsequence: "It's a lovely day, Johnny."

"It's a lovely day to die," Nicolson said sombrely. Then he caught the captain's eye and smiled, briefly. "It's a long time waiting, but the Japanese are polite little gentlemen—ask Miss Drachmann: they always have been polite little gentlemen: I don't think they'll keep us waiting much longer."

*   *   *

But the Japanese did keep them waiting. They kept them waiting a long, long time. Not long, perhaps, as the world reckons seconds and minutes and hours, but when men, despairing men too long on the rack of suspense, momentarily await and expect the inevitable, then the seconds and the minutes and the hours lose any significance as absolute units of time and, instead, become relative only to the razor-edged expectancy of the passing moment, to the ever-present anticipation of what must inexorably come. And so the seconds crawled by and became minutes, and the minutes stretched themselves out interminably and lengthened into an hour, and then another hour, and still the skies were empty and the line of the shimmering horizon remained smooth and still and unbroken. Why the enemy—and Findhorn knew hundreds of ships and planes must be scouring the seas for them—held off so long was quite beyond his understanding: he could only hazard the guess that they must have swept that area the previous afternoon after they had turned back to the aid of the *Kerry Dancer* and were now searching the seas farther to the south. Or perhaps they thought the *Viroma* had been lost in the typhoon—and even as that explanation crossed his mind Findhorn dismissed it as wishful thinking and knew that the Japanese would think nothing of the kind. . . . Whatever the reason, the *Viroma* was still alone, still rolling south-eastwards in a vast expanse of empty sea and sky. Another hour passed, and then another and it was high noon, a blazing, burning sun riding almost vertically overhead in the oven of the sky and for the first time Captain Findhorn was allowing himself the luxury of the first tentative stirrings of hope: the Carimata Straits and darkness and the Java Sea and they might dare begin to think of home again. The sun rolled over its zenith, noon passed, and the minutes crept on again, five, ten, fifteen, twenty, each minute dragging longer and longer as hope began to rise once more. And then, at twenty-four minutes past noon, hope had turned to dust and the long wait was over.

A gunner on the fo'c'sle saw it first—a tiny black speck far to the south-west, materialising out of the heat haze, high above the horizon. For a few seconds it seemed to remain there, stationary in the sky, a black, meaningless dot suspended in the air, and then, almost all at once, it was no longer tiny but visibly swelling in size with every breath the watchers took, and no longer meaningless, but taking shape, hardening in definition through the shimmering haze until the outline of fuselage and wings could be clearly seen, so clearly as to be unmistakable. A Japanese Zero fighter, probably fitted with long-range tanks, and even as the watchers on the *Viroma* recognised it the muted thunder of the aero engine came at them across the stillness of the sea.

The Zero droned in steadily, losing height by the second and heading straight for them. It seemed at first as if the pilot intended flying straight across the *Viroma*, but, less than a mile away, he banked sharply to starboard and started to circle the ship at a height of about five hundred feet. He made no move to attack, and not a gun fired aboard the *Viroma*. Captain Findhorn's orders to his gunners had been explicit— no firing except in self-defence: their ammunition was limited and they had to conserve it for the inevitable bombers. Besides, there was always the chance that the pilot might be deceived by the newly-painted name of *Siyushu Maru* and the large flag of the Rising Sun which had taken the place of *Resistencia* and the flag of the Argentine Republic a couple of days previously—about one chance in ten thousand, Findhorn thought grimly. The brazen effrontery and the sheer unexpectedness that had carried the *Viroma* thus far had outlived their usefulness.

For almost ten minutes the Zero continued to circle the *Viroma*, never much more than half a mile away, banking steeply most of the time. Then two more 'planes—Zero fighters also—droned up from the south-west and joined the first. Twice all three of them circled the ship, then the first pilot broke formation and made two fore-and-aft runs, less than a hundred yards away, the canopy of his cockpit pushed right back so that the watchers on the bridge could see his face—or what little of it was visible behind helmet, goggles on forehead and transmitter mouthpiece—as the pilot took in every detail of the ship. Then he banked away sharply and rejoined the others: within seconds they were in line ahead

95

formation, dipping their wings in mocking salute and heading north-west, climbing steadily all the time.

Nicolson let go his breath in a long, soundless sigh and turned to Findhorn. "That bloke will never know how lucky he is." He jerked his thumb upwards towards the Hotchkiss emplacements. "Even our pop-gun merchants up top could have chewed him into little bits."

"I know, I know." His back against the dodger screen, Findhorn stared bleakly after the disappearing fighters. "And what good would it have done? Just wasted valuable ammunition, that's all. He wasn't doing us any harm—all the harm he could do he'd done long before he came anywhere near us. Our description, right down to the last rivet, our position, course and speed—his command H.Q. got that over the radio long before he came anywhere near us." Findhorn lowered his glasses and turned round heavily. "We can't do anything about our description and position, but we can about our course. 200, Mr. Nicolson, if you please. We'll try for the Macclesfield Channel."

"Aye, aye, sir." Nicolson hesitated. "Think it'll make any difference, sir?"

"None whatsoever." Findhorn's voice was just a little weary. "Somewhere within two hundred and fifty miles from here laden bombers—altitude bombers, dive-bombers, torpedo bombers—are already taking off from Japanese airfields. Scores of them. Prestige is vital. If we escaped, Japan would be the laughing-stock of their precious Greater East Asia Co-Prosperity Sphere, and they can't afford to lose anybody's confidence." Findhorn looked directly at Nicolson, his eyes quiet and sad and remote. "I'm sorry, Johnny, sorry for little Peter and the girl and all the rest of them. They'll get us all right. They got the *Prince of Wales* and the *Repulse*: they'll massacre us. They'll be here in just over an hour."

"So why alter course, sir?"

"So why do anything. Give us another ten minutes, perhaps, before they locate us. A gesture, my boy—empty, I know, but still a gesture. Even the lamb turns and runs before the wolf-pack tears him to pieces." Findhorn paused a moment, then smiled. "And speaking of lambs, Johnny, you might go below and drive our little flock into the fold."

Ten minutes later Nicolson was back on the bridge. Findhorn looked at him expectantly.

"All safely corralled, Mr. Nicolson?"

"Afraid not, sir." Nicolson touched the three golden bars

96

on his epaulets. "The soldiers of to-day are singularly unimpressed by authority. Hear anything, sir?"

Findhorn looked at him in puzzlement, listened, then nodded his head. "Footsteps. Sounds like a regiment up above."

Nicolson nodded. "Corporal Fraser and his two merry men. When I told them to get into the pantry and stay there the corporal asked me to raffle myself. His feelings were hurt, I think. They can muster three rifles and a sub-machine-gun between them, and I suspect they'll be ten times as effective as the two characters with the Hotchkisses up there."

"And the rest?"

"Same story with the other soldiers—off with their guns right aft. No heroics anywhere—all four of them just kind of grim and thoughtful. Just kids. The sick men are still in the hospital—too sick to be moved. Safe there as anywhere, I suppose: there's a couple of nurses with them."

"Four of them?" Findhorn frowned. "But I thought——"

"There were five," Nicolson acknowledged. "Fifth's a shell-shock case, I imagine. Alex something—don't know his name. He's useless—nerves shot to ribbons. I dragged him along to join the others in the pantry.

"All the others accounted for. Old Farnholme wasn't too keen on leaving the engineers' office but when I pointed out that the pantry was the only compartment in the superstructure that didn't open to the outside, that it had steel instead of the usual wooden bulkheads, and that it had a couple of protective bulkheads fore and aft and three on either side he was over there like a shot."

Findhorn's mouth twisted. "Our gallant army. Colonel Blimp to the ramparts, but not when the guns start firing. A bad taste in the mouth, Johnny, and quite out of character. The saving grace of the Blimps of this world is that they don't know what fear is."

"Neither does Farnholme." Nicolson was positive. "I'd take very long odds on that. But I think he's worried about something, badly worried." Nicolson shook his head. "He's a queer old bird, sir, and he's some very personal reason for taking shelter; but it's got nothing to do with saving his own skin."

"Perhaps you're right." Findhorn shrugged. "I don't see that it matters anyway, not now. Van Effen with him?"

"In the dining-saloon. He thought Siran and his pals might pick an awkward time to start trouble. He has his gun on them. They won't start anything." Nicolson smiled faintly.

"Van Effen strikes me as a very competent gentleman indeed."

"You left Siran and his men in the saloon?" Findhorn pursed his lips. "Our suicide parlour. Wide open to fore-and-aft strafing attacks and a cannon shell wouldn't even notice the shuttering on these windows." It was more a question than statement, and Findhorn matched it with his look, half-quizzical, half-expectant, but Nicolson merely shrugged his shoulders and turned away, the cold blue eyes lost in indifference and quartering the sun-hazed horizon to the north.

* * *

The Japanese returned at twelve minutes past two o'clock in the afternoon, and they came in force. Three or four planes would have been enough: the Japanese sent fifty. There were no delays, no tentative skirmishing, no preliminary altitude bombing, just the long curving sweep to the south-west and then that single, shattering attack out of the sun, a calculated, precision-engineered attack of dovetailing torpedo-bombers, dive-bombers and Zeros, an attack the skill of whose execution was surpassed only by its single-minded savagery and ferocity. From the moment that the first Zero swept in at deck level, shells from its twin cannon smashing into the bridge, until the last torpedo-bomber lifted and banked away from the concussive blast of its own detonating torpedo, only three minutes passed. But they were three minutes that transformed the *Viroma* from the finest, most modern tanker of the Anglo-Arabian fleet, from twelve thousand tons of flawless steel with all the guns on deck chattering their puny defiance at the incoming enemy, to a battered, blazing, smoke-enshrouded shambles with all the guns fallen silent, the engines gone and nearly all the crew dying or already dead. Massacre, ruthless, inhuman massacre with but one saving grace—the merciless fury of the attack tempered only by its merciful speed.

Massacre, but massacre aimed not at the ship primarily, but at the men who manned the ship. The Japanese, obviously flying under strict orders, had executed these, and brilliantly. They had concentrated their attacks on the engine-room, bridge, fo'c'sle and gun positions, the first of these suffering grievously: two torpedoes and at least a dozen bombs had entered the machinery space and the decks above: half the stern was blown away and in the after part of the ship there were no survivors at all. Of all the gunners, only two survived —Jenkins, an able seaman who had manned a fo'c'sle gun,

98

and Corporal Fraser. Perhaps Corporal Fraser would not be a survivor for long: half his already crippled left arm had been shot away and he was too weak, too shocked, to make more than a token attempt to stem the welling arterial blood.

On the bridge, crouched flat on the floor behind the armoured steel bulkheads of the wheelhouse, half-stunned with the blast and concussion of exploding cannon shells, both Findhorn and Nicolson dimly realised the significance of the plan of attack, the reason for the overwhelming weight of bombers used in the onslaught and the heavy escort of Zero fighters. They realised, too, why the bridge remained miraculously immune from bombs, why no torpedo had as yet smashed into any of the oil cargo tanks—a target impossible to miss—and torn the heart out of the *Viroma*. The Japanese weren't trying to destroy the *Viroma*: they were trying to save the *Viroma* and to destroy the crew. What matter if they blew the stern off the ship—her nine great oil tanks, still intact, and the fo'c'sle had enough reserve buoyancy to keep the ship afloat: awash, perhaps, but still afloat. And if they could ensure that none of the *Viroma's* crew lived to blow up or scuttle the shattered ship, ten thousand tons of oil would be theirs for the taking: millions of gallons of high grade fuel for their ships and tanks and planes.

And then, quite suddenly, the almost continuous roar and teeth-chattering vibration of bursting bombs and torpedoes were at an end, the off-beat drone of heavy bomber engines faded quickly in the distance and the abrupt, comparative silence was almost as hurting to the ear as the clamour that had just ended. Wearily Nicolson shook his head to clear it of the shock and sound and smoke and choking dust, levered himself groggily to his hands and knees, caught the handle of the screen door and pulled himself to his feet, then dropped to the deck like a stone as cannon shells whistled evilly through the smashed windows just above his head and exploded against the chartroom bulkhead, filling the wheelhouse with the shocking blast of sound and a lethal storm of splintered steel.

For a few seconds Nicolson remained prone on the deck, face down with his hands over his ears and his cradling forearms protecting his head, half-dazed and cursing himself silently for his precipitate, unthinking folly in rising so quickly to his feet. He should have known better than to imagine for a moment that the entire Japanese assault force would withdraw. It had been inevitable that they would leave some planes behind to take care of any survivor who might move out on deck and try to rob them of their prize—and these planes, Zero fighters, would remain to the limit of their long range tanks.

Slowly, this time, moving with infinite caution, Nicolson rose to his feet again and peered out over the jagged glass in the bottom of the shattered window frame. Puzzled for a moment, he tried to orientate himself and the ship, then realised from the black bar of shadow from the foremast what had happened. A torpedo must have blown off or jammed the rudder, for the *Viroma*, losing way rapidly in the water until she was now almost stopped, had swung right round through a hundred and eighty degrees and was facing in the direction she had come. And then, almost at the same time, Nicolson saw something else again, something that made the position of the *Viroma* of no importance at all, something that made a mockery of the vigil of the planes watching and waiting in the sky.

It hadn't been miscalculation on the part of the bomber pilots, just ignorance. When they had attacked the fo'c'sle, destroying guns and gunners and using armour piercing cannon shells to penetrate the fo'c'sle deck and kill any of the crew members sheltering beneath, it must have been a reasonable supposition to them that that was all they were doing. But what they did not know, what they could have had no means of knowing, was that the storage space beneath the fo'c'sle deck, the 'tween-deck cargo hold beneath that and the even larger hold beneath that were not empty. They were full, completely, filled to capacity with hundreds of closely stacked barrels, with tens of thousands of gallons of high-octane aircraft fuel—petrol intended for the shattered, burnt-out wrecks that now littered the Selengar airfield.

The flames rose a hundred, two hundred feet into the still, breathless air, a great, solid column so white, so intensely hot and free from smoke that it was all but invisible in the bright glare of the afternoon sun, not flames really but a broad shimmering band of super-heated air that narrowed as it climbed and ended in a twisting, wavering point that reached far up beyond the tip of the foremast and died in a feathery wisp of pale blue smoke. Every now and then another barrel would explode deep in the hold and, just for a moment, a gout of thick smoke would lace the almost invisible flame and then, as quickly, it would be gone. And the fire, Nicolson knew, was only starting. When the flames really got hold, when the barrels started bursting by the dozen, the aviation spirit in the for'ard fuel tank, number nine, would go up like an exploding ammunition dump. The heat of the flames already fierce on his forehead, he stared at the fo'c'sle a few moments longer, trying to estimate how much time they had left. But it was impossible to know, impossible even to guess. Perhaps only two minutes, perhaps as long as twenty—after two years of war the toughness of tankers, their reluctance to die, had become almost legendary . . . But certainly not more than twenty minutes.

Nicolson's attention was suddenly caught by something moving among the maze of pipes on the deck, just aft of the foremast. It was a man, dressed only in a pair of tattered blue denims, stumbling and falling as he made his way towards a ladder that led up to the catwalk. He seemed dazed and kept rubbing his forearm across his eyes, as if he couldn't see too well, but he managed to reach the foot of the ladder, drag himself to the top and began, at a lurching run, to make his way along the catwalk to the bridge superstructure. Nicolson could see him clearly now—Able Seaman Jenkins, trainer of the fo'c'sle pom-pom. And someone else had seen him too and Nicolson had time only for a desperate shout of warning before he flung himself to the deck and listened, with clenched fists, to the hammerblows of exploding cannon shells as the Zero pulled out of its short, sudden dive and raked the foredeck from fo'c'sle to bridge.

This time Nicolson didn't get to his feet. Getting to his feet inside that wheelhouse, he realised, was a good way of committing suicide. There could be only one good reason for getting to his feet, and that was to see how Jenkins was. But he didn't have to look to know how Jenkins was. Jenkins should have bided his time and chosen his chance for making his dash, but perhaps he had been too dazed: or perhaps the only alternative he'd had was between running and being killed, and staying and being incinerated.

Nicolson shook his head to clear away the fumes and smell of cordite, pushed himself to a sitting position and looked round the scarred and shattered wheelhouse. There were four people in it apart from himself—and there had only been three a moment ago. McKinnon, the bo'sun, had just arrived, just as the last shells had exploded inside the bridge. He was half-crouched, half-lying across the threshold of the chartroom door, propped on one elbow and looking cautiously around him. He was unhurt, but taking no chances before moving any further.

" Keep your head down!" Nicolson advised him urgently.
" Don't stand up or you'll get it blown off." Even to himself
his voice sounded hoarse and whispery and unreal.

Evans, the duty quartermaster, was sitting on his duckboard
grill, his back to the wheel and swearing softly, fluently, continuously in his high-pitched Welsh voice. Blood dripped from
a long gash on his forehead on to his knees, but he ignored it
and concentrated on wrapping a makeshift bandage round his
left forearm. How badly the arm was gashed Nicolson
couldn't tell: but every fresh strip of ragged white linen torn
from his shirt became bright red and saturated the moment it
touched his arm.

Vannier was lying against the deck in the far corner.
Nicolson crawled across the deck and lifted his head, gently.
The fourth officer had a cut and bruised temple, but seemed
otherwise unharmed: he was quite unconscious, but breathing
quietly and evenly. Carefully, Nicolson lowered his head to
the deck and turned to look at Findhorn. The captain was
sitting watching him on the other side of the bridge, back
against the bulkhead, palms and splayed fingers resting on the
deck beside him. The old man looks a bit pale, Nicolson
thought: he's not a kid any longer, not fit for it, especially
this kind of fun and games. He gestured at Vannier.

" Just knocked out, sir. He's as lucky as the rest of us—all
alive, if not exactly kicking." Nicolson made his voice sound
more cheerful than he felt. Even as he stopped speaking he
saw Findhorn bending forward to get up, his fingernails
whitening as he put pressure on his hands. " Easy does it,
sir!" Nicolson called out sharply. " Stay where you are. There
are some characters snooping around outside just begging for a
sight of you."

Findhorn nodded and relaxed, leaning back against the
bulkhead. He said nothing. Nicholson looked at him sharply.
" You all right, sir?"

Findhorn nodded again and made to speak. But no words
came, only a strange gravelly cough and suddenly his lips were
flecked with bright bubbles of blood, blood that trickled down
his chin and dripped slowly on to the fresh, white crispness of
his tunic shirt. Nicolson was on his feet in a moment, crossed
the wheelhouse in a stumbling run and fell on his knees in
front of the captain.

Findhorn smiled at him and tried to speak, but again there
was only the bubbling cough and more blood at his mouth,

102

bright arterial blood that contrasted pitifully with the whiteness of the lips. His eyes were sick and glazed.

Quickly, urgently, Nicolson searched body and head for
evidence of a wound. At first he could see nothing, then all at
once he had it—he'd mistaken it for one of the drops of blood
soaking into Findhorn's shirt. But this was no blood-drip, but
a hole—a small, insignificant looking hole, quite circular and
reddening at the edges. That was Nicolson's first shocked
reaction—how small a hole it was, and how harmless. Almost
in the centre of the captain's chest, but not quite. It was perhaps an inch or so to the left of the breastbone and two inches
above the heart.

CHAPTER SEVEN

GENTLY, CAREFULLY, Nicolson caught the captain by the
shoulders, eased his back off the bulkhead and turned to look
for the bo'sun. But McKinnon was already kneeling by his
side, and one glance at McKinnon's studiously expressionless
face told Nicolson that the stain on the captain's shirt-front
must be spreading. Quickly, without any word from Nicolson,
McKinnon had his knife out and the back of the captain's
shirt slit open in one neat movement, then he closed the knife,
caught the edges of the cut cloth in his hands and ripped the
shirt apart. For a moment he scanned the captain's back, then
he closed the tear together, looked up at Nicolson and shook
his head. As carefully as before Nicolson eased the captain
back against the bulkhead.

" No success, gentlemen, eh?" Findhorn's voice was only a
husky, strained murmur, a fight against the blood welling up in
his throat.

" It's bad enough, not all that bad though." Nicolson picked
his words with care. " Does it hurt much, sir?"

" No." Findhorn closed his eyes for a moment, then opened
them again. " Please answer my question. Did it go right
through?"

Nicolson's voice was detached, almost clinical. " No, sir.
Must have nicked the lung, I think, and lodged in the ribs at the
back. We'll have to dig for it, sir."

" Thank you." ' Nicked ' was a flagrant meiosis and only

a fully equipped hospital theatre could hope to cope with surgery within the chest wall, but if Findhorn appreciated these things he gave no sign by either tone or expression. He coughed painfully, then tried to smile. " The excavations will have to wait. How is the ship, Mr. Nicolson?"

" Going," Nicolson said bluntly. He jerked a thumb over his shoulder. " You can see the flames, sir. Fifteen minutes if we're lucky. Permission to go below, sir?"

" Of course, of course! What am I thinking of?" Findhorn struggled to rise to his feet, but McKinnon held him down, talking to him in his soft Highland voice, looking at Nicolson for guidance. But the guidance came not from Nicolson but in the shape of a crescendoing roar of an aircraft engine, the trip-hammer thudding of aircraft cannon and a shell that screamed through the smashed window above their heads and blasted the top of the chartroom door off its hinges. Findhorn ceased to struggle and leaned back tiredly against the bulkhead, look-ing up at McKinnon and half smiling. Then he turned to speak to Nicolson, but Nicolson was already gone, the chartroom door half closing behind him, swinging crazily on its shattered hinges.

Nicolson dropped down the centre ladder, turned for'ard and went in the starboard door of the dining-saloon. Van Effen was sitting on the deck by the door as he went in, his gun in his hand, unhurt. He looked up as the door opened.

" A great deal of noise indeed, Mr. Nicolson. Finished?"

" More or less. I'm afraid the ship is. Still two or three Zeros outside, looking for the last drop of blood. Any trouble?"

" With them?" Van Effen waved a contemptuous pistol barrel at the crew of the *Kerry Dancer*: five of them lay hud-dled fearfully on the deck at the foot of the for'ard settees, two more were prostrate under the tables. " Too worried about their own precious skins."

" Anyone hurt?"

Van Effen shook his head regretfully. " The devil is good to his own kind, Mr. Nicolson."

" Pity." Nicolson was already on his way across to the port door of the dining-saloon. " The ship's going. We haven't long. Herd our little friends up to the deck above— keep 'em in the passageway for the time being. Don't open the screen doors——" Nicolson broke off suddenly, halted in mid-stride. The wooden serving hatch into the pantry was riddled

104

and smashed in a dozen places. From the other side he could hear the thin, quavering sobbing of a little child.

Within three seconds Nicolson was out in the passage, wrestling with the handle of the pantry door. The handle turned, but the door refused to open—locked, perhaps, more probably jammed and buckled. A providential fire axe hung on the bulkhead outside the fifth engineer's cabin and Nicolson swung it viciously against the lock of the pantry door. On the third blow the lock sprang open and the door crashed back on its hinges.

Nicolson's first confused impressions were of smoke, burning, a sea of smashed crockery and an almost overpowering reek of whisky. Then the rush of fresh air quickly cleared the air and he could see the two nurses sitting on the deck, almost at his feet, Lena, the young Malayan girl, with her dark, sooty eyes wide and shadowed with terror, and Miss Drachmann beside her, her face pale and strained but calm. Nicolson dropped on his knees beside her.

" The little boy?" he asked harshly.

" Do not worry. Little Peter is safe." She smiled at him gravely, eased back the heavy metal door of the hot press, already ajar. The child was inside, snugly wrapped in a heavy blanket, staring out at him with wide, fearful eyes. Nicolson reached in a hand, gently ruffled the blond hair, then rose abruptly to his feet and let his breath go in a long sigh.

" Thank God for that, anyway." He smiled down at the girl. " And thank you, too, Miss Drachmann. Damned clever idea. Take him outside in the passage, will you? It's stifling in here." He swung round, then halted and stared down in disbelief at the tableau at his feet. The young soldier, Alex, and the priest were stretched out on the deck, side by side, both obviously unconscious—at least. Farnholme was just straightening up from examining the priest's head. The smell of whisky from him was so powerful that his clothes might have been saturated in it.

" What the hell's been going on here?" Nicolson demanded icily. " Can't you keep off the bottle for even five minutes, Farnholme?"

" You're a headstrong young man, young man." The voice came from the far corner of the pantry. " You mustn't jump to conclusions, especially wrong conclusions."

Nicolson peered through the gloom. With the dynamos and lighting gone the windowless pantry was half-shrouded in darkness. He could barely distinguish the slight form of Miss Plenderleith sitting straight-backed against the ice-box. Her head was bent over her hands and the busy click-click, click-click of needles seemed unnaturally loud. Nicolson stared at her in utter disbelief.

"What are you doing, Miss Plenderleith?" Even to himself, Nicolson's voice sounded strained, incredulous.

"Knitting, of course. Have you never seen anyone knitting before?"

"Knitting!" Nicolson murmured in awe. "Knitting, of course! Two lumps or three, vicar." Nicolson shook his head in wonder. "If the Japs knew this they'd demand an armistice to-morrow."

"What on earth are you talking about?" Miss Plenderleith demanded crisply. "Don't tell me that you've lost your senses, too."

"Too?"

"This unfortunate young man here." She pointed at the young soldier. "We jammed some trays against the serving hatch when we came in—it's only wood, you know. The Brigadier thought it might give protection from bullets." Miss Plenderleith was talking very rapidly, very concisely, her knitting now laid aside. "When the first bombs hit, this young man tried to get out. The Brigadier locked the door— and very quick he was about it, too. Then he started to pull the trays down—going to go out the hatch, I suppose. The—ah —priest here was trying to pull him back when the bullets came through the hatch."

Nicolson turned away quickly, looked at Farnholme and then nodded down at the Muslim priest. "My apologies, Brigadier. Is he dead?"

"Thank God, no." Farnholme straightened on his knees, his Sandhurst drawl temporarily in abeyance. "Creased, concussed, that's all." He looked down at the young soldier and shook his head in anger. "Bloody young fool!"

"And what's the matter with him?"

"Laid him out with a whisky bottle," Farnholme said succinctly. "Bottle broke. Must have been flawed. Shockin' waste, shockin'."

"Get him outside, will you? The rest of you outside, too." Nicolson turned round as someone entered the door behind him. "Walters! I'd forgotten all about you. Are you all right?"

"All right, sir. Wireless room's a bit of a shambles, I'm

afraid." Walters looked pale and sick, but purposeful as ever.

"Doesn't matter now." Nicolson was grateful for Walters's presence, his solidity and competence. "Get these people up to the boat-deck—in the passage, better still in your office or cabin. Don't let 'em out on deck. If there's anything they want to get from their cabins, give 'em a couple of minutes."

Walters smiled wryly. "We're taking a little trip, sir?"

"Very shortly. Just to be on the safe side." It would hardly benefit the morale of the passengers, Nicolson reflected, by adding what Walters himself must have been aware of—that the only alternatives were cremation or disintegration when the ship went up. He went out the door quickly, then staggered and almost fell as a tremendous detonation, right aft, seemed to lift the stern of the *Viroma* out of the water and sent a shuddering, convulsive shock through her every plate and rivet. Instinctively Nicolson reached out and caught the lintel of the door, caught and held Miss Drachmann and Peter as the nurse fell against him, steadied her and turned quickly to Walters.

"Belay that last order. No one to go to their cabins. Just get 'em up there and see that they stay there." In four strides he was at the after screen door, opening it cautiously. Seconds later he was outside on deck, standing at the top of the iron ladder that led down to the main deck, and staring aft.

The heat struck at him almost with the physical impact of a blow and brought tears of pain to his eyes. No complaints that he couldn't see this fire, he thought grimly. Billowing, convoluted clouds of oily black smoke stretched up hundreds of feet into the sky, reaching higher and higher with the passing of every second, not tailing off to a peak but spreading out at the top in a great, black anvil-head, spreading over the ship like a pall: at the base, however, just at deck level, there was hardly any smoke at all, only a solid wall of flame perhaps sixty feet in diameter, a wall that rose forty feet, then broke into a dozen separate pillars of fire ; fiery, twisting tongues of flame that reached hungrily upwards, their flickering points swallowed up in the rolling darkness of the smoke. In spite of the intense heat, Nicolson's first reaction was to cover not his face but his ears: even at a hundred and fifty feet the roaring of the flames was all but intolerable.

Another miscalculation on the part of the Japs, he thought grimly. A bomb meant for the engine-room had exploded in the diesel oil bunkers, blowing aft through the engine-room

bulkhead and for'ard clear through both walls of the cofferdam into number one cargo tank. And it was almost certainly
number one tank that was on fire, its quarter of a million
gallons of fuel oil ignited and fanned by the fierce down-
draught of air through the wrecked cofferdam. Even if they
had had firefighting apparatus left, and the men to man the
apparatus, tackling that inferno, an inferno that would have
engulfed and destroyed any man before he could have come
within fifty feet of it, would only have been the suicidal gesture
of an imbecile. And then, above the deep, steady roar of the
flames, Nicolson heard another, more deadly sound, the high-
pitched, snarling howl of an aero engine under maximum
boost, caught a momentary glimpse of a Zero arrowing in off
the starboard beam, at mast-top height, flung himself convulsively backward through the open door behind him as cannon-
shells struck and exploded where he had been only two seconds
before.

Cursing himself for his forgetfulness, Nicolson pushed
himself to his feet, clipped the door shut and looked around
him. Already both pantry and passage were quite empty—
Walters was not a man to waste time. Quickly Nicolson made
his way along the passage, through the dining-saloon to the
foot of the companionway leading up to the boat deck. Farn
holme was there, struggling to carry the young soldier up the
stairs. Nicolson helped him in silence, and at the top Walters
met him and relieved him of his share of the burden. Nicolson
glanced along the passage towards the wireless office.

" All safely corralled, Sparks?"

" Yes, sir. The Arab Johnny's just coming to and Miss
Plenderleith's packing her bag as if she were off to Bourne-
mouth for a fortnight."

" Yes, I've noticed. The worrying kind." Nicolson looked
along to the for'ard end of the passage. Siran and his men
were huddled round the ladder that led up to the chartroom,
fearful and unhappy. All, that is, except Siran himself. Despite its cuts and bruises, the brown face still held its expressionless calm. Nicolson looked sharply at Walters. " Where's
Van Effen?"

" No idea, sir. Haven't seen him."

Nicolson walked to face Siran. " Where's Van Effen?"

Siran shrugged his shoulders, twisted his lips into a smile and
said nothing.

Nicolson jammed a pistol into Siran's solar plexus, and the

smile faded from the brown face. " I'd just as soon you died,"
Nicolson said pleasantly.

" He went above." Siran nodded at the ladder. " A minute
ago."

Nicolson swung round. " Got a gun, Sparks?"

" In the office, sir."

" Get it. Van Effen had no right to leave this lot." He
waited till Walters returned. " No reasons required for shooting this bunch. Any flimsy excuse will do."

He went up the stairs three at a time, passed through the
chartroom and into the wheelhouse. Vannier was conscious
now, still shaking his head to free it from muzziness, but recovered enough to help Evans bind his arm. McKinnon and
the captain were still together.

" Seen Van Effen, Bo'sun?"

" Here a minute ago, sir. He's gone up top."

" Up top? What in heaven's name——" Nicolson checked
himself. Time was too short as it was. " How do you feel,
Evans?"

" Bloody well mad, sir," Evans said, and looked it. " If I
could get my hands on those murderin'——"

" All right, all right." Nicolson smiled briefly. " I can see
you'll live. Stay here with the captain. How are you,
Fourth?"

" O.K. now, sir." Vannier was very pale. " Just a crack on
the head."

" Good. Take the bo'sun with you and check the boats.
Just numbers one and two—three and four are finished." He
broke off and looked at the captain. " You said something,
sir?"

" Yes." Findhorn's voice was still weak, but clearer than it
had been. " Three and four gone?"

" Bombed to bits and then burnt to a cinder," Nicolson said
without bitterness. "A very thorough job. Number one
tank's on fire, sir."

Findhorn shook his head. " What hope, boy?"

" None, just none at all." Nicolson turned back to Vannier.
" If they're both serviceable we'll take them both." He glanced
at Findhorn, raised eyebrows seeking confirmation. " We
don't want Siran and his cut-throat pals in the same open
boat as us when night falls."

Findhorn nodded silently, and Nicolson went on: " As many
spare blankets, food, water, arms and ammunition as you can

109

find. And first-aid kits. All these in the better boat—ours.
That clear, Fourth?"

"All clear, sir."

"One other thing. When you're finished, a strap stretcher
for the captain. Don't get yourselves shot full of cannon
holes—they nearly got me a couple of minutes ago. And for
God's sake hurry! Five minutes for the lot."

Nicolson moved just outside the wheelhouse starboard
door and stood there for two or three seconds, taking stock.
The blast of fiery heat struck at him, fore and aft, like the
scorching incalescence of an opened furnace door, but he
ignored it. The heat wouldn't kill him, not yet, but the Zeros
would if they were given any chance at all: but the Zeros
were half a mile away, line ahead and port wings dipped as
they circled the *Viroma*, watching and waiting.

Five steps, running, took him to the foot of the wheelhouse top ladder. He took the first three steps in a stride,
then checked so abruptly that only a swiftly bent arm cush-
ioned the shock as he fell forward against the rungs. Van
Effen, face and shirt streaked with blood, was just beginning
to descend, half supporting, half carrying Corporal Fraser.
The soldier was in a very bad way, a man obviously willing
himself to hang on to the last shreds of consciousness. Beneath the dark tan the pain-twisted face was drained of blood,
and with his right arm he supported what was left of his left
forearm, torn and shredded and horribly maimed—only an
exploding cannon shell could have worked that savage injury.
He seemed to be losing only a little blood: Van Effen had
knotted a tourniquet just above the elbow.

Nicolson met them half-way up the ladder, caught the
soldier and took some of the almost dead weight off Van
Effen. And then, before he realised what was happening, he
had all the weight and Van Effen was on his way back up to
the wheelhouse top.

"Where are you going, man?" Nicolson had to shout to
make himself heard over the roar of the flames. "Damn all
anybody can do up there now. We're abandoning ship. Come
on!"

"Must see if there's anyone else alive," Van Effen yelled.
He shouted something else and Nicolson thought he heard him
mention guns, but couldn't be sure. His voice didn't carry too
well above the roar of the two great fires and Nicolson's attention was already elsewhere. The Zeros—there were only three
of them—were no longer circling the ship but banking steeply,

110

darkness she was a stranger lost in a strange city. Somewhere down there on the waterfront, she had been told, there was a party of soldiers, many of whom urgently required attention—and if they didn't get it that night, they would most certainly never get it inside a Japanese prison camp. But with every minute that passed, it looked more and more as if the Japanese would get to them first. The more they twisted and turned through the deserted streets, the more hopelessly lost she became. Somewhere opposite Cape Ru on the Kallang creek she might expect to find them, she had been told: but, as it was, she couldn't even find the waterfront, far less have any idea where Cape Ru lay in the darkness.

Half an hour passed, an hour, and even her own steps began to flag as despair touched her for the first time. They could never find the soldiers, never, not in this endless confusion and darkness. It was desperately unfair of their doctor, Major Blackley, to have expected it of them. And even with the thought the girl knew that it was not Blackley who was unfair but herself: when dawn came on the outskirts of Singapore, the life of neither man nor woman would be worth a moment's purchase—it all depended on what kind of mood the Japanese had been in: she had met them before and had bitter cause to remember the meeting, and scars that would bear witness of that meeting, for the rest of her life. The further away from the Jap's immediate blood-lust the better: besides, as the Major had pointed out, none of them was in a fit state to remain any longer where they were. Unknowingly, almost, the girl shook her head, quickened her pace again and turned off down another dark and empty street.

* * *

Fear and dismay, sickness and despair—such were the things that coloured and dominated the entire existences of the wandering band of soldiers, the little boy and the nurses, and tens of thousands of others on that midnight of 14th February, 1942, as the exultant, all-conquering Japanese crouched outside the last defences of the city, waiting for the dawn, waiting for the assault, the bloodbath and the victory that must inevitably come. But for one man at least fear and hurt and despair did not exist.

The tall, elderly man in the candle-lit waiting-room of the offices some way south of Fort Canning was conscious of none of these things. He was conscious only of the rapid passage of time, of the most overwhelming urgency he had ever known,

11

of the almost inhuman burden of responsibility that lay in his hands alone. He was conscious of these things, consumed by them to the exclusion of all else, yet no trace of them showed in the expressionless calm of the lined, brick-red face beneath the shock of thick white hair. Perhaps the tip of the Burma cheroot that jutted up jauntily past the bristling white moustache and aquiline nose glowed just a little too brightly, perhaps he sat just that little too relaxed in his cane-bottomed arm-chair, but that was all. To all outward appearances Foster Farnholme, Brigadier-General (Ret.), was at peace with the world.

The door behind him opened and a young, tired-looking sergeant came into the room. Farnholme removed the cheroot from his mouth, turned his head slowly and raised one tufted eyebrow in mute interrogation.

"I've delivered your message, sir." The sergeant sounded as tired as he looked. "Captain Bryceland says he'll be along right away."

"Bryceland?" The white eyebrows met in a bar-straight line across the deep-set eyes. "Who the devil's Captain Bryceland? Look, sonny, I asked, specifically, to see your colonel, and I must see him, immediately. At once. You understand?"

"Perhaps I can be of some help." Another man stood in the doorway now, behind the sergeant. Even in the flickering candle-light it was possible to see the badly bloodshot eyes, the fever-flush that stained the yellow cheeks, but his soft Welsh voice was civil enough.

"Bryceland?"

The young officer nodded, said nothing.

"You certainly can help," Farnholme nodded. "Your colonel, please, and right away. I haven't a moment to lose."

"I can't do it." Bryceland shook his head. "He's having his first sleep for three days and three nights—and God only knows we're going to need him with us to-morrow morning."

"I know. Nevertheless, I must see him." Farnholme paused, waited until the frenetic hammering of a nearby heavy machine-gun had died away, then went on very quietly, very earnestly. "Captain Bryceland, you can't even begin to guess how vitally important it is that I see your colonel. Singapore is nothing—not compared to my business." He slid a hand beneath his shirt, brought out a black Colt automatic—the heavy .45. "If I have to find him myself, I'll use this and I'll find him, but I don't think I'll need it. Tell your colonel that Brigadier Farnholme is here. He'll come."

altering formation to line abreast and heading straight for the midships superstructure. It needed no imagination at all to realise what tempting and completely exposed targets they must be, perched high on top of the ship. Nicolson tightened his hold on Corporal Fraser and pointed urgently out to sea with his free hand.

"You haven't a chance, you crazy fool!" he shouted. Van Effen was now at the top of the ladder. "Are you blind or mad?"

"Look to yourself, my friend," Van Effen called, and was gone. Nicolson waited no longer, he would have to look to himself, and with a vengeance. Only a few steps, only a few seconds to the door of the wheelhouse, but Fraser was now only a limp, powerless weight in his arms, and it would take a Zero perhaps six seconds, no more, to cover the intervening distance. Already he could hear the thin, high snarl of the engines, muted but menacing over the steady roar of the flames, but he didn't dare look, he knew where they were anyway, two hundred yards away and with the gunsights lined up on his unprotected back. The wheelhouse sliding door was jammed, he could get only a minimal purchase on it with his left hand, then it was suddenly jerked open, the bo'sun was dragging Corporal Fraser inside and Nicolson was catapulting himself forward on to the deck, wincing involuntarily as he waited for the numbing shock of cannon shells smashing into his back. And then he had rolled and twisted his way into shelter and safety, there was a brief, crescendoing thunder of sound and the planes had swept by only feet above the wheelhouse. Not a gun had been fired.

Nicolson shook his head in dazed incredulity and rose slowly to his feet. Maybe the smoke and the flame had blinded the pilots, perhaps even they had exhausted their ammunition— the number of cannon shells a fighter could carry was limited. Not that it mattered anyway, not any more. Farnholme was on the bridge now, Nicolson saw, helping McKinnon to carry the soldier below. Vannier was gone, but Evans was still there with the captain. Then the chartroom door swung open on its shattered hinges, and once again Nicolson's face tightened in disbelief.

The man who stood before him was almost naked, clad only in the charred tatters of what had been a pair of blue trousers: they were still smoking, smouldering at the edges. Eyebrows and hair were singed and frizzled and the chest and arms red and scorched: the chest rose and fell very quickly in

111

small shallow breaths, like a man whose lungs have been so long starved of air that he cannot find time to breathe deeply. His face was very pale.

"Jenkins!" Nicolson had advanced, seized the man by the shoulders then dropped his hands quickly as the other winced with pain. "How on earth—I saw the 'planes——"

"Somebody trapped, sir!" Jenkins interrupted. "For'ard pump-room." He spoke hurriedly, urgently but jerkily, only a word or two for every breath. "Dived off the catwalk—landed on the hatch. Heard knocking, sir."

"So you got the hell out of it? Is that it?" Nicolson asked softly.

"No, sir. Clips jammed." Jenkins shook his head tiredly. "Couldn't open them, sir."

"There's a pipe clipped to the hatch," Nicolson said savagely. "You know that as well as I do."

Jenkins said nothing, turned his palms up for inspection. Nicolson winced. There was no skin left, none at all, just red, raw flesh and the gleam of white bone.

"Good God!" Nicolson stared at the hands for a moment, then looked up at the pain-filled eyes. "My apologies, Jenkins. Go below. Wait outside the wireless office." He turned round quickly as someone touched him on the shoulder. "Van Effen. I suppose you know that apart from being a bloody fool you're the luckiest man alive?"

The tall Dutchman dropped two rifles, an automatic carbine and ammunition on the deck and straightened up. "You were right," he said quietly. "I was wasting my time. All dead." He nodded at Jenkins's retreating back. "I heard him. That's the small deckhouse just for'ard of the bridge, isn't it? I'll go."

Nicolson looked at the calm grey eyes for a moment, then nodded. "Come with me if you like. Might need help to get him out, whoever he is."

In the passage below they bumped into Vannier, staggering under the weight of an armful of blankets. "How are the boats, Fourth?" Nicolson asked quickly.

"Remarkable, sir. They're hardly scratched. You'd think the Japs had left them alone on purpose."

"Both of them?" Nicolson asked in astonishment.

"Yes, sir."

"Gift horses," Nicolson muttered. "Carry on, Fourth. Don't forget the stretcher for the captain."

Down on the main deck the heat was almost suffocating,

and both men were gasping for oxygen before ten seconds had passed. The petrol fire in the cargo holds was twice, three times as fierce as it had been five minutes ago, and dimly, through the roar of the flames, they could hear an almost continuous rumble of explosions as the metal fuel barrels ruptured and burst in the intense heat. But Nicolson noticed these things with only a corner of his mind. He was standing by the water-tight steel door of the entrance house to the hatch, rapping on the surface with the end of the two-foot length of pipe that served as clip levers for these doors. As he waited for a reply, bent low over the hatch, he could see the sweat from his forehead dripping on to the hatch in an almost continuous trickle. The air was so dry and parched, the metal so hot—they could feel the heat of the deck even through the soles of their shoes—that the drips of perspiration evaporated and vanished almost as they touched the deck . . . And then, so suddenly that both men started in spite of their tense expectation, there came an answering rap from inside, very faint but quite unmistakable, and Nicolson waited no longer. The clips were very stiff indeed—some explosive shock must have warped or shifted the metal—and it took a dozen powerful strokes from the sledge he carried to free the two jammed clips: the last retaining clip sheered at the first blow.

A gust of hot, fetid air swept up from the gloomy depths of the pump-room, but Nicolson and Van Effen ignored it and peered into the darkness. Then Van Effen had switched on his torch and they could clearly see the oil-streaked grey hair of a man climbing up towards the top of the ladder. And then two long arms reached down and, a moment later, the man was standing on deck beside him, a forearm flung up in reflex instinct to shield himself from the heat of the flames. He was drenched in oil from head to foot, the whites of his eyes almost comically prominent in the black, smeared face.

Nicolson peered at him for a moment, and then said in astonishment: "Willy!"

"Even so," Willoughby intoned. "None other. Good old Willy. Golden lads and lasses must, etc., but not superannuated second engineers. No ordinary mortals we." He wiped some oil from his face. "Sing no sad songs for Willoughby."

"But what the hell were you doing?—never mind. It can wait. Come on, Willy. No time to lose. We're leaving."

Willoughby panted for air as they climbed up to the bridge. "Dived in for shelter, my boy. Almost cut off in my prime. Where are we going?"

113

"As far away from this ship as possible," Nicolson said grimly. "She's due to go up any moment now."

Willoughby turned round, shielding his eyes with his hand. "Only a petrol fire, Johnny. Always a chance that it'll burn itself out."

"Number one cargo tank's gone up."

"The boats, and with all speed," Willoughby said hastily. "Old Willy would live and fight another day."

* * *

Within five minutes both boats had been provisioned and lowered for embarkation. All the survivors, including the wounded, were gathered together, waiting. Nicolson looked at the captain.

"Ready when you give the word, sir."

Findhorn smiled faintly: even that seemed an effort, for the smile ended in a grimace of pain. "A late hour for this modesty, Mr. Nicolson. You're in charge, my boy." He coughed, screwed shut his eyes, then looked up thoughtfully. "The 'planes, Mr. Nicolson. They could cut us to ribbons when we're lowering into the water."

"Why should they bother when they can have a far better go at us once we're in the water?" Nicolson shrugged his shoulders. "We've no option, sir."

"Of course. Forgive a foolish objection." Findhorn leaned back and closed his eyes.

"There will be no trouble from the 'planes." It was Van Effen speaking, and he seemed oddly sure of himself. He smiled at Nicolson. "You and I could have been dead twice over: they either cannot fire or do not wish to fire. There are other reasons, too, but time is short, Mr. Nicolson."

"Time is short." Nicolson nodded, then clenched his fists as a deep, rumbling roar reverberated throughout the ship. A heavy, prolonged shudder ran through the superstructure of the *Viroma*, a shudder that culminated in a sudden, sickening lurch as the deck dropped away under their feet, towards the stern. Nicolson smiled faintly at Van Effen. "Time is indeed short, Van Effen. Must you illustrate your points quite so thoroughly?" He raised his voice. "Right, everybody, into the boats."

The need for speed had been urgent before: it was desperate now. The bulkheads of number two tank had ruptured, and one of the tanks, possibly both, were open to the sea: the *Viroma* was already settling by the stern. But speed was a

114

double-edged weapon and Nicolson only too clearly realised that undue haste and pressure would only drive the untrained passengers into panic, or, at best—and equally delaying—confusion. McKinnon and Van Effen were invaluable, shepherding the passengers to their positions, carrying the wounded and laying them down between the thwarts, talking quietly, encouragingly all the time. Inside, that is—outside they had to shout to make themselves heard above the sound of the flames—a weird, terrifying noise compounded of a thin, high-pitched hissing noise that set teeth and nerves on edge and a deep, continuous tearing sound like the ripping of calico, only magnified a thousand times.

The heat was no longer uncomfortable. It was intense, and the two great curtains of flame were beginning to sweep irresistibly together—the pale-blue transparent gauze, shimmering and unreal, of the petrol fire from the bows, and the blood-red, smoke-shot flames from the stern. Breathing became a rasping, throat-tearing agony, and Jenkins, especially, suffered terribly as the super-heated air laid agonising fingers on his scorched skin and raw, bleeding hands. Of them all, young Peter Tallon suffered the least discomfort: McKinnon had dipped a large, fleecy blanket in the pantry sink and wrapped it round the little boy, covering him from head to toe.

Within three minutes of giving the order both boats were in the water. The port lifeboat, manned only by Siran and his six men, was first away—with fewer men, and none of these injured, it had taken less time to embark them, but, from the glimpse Nicolson had of them before he ran back to the starboard lifeboat, it was going to take them a long time to get clear of the burning ship. They were having difficulty in clearing the falls, although Nicolson had given instructions about the patent release gear, two of them were swinging fear-maddened blows at one another and all of them gesticulating and shouting at the tops of their voices. Nicolson turned away, heedless, indifferent. Let them sort it out themselves and if they failed the world would be the better for their failure. He had given them what they had denied the little boy—a chance to live.

Less than a minute later Nicolson, the last man to leave, was sliding down the knotted lifeline into the waterborne number one lifeboat. He could see the lifeboat beneath him, jammed with passengers and equipment, and realised how difficult it would be to ship the oars and pull away, especially with only three or four people fit or able to use an oar, but even as his feet touched a thwart the engine coughed, sputtered, coughed again, caught and settled down to a gentle murmur he could barely hear above the flames.

Within a minute they were well away from the *Viroma's* side, circling anti-clockwise round the bows. Abreast the fo'c'sle, with two hundred feet of intervening sea, the heat from the flames still stung their eyes and caught at their throats but Nicolson still held the lifeboat in, rounding the bows as closely as they dared. And then, all at once, the long length of the port side of the *Viroma* opened up and they could see number two lifeboat. Three minutes, at least, had passed since she had been launched: she was still less than twenty yards from the side of the ship. Siran had finally succeeded in restoring order with the lash of his tongue and the heavy and indiscriminate use of the boathook, but, with two men lying groaning on the bottom-boards and a third nursing a numbed and, for the moment, useless arm, Siran had only three men left to man the heavy sweeps. On board number one boat Nicolson compressed his lips and looked at Findhorn. The captain interpreted the look correctly and nodded heavily and reluctantly.

Half a minute later McKinnon sent a coil of rope snaking expertly over the water. Siran himself caught it and made it fast to the mast thwart, and almost at once the motorboat took up the slack and started towing Siran and his men clear of the ship's side. This time Nicolson made no attempt to circle the ship but moved straight out to sea intent on putting the maximum possible distance between themselves and the *Viroma* in the least possible time.

Five minutes and five hundred yards passed and still nothing happened. The motorboat, with the other lifeboat in tow, was making a top speed of perhaps three and a half knots, but every foot covered was a foot nearer safety. The fighters still cruised overhead, but aimlessly: they had made no move to attack since the embarkation had begun and obviously had no intention of making any now.

Two more minutes passed, and the *Viroma* was burning more fiercely than ever. The flames from the fo'c'sle were now clearly visible, no longer swallowed up by the brilliance of the sunlight: the dense pall of smoke from the two after cargo tanks now spread over half a square mile of sea and not even the fierce tropical sun could penetrate its black intensity. Under this dark canopy the two great pillars of flame swept

116

more and more closely together, remorseless, majestic in the splendour of their inexorable progress. The tips of the two great fires leaned in towards one another—some curious freak of the superheated atmosphere—and Findhorn, twisted round in his seat and watched his ship die, knew with sudden certainty that when these two flames touched the end would come. And so it was.

After the barbaric magnificence of the dying, the death was strangely subdued and unspectacular. A column of white flame streaked upwards just abaft the bridge, climbing two, three, four hundred feet, then vanishing as suddenly as it had come. Even as it vanished a low, deep, prolonged rumble came at them across the stillness of the sea ; by and by the echoes vanished away in the empty distance and there was only then the silence. The end came quietly and without any fuss, even with a certain grace and dignity, the *Viroma* slipping gently under the surface of the sea on an even steady keel, a tired and dreadfully wounded ship that had taken all it could and was glad to go to rest. The watchers in the lifeboats could hear the gentle hissing, quickly extinguished, of water pouring into red-hot holds, could see the tips of the two slender masts sliding down vertically into the sea, then a few bubbles and then nothing at all, no floating wood or flotsam on the oily waters, just nothing at all. It was as if the *Viroma* had never been.

Captain Findhorn turned to Nicolson, his face like a stone, his eyes drained and empty of all expression. Almost everybody in the lifeboat was looking at him, openly or covertly, but he seemed completely unaware of it, a man sunk in a vast and heedless indifference.

" Unaltered course, Mr. Nicolson, if you please." His voice was low and husky, but only from weakness and blood. " 200, as I remember. Our objective remains. We should reach the Macclesfield Channel in twelve hours."

CHAPTER EIGHT

HOURS PASSED, interminable, breathless hours under a blue, windless sky and the fierce glare of the tropical sun and still number one lifeboat chugged steadily south, towing the other boat behind it. Normally a lifeboat carries a fuel supply good only for a hundred miles steaming at about four knots, and is used solely for emergencies, such as towing other boats clear of a sinking ship, cruising around for survivors, going for immediate help or keeping the boat itself hove to in heavy seas. But McKinnon had had the foresight to throw in extra cans of petrol and, even allowing for the possibility of bad weather, they had enough, and more than enough, to carry them to Lepar, an island about the size of the Isle of Sheppey on the starboard hand as they passed through the Macclesfield Channel. Captain Findhorn, with fifteen years in the Archipelago behind him, knew where he could find petrol on Lepar, and plenty of it. The only unknown quantity was the Japanese: they might have already taken over the island, but with their land forces already so widespread and thinly stretched it seemed unlikely that they could yet have had the time or sufficient reason to garrison so small a place. And with plenty of petrol and fresh water there was no saying how far they might go: the Sunda Straits between Sumatra and Java was not impossible, especially when the north-east trades started up again and helped them on their way.

But there were no trades just now, not even the lightest zephyr of a breeze; it was absolutely still and airless and suffocatingly hot and the tiny movement of air from their slow passage through the water was only a mockery of coolness and worse than nothing at all. The blazing sun was falling now, slipping far to the west, but still burning hot: Nicolson had both sails stretched as awnings, the jib for the fore end and the lug-sail, its yard lashed half-way up the mast, stretched aft as far as it would go, but even beneath the shelter of these the heat was still oppressive, somewhere between eighty and ninety degrees with a relative humidity of over 85 per cent. It was seldom enough in the East Indies, at any time of the year, that the temperature dropped below eighty degrees. Nor was there any relief to be obtained, any chance of cooling off by

118

plunging over the side into the water, the temperature of which lay somewhere between eighty degrees and eighty-five. All the passengers could do was to recline limply and listlessly in the shade of awnings, to sit and suffer and sweat and pray for the sun to go down.

The passengers. Nicolson, sitting in the sternsheets with the tiller in his hand, looked slowly round the people in the boat, took in their condition and lifeless inertia and tightened his lips. If he had to be afloat in an open boat in the tropics, hundreds—thousands—of miles from help and surrounded by the enemy and enemy-held islands, he could hardly have picked a boatload of passengers less well equipped for handling a boat, with a poorer chance of survival. There were exceptions, of course, men like McKinnon and Van Effen would always be exceptions, but as for the remainder . . .

Excluding himself, there were seventeen people aboard. Of these, as far as sailing and fighting the boat were concerned, only two were definite assets: McKinnon, imperturbable, competent, infinitely resourceful, was worth any two men, and Van Effen, an otherwise unknown quantity, had already proved his courage and value in an emergency. About Vannier it was difficult to say: no more than a boy, he might possibly stand up to prolonged strain and hardship, but time alone would show. Walters, still looking sick and shaken, would be a useful man to have around when he had recovered. And that, on the credit side, was just about all.

Gordon, the second steward, a thin-faced, watery-eyed and incurably furtive individual, a known thief who had been conspicuously and mysteriously absent from his action stations that afternoon, was no seaman, no fighter and could be trusted to do nothing whatsoever that didn't contribute to the immediate safety and benefit of himself. Neither the Muslim priest nor the baffling, enigmatic Farnholme—they were seated together on the same thwart, conversing in low murmurs—had shown up too well that afternoon either. There was no more kindly nor better-meaning man than Willoughby, but, outside his engine room and deprived of his beloved books and for all his rather pathetic eagerness to be of assistance, there was no more ineffectual and helpless person alive than the gentle second engineer. The captain, Evans, the quartermaster, Fraser and Jenkins, the young able seaman, were too badly hurt to give any more than token assistance. Alex, the young soldier—Nicolson had discovered that his name was Sinclair—was as jittery and unstable as ever, his wide, staring eyes darting restlessly, ceaselessly, from one member of the boat's company to the next, the palms of his hands rubbing constantly up and down the thighs of his trousers, as if desperately seeking to rub off some contamination. That left only the three women and young Peter—and if anyone wanted to stack the odds even higher, Nicolson thought bitterly, there was always Siran and his six cut-throat friends not twenty feet away. The prospects, overall, were not good.

The one happy, carefree person in the two boats was young Peter Tallon. Clad only in a haltered pair of white, very short shorts, he seemed entirely unaffected by the heat or anything else, bouncing incessantly up and down on the sternsheets and having to be rescued from falling overboard a dozen times a minute. Familiarity breeding trust, he had quite lost his earlier fear of the other members of the crew but had not yet given him his unquestioning confidence: whenever Nicolson, whose seat by the tiller was nearest to the youngster, offered him a piece of ship's biscuit or a mug with some watered down sweet condensed milk, he would smile at him shyly, lean forward, snatch the offering, retreat and eat or drink it, head bent and looking suspiciously at Nicolson under lowered eyelids. But if Nicolson reached out a hand to touch or catch him he would fling himself against Miss Drachmann, who sat on the starboard side of the sternsheets, entwine one chubby hand in the shining black hair, often with a force that brought a wince and an involuntary ' ouch ' from the girl, twist his head round and regard him gravely through the spread fingers of his left hand. It was a favourite trick of his, this peeping from behind his fingers, one which he seemed to imagine made him invisible. For long moments at a time Nicolson forgot the war, the wounded men and their own near-hopeless situation, absorbed in the antics of the little boy but always he came back to the bitter present, to an even keener despair, to a redoubled fear of what would happen to the child when the Japanese finally caught up with them.

And they would catch up with them. Nicolson had known that, known it beyond any shadow of doubt, known that Captain Findhorn knew it also despite his encouraging talk of sailing for Lepar and the Sunda Straits. The Japanese had their position to within a few miles, could find them and pick them off whenever they wished. The only mystery was why they had not already done so. Nicolson wondered if the others knew that their hours of freedom and safety were limited, that the cat was playing with the mouse. If they did, it was impossible to tell by their behaviour and appearance. A helpless, useless bunch in many ways, a crushing liability to any man who hoped to sail his boat to freedom, but Nicolson had to concede them one saving grace: Gordon and the shocked Sinclair apart, their morale was magnificent.

They had worked hard and uncomplainingly to get all the blankets and provisions stowed away as neatly as possible, had cleared spaces at the expense of their own comfort for the wounded men—who themselves, in spite of obvious agony, had never complained once—and accepted all Nicolson's orders and their own cramped positions cheerfully and willingly. The two nurses, surprisingly and skilfully assisted by Brigadier Farnholme, had worked for almost two hours over the wounded men and done a splendid job. Never had the Ministry of Transport's insistence that all lifeboats carry a comprehensive first-aid kit been more fully justified, and seldom could it have been put to better use: collapse revivers, ' Omnopon,' sulphanilamide powder, codeine compounds, dressings, bandages, gauze, cotton wool and jelly for burns—they were all there and they were all used. Surgical kit Miss Drachmann carried herself: and with the lifeboat's hatchet and his own knife McKinnon had perfectly adequate splints improvised from the bottom-boards for Corporal Fraser's shattered arm within ten minutes of being asked for them.

And Miss Plenderleith was magnificent. There was no other word for it. She had a genius for reducing circumstances and situations to reassuring normality, and might well have spent her entire life in an open boat. She accepted things as they were, made the very best of them, and had more than sufficient authority to induce others to do the same. It was she who wrapped the wounded in blankets and pillowed their heads on lifebelts, scolding them like unruly and recalcitrant little children if they showed any signs of disobeying: Miss Plenderleith never had to scold anyone twice. It was she who had taken over the commissariat and watched over the wounded until they had eaten the last crumb and drunk the last drop of what she had offered them. It was she who had snatched Farnholme's gladstone bag from him, stowed it beneath her side bench, picked up the hatchet McKinnon had laid down, and informed the seething Brigadier, with the light of battle in her eyes, that his drinking days were over and that the contents of the bag, which he had been on the point of broaching, would be in future reserved for medicinal use only—and thereafter, incredibly, had produced needles and wool from the depths of her own capacious bag and calmly carried on with her knitting. And it was she who was now sitting with a board across her knees, carefully slicing bully beef and bread, doling out biscuits, barley sugar and thinned down condensed milk and ordering around a grave and carefully unsmiling McKinnon, whom she had pressed into service as her waiter, as if he were one of her more reliable but none too bright school children. Magnificent, Nicolson thought, trying hard to match his bo'sun's deadpan expression, just magnificent: there was no other word for her. Suddenly her voice sharpened, rose almost an octave.

"Mr. McKinnon! What on earth are you doing?" The bo'sun had dropped his latest cargo of bread and corned beef to the bottom-boards and sunk down on his knees beside her, peering out below the awning, ignoring Miss Plenderleith as she repeated her question. She repeated it a third time, received no answer, tightened her lips and jabbed him ferociously in the ribs with the haft of her knife. This time she got a reaction.

"Will you look what you've done, you clumsy idiot?" She pointed her knife angrily at McKinnon's knee: between it and the side bench half a pound of meat was squashed almost flat.

"Sorry, Miss Plenderleith, sorry." The bo'sun stood up, absently rubbing shreds of beef off his trousers, and turned to Nicolson. "'Plane approaching, sir. Green ninety, near enough."

Nicolson glanced at him out of suddenly narrowed eyes, stopped and stared out to the west under the awning. He saw the plane almost at once, not more than two miles away, at about two thousand feet. Walters, the lookout in the bows, had missed it, but not surprisingly: it was coming at them straight out of the eye of the sun. McKinnon's sensitive ears must have picked up the faraway drone of the engine. How he had managed to detect it above the constant flow of Miss Plenderleith's talk and the steady putt-putt of their own engine Nicolson couldn't imagine. Even now he himself could hear nothing.

Nicolson drew back, glanced over at the captain. Findhorn was lying on his side, either asleep or in a coma. There was no time to waste finding out which.

"Get the sail down, Bo'sun," he said quickly. "Gordon, give him a hand. Quickly, now. Fourth?"

. " Sir?" Vannier was pale, but looked eager and steady enough.

"The guns. One each for yourself, the brigadier, the bo'sun, Van Effen, Walters and myself." He looked at Farnholme. "There's some sort of automatic carbine there, sir. You know how to handle it?"

"I certainly do!" Pale blue eyes positively gleaming, Farnholme stretched out a hand for the carbine, cocked the bolt with one expert flick of his fingers and cradled the gun in his arms, glaring hopefully at the approaching plane: the old warhorse sniffing the scent of battle and loving it. Even in that moment of haste Nicolson found time to marvel at the complete transformation from the early afternoon: the man who had scuttled thankfully into the safe refuge of the pantry might never have existed. It was incredible, but there it was: far back in his mind Nicolson had a vague suspicion that the brigadier was just too consistent in his inconsistencies, that a purposeful but well-concealed pattern lay at the root of all his odd behaviour. But it was only a suspicion, he couldn't make sense of it and maybe he was reading into Farnholme's strange, see-saw conduct something that didn't exist. Whatever the explanation, now was not the time to seek it.

"Get your gun down," Nicolson said urgently. "All of you. Keep them hidden. The rest of you flat on the boards, as low down as you can get." He heard the boy's outraged wail of protest as he was pulled down beside the nurse and deliberately forced all thought of him out of his mind. The aircraft—a curious looking seaplane of a type he had never seen before—was still heading straight for them, perhaps half a mile distant now. Losing height all the time, it was coming in very slowly: that type of plane was not built for speed.

It was banking now, beginning to circle the lifeboats, and Nicolson watched it through his binoculars. On the fuselage the emblem of the rising sun glinted as the plane swung first to the south and then to the east. A lumbering, clumsy plane, Nicolson thought, good enough for low-speed reconnaissance, but that was about all. And then Nicolson remembered the three Zeros that had circled indifferently overhead as they had abandoned the burning *Viroma* and all at once he had a conviction that amounted to complete certainty.

"You can put your guns away," he said quietly. "And you can all sit up. This character isn't after our lives. The Japs have plenty of bombers and fighters to make a neat, quick job of us. If they wanted to finish us off, they wouldn't have sent an old carthorse of a seaplane that has more than an even chance of being shot down itself. They'd have sent the fighters and bombers."

"I'm not so sure about that." Farnholme's blood was roused, and he was reluctant to abandon the idea of lining the Japanese 'plane up over the sights of his carbine. "I wouldn't trust the beggars an inch!"

"Who would?" Nicolson agreed. "But I doubt whether this fellow has more than a machine-gun." The seaplane was still circling, still at the same circumspect distance. "My guess is they want us, but they want us alive, lord only knows why. This bloke here, as the Americans would say, is just keeping us on ice." Nicolson had spent too many years in the Far East not to have heard, in grisly detail, of Japanese atrocities and barbaric cruelties during the Chinese war and knew that, for an enemy civilian, death was a pleasant, a desirable end compared to being taken prisoner by them. "Why we should be all that important to them I can't even begin to guess. Just let's count our blessings and stay alive a little longer."

"I agree with the chief officer." Van Effen had already stowed away his gun. "This plane is just—how do you say— keeping tabs on us. He'll leave us alone, Brigadier, don't you worry about that."

"Maybe he will and maybe he won't." Farnholme brought his carbine into plain view. "No reason then why I shouldn't have a pot at him. Dammit all, he's an enemy, isn't he?" Farnholme was breathing hard. "A bullet in his engine——"

"You'll do no such thing, Foster Farnholme." Miss Plenderleith's voice was cold, incisive and imperious. "You're behaving like an idiot, an irresponsible child. Put that gun down at once." Farnholme was already wilting under her glare and the lash of her tongue. "Why kick a wasp's nest? You fire at him and the next thing you know he loses his temper and fires at us and half of us are dead. Unfortunately there's no way of guaranteeing that you'll be among that half."

Nicolson struggled to keep his face straight. Where their journey would end he had no idea, but as long as it lasted the violent antipathy between Farnholme and Miss Plenderleith promised to provide plenty of light entertainment: no one had yet heard them speak a civil word to each other.

"Now, then, Constance." The brigadier's voice was half truculent, half placating. "You've no right——"

" Don't you ' Constance ' me," she said icily. " Just put that gun away. None of us wishes to be sacrificed on the altar of your belated valour and misplaced martial ardour." She gave him the benefit of a cold, level stare, then turned ostentatiously away. The subject was closed and Farnholme suitably crushed.

" You and the brigadier—you've known each other for some time?" Nicolson ventured.

For a moment she transferred her glacial stare to Nicolson, and he thought he had gone too far. Then she pressed her lips together and nodded. " A long time. For me, far too long. He had his own regiment in Singapore, years before the war, but I doubt whether they ever saw him. He practically lived in the Bengal Club. Drunk, of course. All the time."

" By heaven, madam!" Farnholme shouted. His bristly white eyebrows were twitching furiously. " If you were a man——"

" Oh, do be quiet," she interrupted wearily. " When you repeat yourself so often, Foster, it becomes downright nauseating."

Farnholme muttered angrily to himself, but everybody's attention was suddenly transferred to the plane. The engine note had deepened, and for one brief moment Nicolson thought it was coming in to attack, but realised almost at once that its circle round the boats was widening, if anything. The seaplane had cut its engine booster, but only for extra power for climb. It was still circling, but rising steadily all the time, making a laborious job of it, but nonetheless climbing. At about five thousand feet it levelled off and began to cruise round in great circles four or five miles in diameter.

" Now what do you think he's done that for?" It was Findhorn talking, his voice stronger and clearer than it had been at any time since he had been wounded. " Very curious, don't you think, Mr. Nicolson?"

Nicolson smiled at him. " Thought you were still asleep, sir. How do you feel now?"

" Hungry and thirsty. Ah, thank yóu, Miss Plenderleith." He stretched out his hand for a cup, winced at the sudden pain the movement caused him, then looked again at Nicolson. " You haven't answered my question."

" Sorry, sir. Difficult to say. I suspect he's bringing some of his pals along to see us and he's giving himself a spot of elevation, probably to act as a marker. Only a guess, of course."

" Your guesses have an unfortunate habit of being too

125

damned accurate for my liking." Findhorn lapsed into silence and sank his teeth into a corned beef sandwich.

Half an hour passed, and still the scout seaplane stayed in the same relative position. It was all rather nerve-racking and necks began to ache from staring up so fixedly into the sky. But at least it was obvious now that the 'plane had no directly hostile intentions towards them.

Another half-hour passed and the blood-red sun was slipping swiftly, vertically down towards the rim of the sea, a mirror-smooth sea that faded darkly towards the blurred horizon to the east, but a great motionless plain of vermilion to the west, stretching far away into the eye of the setting sun. Not quite mirror-smooth on this side—one or two tiny islets dimpled the red sheen of the water, standing out black against the level rays of the sun, and away to the left, just off the starboard bow and maybe four miles to the south-south-west a larger, low-lying island was beginning to climb imperceptibly above the tranquil surface of the sea.

It was soon after sighting this last island that they saw the seaplane begin to lose height and move off to the east in a long shallow dive. Vannier looked hopefully at Nicolson.

"Knocking-off time for the watch-dog, sir? Off home to bed, likely enough."

"Afraid not, Fourth." Nicolson nodded in the direction of the retreating plane. "Nothing but hundreds of miles of sea in that direction, and then Borneo—and that's not where our friend's home is. He's spotted a pal, a hundred to one." He looked at the captain. "What do you think, sir?"

"You're probably right again, damn you." Findhorn's smile robbed the words of any offence, and then the smile slowly vanished and the eyes became bleak as the seaplane levelled off about a thousand feet and began to circle. "You are right, Mr. Nicolson," he added softly. He twisted painfully in his seat and stared ahead. "How far off would you say that island there is?"

"Two and a half miles, sir. Maybe three."

"Near enough three." Findhorn turned to look at Willoughby, then nodded at the engine. "Can you get any more revs out of that sewing machine of yours, Second?"

"Another knot, sir, if I'm lucky." Willoughby laid a hand on the tow-rope that stretched back to Siran's boat. "Two, if I cut this."

"Don't tempt me, Second. Give her all you can, will you?"

126

Bryceland looked at him for a long moment, hesitated, nodded, then turned away without a word. He was back inside three minutes and stood aside at the doorway to let the man following him precede him into the room.

The colonel, Farnholme guessed, must have been a man of about forty-five—fifty at the most. He looked about seventy, and walked with the swaying, half-inebriated gait of a man who has lived too long with exhaustion. He had difficulty in keeping his eyes open, but he managed to smile as he walked slowly across the room and extended a courteous hand.

"Good evening, sir. Where in the world have you come from?"

"Evening, Colonel." On his feet now, Farnholme ignored the question. "You know of me, then?"

"I know of you. I heard about you for the first time, sir— just three nights ago."

"Good, good." Farnholme nodded in satisfaction. "That will save a lot of explaining—and I've no time for explanations. I'll come to the point right away." He half-turned as the explosion of a shell landing very close shook the room, the shock wave of displaced air almost blowing the candles out, then looked back at the colonel. "I want a 'plane out of Singapore, Colonel. I don't care what kind of 'plane, I don't care who you've got to shove off to get me on board, I don't care where it's going—Burma, India, Ceylon, Australia—it's all the same to me. I want a 'plane out of Singapore—immediately."

"You want a 'plane out of Singapore." The colonel echoed the words tonelessly, his voice as wooden as the expression on his face, then he suddenly smiled, tiredly, as if the effort had cost him a great deal. "Don't we all, Brigadier."

"You don't understand." Slowly, with a gesture of infinitely controlled patience, Farnholme ground out his cheroot on an ashtray. "I know there are hundreds of wounded and sick, women and children——"

"The last 'plane has already gone," the colonel interrupted flatly. He rubbed a bare forearm across exhausted eyes. "A day, two days ago—I'm not sure."

"11th February," Bryceland supplied. "The Hurricanes, sir. They left for Palembang."

"That's right," the colonel remembered. "The Hurricanes. They left in a great hurry."

"The last plane." Farnholme's voice was empty of all emo-

13

tion. " The last 'plane. But—but there were others, I know. Brewster fighters, Wildebeestes——"

" All gone, all destroyed." The colonel was watching Farnholme now with some vague curiosity in his eyes. " Even if they weren't, it would make no difference. Seletar, Semba-wang, Tengah—the Japs have all these aerodromes. I don't know about Kallang airport—but I do know it's useless."

" I see. I see indeed." Farnholme stared down at the glad-stone bag beside his feet, then looked up again. " The flying-boats, Colonel? The Catalinas?"

The colonel shook his head in slow finality. Farnholme gazed at him for long seconds with unwinking eyes, nodded his head in understanding and acceptance, then glanced at his watch. " May I see you alone, Colonel?"

" Certainly." The colonel didn't even hesitate. He waited until the door had closed softly behind Bryceland and the sergeant, then smiled faintly at Farnholme. " I'm afraid the last 'plane has still gone, sir."

" I never doubted it." Farnholme, busy unbuttoning his shirt, paused and glanced up. " You know who I am, Colonel —not just my name, I mean?"

" I've known for three days. Utmost secrecy, and all that— it was thought you might be in the area." For the first time the colonel regarded his visitor with open curiosity. " Seven-teen years counter-espionage-chief in South-East Asia, speak more Asiatic languages than any other——"

" Spare my blushes." His shirt unbuttoned, Farnholme was unfastening a wide, flat rubber-covered belt that encircled his waist. " I don't suppose you speak any Eastern languages yourself, Colonel?"

" For my sins, yes. That's why I'm here. Japanese." The colonel grinned mirthlessly. " It'll come in very handy in the concentration camps, I should think."

" Japanese, eh? That's a help." Farnholme unzipped two pouches on the belt, placed their contents on the table before him. " See what you make of these, will you, Colonel?"

The colonel glanced sharply at him, glanced down at the photostats and rolls of film that lay on the table, nodded, went out of the room and returned with a pair of spectacles, a magnifying glass and a torch. For three minutes he sat at the table without looking up or speaking. From outside came the occasional crump of an exploding shell, the staccato chattering of a distant machine-gun and the evil whine of some mis-

14

shapen ricochet whistling blindly through the smoke-filled night. But no noise whatsoever came from inside the room itself. The colonel sat at his table like a man carved from stone, only his eyes alive: Farnholme, a fresh cheroot in his mouth, was stretched out in his wicker chair, lost in a seeming vast indifference.

By and by the colonel stirred and looked across at Farnholme. When he spoke both his voice and the hands that held the photostats were unsteady.

"I don't need Japanese to understand these. My God, sir, where did you get them?"

"Borneo. Two of our best men, and two Dutchmen, died to get these. But that's not important now, and quite irrelevant." Farnholme puffed at his cheroot. "All that matters is that I have them and the Japs don't know it."

The colonel didn't seem to have heard him. He was staring down at the papers in his hands, shaking his head slowly from side to side. Finally he laid the papers down on the desk, folded his spectacles away into their case and lit a cigarette. His hands were still trembling.

"This is fantastic," he muttered. "This is quite fantastic. There can only be a few of these in existence. All Northern Australia—blueprints for invasion!"

"Complete in every relevant detail," Farnholme assented. "The invasion ports and airfields, the times to the last minute, the forces to be used down to the last battalion of infantry."

"Yes." The colonel stared down at the photostats, his brows wrinkling. "But there's something that——"

"I know, I know," Farnholme interrupted bitterly. "We haven't got the key. It was inevitable. The dates and primary and secondary objectives are in code. They couldn't take the risk of having these in plain language—and Japanese codes are unbreakable, all of them. All of them, that is, except to a little old man in London who looks as if he couldn't write his own name." He paused and puffed some more blue smoke into the air. "Still, it's quite something, isn't it, Colonel?"

"But—but how did you happen to get——"

"That's quite irrelevant, I've told you." The steel below was beginning to show through the camouflage of lazy indifference. He shook his head, then laughed softly. "Sorry, Colonel. Must be getting edgy. There was no 'happen' about it, I assure you. I've worked for five years on one thing and one thing only—to get these delivered me at the right time and the right place: the Japanese are not incorruptible. I managed to get them at the right time: not at the right place. That's why I'm here."

The colonel hadn't even been listening. He had been staring down at the papers, shaking his head slowly from side to side, but now he looked up again. All at once his face was haggard and defeated and very old.

"These papers—these papers are priceless, sir." He lifted the photostats in his hand and stared unseeingly at Farnholme. "God above, all the fortunes that ever were are nothing compared to these. It's all the difference between life and death, victory and defeat. It's—it's—great heavens, sir, think of Australia! Our people must have these—they must have them!"

"Exactly," Farnholme agreed. "They must have them."

The colonel stared at him in silence, the tired eyes slowly widening in shocked understanding, then slumped back into his chair, his head resting on his chest. The spiralling cigarette smoke laced painfully across his eyes, but he didn't even seem to notice it.

"Exactly, once again," Farnholme said dryly. He reached out for the films and photostats and began to replace them carefully in the waterproof pouches of his belt. "You begin to understand, perhaps, my earlier anxiety for—ah—aerial transport out of Singapore." He zipped the pouches shut. "I'm still as anxious as ever, I assure you."

The colonel nodded dully, but said nothing.

"No 'plane at all?" Farnholme persisted. "Not even the most dilapidated, broken down——" He stopped abruptly at the sight of the expression on the colonel's face, then tried again. "Submarine?"

"No."

Farnholme's mouth tightened. "Destroyer, frigate, any naval vessel at all?"

"No." The colonel stirred. "And not even a merchant ship. The last of them—the *Grasshopper, Tien Kwang, Katydid, Kuala, Dragonfly* and a few other small coastal vessels like these—pulled out of Singapore last night. They won't be back. They wouldn't get a hundred miles, even, the Jap air force is everywhere round the archipelago. Wounded, women and children aboard all these vessels, Brigadier. Most of them will finish up at the bottom of the sea."

"A kindly alternative to a Japanese prison camp. Believe me, Colonel, I know." Farnholme was buckling on the heavy belt again. He sighed. "This is all very handy, Colonel. Where do we go from here?"

"Why in God's name did you ever come here?" the colonel demanded bitterly. "Of all places, of all times, you had to come to Singapore now. And how in the world did you manage to get here anyway?"

"Boat from Banjermasin," Farnholme replied briefly. "The *Kerry Dancer*—the most dilapidated floating death-trap that was ever refused a certificate of seaworthiness. Operated by a smooth, dangerous character by the name of Siran. Hard to say, but I'd almost swear he was a renegade Englishman of some kind, and on more than nodding terms with the Japs. He stated he was heading for Kota Bharu—lord knows why—but he changed his mind and came here."

"He changed his mind?"

"I paid him well. Not my money, so I could afford it. I thought Singapore would be safe enough. I was in North Borneo when I heard on my own receiver that Hong Kong and Guam and Wake had fallen, but I had to move in a considerable hurry. A long time passed before I heard the next item of news, and that was on board the *Kerry Dancer*. We waited ten days in Banjermasin before Siran condescended to sail," Farnholme went on bitterly. "The only respectable piece of equipment and the only respectable man on that ship were both to be found in the radio room—Siran must have considered them both necessary for his nefarious activities—and I was in the radio room with this lad Loon on our second day aboard the ship—29th January, it was, when we picked up this B.B.C. broadcast that Ipoh was being bombarded, so, naturally, I thought the Japs were advancing very slowly and that we'd plenty of time to go to Singapore and pick up a 'plane."

The colonel nodded in understanding. "I heard that communiqué, too. Heaven only knows who was responsible for that appalling claptrap. Ipoh had actually fallen to the Japs more than a month before that, sir. The Japs were only a few miles north of the causeway at the time. My God, what a damnable mess!" He shook his head slowly. "A damnable, damnable mess!"

"You put things very mildly," Farnholme agreed. "How long have we got?"

"We're surrendering to-morrow." The colonel stared down at his hands.

"To-morrow!"

" We're all washed up, sir. Nothing more we can do. And we've no water left. When we blew up the causeway we blew up the only water-pipe from the mainland."

" Very clever, far-seeing chaps who designed our defences here," Farnholme muttered. " And thirty million quid spent on it. Impregnable fortress. Bigger and better than Gib. Blah, blah, blah. God, it all makes you sick!" He snorted in disgust, rose to his feet and sighed. " Ah, well, nothing else for it. Back to the dear old *Kerry Dancer*. God help Australia!"

" The *Kerry Dancer*!" The colonel was astonished. " She'll be gone an hour after dawn, sir. I tell you, the Straits are swarming with Japanese 'planes."

" What alternative can you offer?" Farnholme asked wearily.

" I know, I know. But even if you are lucky, what guarantee have you that the captain will go where you want him to?"

" None," Farnholme admitted. " But there's a rather handy Dutchman aboard, by the name of Van Effen. Together we may be able to persuade our worthy captain where the path of duty lies."

" Perhaps." A sudden thought occurred to the colonel. " Besides, what guarantee have you that he'll even be waiting when you get back down to the waterfront?"

" Here it is." Farnholme prodded the shabby valise lying by his feet. " My guarantee and insurance policy—I hope. Siran thinks this thing's stuffed full of diamonds—I used some of them to bribe him to come here—and he's not so far out. Just so long as he thinks there's a chance of separating me from these, he'll hang on to me like a blood brother."

" He—he doesn't suspect——"

" Not a chance. He thinks I'm a drunken old reprobate on the run with ill-gotten gains. I have been at some pains to— ah—maintain the impersonation."

" I see, sir." The colonel came to a decision and reached out for a bell. When the sergeant appeared, he said, " Ask Captain Bryceland to come here."

Farnholme lifted an eyebrow in silent interrogation.

" It's the least I can do, sir," the colonel explained. " I can't provide a plane. I can't guarantee you won't all be sunk before noon to-morrow. But I can guarantee that the captain of the *Kerry Dancer* will follow your instructions implicitly. I'm going to detail a subaltern and a couple of dozen men from a Highland regiment to accompany you on the *Kerry*

18

He jerked his head at Nicolson, who handed over the tiller to Vannier and moved over beside the captain. "What's your guess, Johnny?" Findhorn murmured.

"What do you mean, sir? Kind of ship it is, or what's going to happen?"

"Both."

"No idea about the first—destroyer, M.T.B., fishing boat, anything. As to the other—well, it's clear now that they want us, and not our blood." Nicolson grimaced. "The blood will come later. Meantime, they take us prisoner—then the old green bamboo torture, the toenails and teeth, the water treatment, the silos and all the usual refinements." Nicolson's mouth was only a white gash in his face and his eyes were gazing at the sternsheets where Peter and Miss Drachmann were playing together, laughing at each other, the girl as if she hadn't a care in the world. Findhorn followed his gaze and nodded slowly.

"Yes, me too, Johnny. It hurts—just to look at them hurts. They go well together." He rubbed his grey-grizzled chin thoughtfully. 'Translucent amber'—that was the phrase some writing johnny used once about his heroine's complexion. Blasted fool—or that was what I thought then. I'd like to apologise to him some day. Really incredible, isn't it." He grinned. "Imagine the traffic jam if you brought her back to Piccadilly."

Nicolson smiled in turn. "It's just the sunset, sir, and your bloodshot eyes." He was grateful to the older man for deliberately diverting his train of thought and, remembering, he quickly became serious again. "That bloody awful gash. Our yellow brethren. I think there should be some payment on account."

Findhorn nodded slowly. "We should—ah—postpone our capture, perhaps? Let the thumb-screws rust a while longer? The idea is not without its attractions, Johnny." He paused, then went on quietly: "I think I can see something."

Nicolson had his glasses to his eyes at once. He stared through them for a moment, caught a glimpse of a craft hull-down on the horizon with the golden gleams of the setting sun striking highlights off its superstructure, lowered the glasses, rubbed his eyes and looked again. Seconds passed, then he lowered the binoculars, his face expressionless, and handed them in silence to the captain. Findhorn took them, held them steady to his eyes, then handed them back to Nicolson. "No signs of our luck turning, is there? Tell them, will you? Trying to raise my voice above that damned engine is like having a set of fish-hooks dragged up my throat."

Nicolson nodded and turned round.

"Sorry, everybody, but—well, I'm afraid there's some more trouble coming along. It's a Jap submarine, and it's over-taking us as if we were standing still. If he'd appeared fifteen minutes later we might have made that island there." He nodded forward over the starboard bow. "As it is, he'll be up on us before we're much more than half-way there."

"And what do you think will happen then, Mr. Nicolson?" Miss Plenderleith's voice was composed almost to the level of indifference.

"Captain Findhorn thinks—and I agree with him—that they will probably try to take us prisoner." Nicolson smiled wryly. "All I can say just now, Miss Plenderleith, is that we'll try not to be taken prisoner. It will be difficult."

"It will be impossible." Van Effen spoke from his seat in the bows, and his voice was cold. "It's a submarine, man. What can our little pop-guns do against a pressure hull. Our bullets will just bounce off."

"You propose that we give ourselves up?" Nicolson could see the logic of Van Effen's words and knew that the man was without fear: nevertheless he felt vaguely disappointed.

"Why commit outright suicide—which is what you suggest we do." Van Effen was pounding the heel of his fist gently on the gunwale, emphasising his point. "We can always find a better chance to escape later."

"You obviously don't know the Japs," Nicolson said wearily. "This is not only the best chance we'll ever have—it's also the last."

"And I say you're talking nonsense!" There was hostility now in every line in Van Effen's face. "Let us put it to the vote, Mr. Nicolson." He looked round the boat. "How many of you are in favour of——"

"Shut up and don't talk like a fool!" Nicolson said roughly. "You're not attending a political meeting, Van Effen. You're aboard a vessel of the British Mercantile Marine, and such vessels are not run by committees but by the authority of one man only—the captain. Captain Findhorn says we offer resistance—and that's that."

"The captain is absolutely determined on that?"

"He is."

Dancer." He smiled. "They're a tough bunch at the best of times, but they're in an especially savage mood just now. I don't think Captain Siran will give you very much trouble."

"I'm sure he won't. Damned grateful to you, Colonel. It should help a lot." He buttoned his shirt, picked up his gladstone and extended his hand. "Thanks for everything, Colonel. It sounds silly knowing a concentration camp is waiting you—but, well, all the best."

"Thank you, sir. And all the luck to you—God knows you're going to need it." He glanced down in the region of the concealed belt that held the photostats, then finished sombrely. "We've at least got a chance."

*   *   *

The smoke was slowly clearing when Brigadier Farnholme wnet out again into the darkness of the night, but the air still held that curious, unpleasant amalgam of cordite and death and corruption that the old soldier knows so well. A subaltern and a company of men were lined up outside waiting for him.

Musketry and machine-gun fire had increased now, visibility was far better, but the shell-fire had ceased altogether—probably the Japanese saw no sense in inflicting too much damage on a city which would be theirs on the following day anyway. Farnholme and his escort moved quickly through the deserted streets through the now gently falling rain, the sound of gunfire in their ears all the time, and had reached the waterfront within a few minutes. Here the smoke, lifted by a gentle breeze from the east, was almost entirely gone.

The smoke was gone, and almost at once Farnholme realised something that made him clutch the handle of the gladstone until his knuckles shone white and his forearms ached with the strain. The small lifeboat from the *Kerry Dancer*, which he had left rubbing gently against the wharf, was gone also, and the sick apprehension that at once flooded through his mind made him lift his head swiftly and stare out into the roads but there was nothing there for him to see. The *Kerry Dancer* was gone as if she had never existed. There was only the falling rain, the gentle breeze in his face and, away to his left, the quiet, heart-broken sobs of a little boy crying alone in the darkness.

CHAPTER TWO

THE SUBALTERN in charge of the soldiers touched Farnholme on the arm and nodded out to sea. "The boat, sir—she's gone!"

Farnholme restrained himself with an effort. His voice, when he spoke, was as calm and as matter-of-fact as ever.

"So it would appear, Lieutenant. In the words of the old song, they've left us standing on the shore. Deuced inconvenient, to say the least of it."

"Yes, sir." Farnholme's reaction to the urgency of the situation, Lieutenant Parker felt, was hardly impressive. "What's to be done now, sir?"

"You may well ask, my boy." Farnholme stood still for several moments, a hand rubbing his chin, an abstracted expression on his face. "Do you hear a child crying there, along the waterfront?" he asked suddenly.

"Yes, sir."

"Have one of your men bring him here. Preferably," Farnholme added, "a kindly, fatherly type that won't scare the living daylights out of him."

"Bring him here, sir?" The subaltern was astonished. "But there are hundreds of these little street Arabs——" He broke off suddenly as Farnholme towered over him, his eyes cold and still beneath the jutting brows.

"I trust you are not deaf, Lieutenant Parker," he inquired solicitously. The low-pitched voice was for the lieutenant's ears alone, as it had been throughout.

"Yes, sir! I mean, no, sir!" Parker hastily revised his earlier impression of Farnholme. "I'll send a man right away, sir."

"Thank you. Then send a few men in either direction along the waterfront, maybe half a mile or so. Have them bring back here any person or persons they find—they may be able to throw some light on the missing boat. Let them use persuasion if necessary."

"Persuasion, sir?"

"In any form. We're not playing for pennies to-night, Lieutenant. And when you've given the necessary orders, I'd like a private little talk with you."

20

" My apologies." Van Effen bowed. " I bow to the authority of the captain."

" Thank you." Feeling vaguely uncomfortable, Nicolson transferred his gaze to the submarine. It was clearly visible now, in all its major details, less than a mile distant. The seaplane was still circling overhead. Nicolson looked at it and scowled.

" I wish that damn' snoop would go on home," he muttered.

" He does complicate things rather," Findhorn agreed. " Time is running out, Johnny. He'll be up with us in five minutes."

Nicolson nodded absently. " We've seen that type of sub before, sir?"

" I rather think we have," Findhorn said slowly.

" We have." Nicolson was certain now. " Light A.A. gun aft, machine-gun on the bridge and a heavy gun for'ard—3.7 or 4-inch, something like that, I'm not sure. If they want to take us aboard we'll have to go right alongside the hull—beneath the conning-tower, probably. Neither of the two guns can depress that far." He bit his lip and stared ahead. " It'll be dark in twenty minutes—and that island won't be much more than half a mile away by the time he stops us. It's a chance, a damn' poor chance at that, but still . . ." He raised the glasses again and stared at the submarine, then shook his head slowly. " Yes, I thought I remembered that. That 3.7 or whatever it is has a big armoured shield for its gun-crew. Some sort of hinged, collapsible thing, probably." His voice trailed off and his fingers beat an urgent tattoo on the rim of the gunwale. He looked absently at the captain. " Complicates things rather, doesn't it, sir?"

" I'm not with you, Johnny." Findhorn was beginning to sound tired again. " Afraid my head's not at its best for this sort of thing. If you've got any idea at all——"

" I have. Crazy, but it might work." Nicolson explained rapidly, then beckoned to Vannier, who handed the tiller to the bo'sun and moved across. " Don't smoke, do you, Fourth?"

" No, sir." Vannier looked at Nicolson as if he had gone off his head.

" You're starting to-night." Nicolson dug into his pocket, fished out a flat tin of Benson and Hedges and a box of matches. He gave them to him, along with a few quick instructions. " Right up in the bows, past Van Effen. Don't forget, everything depends on you. Brigadier? A moment, if you please."

Farnholme looked up in surprise, lumbered over a couple of thwarts and sat down beside them. Nicolson looked at him for a second or two in silence and then said seriously: "You really know how to use that automatic carbine, Brigadier?"

"Good God, man, yes!" the Brigadier snorted. "I practically invented the bloody thing."

"How accurate are you?" Nicolson persisted quietly.

"Bisley," Farnholme answered briefly. "Champion. As good as that, Mr. Nicolson."

"Bisley?" Nicolson's eyebrows reflected his astonishment.

"King's marksman." Farnholme's voice was completely out of character now, as quiet as Nicolson's own. "Chuck a tin over the side, let it go a hundred feet and I'll give you a demonstration. Riddle it with this carbine in two seconds." The tone was matter-of-fact; more, it was convincing.

"No demonstration," Nicolson said hastily. "That's the last thing we want. As far as brother Jap is concerned, we haven't even a fire-cracker between us. This is what I want you to do." His instructions to Farnholme were rapid and concise, as were those given immediately afterwards to the rest of the boat's company. There was no time to waste on lengthier explanations, to make sure he was fully understood: the enemy was almost on them.

The sky to the west was still alive and glowing, a kaleidoscopic radiance of red and orange and gold, the barred clouds on the horizon ablaze with fire, but the sun was gone, the east was grey and the sudden darkness of the tropical night was rushing across the sea. The submarine was angling in on their starboard quarter, grim and black and menacing in the gathering twilight, the glassy sea piling up in phosphorescent whiteness on either side of its bows, the diesels dying away to a muted murmur, the dark, evil mouth of the big for'ard gun dipping and moving slowly aft as it matched the relative movement of the little lifeboat, foot by remorseless foot. And then there had come some sharp, unintelligible command from the conning-tower of the submarine; McKinnon cut the engine at a gesture from Nicolson and the iron hull of the submarine scraped harshly along the rubbing piece of the lifeboat.

Nicolson craned his neck and looked swiftly along the deck and conning-tower of the submarine. The big gun for'ard was pointing in their direction, but over their heads, as he had guessed it would: it had already reached maximum depression. The light A.A. gun aft was also lined up at them—lined up into the heart of their boat: he had miscalculated about that one, but it was a chance they had to take. There were three men in the conning-tower, two of them armed—an officer with a pistol and a sailor with what looked like a sub-machine gun—and five or six sailors at the foot of the conning-tower, only one of them armed. As a reception committee it was dismaying enough, but less than what he had expected. He had thought that the lifeboat's abrupt, last-minute alteration of course to port—a movement calculated to bring them alongside the port side of the submarine, leaving them half-shadowed in the gloom to the east while the Japanese were silhouetted against the after-glow of sunset—might have aroused lively suspicion: but it must have been almost inevitably interpreted as a panic-stricken attempt to escape, an attempt no sooner made than its futility realised. A lifeboat offered no threat to anyone and the submarine commander must have thought that he had already taken far more than ample precautions against such puny resistance as they could possibly offer.

The three craft—the submarine and the two lifeboats—were still moving ahead at about two knots when a rope came spinning down from the deck of the submarine and fell across the bows of number one lifeboat. Automatically Vannier caught it and looked back at Nicolson.

" Might as well make fast, Fourth." Nicolson's tone was resigned, bitter. " What good's fists and a couple of jack-knives against this lot?"

" Sensible, so sensible." The officer leaned over the conning-tower, his arms folded, the barrel of the gun lying along his upper left arm: the English was good, the tone self-satisfied, and the teeth a white gleaming smirk in the dark smudge of the face. " Resistance would be so unpleasant for all of us, would it not?"

" Go to hell!" Nicolson muttered.

" Such incivility! Such lack of courtesy—the true Anglo-Saxon." The officer shook his head sadly, vastly enjoying himself. Then he suddenly straightened, looked sharply at Nicolson over the barrel of his gun. " Be very careful!" His voice was like the crack of a whip.

Slowly, unhurriedly, Nicolson completed his movement of extracting a cigarette from the packet Willoughby had offered him, as slowly struck a match, lit his own and Willoughby's cigarettes and sent the match spinning over the side.

"So! Of course!" The officer's laugh was brief, contemptuous. "The phlegmatic Englishman! Even though his teeth chatter with fear, he must maintain his reputation—especially in front of his crew. And another of them!" Up in the bows of the lifeboat Vannier's bent head, a cigarette clipped between his lips, was highlit by the flaring match in his hand. "By all the gods, it's pathetic, really pathetic." The tone of his voice changed abruptly.. "But enough of this—this foolery. Aboard at once—all of you." He jabbed his gun at Nicolson. "You first."

Nicolson stood up, one arm propping himself against the hull of the submarine, the other pressed close by his side.

"What do you intend to do with us, damn you?" His voice was loud, almost a shout, with a nicely-induced tremor in it. "Kill us all? Torture us? Drag us to those damned prison camps in Japan?" He was shouting in earnest now, fear and anger in the voice: Vannier's match hadn't gone over the side, and the hissing from the bows was even louder than he had expected. "Why in the name of God don't you shoot us all now instead of——"

With breath-taking suddenness there came a hissing roar from the bows of the lifeboat, twin streaks of sparks and smoke and flame lancing upwards into the darkening sky across the submarine's deck and at an angle of about thirty degrees off the vertical and then two incandescent balls of flame burst into life hundreds of feet above the water as both the lifeboat's rocket parachute flares ignited almost at the same instant. A man would have had to be far less than human to check the involuntary, quite irresistible, impulse to look at the two rockets exploding into flame far up in the skies, and the Japanese crew of the submarine were only human. To a man, like dolls in the hands of a puppet master, they twisted round to look, and to a man they died that way, their backs half-turned to the lifeboat and their necks craned back as they stared up into the sky.

The crash of automatic carbines, rifles and pistols died away, the echoes rolled off into distant silence across the glassy sea and Nicolson was shouting at everyone to lie flat in the boat. Even as he was shouting, two dead sailors rolled off the sloping deck of the submarine and crashed into the stern of the lifeboat, one of them almost pinning him against the gunwale. The other, lifeless arms and legs flailing, was heading straight

132

Farnholme strolled off some yards into the gloom. Lieutenant Parker rejoined him within a minute. Farnholme lit a fresh cheroot and looked speculatively at the young officer before him.

"Do you know who I am, young man?" he asked abruptly.

"No, sir."

"Brigadier Farnholme." Farnholme grinned in the darkness as he saw the perceptible stiffening of the lieutenant's shoulders. "Now that you've heard it, forget it. You've never heard of me. Understand?"

"No, sir," Parker said politely. "But I understand the order well enough."

"That's all you need to understand. And cut out the 'sirs' from now on. Do you know my business?"

"No, sir, I——"

"No 'sirs,' I said," Farnholme interrupted. "If you cut them out in private, there's no chance of your using them in public."

"I'm sorry. No, I don't know your business. But the colonel impressed upon me that it was a matter of the utmost importance and gravity."

"The colonel was in no way exaggerating," Farnholme murmured feelingly. "It is better, much better, that you don't know my business. If we ever reach safety I promise you I'll tell you what it's all about. Meantime, the less you and your men know the safer for all of us." He paused, drew heavily on the cheroot and watched the tip glow redly in the night. "Do you know what a beachcomber is, Lieutenant?"

"A beachcomber?" The sudden switch caught Parker off balance, but he recovered quickly. "Naturally."

"Good. That's what I am from now on, and you will kindly treat me as such. An elderly, alcoholic and somewhat no-account beachcomber hell-bent on saving his own skin. Good-natured and tolerant contempt—that's your line. Firm, even severe when you've got to be. You found me wandering about the streets, searching for some form of transport out of Singapore. You heard from me that I had arrived on a little inter-island steamer and decided that you would commandeer it for your own uses."

"But the ship's gone," Parker objected.

"You have a point," Farnholme admitted. "We may find it yet. There may be others, though I very much doubt it. The point is that you must have your story—and your attitude—

21

ready, no matter what happens. Incidentally, our objective is Australia."

"Australia!" Parker was startled into momentary forgetfulness. "Good lord, sir, that's thousands of miles away!"

"It's a fairish bit," Farnholme conceded. "Our destination, nevertheless, even if we can't lay hands on anything larger than a rowing boat." He broke off and swung round. "One of your men returning, I think, Lieutenant."

It was. A soldier emerged out of the darkness, the three white chevrons on his arms easy to see. A very big man, over six feet tall and broad in proportion, he made the childish figure in his arms tiny by comparison. The little boy, face buried in the soldier's sun-burned neck, was still sobbing, but quietly now.

"Here he is, sir." The burly sergeant patted the child's back. "The little duffer's had a bad fright, I think, but he'll get over it."

"I'm sure he will, Sergeant." Farnholme touched the child's shoulder. "And what's your name, my little man, eh?"

The little man took one quick look, flung his arms round the sergeant's neck and burst into a fresh torrent of tears. Farnholme stepped back hastily.

"Ah, well." He shook his head philosophically. "Never had much of a way with children, I'm afraid. Crusty old bachelors and what have you. His name can wait."

"His name is Peter," the sergeant said woodenly. "Peter Tallon. He's two years and three months old, he lives in Mysore Road in north Singapore and he's a member of the Church of England."

"He told you all that?" Farnholme asked incredulously.

"He hasn't spoken a word, sir. There's an identity disc tied round his neck."

"Quite," Farnholme murmured. It seemed the only appropriate remark in the circumstances. He waited until the sergeant had rejoined his men, then looked speculatively at Parker.

"My apologies." The lieutenant's tone was sincere. "How the devil did you know?"

"Be damned funny if I didn't know after twenty-three years in the East. Sure, you'll find Malay and Chinese waifs, but waifs only of their own choice. You don't find them crying. If they did, they wouldn't be crying long. These people always look after their own—not just their own children, but their own kind." He paused and looked quizzically at Parker.

" Any guesses as to what brother Jap would have done to that kid, Lieutenant?"

" I can guess," Parker said sombrely. " I've seen a little and I've heard a lot."

" Believe it all, then double it. They're an inhuman bunch of fiends." He changed the subject abruptly. " Let's rejoin your men. Berate me as we go. It'll create no end of a good impression—from my point of view, that is."

Five minutes passed, then ten. The men moved about restlessly, some smoked, some sat on their packs, but no one spoke. Even the little boy had stopped crying. The intermittent crackle of gunfire carried clearly from the north-west of the town, but mostly the night was very still. The wind had shifted, and the last of the smoke was clearing slowly away. The rain was still falling, more heavily than before, and the night was growing cold.

By and by, from the north-east, the direction of Kallang creek, came the sound of approaching footsteps, the measured paces of three soldiers marching in step and the quicker, more erratic click of feminine heels. Parker stared as they emerged out of the darkness, then turned to the soldier who had been leading the party.

" What's all this? Who are these people?"

" Nurses, sir. We found them wandering a little way along the front." The soldier sounded apologetic. " I think they were lost, sir."

" Lost?" Parker peered at the tall girl nearest him. " What the dickens are you people doing wandering about the town in the middle of the night?"

" We're looking for some wounded soldiers, sir." The voice was soft and husky. " Wounded and sick. We—well, we don't seem able to find them."

" So I gather," Parker agreed dryly. " You in charge of this party?"

" Yes, sir."

" What's your name, please?" The lieutenant's tone was a shade less peremptory now; the girl had a pleasant voice, and he could see that she was very tired, and shivering in the cold rain.

" Drachmann, sir."

" Well, Miss Drachmann, have you seen or heard anything of a small motorboat or a coastal steamer, anywhere offshore?"

23

"No, sir." Her tone held tired surprise. "All the ships have left Singapore."

"I hope to heaven you're wrong," Parker muttered. Aloud, he said, "Know anything about kids, Miss Drachmann?"

"What?" She sounded startled.

"The sergeant there has found a little boy." Parker nodded to the child still in the sergeant's arms, but wrapped now in a waterproof cape against the cold and rain. "He's lost, tired, lonely and his name is Peter. Will you look after him for the present?"

"Why, of course I will."

Even as she was stretching out her hands for the child, more footsteps were heard approaching from the left. Not the measured steps of soldiers, nor the crisp clickety-clack of women's heels, but a shambling, shuffling sound such as very old men might make. Or very sick men. Gradually there emerged out of the rain and the darkness a long, uncertain line of men, weaving and stumbling, in token column of twos. They were led by a little man with a high, hunched left shoulder, with a Bren gun dangling heavily from his right hand. He wore a balmoral set jauntily on his head, and a wet kilt that flapped about his bare, thin knees. Two yards away from Parker he stopped, shouted out a command to halt, turned round to supervise the lowering of the stretchers—it was then that Parker saw for the first time that three of his own men were helping to carry the stretchers—then ran backwards to intercept the straggler who brought up the end of the column and was now angling off aimlessly into the darkness. Farnholme stared after him, then at the sick, maimed and exhausted men who stood there in the rain, each man lost in his suffering and silent exhaustion.

"My God!" Farnholme shook his head in wonder. "The Pied Piper never had anything on this bunch!"

The little man in the kilt was back at the head of the column now. Awkwardly, painfully, he lowered his Bren to the wet ground, straightened and brought his hand up to his balmoral in a salute that would have done credit to a Guards' parade ground. "Corporal Fraser reporting, sir." His voice had the soft burr of the north-east Highlands.

"At ease, Corporal." Parker stared at him. "Wouldn't it—wouldn't it have been easier if you'd just transferred that gun to your left hand?" A stupid question, he knew, but the sight of that long line of haggard, half-alive zombies materialising

24

for little Peter and the two nurses, but McKinnon got there first. The two heavy splashes sounded almost like one.

One second passed, two, then three. Nicolson was on his knees, staring upwards, fists clenched as he waited in tense expectation. At first he could hear the shuffle of feet and the fast, low-pitched murmur of voices behind the shield of the big gun. Another second passed, and then another. His eyes moved along the submarine deck, perhaps there was someone still alive, still seeking a glorious death for his Emperor—Nicolson had no illusions about the fanatical courage of the Japanese. But now everything was still, still as death. The officer hanging tiredly over the conning-tower, gun still locked in a dangling hand—Nicolson's pistol had got him, and the other two had fallen inside. Four shapeless forms lay in a grotesque huddle about the foot of the conning-tower. Of the two men who had manned the light A.A. gun there was no sign: Farnholme's automatic carbine had blasted them over the side.

The tension was becoming intolerable. The big gun, Nicolson knew, couldn't depress far enough to reach the boat, but he had vague memories of stories told him by naval officers of the almost decapitating effects of a naval gun fired just above one's head. Perhaps the blast of the concussion would be fatal to those directly beneath, there was no way of knowing. Suddenly, silently, he began to curse his own stupidity and turned quickly to Willoughby.

" Start the engine up, Bo'sun. Then reverse—fast as you can. The conning-tower can block off that gun if we——"

The words were lost, obliterated in the roar of the firing gun. It wasn't a roar, really, but a flat, violent whip-lash crack that stabbed savagely at the eardrums and almost stunned in its intensity. A long red tongue of flame flickered evilly out of the mouth of the barrel, reaching down almost to the boat itself. The shell smashed into the sea, throwing up a fine curtain of spray and a spout of water that reached fifty feet up into the sky, and then the sound had died, the smoke had cleared, and Nicolson, desperately shaking a dazed head, knew that they were alive, that the Japanese were frantically trying to load again, knew that the time had come.

" Right, Brigadier." He could see Farnholme heaving himself to his feet. " Wait till I give the word." He looked up swiftly towards the bows as a rifle boomed.

" Missed him." Van Effen was disgusted. " An officer looked over the edge of the conning-tower just now."

"Keep your gun lined up," Nicolson ordered. He could hear the boy wailing with fear and knew that the blast of the big gun must have terrified him: his face twisted savagely as he shouted to Vannier. "Fourth! The signal set. A couple of red hand flares and heave them into the conning-tower. That'll keep 'em busy." He was listening all the time to the movements of the gun crew. "All of you—watch the tower and the fore and aft hatches."

Perhaps another five seconds passed and then Nicolson heard the sound he had been waiting for—the scrape of a shell in the breech and the block swinging solidly home. "Now!" he called sharply.

Farnhome didn't even bother to raise the gun to his shoulder but fired with the stock under his arm, seemingly without taking any aim whatsoever. He didn't need to, he was even better than he had claimed to be. He ripped off perhaps five shots, no more, deflected them all down the barrel of the big gun then dropped to the bottom of the lifeboat like a stone as the last bullet found the percussion nose of the shell and triggered off the detonation. Severe enough in sound and shock at such close range, the explosion of the bursting shell inside the breech was curiously muffled, although the effects were spectacular enough. The whole big gun lifted off its mounting and flying pieces of the shattered metal clanged viciously against the conning-tower and went whistling over the sea, ringing the submarine in an erratic circle of splashes. The gun-crew must have died unknowing: enough T.N.T. to blow up a bridge had exploded within arm's length of their faces.

"Thank you, Brigadier." Nicolson was on his feet again, forcing his voice to steadiness. "My apologies for all I ever said about you. Full ahead, Bo'sun." A couple of sputtering crimson hand flares went arching through the air and landed safely inside the conning-tower, silhouetting the coaming against a fierce red glow. "Well done, Fourth. You've saved the day to-day."

"Mr. Nicolson?"

"Sir?" Nicolson glanced down at the captain.

"Wouldn't it be better, perhaps, if we stayed here a little longer? No one dare show his head through the hatches or over the tower. In ten or fifteen minutes it'll be dark enough for us to reach that island there without the beggars taking pot-shots at us all the time."

"Afraid that wouldn't do, sir." Nicolson was apologetic. "Right now the lads inside there are shocked and stunned, but
134

pretty soon someone's going to start thinking, and as soon as he does we can look for a shower of hand grenades. They can shuck them into the boat without having to show a finger—and even one would finish us."

"Of course, of course." Findhorn sank back wearily on his bench. "Carry on, Mr. Nicolson."

Nicolson took the tiller, came hard round with both life-boats through a hundred and eighty degrees, circled round the slender, fish-tail stern of the submarine while four men with guns in their hands watched the decks unblinkingly, and slowed down just abaft the submarine's bridge to allow Farnholme to smash the A.A. gun's delicate firing mechanism with a long, accurate burst from his automatic carbine. Captain Findhorn nodded in slow realisation.

"Exit their siege gun. You think of everything, Mr. Nicolson."

"I hope so, sir." Nicolson shook his head. "I hope to God I do."

The island was perhaps half-a-mile distant from the sub-marine. A quarter of the way there Nicolson stooped, brought up one of the lifeboat's two standard Wessex distress signal floats, ripped away the top disc seal, ignited it by tearing off the release fork and immediately threw it over the stern, just wide enough to clear Siran's boat. As soon as it hit the water it began to give off a dense cloud of orange-coloured smoke, smoke that hung almost without moving in the windless twi-light, an impenetrable screen against the enemy. A minute or two later bullets from the submarine began to cut through the orange smoke, whistling overhead or splashing into the water around them, but none came near enough to do any damage ; the Japanese were firing at random and in blind anger. Four minutes after the first smoke float, now fizzling to extinction, had been thrown overboard the second one followed it, and long before it, too, had burnt out they had beached their boats and landed safely on the island.

CHAPTER NINE

IT HARDLY deserved the name of island. An islet, perhaps, but no more. Oval in shape, lying almost due east and west, it was no more than three hundred yards long, and about a hundred and fifty from north to south. It wasn't a perfect oval, however: about a hundred yards along from the apex the sea had cut deep notches on both sides, at points practically opposite one another, so that the islet was all but bisected. It was in the southerly bight—Nicolson had taken the precaution of rounding the island before landing—that they had beached their boats and moored them to a couple of heavy stones.

The narrow end of the island, east beyond the bights, was low and rocky and bare, but the west had some vegetation—scrub bushes and stunted lalang grass—and rose to a height of perhaps fifty feet in the middle. On the southern side of this hill there was a little hollow, hardly more than a shelf, about half-way up the slope, and it was towards this that Nicolson urged the passengers as soon as the boat had grounded. The Captain and Corporal Fraser had to be carried, but it was only a short trip and within ten minutes of the boats' grounding the entire party had taken refuge in the hollow, surrounded by all the food, water supplies and portable equipment, even the oars and the crutches.

A light breeze had sprung up with the going down of the sun, and clouds were slowly filling up the sky from the northeast, blanketing the early evening stars, but it was still light enough for Nicolson to use his glasses. He stared through them for almost two minutes, then laid them down, rubbing his eyes. He was aware, without being able to see, that everybody in the hollow was watching him anxiously—all except the boy who was bundled up in a blanket and already drowsing off to sleep.

"Well?" Findhorn broke the silence.

"They're moving round the western tip of the island, sir, Pretty close inshore, too."

"I can't hear them.".

"Must be using their batteries. Why, I don't know. Just because they can't see us it doesn't mean that we can't see them. It's not all that dark."

Van Effen cleared his throat. And what do you think the next move is going to be, Mr. Nicolson?"

" No idea. It's up to them, I'm afraid. If they had either their big gun or A.A. gun left they could blast us out of here in two minutes." Nicolson gestured at the low ridge that bounded the hollow to the south, barely visible in the gloom even six feet away. " But with a little luck I think that'll stop rifle bullets."

" And if it doesn't?"

" Time enough to worry about that when it happens," Nicolson answered shortly. " Maybe they'll try to land men at various points and surround us. Maybe they'll try a frontal attack." He had the glasses to his eyes again. " Whatever happens they can't just go home and say they left us here— they'd get their heads in their hands, perhaps literally. Either that or hara-kiri all over the shop."

" They won't go home." Captain Findhorne's voice was heavy with certainty. " Too many of their shipmates have died."

For some time there had been a murmur of voices behind them, and now the murmur died away and Siran spoke.

" Mr. Nicolson?"

Nicolson lowered his binoculars and looked over his shoulder.

" What do you want?"

" My men and I have been having a discussion. We have a proposition to make to you."

" Make it to the captain. He's in charge." Nicolson turned away abruptly and raised the binoculars again.

" Very well. It is this, Captain Findhorn. It is obvious— painfully obvious, if I may say so—that you do not trust us. You force us to occupy a separate lifeboat—and not, I think, because we don't bathe twice a day. You feel—wrongly, I assure you—that you must watch us all the time. We are a heavy—ah—responsibility, a liability, I should say. We propose, with your permission, to relieve you of this liability."

" For heaven's sake get to the point," Findhorn snapped irritably.

" Very well. I suggest you let us go, have no more worry about us. We prefer to be the prisoners of the Japanese."

" What!" The angry interjection came from Van Effen. " God in heaven, sir, I'd shoot the lot of them first!"

" Please!" Findhorn waved a hand in the darkness, looking curiously at Siran, but it was too dark to see his expression.

137

"As a matter of interest, how would you propose to surrender yourselves. Just walk off down the hill towards the beach?"

"More or less."

"And what guarantee would you have that they wouldn't shoot you before you surrendered? Or, if you did succeed in surrendering, that they wouldn't torture or kill you afterwards?"

"Don't let them go, sir." Van Effen's voice was urgent.

"Do not distress yourself," Findhorn said dryly. "I've no intention of complying with his ridiculous request. You stay, Siran, although heaven knows we don't want you. Please don't insult our intelligence."

"Mr. Nicolson!" Siran appealed. "Surely you can see——"

"Shut up!" Nicolson said curtly. "You heard what Captain Findhorn said. How naïve and dim-witted do you think we are? Not one of you would risk his precious neck if there was the slightest chance of being shot or ill-treated by the Japs. It's a hundred to one——"

"I assure you——" Siran made to interrupt but Nicolson stopped him.

"Save your breath," he said contemptuously. "Do you think anyone would believe you? You're obviously in cahoots with the Japs, one way or another—and we have enough on our plates without making ourselves the present of another seven enemies." There was a pause, then Nicolson went on thoughtfully, "A pity you promised this man to the gallows, Captain Findhorn. I think Van Effen went to the heart of the matter at once—it would simplify things all round if we shot the lot of them now. We'll probably have to do it later on anyway."

There was a long pause, then Findhorn said quietly: "You are very silent, Siran. You miscalculated, perhaps? Almost your last blunder? You can be very grateful, Captain Siran, for the fact that we are not callous murderers of your own stamp. But please bear in mind that it will require very little provocation indeed for us to carry out the suggestion just made."

"And just move back a bit, will you?" Nicolson asked. "Right to the edge, there. And maybe a quick search of your pockets wouldn't do any harm, either."

"Already done, Mr. Nicolson," the captain assured him. "We took a whole arsenal off them after you left the saloon last night . . . Still see that sub?"

"Almost due south of us now, sir. About two hundred yards offshore."

He suddenly dropped the binoculars and pushed himself back down into the hollow. A searchlight had just been switched on in the conning-tower of the submarine, its dazzling white beam swinging rapidly along the rocky shore of the island. Almost at once it found the little notch in the shoreline where the lifeboats lay, steadied there for a couple of seconds, then started moving slowly up the hill, almost in a line with the hollow where they lay hidden.

"Brigadier!" Nicolson's voice was sharp, urgent.

"It'll be a pleasure," Farnholme grunted. He slid the carbine forward along the ground, cradled it to his shoulder, sighted and fired, all in one swift movement. It was set for single shot firing, but the single shot was enough: through the fading echoes of the crash of the carbine they caught the distant tinkle of glass, and the white glare of the light faded quickly to a dull red glow, then died away altogether.

"Stay with us a few more days, will you, Brigadier?" Findhorn said dryly. "I can see that we're going to need you around . . . Hardly a very bright move on their part, was it, Mr. Nicolson? I mean, they've already had a sample from the Brigadier here."

"Bright enough," Nicolson differed. "A calculated risk, and it paid off. They've found out where the boats are and they know now, from the flash of the brigadier's rifle, where we are —two facts it might have cost a landing party a long time and a good few lives to find out. But it was really the boats they were worried about, not us. If they can stop us from leaving the island, they can get us at their leisure, preferably in daylight."

"I'm afraid I agree with you," Findhorn said slowly. "The boats come next. Sink them from the sub, you reckon? We can't stop them if they do."

"Not from the sub." Nicolson shook his head. "They can't see the boats and it would take them all night to sink them with random fire: a hundred lucky shots at least. A landing party to knock the bottom out of the boats and spike the air tanks is more likely—or tow them or row them out to sea."

"But—but how do they get ashore?" Vannier asked.

"Swim if they have to, but they don't have to. Most subs carry collapsible or inflatable dinghies of some kind. For a sub operating in close waters, almost certainly in contact with their own troops on a score of different islands, it would be essential."

No one spoke for several minutes. The little boy was muttering to himself in his sleep, and Siran and his men were whispering in the far corner of the hollow, their words indistinguishable. Then Willoughby coughed to catch their attention.

"The flood of time is rolling on, etc., etc.," he quoted. "I have an idea."

Nicolson smiled in the darkness. "Careful, Willy."

"Base envy hates that excellence it cannot reach," Willoughby said loftily. "My plan has the simplicity of true genius. Let us sail away."

"Brilliant." Nicolson was heavily sarcastic. "Muffled oars in the moonlight. How far do you reckon we get?"

"Tush! You underrate me. Willoughby soaring in the realms of pure thought and our worthy chief officer still trudging in the mire. We use the engine, of course!"

"Oh, of course! And how do you propose to persuade our pals out there to wear ear-plugs?"

"I don't. Give me an hour on that exhaust-pipe and baffle plates and I guarantee you won't hear that engine a hundred yards away. Lose some speed of course, but not much. And even if they do hear it, you know yourself how difficult it is to get a bearing on a faint sound over the sea at night. Freedom beckons, gentlemen. Let us no longer delay."

"Willy," Nicolson said gently, "I have news for you. The human ear is not to be depended on for finding bearings at night, but then the Japs don't have to depend on it. They use hydrophones, which are very accurate indeed—and which couldn't care less whether you muffle the exhaust or not as the propeller thrash in the water will serve them excellently."

"Damn them," Willoughby said with feeling. He lapsed into silence, then spoke again. "Let no one despair. Willoughby shall think of something else."

"I've no doubt you will," Nicolson said kindly. "Don't forget that the north-west monsoon only lasts for another couple of months or so and it would be handy if—down, everybody, down!"

The first bullets were thudding soggily into the earth around them, ricocheting with a vicious whine off the rocks and whistling evilly overhead as they heard the barrage opening up from the deck of the submarine. It had moved a good deal closer inshore and it sounded as if at least a dozen different guns, machine-guns, two at least, included, were all firing at once. And someone aboard the ship had been fast enough to take a bearing on the flash of Farnholme's carbine: the fire was as accurate as it was heavy.

"Anybody hurt? Anybody hurt at all?" It was difficult to hear the captain's low, hoarse voice above the crackle of gunfire.

There was no immediate reply, and Nicolson answered for the others. "I don't think so, sir. I was the only one exposed at the time."

"Good enough—and no retaliation just now," Findhorn warned. "No reason for anybody to get his head blown off." He lowered his voice with evident relief. "Mr. Nicolson, this baffles me completely. The Zeros didn't touch us when we left the *Viroma*: the sub didn't try to sink us: and the seaplane left us alone even after we'd thumped their pals. And now they're trying their best to massacre us. It doesn't make any kind of sense at all to me."

"Still less to me," Nicolson admitted. He winced involuntarily as a bullet thudded into the earth a couple of feet above his head. "And we can't stay here and do an ostrich act, sir. This is a cover for an attack on the boats. Pointless otherwise."

Findhorn nodded heavily in the darkness. "What do you want to do? I'm afraid I'm a dead loss, Johnny."

"As long as you're not just dead," Nicolson said grimly. "Permission to take some men down to the shore, sir. We must stop them."

"I know, I know . . . Good luck, boy."

Seconds later, in a brief lull in the firing, Nicolson and six men slithered over the edge of the bank and started downhill. They hadn't gone five paces when Nicolson whispered in Vannier's ear, caught the Brigadier by the arm and retraced his steps with him to the eastern edge of the hollow. They lay down on the edge, peering into the darkness. Nicolson put his mouth to the Brigadier's ear. "Remember, we play for keeps."

He could just sense Farnholme nodding in the darkness.

They didn't have to wait long. Within fifteen seconds they heard the first faint, cautious slither, followed at once by Findhorn's voice, sharp and hoarse, jerking out a question. There was no reply, just another ominous movement, a swift rush of feet, the sudden click as Nicolson's torch switched on, the brief glimpse of two running stooping figures with upraised arms, the stuttering crash of Farnholme's automatic carbine, the heavy thud of falling bodies and then the silence and the darkness together.

"Bloody fool that I am! I'd forgotten all about these." Nicolson was crawling about the hollow, torch hooded in his hand, tearing away weapons still clenched in dead hands. He let the light play on them for a moment. "The two hatchets from number two lifeboat, sir. They'd have made a pretty mess at close quarters." He shone his torch at the other end of the hollow. Siran was still sitting there, his face smooth and expressionless. Nicolson knew that he was guilty, guilty as hell, that he had sent his three men to do the hatchet-work—literally—while he remained safely behind. He also knew that the bland, inscrutable face would remain that way as Siran denied all knowledge of the attack: dead men couldn't talk, and the three men were quite dead. There was no time to waste.

"Come here, Siran." Nicolson's voice was as expressionless as Siran's face. "The rest won't give any trouble, sir." Siran rose to his feet, walked the few paces forward and toppled to the ground like a falling tree trunk as Nicolson struck him viciously behind the ear with the butt of his Navy Colt. The blow had carried sufficient weight to crush the skull, and it had sounded like it, but Nicolson was on his way even before Siran had fallen, Farnholme at his heels. The whole episode hadn't taken thirty seconds from start to finish.

They ran at full speed, uncaringly, down the slope, stumbling, slipping, recovering and racing on again. Thirty yards from the beach they heard a sudden flurry of shots, screams of pain, oaths, high-pitched voices shouting some insane gibberish, another volley of shots then the sounds of more blows, of struggling and violent splashing as men fought hand to hand in the water. Ten yards from the water's edge, well ahead of Farnholme by this time, and still pounding along at the full stretch of his legs, Nicolson switched on his torch. He had a confused impression of men struggling furiously in the shallow water round the boats, caught a brief glimpse of an officer poised above a fallen McKinnon with a sword or bayonet swung back for a decapitation stroke and then leapt, one arm round the officer's throat and the gun exploding in his back, before he landed cat-like on his feet. Again his torch swung up, steadied for a moment on Walters and a Japanese sailor thrashing and splashing as they rolled over and over in the

142

mud-stained water: nothing to be done there—as easy to kill the one as the other. The beam lifted, and stopped again.

One of the lifeboats, well aground, was lying almost parallel to the shore. Two Japanese sailors, knee-deep in the water and sharply profiled in the harsh glare of the torch, were standing close by the stern, one of them stooping with bent head, the other upright, arm upraised, his right hand far behind his head. For a long second of time, all volition inhibited by the light that blinded their shrinking eyes, the two men held their respective positions, a frozen sequence from some nightmare ballet: and then, in perfect unison, petrified stillness yielded to convulsive action, the stooped man straightening with his right hand clutching something snatched from the net bag tied to his belt, the other dropping his left shoulder and lunging forward as his throwing arm came flashing over, and Nicolson, even as he brought his Colt up, his finger tightening on the trigger, knew that he was already too late.

Too late for Nicolson, too late for the Japanese sailors. For a second time they stiffened into immobility, brought up short by the savage jerk of some invisible hand, then they began to move again, slowly, this time, very slowly, pivoting forward with an almost ponderous deliberation on rooted, lifeless legs: Nicolson's torch had switched off and the crash of Farn-holme's carbine was only an echoing memory as they fell on their faces, one full length into the water, the other jack-knifing heavily over the gunwale of the lifeboat and crashing on to the sternsheets, the sound of his falling lost in a flat explosive crack and sheet of blinding white as the grenade exploded in his hand.

After the bright light of the bursting grenade the darkness was doubly dark. Darkness everywhere, on land, over the sea and in the sky, complete and, for the moment, impenetrable. Away to the south-west a last few stars winked faintly in an indigo sky, but they too were going, extinguished one by one as the unseen blanket of cloud closed with the horizon. Dark, and very silent; there was no sound, no movement at all.

Nicolson risked one quick sweep with his lighted torch, then clicked off the switch. His men were all there, all on their feet, and the enemy were the enemy no longer, just little dead men lying still in the shadows. They had had next to no chance at all: they had expected no attack, deeming the *Viroma's* crew safely pinned in the hollow by the submarine's covering

143

fire: they had been silhouetted against the sea, always lighter by night than the land: and they had been caught at a crippling disadvantage in the moment of stepping from their rubber boats into the sea.

"Anybody hurt?" Nicolson kept his voice low.

"Walters is, sir." Vannier matched his tone with Nicolson's. "Pretty badly, I think."

"Let me see." Nicolson moved across to the source of the voice, hooded the torch with his fingers and clicked the switch. Vannier was cradling Walters's left wrist in his hand: it was a gaping, gory wound just below the ball of the thumb, and half the wrist was severed. Vannier already had a handkerchief twisted as a tourniquet, and the bright red blood was pulsing only very slowly from the wound. Nicolson switched off the light.

"Knife?"

"Bayonet." Walters's voice was a good deal steadier than Vannier's had been. He prodded something lying still and shapeless at his feet in the water. "I took it from him."

"So I gathered," Nicolson said dryly. "Your wrist's a mess. Get Miss Drachmann to fix it for you. It'll be some time before you can use that hand, I'm afraid." Which was one way of saying 'never,' Nicolson thought bitterly to himself. The clenching tendons had been severed clean through, and it was a certainty that the radial nerve had gone also. Paralysis, in any event.

"Better than the heart," Walters said cheerfully. "I really need that."

"Get up there as fast as you can. The rest of you go with him—and don't forget to announce yourselves. For all the captain knows we lost—and he's got a gun lying handy. Bo'sun, you stay with me." He broke off suddenly as he heard splashing in the vicinity of the nearest lifeboat. "Who's there?"

"Me, Farnholme. Just investigatin', old boy. Dozens of them, actually dozens of them."

"What the devil are you talking about?" Nicolson asked irritably.

"Grenades. Bags full of 'em. Fellow here like a walkin' arsenal."

"Take them away, will you? We may need them. Get someone to help you." Nicolson and McKinnon waited till the last of the men had gone, then waded out towards the nearest lifeboat. Just as they reached it, two machine-guns opened up

144

from the darkness to the south, tracer bullets burning white then extinguishing in vicious plops and gouts of water. Now and then a freak ricocheted off the water and whined thinly into the darkness: more rarely still a bullet thudded solidly into one or other of the lifeboats.

Stretched full length behind a boat, only his head above water, McKinnon touched Nicolson on the arm. "What's all this in aid of, sir?" The soft Highland voice was puzzled, but completely unworried. Nicolson grinned to himself in the darkness.

"Anybody's guess, Bo'sun. Chances are that their landing party was supposed to signal—torch or something—if they landed safely. Alarums and excursions ashore and our pals on the sub climbing the walls with uncertainty. Finally, they open up—no signal."

"And if that's all they're wanting, why shouldn't we be sending them one?"

Nicolson stared at him for a moment in the darkness, then laughed softly. "Genius, McKinnon, pure genius. If they're all confused, and if they imagine their pals ashore are as confused as they are themselves, any old signal has a chance of getting by."

And so it proved. Nicolson raised his hand above the lifeboat gunwale, flashed the torch irregularly on and off, then hurriedly withdraw his arm. To any trigger-happy machine-gunner that pinpoint of light must have been the answer to a prayer, but no line of tracers came lancing at them out of the darkness. Instead, both machine-guns abruptly ceased fire and all at once the night was silent and still. Land and sea alike might have been deserted; empty of all life: even the blurred silhouette of the submarine lying quietly out to sea was only a shadow, insubstantial and quite unreal, more imagined than seen.

Furtive attempts at concealment seemed not only unnecessary but dangerous. Unhurriedly both men rose to their feet and inspected the lifeboats in the light of the torch. Number two, Siran's boat, had been holed in several places, but all above the water-line, and she appeared to be making little or no water: several of her airtight tanks had been punctured, but sufficient were undamaged to provide a still reasonable margin of safety.

It was a different story altogether with number one, the motor lifeboat. If anything, even fewer random shots had pierced her hull, but she was already settled deeply, heavily in the shallow water, her floorboards covered. The water inside the boat was stained and streaked with red blood from the shockingly mutilated Japanese sailor who lay draped over the gunwale, and it was below this barely recognisable remains of a human being that Nicolson found the cause of the trouble. The same grenade that had blown off a hand and most of a face had also blown a hole clear through the bottom of the boat, shattering the garboard strake for eighteen inches of its length and the adjacent planks right up to the bilge-stringer on the starboard side. Nicolson straightened slowly and looked at McKinnon in the backwash of reflected light.

"Holed," he murmured briefly. "I could stick my head and shoulders through that gap in the bottom. Take us days to patch the damn' thing."

But McKinnon wasn't listening. The beam of the torch had shifted and he was staring down into the boat. When he spoke, he sounded remote, indifferent.

"It doesn't matter anyway, sir. The engine's finished." He paused, then went on quietly: "The magneto, sir: the grenade must have gone off just beneath it."

"Oh, lord, no! The magneto? Perhaps the second engineer——"

"No one could repair it, sir," McKinnon interrupted patiently. "There's damn all left to repair."

"I see." Nicolson nodded heavily and gazed down at the shattered magneto, his mind dull and heavy with all the appalling implications that smashed magneto carried with it. "There isn't very much left of it, is there?"

McKinnon shivered. "Somebody's walking over my grave," he complained. He shook his head slowly, stared down into the boat even after Nicolson had switched the light off, then touched Nicolson lightly on the arm. "You know something, sir? It's a long, long row to Darwin."

*   *   *

Gudrun was her name, she told him, Gudrun Jörgensen Drachmann, the Jörgensen being for her maternal grandfather. She was three parts Danish, twenty-three years old and had been born in Odense on Armistice Day, 1918. Apart from two short stays in Malaya, she had lived in Odense all her life until she had qualified as a nurse and come out to her father's plantations near Penang. That had been in August, 1939.

Nicolson, lying on his back against the bank of the hollow, clasped hands beneath his head and staring up unseeingly at the dark canopy of clouds, waited for her to go on, waited till she would begin again and hoped she would begin again. What was that quotation that old Willoughby, a hopeless, inveterate bachelor if ever there had lived one, had thrown at him so often in the past? "Her voice was ever soft"—that was it. *King Lear*. "Her voice was ever soft, gentle and low." Willoughby's stock excuse for avoiding the accursed snares—his own words—of holy matrimony: a female—Willoughby could invest that word with a wealth of scorn—with a voice ever soft, gentle and low—he had never found one. But maybe if Willoughby had been sitting where he'd been in the twenty minutes that had elapsed since he'd reported back to Findhorn and then come to see how the young boy was, he might have changed his mind.

Two minutes passed, three and she had said no more. By and by Nicolson stirred and turned towards her.

"You're a long way from home, Miss Drachmann. Denmark—you liked it?" It was just something to say, but the vehemence of her answer surprised him.

"I loved it." There was finality in her voice, the tone of someone speaking of something lost beyond recall. Damn the Japanese, damn that waiting submarine, Nicolson thought viciously. He changed the subject abruptly.

"And Malaya? Hardly the same high regard for that, eh?"

"Malaya?" The tone changed, was the vocal accompaniment of an indifferent shrug. "Penang was all right, I suppose. But not Singapore. I—I hated Singapore." She was suddenly vehement, all indifference gone, and had no sooner shown the depths of her feelings than she had realised what she had done, for voice and subject changed again. She reached out and touched him on the arm. "I would love a cigarette too. Or does Mr. Nicolson disapprove."

"Mr. Nicolson is sadly lacking in old world courtesy, I'm afraid." He passed over a packet of cigarettes, struck a match and as she bent to dip her cigarette in the pool of flame he could smell the elusive sandalwood again and the faint fragrance of her hair before she straightened and withdrew into the darkness. He ground out his match into the soil and asked her gently: "Why do you hate Singapore?"

Almost half a minute passed before she replied. "Don't you think that that might be a very personal question?"

"Very possibly." He paused a moment, then went on quietly, "What does it matter now?"

She took his meaning at once. "You're right, of course.

Even if it's only idle curiosity on your part, what does it matter now? It's funny, but I don't mind telling you—probably because I can be sure that you wouldn't waste false sympathy on anyone, and I couldn't stand that." She was silent for a few seconds, and the tip of her cigarette burnt brightly in the gloom. " It's true what I say. I do hate Singapore. I hate it because I have pride, personal pride, because I have self-pity and because I hate not to belong. You wouldn't know about any of these things, Mr. Nicolson."

" You know an awful lot about me," Nicolson murmured mildly. " Please go on."

" I think you know what I mean," she said slowly. " I am European, was born in Europe, brought up and educated in Europe, and thought of myself only as a Dane—as did all the Danish people. I was welcome in any house in Odense. I have never been asked to any European's house in Singapore, Mr. Nicolson." She tried to keep her voice light. " A drug on the social market, you might say. I wasn't a nice person to be seen with. It's not funny when you hear someone say, ' A touch of the tarbrush, old man." And say it without bothering to lower their voice, and then everybody looks at you and you never go back there again. I know my mother's mother was Malay, but she is a wonderful, kind old lady and——"

" Easy, take it easy. I know it must have been rotten. And the British were the worst, weren't they?"

" Yes, yes they were." She was hesitant. " Why do you say that?"

" When it comes to empire-building and colonialism we are the world's best—and the world's worst. Singapore is the happy hunting ground of the worst, and our worst is something to wonder at. God's chosen people and with a dual mission in life—to pickle their livers in an impossibly short time and to see to it that those who are not of the chosen remain continually aware of the fact—the sons of Ham to be hewers of wood and drawers of water to the end of their days. Good Christians all, of course, and staunch pillars and attenders of the church—if they can sober up in time on the Sunday morning. They're not all like that, not even in Singapore : but you just didn't have the luck to run into any of the others."

" I didn't expect to hear you say that." Her voice was slow, surprised.

" Why not? It's true."

" That's not what I mean. It's just that I didn't expect to

148

hear you talking like—oh, well, never mind." She laughed, self-consciously. " The colour of my skin is not all that important."

" That's right. Go on. Give the knife a good twist." Nicolson ground out his cigarette beneath his heel. His voice was deliberately rough, almost brutal. " It's damned important to you, but it shouldn't be. Singapore's not the world. We like you, and we don't give two hoots if you're heliotrope."

" Your young officer—Mr. Vannier—he gives two hoots," she murmured.

" Don't be silly—and try to be fair. He saw that gash and he was shocked—and ever since he's been ashamed of showing that shock. He's just very young, that's all. And the captain thinks you're the cat's pyjamas. ' Translucent amber,' that's what he says your skin's like." Nicolson tut-tutted softly. " Just an elderly Lothario."

" He is not. He's just very, very nice and I like him very much." She added, inconsequentially: " You make him feel old."

" Nuts!" Nicolson said rudely. " A bullet in the lungs would make anyone feel old." He shook his head. " Oh, lord, there I go again. Sorry, sorry, didn't mean to snap at you. Daggers away, shall we, Miss Drachmann?"

" Gudrun." The one word was both his answer and a request, and completely innocent of any hint of coquetry.

" Gudrun? I like it, and it suits you."

" But you don't—what is the word—reciprocate?" There was mischief now in the husky voice. " I have heard the captain call you ' Johnny.' Nice," she said consideringly. " In Denmark it is the kind of name we would give to a very little boy. But I think I might manage to become used to it."

" No doubt," Nicolson said uncomfortably. " But you see——"

" Oh, but of course!" She was laughing at him, he knew, and he felt still more uncomfortable. " ' Johnny ' in front of the members of your crew—unthinkable! But then, of course, it would be Mr. Nicolson," she added demurely. " Or perhaps you think ' sir ' would be better?"

" Oh, for heaven's sake!" Nicolson began, then stopped short and found himself echoing the girl's barely audible laughter. " Call me anything you like. I'll probably deserve it."

149

He rose to his feet, crossed to the front of the hollow where the Muslim priest was keeping watch, spoke briefly to him then moved down the hill to where Van Effen was keeping watch over the one serviceable lifeboat. He sat there with him for a few minutes, wondering what point there was anyway in guarding the boat, then made his way back up to the hollow. Gudrun Drachmann was still awake, sitting close by the little boy. He sat down quietly beside her.

"There's no point in sitting up all night," he said gently. "Peter will be all right. Why don't you go to sleep?"

"Tell me straight." Her voice was very low. "How much chance have we got?"

"None."

"Honest and blunt enough," she acknowledged. "How long?"

"Noon to-morrow—and that's a very late estimate. The submarine will almost certainly send a landing party ashore first—or try to. Then they'll call up help—but probably the planes will be here at first light anyway."

"Perhaps the men from the submarine will be enough. Perhaps they won't require to call up help. How many——"

"We'll cut them to ribbons," Nicolson said matter-of-factly. "They'll need help, all right. They'll get it. Then they'll get us. If they don't kill us all by bombing or shelling, they may take you and Lena and Miss Plenderleith prisoner. I hope not."

"I saw them at Kota Bharu." She shivered at the memory. "I hope not too. And little Peter?"

"I know. Peter. Just another casualty," Nicolson said bitterly. "Who cares about a two-year-old kid?" He did, he knew; he was becoming more attached to the youngster than he would ever have admitted to anybody, and one day, had Caroline lived——

"Is there nothing we can do?" The girl's voice cut through his wandering thoughts.

"I'm afraid not. Just wait, that's all."

"But—but couldn't you go out to the submarine and—and do something?"

"Yes, I know. Cutlasses in teeth, capture it and sail it home in triumph. You've been reading the wrong comic books, lady." Before she could speak, he stretched out and caught her arm. "Cheap and nasty. I'm sorry. But they'll be just begging for us to do something like that."

"Couldn't we sail the boat away without being heard or seen?"

"My dear girl, that was the first thing we thought of. Hopeless. We might get away, but not far. They or the planes would get us at dawn—and then those who weren't killed would be drowned. Funny, Van Effen was very keen on the idea too. It's a fast way of committing suicide," he ended abruptly.

She thought for a few more moments. "But you think it's possible to leave here without being heard?"

Nicolson smiled. "Persistent young so-and-so, aren't you? Yes, it's possible, especially if someone were creating some sort of diversion elsewhere on the island to distract their attention. Why?"

"The only way out is to make the submarine think we're gone. Couldn't two or three of you take the boat away— maybe to one of these little islands we saw yesterday—while the rest of us make some kind of diversion." She was speaking quickly, eagerly now. "When the submarine saw you were gone, it would go away and——"

"And go straight to these little islands—the obvious place to go—see that there was only a few of us, kill us, sink the boat, come back here and finish the rest of you off."

"Oh!" Her voice was subdued. "I never thought of that."

"No, but brother Jap would. Look, Miss Drachmann——"

"Gudrun. We've stopped fighting, remember?"

"Sorry. Gudrun. Will you stop trying to beat your head against a brick wall? You'll just give yourself a headache. We've thought of everything ourselves, and it's no good. And if you don't mind now I'll try to get some sleep. I have to relieve Van Effen in a little while."

He was just dropping off when her voice came again. "Johnny?"

"Oh lord," Nicolson moaned. "Not another flash of inspiration."

"Well, I've just been thinking again and——"

"You're certainly a trier." Nicolson heaved a sigh of resignation and sat up. "What is it?"

"It wouldn't matter if we stayed here as long as the submarine went away, would it?"

"What are you getting at?"

"Answer me please, Johnny."

"It wouldn't matter, no. It would be a good thing—and if

we could hole up here, unsuspected, for a day or so they'd probably call off the search. From this area, at least. How do you propose to make them sail away, thinking we're gone? Going to go out there and hypnotise them?"

"That's not even a little bit funny," she said calmly. "If dawn came and they saw that our boat was gone—the good one, I mean—they'd think we were gone too, wouldn't they."

"Sure they would. Any normal person would."

"No chance of them being suspicious and searching the island?"

"What the devil are you getting at?"

"Please, Johnny."

"All right," he growled. "Sorry again and again and again. No, I don't think they'd bother to search. What are you after, Gudrun?"

"Make them think we've gone," she said impatiently. "Hide the boat."

"'Hide the boat,' she says! There's not a place on the shores of this island where we could put it that the Japs wouldn't find in half-an-hour. And we can't hide it on the island—it's too heavy to drag up and we'd make such a racket trying that they'd shoot the lot of us, even in the darkness, before we'd moved ten feet. And even if we could, there isn't a big enough clump of bushes on this blasted rock to hide a decent-sized dinghy, far less a twenty-four foot lifeboat. Sorry and all that, but it's no go. There's nowhere you could hide it, either on sea or land, that the Japs couldn't find it with their eyes shut."

"These were your suggestions, not mine," she said tranquilly. "Impossible to hide it on or around the island, and I agree. My suggestion is that you should hide it *under* the water."

"What!" Nicolson half sat up, stared at her in the darkness.

"Make some sort of diversion at one end of the island," she said quickly. "Sail the boat round the other end to that little bay in the north, fill it with stones, pull out the plug or whatever you call it, sink it in pretty deep water and then after the Japs have gone——"

"Of course!" Nicolson's voice was a slow, considering whisper. "Of course it would work! My God, Gudrun, you've got it, you've got it!" His voice almost a shout now, he sat up with a jerk, caught the protesting, laughing girl in a bear hug of sheer joy and splendidly renewed hope, scrambled to his
152

feet and ran across to the other side of the hollow. "Captain!
Fourth! Bo'sun! Wake up, wake up all of you!"

*　　　*　　　*

Luck was with them at last, and it went off without a hitch.
There had been some argument about the nature of the diversion—some held that the captain of the submarine, or the man
who had taken over since the captain's death, would be suspicious of a straightforward diversion, but Nicolson insisted that
any man stupid enough to send a landing party straight ashore
to where the boats had been instead of making a flank attack,
was unlikely to be acute enough not to fall for the deception,
and his insistence carried the day. Moreover, the wind, which
had backed to the north, lent strength to his arguments, and
the events proved him right.

Vannier acted as decoy and carried out his part intelligently
and with perfect timing. For about ten minutes he moved
around the shore of the south-west tip of the island, flashing
his hooded torch furtively and at infrequent intervals. He had
Nicolson's night glasses with him, and as soon as he saw the
dark shadow of the submarine begin to creep silently forward
on her batteries he laid aside the torch altogether and took
shelter behind a boulder. Two minutes later, with the submarine directly abreast of him and not more than a hundred
yards off-shore, he stood up, twisted off the release fork of one
of number two lifeboat's smoke floats and hurled it as far out
to sea as he could: within thirty seconds the light northerly
breeze had carried the dense orange smoke out to the submarine, smoke that swirled chokingly round the men in the
conning-tower and made them blind.

Four to five minutes is the normal burning time for a
smoke-float, but it was more than enough. Four men and
muffled oars had number two lifeboat well round to the northern side of the island a full minute before the canister hissed
softly to extinction. The submarine remained where it was,
motionless. Nicolson eased the lifeboat quietly alongside a
steep shelf in the deep bight to the north, and found Farnholme, Ahmed the priest, Willoughby and Gordon waiting for
them, a huge pile of smooth round stones lying ready at their
feet.

Willoughby had insisted on removing the aircases—the idea
of driving holes into them had wounded his engineer's soul.
It would take time with the limited tools at their disposal,
require light for working by, would inevitably cause too much

noise—and the submarine commander might at any moment take it into his head to make a quick cruise round the island, lighting his way with flares. But the risk had to be taken.

Quickly the plugs were pulled out of the garboard strake, the men working at breakneck speed, and in almost complete silence, loading the bottom-boards with the stones passed down from the shelf, carefully avoiding blocking the gushing plug holes. After two minutes Nicolson spoke softly to Farnholme, and the Brigadier went running off up the hill: only seconds later he was firing spaced shots in the direction of the submarine, the flat, explosive crack of the carbine roughly synchronising with and covering the metallic rings from the north side of the island as Nicolson and the others removed the shuttering of the buoyancy tanks and withdrew the yellow metal aircases, but leaving enough of the tanks in place to give the boat a strong positive buoyancy.

More stones into the boat, more water through the plug holes, and the level inside and out was just the same, lipping the lowest part of the gunwale, and then a few last stones and she was gone, slipping gently below the surface of the sea, steadied by fore and aft painters, settling in fifteen feet of water, on an even keel and a fine, shingly bottom. As they returned to the hollow on the hill, they saw a rocket parachute flare soaring up from the eastern tip of the island, curving away to the north-east. Vannier had timed it well, and if the submarine investigated there it would find it as quiet and empty of life as was now the other end. It would also have the effect of confusing them utterly, filling their minds with half a dozen conflicting suspicions, and, when morning came, would lend colour to the obvious conclusion that the survivors on the island had outwitted them and made off during the night.

And that was the conclusion to which they unmistakably came in the morning—a grey, overcast dawn with a strengthening wind and no sign of the sun. As soon as it was light, the carefully hidden watchers on the island, securely screened behind thick bushes, could see the figures manning the conning-tower raising binoculars to their eyes—the submarine had moved much farther out during the night—and gesticulating at each other. Shortly afterwards the sound of the diesel motors could be heard, and the submarine moved off, circling quickly round the island. Abreast the remaining lifeboat once more it came to a stop and the A.A. gun lined up on the boat and started firing—artificers must have repaired the damaged firing mechanism during the night. Only six shots in all were fired, but they were enough to reduce the boat to a holed and splintered wreck, and immediately after the last shell had exploded in the shallows the heavy diesels throbbed again and the submarine moved off due west, travelling at high speed, and investigated the two little islands there. Half an hour later it was lost to sight over the southern horizon.

CHAPTER TEN

THE LIFEBOAT lay motionless and dead on the motionless mirror of the sea. Nothing moved, nothing stirred, not the faintest ghost of a catspaw to ruffle the shining, steel-blue metal of the ocean that reflected every tiniest detail of the clincher sides with faithful and merciless accuracy. A dead boat on a dead sea, in a dead and empty world. An empty sea, a vast, shimmering plain of nothingness that stretched away endlessly on every side until it blurred in the far distance into the hazed rim of a vast and empty sky. No cloud in sight, and none for three days past. An empty and a terrible sky, majestic in its cruel indifference, and all the emptier for the blinding sun that beat down like an open furnace on the sweltering sea beneath.

A dead boat, too, it seemed, but not empty. It seemed full, rather, packed to capacity, but the impression was misleading. Under such pitiful shade as the remaining tatters of sail provided, men and women lay sprawled or stretched their full length on the benches, thwarts and bottom-boards, spent beyond words and prostrate with the heat, some in coma, some in nightmare sleep, others half-asleep, half-waking, making no movement at all, carefully hoarding what little spark of life was left them and the will to keep it burning. They were waiting for the sun to go down.

Of all that emaciated, sun-blackened shipload of survivors, only two could be seen to be alive. They were in as bad case as the others, gaunt-cheeked, hollow-eyes, with cracked and purpled lips and ugly red suppurating blisters where their salt-water and heat-rotted clothes had laid open patches of untanned skin to the burning sun. Both men were right aft in the boat, and they could be seen to be alive only because they were sitting upright in the sternsheets. But for all the movement

155

they made they too might have been dead, or carved from stone. One man sat with his arm leaning on the tiller, though there had been neither wind to fill the torn sails nor men with strength to man the oars for almost four days: the other had a gun in his hand, unwavering, rock-like, and only his eyes showed that he was alive.

There were twenty people in the boat. There had been twenty-two when they had set sail from that little island in the South China Sea six days ago, but only twenty now. Two had died. There never had been any hope for Corporal Fraser, he had already been weakened and ravaged with fever long before the cannon shell from the Zero had all but blown his left arm off as he had fought back at it with his puny rifle from the wheelhouse top of the *Viroma*. There had been no medical supplies, no anæsthetics at all left, but he had hung on for a lifetime of four days and had died only forty-eight hours ago, cheerfully and in great agony, his arm blackened right to the shoulder. Captain Findhorn had said as much of the burial service as he could remember, almost his last conscious act before he had fallen into the restless, muttering coma from which it seemed unlikely that he would ever emerge.

The other man, one of Siran's three remaining crew members, had died the previous afternoon. He had died violently and because he had completely misinterpreted McKinnon's slow smile and soft Highland voice. Shortly after Fraser's death, McKinnon, whom Nicolson had made responsible for the water supplies, had discovered that one of the tanks had been damaged during the previous night, probably broached, but it was impossible to say: in any event it was empty, and they were left with less than three gallons in the remaining tank. Nicolson had at once suggested that each person in the boat should be limited to one and a half ounces of water twice a day, taken from the graduated drinking cup —part of every lifeboat's standard equipment: all except the little boy—he was to have as much as he wanted. There had been only one or two murmurs of dissent, but Nicolson had ignored them completely. The following day when McKinnon had handed Miss Drachmann the child's third drink of the afternoon, two of Siran's men had made their way down the boat from their place in the bows, armed with a heavy metal crutch apiece. McKinnon had glanced quickly at Nicolson, seen that he was asleep—he had kept guard almost all the previous night—and quietly asked them to get back, the revolver in his hand backing up his suggestion. One man had hesitated, but the other had flung himself forward, snarling like an animal, the crutch sweeping down in a vicious arc that would have crushed the bo'sun's skull like a rotten melon if it had landed, but McKinnon had flung himself to one side even as his finger had squeezed down on the trigger and the man's own impetus carried him headlong over the stern. He was dead before he hit the water. Then McKinnon had word-lessly lined up the Colt on the other man, but the gesture was unnecessary; the man was staring down at the thin blue smoke still wisping from the barrel of the gun, and his face was con-torted with fear. He turned quickly and stumbled back to his seat in the bows. After that there had been no more trouble about the water.

At the beginning, six days ago, there had been no trouble at all. Morale had been high, hopes higher, and even Siran, still suffering from the after-effects of concussion, had been as co-operative as possible and seen to it that his men were the same: Siran was nobody's fool and realised as clearly as any that their survival depended upon common and combined effort: an alliance of expediency, it would last just as long as it suited him.

They had left thirty-six hours after the submarine, twenty-four hours after the last reconnaissance 'plane had passed over the tiny island and failed to find any sign of life. They had sailed at sunset, in a light following swell and the monsoon blowing steadily from the north. All night long and nearly all of the following day they had run free before the wind, and all this time the skies had remained empty and the only boat they had seen had been a prahu, lying far to the east. In the evening, with the eastern tip of Banka Island just lifting over the red and gold horizon to the west, they had seen a sub-marine surface not two miles away, then move away steadily to the north. Perhaps it had seen them, perhaps not—the life-boat might have been lost against the darkening sea and sky to the east and Nicolson had dropped the tell-tale orange sails —the lug stamped with the even more damning " VA "—as soon as the submarine had broken water: either way it showed no suspicion, and was lost to sight before the sun had gone down.

That night they had gone through the Macclesfield Channel. This, they had thought, would be the most danger-ous and difficult part of all, and had the wind dropped or backed or veered a few points either way they would have been lost, and found in clear sight of land when morning came. But the trades had held steadily from the north, they had left Liat on the port hand shortly after midnight and cleared the island of Lepar long before sunrise. It was just on noon of that same day that their luck finally ran out.

The wind had dropped then, suddenly and completely, and all day long they lay becalmed, not more than twenty-five miles from Lepar Island. Late in the afternoon a slow, lumbering seaplane—it might have been the same one as they had seen previously—appeared out of the west, circled overhead for almost an hour, then moved off without making any attempt to molest them. The sun was just sinking and a faint breeze beginning to spring up, again from the north, when another aeroplane appeared, again out of the west, flying about three thousand feet and straight at them. No seaplane this, but a Zero, and in no mood for either preliminaries or time-wasting. Less than a mile away it had dropped its nose and come screaming down out of the sky, twin cannon at its wing roots stabbing daggers of red in the gathering dusk, cannon-shells stitching parallel patterns of splashes and spouting spray across the placid surface of the sea right up to the centre of the helplessly waiting lifeboat, through it and away beyond. Or perhaps not so helpless—not while the Brigadier held the machine-carbine in his hands, for the Zero swung round in a tight turn and headed off back against towards the west in the direction of Sumatra, its sleek fuselage black-streaked with pouring engine oil: less than two miles away it met the seaplane returning, and the two planes disappeared together into the pale golden afterwash of sunset. The boat had been holed, severely, in two places but, remarkably, only one person hurt—Van Effen's thigh had been badly gashed by a jagged splinter of shrapnel.

Not an hour afterwards the wind had started gusting up to force six or seven, and the sudden tropical storm was upon them almost before they had realised what was coming. It lasted for ten hours, ten interminable hours of wind and darkness and rain strangely cold, then interminable hours of yawing and pitching while the exhausted boat's company baled for their lives all night long as pooping seas swept over the sternsheets and swirled over the sides and water gushed continuously through the jury patches in the bottom of the lifeboat—the supply of wooden plugs in the repair outfit hadn't gone very far. Nicolson sailed south before the storm with the jib down and the lug sail reefed until he had steerage way and just no more. Every mile south was a mile nearer the

Sunda Strait, but he could have done nothing else than let the storm drive him along even if he had wished to: holed by the stern and deep down by the stern, a sea anchor streamed aft would have pulled them under, and it was quite impossible to heave to with a bow anchor out: enough speed, enough steerage way to get them round would have meant enough sail to dismast the boat or capsize her on the turn, and without that steerage way the sluggish, waterlogged boat would have broached to and been driven under in the troughs. The long agony of the night had ended as abruptly as it had begun, and it was then that the real agony had started.

And now, leaning on the useless tiller, McKinnon sitting armed and still watchful by his side. Nicolson tried to thrust aside the nagging, dominating pains of thirst and swollen tongue and cracked lips and sunblistered back and to assess the damage caused, the complete change brought about by those terrible days that had elapsed since the storm had ended, endless, torturing hours under the pitiless lash of the sun, a sun at once dreadfully impersonal and malignant beyond belief, a sun that steadily grew more and more intolerable until it drove helpless, uncaring men over the edge of breakdown and collapse, physical, moral and mental.

The old spirit of comradeship had gone, vanished completely as if it had never been. Where earlier every man had sought only to help his neighbour, now most sought only to help themselves, and their indifference to their neighbour's welfare was absolute. As each man received his pitiful portion of water or condensed milk or barley sugar—the biscuits had come to an end two days ago—a dozen greedy, hostile eyes followed every movement of thin clawed hands and thirst-cracked lips, intent on making sure that he received his exact ration and not a drop or nibble more. The greed, the starvation lust in bloodshot eyes, the ivory-knuckled clenching of sun-dark wasting hands, became especially terrible to see whenever young Peter was given an extra drink and some of the water dribbled down his chin and dripped on to the hot bench, evaporating almost as it touched. They were at the stage now when even death appeared an almost attractive alternative to the excruciating torture of their thirst. McKinnon had need of the gun in his hand.

The physical change for the worse was, if anything, even more serious than the moral collapse. Captain Findhorn was deep sunk in coma, but a restless pain-filled coma, and Nicolson had taken the precaution of tying him loosely to the gun-

159

wale and one of the thwarts. Jenkins, too, was tied down, although still conscious. Conscious, but in a private hell of indescribable agony: there were no bandages, no protection left for the terrible burns he had received just before they had abandoned the *Viroma*, and the blazing sun had lacerated every inch of exposed flesh until he had gone crazy with the pain. His finger-nails were blood-stained from his insane clawing of raw burning flesh. His wrists were now lashed together, the rope tied to a thwart, not to prevent further pain-maddened scratching but to prevent him from throwing himself overboard, as he had twice tried to do. For long minutes he would sit without moving, then he would fling all his strength against the rope that held his bleeding wrists, his breathing hoarse and quick with agony. Already Nicolson was wondering whether he should just cut him loose, wondering what moral justification he had for condemning the seaman to die a slow lingering death on the rack instead of letting him finish it all, finish it quickly and cleanly, in the waiting waters over the side. For he was going to die anyway: he had the look of death about him.

Evans's gashed arm and Walters's savagely mutilated wrist were becoming steadily worse. All medical supplies were gone, their recuperative powers were gone and salt-water drying in tattered bandages had inflamed the open wounds. Van Effen was in little better case, but his wound had been more recent and he had innate toughness and reserves of stamina far beyond the ordinary: he lay still for hours at a time, reclining on the bottomboards, shoulders braced against a thwart and staring for'ard. He seemed to have passed beyond the need for sleep.

And the mental breakdown had gone furthest of all. Vannier and the old second engineer had not yet slid over the edge of sanity, but both showed the same symptoms of increasing lack of contact with reality, the same long periods of withdrawn melancholy silence, the same occasional aimless mutterings to themselves, the brief, apologetic half-smiles if they realised they were being overheard, then the relapse once more into melancholy and silence. Lena, the young Malayan nurse, showed only the melancholy, the utter disinterest, but never talked, to herself or anyone, at any time. The Muslim priest, on the contrary, showed no melancholy, no emotion whatsoever, but was silent all the time: but then he was always silent, so it was impossible to be sure of him one way or the other. It was impossible, too, to be sure about Gordon, one moment widely smiling with staring, unfocused eyes, the next head sunk in unmoving despair. Nicolson, who had the profoundest distrust for Gordon's calculated cunning and who had tried more than once, without success, to persuade Findhorn to get rid of him, watched him with expressionless face: the symptoms might be real enough, but they might equally well be the symptoms of a man who had read some quasi-medical article on manic-depressives and hadn't quite got the hang of it. But there was, tragically, no doubt about the young soldier, Sinclair: all contact with reality lost, he was quite insane and had all the classic symptoms of acute schizophrenia.

But the collapse, the physical and mental breakdown, was not complete. Not quite. Apart from Nicolson, there were two men who remained quite untouched by weakness and doubt and despair—the bo'sun and the brigadier. McKinnon was the McKinnon of old, unchangeable, apparently indestructible, still with the slow smile and the soft voice and the gun always in his hand. And the brigadier—Nicolson looked at him for the hundredth time and shook his head in unconscious wonder. Farnholme was magnificent. The more their circumstances deteriorated into hopelessness, the better the brigadier became. When there was pain to be eased, sick men to be made more comfortable or shielded from the sun, or water to be baled—it was seldom enough, now, that the floorboards weren't covered, and a random bullet on the island had smashed the manual pump—the brigadier was there, helping, encouraging, smiling and working without complaint or hope of thanks or reward. For a man of his age—Farnholme would never see sixty again—it was a quite incredible performance. Nicolson watched him in a kind of bewildered fascination. The fiery and fatuous Colonel Blimp of the up-and-at-'em-sir school he had met aboard the sinking *Kerry Dancer* might never have existed. Strangely enough, too, the affected Sandhurst drawl had vanished so completely that Nicolson found himself wondering whether he had imagined it in the first place: but there was no questioning the fact that the military expressions and Victorian oaths that had so heavily larded his conversation only a week ago were now so rare as to occasion comment whenever he used them. Perhaps the most convincing proof of his conversion—if that was the word—was the fact that he had not only buried the hatchet with Miss Plenderleith but spent most of his time sitting beside her and talking softly in her ear. She was now very weak, though her tongue had lost none of its power for pungent and acid comment, and she graciously accepted the innumerable small services Farnholme performed for her. They were together now, and Nicolson looked at them, his face expressionless, but smiling to himself. Had they been thirty years younger, he'd have laid odds on the brigadier having designs on Miss Plenderleith. Honourable designs, of course.

Something stirred against his knee, and Nicolson glanced down. Gudrun Drachmann had been sitting there for almost three days now, on the lower cross seat, holding on to the little boy when he jumped about the thwart in front of her—thanks to the unstinted supplies of food and water he received from Miss Plenderleith and McKinnon, Peter Tallon was the only person on the boat with excess energy to dispose of—and cradling him in her arms for hours at a time as he slept. She must have suffered severely from cramp, but never complained. Her face was thinned down now, the cheekbones very prominent, and the great scar on her left cheek more livid and uglier every hour as her skin darkened under the burning sun. She was smiling at him now, a small painful smile through sun-cracked lips, then looked away and nodded at Peter. But it was McKinnon who caught the look, interpreted it correctly, smiled in return and lowered the dipper into the little warm, brackish water that was left in the tank. Almost as if by a pre-arranged signal, a dozen heads lifted and followed every movement of the dipper, McKinnon's careful transfer of the water from the dipper to a cup, the eagerness with which the little boy clasped the cup in his pudgy hands and gulped the water down. Then they looked away from the child and the empty cup and looked at McKinnon instead, bloodshot eyes dulled with suffering and hate, but McKinnon just smiled his slow, patient smile and the gun in his hand never moved.

*   *   *

Night, when it came at last, brought relief, but relief only of a very limited nature. The burning heat of the sun was gone, but the air was still very hot and stifling and oppressive, and the pitiful ration of water each had received just as the sun had gone down had only whetted their appetite for more, made their raging thirsts all the more painful and intolerable. For two or three hours after sunset people shifted restlessly in their seats in the lifeboat, and some even tried to talk with others, but the talk didn't last very long: their throats were too parched, their blistered mouths too sore, and always, at the back of everybody's mind must have been the hopeless thought that, unless some miracle occurred, for some of them to-night's would have been the last sunset they would ever see. But nature was merciful, their minds and bodies were exhausted by hunger and thirst and by the day-long energy-sapping power of the sun, and by and by nearly all of them dropped off into a restless muttering sleep.

Nicolson and McKinnon went to sleep too. They hadn't intended to, it had been their purpose to share the night watches, but exhaustion had dug its fingers as deeply into them as any, and they dozed off from time to time, heads nodding on their chests, then waking with a start. Once, waking out of a short sleep, Nicolson thought he heard someone moving around the boat, and called out softly. There was no reply, and when he called out again and was again answered with silence, he reached under his seat and brought out his torch. The battery was almost gone now, but the feeble yellow beam was enough to show him that all was quiet, that nobody was out of his or her place, every black and shapeless shadow lying sprawled lifelessly across thwarts and bottomboards almost exactly where it had been when the sun had gone down. Not long afterwards, just as he was dozing off again, he could have sworn he heard a splash reaching down through his deep-drugged mists of sleep, and again he reached for his torch. But again there was no one there, no one moving around, no one even moving at all. He counted all the huddled shadows, and the number was right: nineteen, excluding himself.

He stayed awake for the remainder of the night, consciously fighting against an almost overpowering tiredness, against leaden eyelids and a woolly, fuzzy mind, ignoring the demands of a parched throat and dry, swollen tongue that seemed to fill all his mouth that he should let go, let his quivering eyelids fall and bring a few hours' blessed oblivion. But something far back in his mind kept telling him that he mustn't let go, that the lifeboat and the lives of twenty people were in his hands, and when these urgings were not enough he thought of the little boy asleep less than two feet away, and then he was wide awake again. And so a night that was the epitome of all the sleepless nights he had ever known dragged endlessly by, and after a long, long time the first faint streaks of grey began to lighten the eastern horizon.

Minutes passed, and he was beginning to see the mast clearly

silhouetted against the greying sky, then the line of the gunwale of the boat, then the separate and distinct forms of the
people lying about the boat. He looked first at the boy. He
was still sleeping peacefully in the sternsheets beside him,
wrapped in a blanket, his face only a white blur in the darkness, his head lying pillowed in the crook of Gudrun Drachmann's arm. She herself was still sitting on the lower cross
seat, twisted round at an uncomfortable angle, her head on
the sternsheets. Bending down more closely, Nicolson could
see that her head wasn't resting squarely on the seat but
against it, the edge of the wood cutting cruelly into her right
cheek. Carefully he raised her head, eased a doubled corner
of the blanket over the edge of the seat and then, moved by
some strange impulse, gently moved back the wave of blue-
black hair that had fallen forward over her face, concealing
the long, ragged scar. For a moment he let his hand rest there,
lightly, then he saw the sheen of her eyes in the gloom and
knew that she had not been asleep. He felt no embarrassment,
no guilt, just smiled down at her without speaking: she must
have seen the gleam of his teeth against his darkly-tanned
face, for she smiled in return, rubbed the scarred cheek softly,
twice, against his hand then slowly straightened, careful not to
disturb the sleeping boy.

The boat was settling deeper in the water, the level inside
already two or three inches above the floorboards, and
Nicolson knew it was time and past time to bale it out. But
baling was a noisy business, and it seemed pointless to wake
people from the forgetfulness of sleep to the iron realities of
another day when the boat could go at least another hour
without being emptied: true, many people were up to their
ankles in water, and one of two actually sitting in it, but these
were only tiny discomforts compared to what they would
have to suffer before the sun went down again.

And then, suddenly, he saw something that drove away all
thought of inaction, all thought of sleep. Quickly he shook
McKinnon awake—he had to, for McKinnon had been
leaning against him and would have fallen had Nicolson
risen without warning—rose, stepped over the after thwart
and dropped down on his knees on the next lower cross seat.
Jenkins, the seaman who had been so dreadfully burnt, was
lying in a most peculiar position, half-crouched, half-kneeling,
his bloodied wrists still tied to the thwart, his head jammed
against the tank leading. Nicolson stooped and shook him

by the shoulder: the seaman fell further over on his side, but made no other movement. Again Nicolson shook him, more urgently this time, calling his name, but Jenkins would never be shaken awake nor hear his name again. By accident or design—probably by design, and in spite of the ropes that bound him—he had slipped off the thwart some time during the night and drowned in a few inches of bilge-water.

Nicolson straightened his back and looked at McKinnon, and the bo'sun nodded, understanding at once. It wouldn't do the lifeboat's morale any good at all if the survivors woke and found a dead man in their midst, and that they should slip him quietly over the side without even a shred of a burial service seemed a small price to pay for preserving the already fading reason of more than one who might lose it entirely if he opened his eyes only to find already in their midst what he knew must eventually come to all.

But Jenkins was heavier than he looked, and his body was awkwardly jammed between the thwarts. By the time McKinnon had cut free the securing ropes with his jack-knife and helped Nicolson drag him to a side bench, at least half the people in the lifeboat were awake, watching them struggle with the body, knowing that Jenkins was dead, yet looking on with eyes lack-lustre and strangely uncomprehending. But no one spoke; it seemed as if they might get Jenkins over the side without any hysterical outbursts or demonstrations, when a sudden high-pitched cry from for'ard, a cry that was almost a scream, made even the most tired and lethargic jerk their heads round and stare up towards the bows of the boat. Both Nicolson and McKinnon, startled, dropped the body and swung round: in the hushed stillness of the tropical dawn, the cry had seemed unnaturally loud.

The cry had come from the young soldier, Sinclair, but he wasn't looking at Jenkins, or anywhere in that direction. He was on his knees on the floorboards, rocking gently to and fro, staring down at somebody lying stretched on his back. Even as Nicolson watched, he flung himself to one side and pillowed his head on his forearms and the gunwale, moaning softly to himself.

In three seconds Nicolson was by his side, gazing down at the man in the bottom of the boat. Not all of his body was lying on the boards—the backs of his knees were hooked over a thwart, the legs pointing incongruously skywards, as if he had fallen backwards from the seat on which he had been sitting: the back of his head rested in a couple of inches of water. It was Ahmed the priest, Farnholme's strange and taciturn friend, and he was quite dead.

Nicolson stooped over the priest, quickly thrust his hand inside the man's black robe to feel for the heart and as quickly withdrew. The flesh was cold and clammy: the man had been dead for hours.

Unconsciously, almost, Nicolson shook his head in bewilderment, glanced up at McKinnon and saw his own expression reflected there. He looked down again, bent over the body to lift up the head and the shoulders, and it was then that the shock came. He couldn't shift the body more than a couple of inches. Again he tried and again he failed. At his signal, McKinnon lifted one side of the body while Nicolson knelt down till his face was almost in the water, and then he saw why he had failed. The jack-knife between the shoulder-blades was buried clear up to the hilt, and the handle was caught between the planks of the bottom-boards.

CHAPTER ELEVEN

NICOLSON ROSE slowly to his feet and drew his forearm across his forehead. It was already hot for the time of the day, but not that hot. His right arm hung loosely by his side, the butt of the Colt gripped tightly in his hand. He had no recollection of pulling it out of his belt. He gestured at the fallen priest.

"This man is dead." His quiet voice carried easily in the hushed silence. "He has a knife in his back. Someone in this boat murdered him."

"Dead! You said he was dead? A knife in his back?" Farnholme's face wasn't pleasant as he pushed for'ard and knelt at the priest's side. He was on his feet in a moment, his mouth a thin white line in the darkness of his face. "He's dead all right. Give me that gun, Nicolson. I know who did it."

"Leave that gun alone!" Nicolson held him off with a stiff arm, then went on: "Sorry, Brigadier. As long as the captain's unwell I am in charge of this boat. I can't let you take the law into your own hands. Who did it?"

166

" Siran, of course!" Farnholme was back on balance again, but there was no masking the cold rage in his eyes. " Look at the damn' murdering hound, sitting there smirking."

"'The smiler with the knife beneath the cloak'." It was Willoughby who spoke. His voice was weak and husky, but he was quiet and composed enough: the night's sleep seemed to have done him some good.

" It's not under anyone's cloak," Nicolson said matter-of-factly. " It's sticking in Ahmed's back—and it's because of my damn' criminal carelessness that it is," he added in the bitterness of sudden recollection and understanding. " I forgot that there was a boat jack-knife as well as two hatchets in number two lifeboat . . . Why Siran, Brigadier?"

" Good God, man, of course it's Siran!" Farnholme pointed down at the priest. " We're looking for a cold-blooded murderer, aren't we? Who else, but Siran?"

Nicolson looked at him. " And what else, Brigadier?"

" What do you mean, ' what else'?"

" You know very well. I wouldn't shed any more tears than you if we had to shoot him, but let's have some little shred of evidence first."

" What more evidence do you want? Ahmed was facing aft, wasn't he? And he was stabbed in the back. So somebody in the front of the boat did it—and there were only three people farther for'ard than Ahmed. Siran and his two killers."

" Our friend is overwrought." It was Siran who spoke, his voice as smooth and expressionless as his face. " Too many days in an open boat in tropical seas can do terrible things to a man."

Farnholme clenched his fists and started for'ard, but Nicolson and McKinnon caught him by the arms.

" Don't be a fool," Nicolson said roughly. " Violence won't help matters, and we can't have fighting in a small boat like this." He relased his grip on Farnholme's arm, and looked thoughtfully at the man in the bows. " You may be right, Brigadier. I did hear someone moving about the boat, up for'ard, last night, and I did hear something like a thud. Later on I heard a splash. But I checked where the priest had been sitting."

" His bag is gone, Nicolson. I wonder if you can guess where?"

" I saw his bag," Nicolson said quietly. " Canvas, and very light. It wouldn't sink."

167

"I'm afraid it would, sir." McKinnon nodded towards the bows. "The grapnel's gone."

"Weighted to the bottom, eh, Bo'sun? That would sink it all right."

"Well, there you are then," Farnholme said impatiently. "They killed him, took his bag and flung it over the side. You looked both times you heard a noise and both times you saw Ahmed sitting up. Somebody must have been holding him up—probably by the handle of the knife stuck in his back. Whoever was holding him must have been sitting behind him —in the bows of the boat. And there were only these three damned murderers sitting there." Farnholme was breathing heavily, his fists still white-knuckled, and his eyes not leaving Siran's face.

"It sounds as if you were right," Nicolson admitted. "How about the rest of it?"

"How about the rest of what?"

"You know quite well. They didn't kill him just for the exercise. What was their reason?"

"How the devil should I know why they killed him?"

Nicolson sighed. "Look Brigadier, we're not all morons. Of course you know. You suspected Siran immediately. You expected Ahmed's bag to be missing. And Ahmed was your friend."

Just for a moment something flickered far back in Farnholme's eyes, a faint shadow of expression that seemed to be reflected in the sudden tense tightening of Siran's mouth, almost as if the two men were exchanging a guarded look, maybe of understanding, maybe of anything. But the sun was not yet up, and Nicolson couldn't be sure that he wasn't imagining the exchange of glances, and, besides, any idea or suspicion of collusion between the two was preposterous. Give Farnholme a gun and Siran would be only a memory.

"I suppose you have a right to know." Farnholme appeared to be holding himself tightly under control but his mind was racing furiously, fabricating a story that would bear examination. "It won't do any harm, not now, not any more." He looked away from Siran and stared down at the dead man at his feet, and his expression and tone softened. "Ahmed was my friend, you say. He was, but a very new friend, and only then because he desperately needed a friend. His name is Jan Bekker, a countryman of Van Effen's here. Lived in Borneo— Dutch Borneo—near Samarinda, for many years. Representa-

out of the darkness had had a curiously upsetting effect on him.

"Yes, sir. Sorry, sir. I think my left shoulder is kind of broken, sir."

"Kind of broken," Parker echoed. With a conscious effort of will he shook off the growing sense of unreality. "What regiment, Corporal?"

"Argyll and Sutherlands, sir."

"Of course." Parker nodded. "I thought I recognised you."

"Yes, sir. Lieutenant Parker, isn't it, sir."

"That's right." Parker gestured at the line of men standing patiently in the rain. "You in charge, Corporal?"

"Yes, sir."

"Why?"

"Why?" The corporal's fever-wasted face creased in puzzlement. "Dunno, sir. Suppose it's because I'm the only fit man here."

"The only fit——" Parker broke off in mid-sentence, lost in incredulity. He took a deep breath. "That's not what I meant, Corporal. What are you doing with these men? Where are you going with them?"

"I don't rightly know, sir," Fraser confessed. "I was told to lead them back out of the line to a place of safety, get them some medical attention if I could." He jerked a thumb in the direction of the intermittent firing. "Things are a little bit confused up there, sir," he finished apologetically.

"They're all of that," Parker agreed. "But what are you doing down here at the waterfront?"

"Looking for a boat, a ship, anything." The little corporal was still apologetic. "'Place of safety' was my orders, sir. I thought I'd have a real go at it."

"A real go at it." The feeling of unreality was back with Parker once again. "Aren't you aware, Corporal, that by the time you get anywhere the nearest place of safety would be Australia—or India?"

"Yes, sir." There was no change of expression on the little man's face.

"Heaven give me strength." It was Farnholme speaking for the first time, and he sounded slightly dazed. "You were going to set out for Australia in a rowing-boat with that—that——" He gestured at the line of patient, sick men, but words failed him.

"Certainly I was," Fraser said doggedly. "I've got a job to do."

"My God, you don't give up easy, do you, Corporal?" Farnholme stared at him. "You'd have a hundred times more chance in a Jap prison camp. You can thank your lucky stars that there isn't a boat left in Singapore."

"Maybe there is and maybe there isn't," the corporal said calmly. "But there's a ship lying out there in the roads." He looked at Parker. "I was just planning how to get out to it when your men came along, sir."

"What!" Farnholme stepped forward and gripped him by his good shoulder. "There's a ship out there? Are you sure, man?"

"Sure I'm sure." Fraser disengaged his shoulder with slow dignity. "I heard it's anchor going down not ten minutes ago."

"How do you know?" Farnholme demanded. "Perhaps the anchor was coming up and——"

"Look, pal," Fraser interrupted. "I may look stupid, I may even be stupid, but I know the bloody difference between——"

"That'll do, Corporal, that'll do!" Parker cut him off hastily. "Where's this ship lying?"

"Out behind the docks, sir. About a mile out, I should say. Bit difficult to be sure—still some smoke around out there."

"The docks? In the Keppel Harbour?"

"No, sir. We haven't been near there to-night. Only a mile or so away—just beyond Malay Point."

*   *   *

Even in the darkness the journey didn't take long—fifteen minutes at the most. Parker's men had taken over the stretchers, and others of them helped the walking wounded along. And all of them, men and women, wounded and well, were now possessed of the same overwhelming sense of urgency. Normally, no one among them would have placed much hope on any evidence so tenuous as the rattle of what might, or might not have been an anchor going down: but, so much had their minds been affected by the continuous retreats and losses of the past weeks, so certain had they been of capture before that day was through, capture and God only knew how many years of oblivion, so complete was their sense of hopelessness that even this tiny ray of hope was a blazing beacon in the dark despair of their minds. Even so the spirit of the sick men far exceeded their strength, and most of them

26

were spent and gasping and glad to cling to their comrades for support by the time Corporal Fraser came to a halt.

"Here, sir. It was just about here that I heard it."

"What direction?" Farnholme demanded. He followed the line indicated by the barrel of the corporal's Bren, but could see nothing: as Fraser had said, smoke still lay over the dark waters . . . He became aware that Parker was close behind him, his mouth almost touching his ear.

"Torch? Signal?" He could barely catch the lieutenant's soft murmur. For a moment Farnholme hesitated, but only a moment: they had nothing to lose. Parker sensed rather than saw the nod, and turned to his sergeant.

"Use your torch, Sergeant. Out there. Keep flashing until you get an answer or until we can see or hear something approaching. Two or three of you have a look round the docks—maybe you might find some kind of boat."

Five minutes passed, then ten. The sergeant's torch clicked on and off, monotonously, but nothing moved out on the dark sea. Another five minutes, then the searchers had returned to report that they were unable to find anything. Another five minutes passed, five minutes during which the rain changed from a gentle shower to a torrential downpour that bounced high off the metalled roadway, then Corporal Fraser cleared his throat.

"I can hear something coming," he said conversationally.

"What? Where?" Farnholme barked at him.

"A rowing-boat of some sorts. I can hear the rowlocks. Coming straight at us, I think."

"Are you sure?" Farnholme tried to listen over the drumming of the rain on the road, the hissing it made as it churned the surface of the sea to a white foam. "Are you sure, man?" he repeated. "I can't hear a damn' thing."

"Aye, I'm sure. Heard it plain as anything."

"He's right!" It was the big sergeant who spoke, his voice excited. "By God, he's right, sir. I can hear it, too!"

Soon everybody could hear it, the slow grinding creak of rowlocks as men pulled heavily on their oars. The tense expectancy raised by Fraser's first words collapsed and vanished in the almost palpable wave of indescribable relief that swept over them and left them all chattering together in low ecstatic voices. Lieutenant Parker took advantage of the noise to move closer to Farnholme.

"What about the others—the nurses and the wounded?"

"Let 'em come, Parker—if they want to. The odds are high

27

against us. Make that plain—and make it plain that it must be their own choice. Then tell them to keep quiet, and move back out of sight. Whoever it is—and it *must* be the *Kerry Dancer*—we don't want to scare 'em away. As soon as you hear the boat rubbing alongside, move forward and take over."

Parker nodded and turned away, his low urgent tones cutting through the babble of voices.

"Right. Take up these stretchers. Move back, all of you, to the other side of the road—and keep quiet. Keep very quiet, if you ever want to see home again. Corporal Fraser?"

"Sir?"

"You and your men—do you wish to come with us? If we go aboard that ship it's highly probably that we'll be sunk within twelve hours. I must make that clear."

"I understand, sir."

"And you'll come, then?"

"Yes, sir."

"Have you asked the others?"

"No, sir." The corporal's injured tone left no doubt about his contempt for such ridiculously democratic procedures in the modern army, and Farnholme grinned in the darkness. "They'll come too, sir."

"Very well. On your head be it. Miss Drachmann?"

"I'll come, sir," she said quietly. She lifted her left hand to her face in a strange gesture. "Of course I'll come."

"And the others?"

"We've discussed it." She indicated the young Malayan girl by her side. "Lena here wants to go too. The other three don't care much, sir, one way or another. Shock, sir—a shell hit our lorry to-night. Better if they come, I think."

Parker made to answer, but Farnholme gestured him to silence, took the torch from the sergeant and advanced to the edge of the dock. The boat could be seen now, less than a hundred yards away, vaguely silhouetted by the distant beam of the torch. Even as Farnholme peered through the heavy rain, he could see the flurry of white foam as someone in the sternsheets gave an order and the oars dug into the sea, back-watering strongly until the boat came to a stop and lay silently, without moving, a half-seen blur in the darkness.

"Ahoy, there!" Farnholme called. "The *Kerry Dancer*?"

"Yes." The deep voice carried clearly through the falling rain. "Who's there?"

"Farnholme, of course." He could hear the man in the

28

sternsheets giving an order, could see the rowers starting to pull strongly again. " Van Effen?"

" Yes, Van Effen."

" Good man!" There was no questioning the genuineness of the warmth in Farnholme's voice. " Never been so glad to see anyone in all my life. What happened?" The boat was only twenty feet away now, and they could talk in normal tones.

" Not much." The Dutchman spoke perfect, colloquial English, with a scarcely discoverable trace of accent. " Our worthy captain changed his mind about waiting for you, and had actually got under way before I persuaded him to change his mind."

" But—but how do you know the *Kerry Dancer* won't sail before you get back? Good God, Van Effen, you should have sent someone else. You can't trust that devil an inch."

" I know." Hand steady on the tiller, Van Effen was edging in towards the stonework. " If she sails, she sails without her master. He's sitting in the bottom of the boat here, hands tied and with my gun in his back. Captain Siran is not very happy, I think."

Farnholme peered down along the beam of the torch. It was impossible to tell whether Captain Siran was happy or not, but it was undoubtedly Captain Siran. His smooth, brown face was as expressionless as ever.

" And just to make certain," Van Effen continued, " I've got the two engineers tied in Miss Plenderleith's room—tied hand and foot by myself, I may say. They won't get away. The door's locked, and Miss Plenderleith's in there with them, with a gun in her hand. She's never fired a gun in her life, but she's perfectly willing to try, she says. She's a wonderful old lady, Farnholme."

" You think of everything," Farnholme said admiringly. " If only——"

" All right, that'll do! Stand aside, Farnholme." Parker was by his side, a powerful torch shining down on to the upturned faces below. " Don't be a bloody fool!" he said sharply, as Van Effen made to bring up his pistol. " Put that thing away—there's a dozen machine-guns and rifles lined up on you."

Slowly Van Effen lowered his gun and looked up bleakly at Farnholme.

" That was beautifully done, Farnholme," he said slowly. " Captain Siran here would have been proud to claim such a masterpiece of treachery."

" It wasn't treachery," Farnholme protested. " They're British troops, our friends, but I'd no option. I can explain——"

" Shut up!" Parker cut in brusquely. " You can do all your explaining later." He looked down at Van Effen. " We're coming with you, whether you like it or not. That's a motor lifeboat you have there. Why were you using your oars?"

" For silence. Obviously. Much good it did us," Van Effen added bitterly.

" Start the motor," Parker ordered.

" I'll be damned if I will!"

" Perhaps. You'll probably be dead if you don't," Parker said coldly. " You look an intelligent man, Van Effen. You've got eyes and ears and should realise we're desperate men. What's to be gained by childish obstinacy at this stage?"

Van Effen looked at him for a long moment in silence, nodded, jammed his gun hard into Siran's ribs and gave an order. Within a minute the engine had come to life and was putt-putting evenly away as the first of the wounded soldiers was lowered on to the thwarts. Within half an hour the last of the men and women who had been standing on the dockside were safely aboard the *Kerry Dancer*. It had taken two trips, but short ones: Corporal Fraser had been about right in his estimate of distance, and the ship was anchored just outside the three-fathom shoal line of the Pagar Spit.

The *Kerry Dancer* got under way just before half-past two in the morning, the last ship out of the city of Singapore before she fell into the hands of the Japanese later on that same day of 15th February, 1942. The wind had dropped away now, the rain fined to a gentle drizzle and a brooding hush lay over the darkened city as it faded swiftly into the gloom of the night. There were no fires to be seen now, no lights at all, and even the crackle of desultory gunfire had died away completely. Everything was unnaturally, uncannily silent, silent as death itself, but the storm would break when the first light of day touched the rooftops of Singapore.

*　　　*　　　*

Farnholme was in the bleak, damp aftercastle of the *Kerry Dancer*, helping two of the nurses and Miss Plenderleith to attend to the bandaging and care of the wounded soldiers, when a knock came to the door—the only door, the one that led out into the deep after well. He switched out the light,

tive of a big Amsterdam firm and supervisor of a whole string of river rubber plantations. And a lot more besides."

He paused, and Nicolson prompted him: "Meaning?"

"I'm not quite certain. He was some kind of agent for the Dutch Government. All I know is that some weeks ago he broke up and exposed a well-organised Japanese Fifth Column in Eastern Borneo. Dozens of them arrested and shot out of hand—and he also managed to get hold of their complete list of every Japanese agent and fifth-columnist in India, Burma, Malaya and the East Indies.

"He carried it in his bag, and it would have been worth a fortune to the allies. The Japs knew he had it, and they've put a fantastic price on his head—dead or alive—and offered a similar reward for the return or destruction of the lists. He told me all this himself. Somehow or other Siran knew of all this, and that's what he's been after. He's earned his money, but I swear before God he'll never live to collect."

"And that's why Bekker or whatever his name is was disguised?"

"It was my idea," Farnholme said heavily. "I thought I was being very, very clever. Muslim priests are as good as any other priests in the world: a renegade, whisky-drinking priest is an object of contempt and everybody shuns him. I tried as best I could to be the kind of dissolute drinking companion a man like that would have. We weren't clever enough. I don't think we could have been anyway. The alarm call was out for Bekker the length and breadth of the Indies."

"He was a very lucky man to have got even this far," Nicolson acknowledged. "That's why the Japs have been at such pains to get us?"

"Heavens above, man, surely it's all obvious enough now!" Farnholme shook his head impatiently, then looked again at Siran: there was no anger in his eyes now, only cold, implacable purpose. "I'd sooner have a king cobra loose in this boat than that murderous swine there. I don't want you to have any blood on your hands, Nicolson. Give me your gun."

"How very convenient," Siran murmured. Whatever he lacked, Nicolson thought, it wasn't courage. "Congratulations, Farnholme. I salute you."

Nicolson looked at him curiously, then at Farnholme. "What's he talking about?"

"How the devil should I know," Farnholme answered impatiently. "We're wasting time, Nicolson. Give me that gun!"

"No."

"For God's sake, why not? Don't be a fool, man. There's not one of our lives worth a snuff of a candle as long as this man's at large in the boat."

"Very likely," Nicolson agreed. "But suspicion, no matter how strong, is not proof. Even Siran is entitled to a trial."

"In the name of heaven!" Farnholme was completely exasperated. "Don't you know that there's a time and place for these quaint old Anglo-Saxon notions about fair play and justice. This is neither the time nor the place. This is a matter of survival."

Nicolson nodded. "I know it is. Siran wouldn't recognise a cricket bat if he saw one. Get back in your seat, Brigadier, please. I'm not completely indifferent to the safety of the others in the boat. Cut one of the heaving lines in three, bo'sun, and make a job on these characters. It doesn't matter if the knots are a bit tight."

"Indeed?" Siran raised his eyebrows. "And what if we refuse to subject ourselves to this treatment?"

"Suit yourselves," Nicolson said indifferently. "The brigadier can have the gun."

McKinnon made a very thorough job of immobilising Siran and his two men, and took a great deal of grim satisfaction in hauling the ropes tight. By the time he was finished the three men were trussed hand and foot and quite unable to move: as a further precaution he had secured the three rope ends to the ring-bolt in the for'ard apron. Farnholme had made no further protest. It was noticeable, however, that when he resumed his seat on the benches beside Miss Plenderleith, he changed his position so that he was between her and the stern, and from there he could watch both her and the bows of the boat at the same time: his carbine was lying on the seat beside him.

His work done, McKinnon came aft to the sternsheets and sat down beside Nicolson. He brought out dipper and graduated cup, ready to serve out the morning ration of water, then turned suddenly to Nicolson. Half-a-dozen people in the boat were talking—the babble wouldn't last long after the sun cleared the horizon—and his low pitched words could not have been heard two feet away.

"It's a desperate long way to Darwin, sir," he said obliquely.

stepped outside and closed the door carefully behind him. He turned to look at the shadowy figure standing in the gloom.

"Lieutenant Parker?"

"Yes." Parker gestured in the darkness. "Perhaps we'd better go up on the poop-deck here—we can't be overheard there."

Together they climbed the iron ladder and walked right aft to the taffrail. The rain had quite stopped now, and the sea was very calm. Farnholme leaned over the rail, gazed down at the phosphorescence bubbling in the *Kerry Dancer's* creaming wake and wished he could smoke. It was Parker who broke the silence.

"I've a rather curious item of news for you, sir—sorry, no ' sir '. Did the corporal tell you?"

"He told me nothing. He only came into the aftercastle a couple of minutes ago. What is it?"

"It appears that this wasn't the only ship in the Singapore roads to-night. While we were coming out to the *Kerry Dancer* with the first boatload, it seems that another motor-boat came in and tied up less than a quarter of a mile away. A British crew."

"Well, I'll be damned!" Farnholme whistled softly in the darkness. "Who were they? What the hell were they doing there anyway? And who saw them?"

"Corporal Fraser and one of my own men. They heard the engine of the motor-boat—we never heard it, obviously, because the sound of our own drowned it—and went across to investigate. Only two men in it, both armed with rifles. The only man who spoke was a Highlander—chap from the Western Isles, Fraser says, and he'd know. Very uncommunicative indeed, Fraser says, although he asked plenty of questions himself. Then Fraser heard the *Kerry Dancer's* boat coming back, and they had to go. He thinks one of the men followed him, but he can't be sure."

"' Curious ' is hardly the word to describe it, Lieutenant." Farnholme bit his lower lip thoughtfully and stared out to sea. "And Fraser has no idea where they came from, or what kind of ship they had or where they were going?"

"He knows nothing," Parker said positively. "They might have come straight from the moon for all Fraser knows."

They talked about it for a few minutes, then Farnholme dismissed the matter.

"No good talking about it, Parker, so let's forget it. It's

over and done with and no harm to anyone—we got clear away, which is all that matters." Deliberately he changed the subject. " Got everything organised?"

" Yes, more or less. Siran's going to co-operate, no doubt about that—his own neck's at stake just as much as ours and he's fully aware of it. The bomb or torpedo that gets us isn't very likely to miss him. I've a man watching him, one watching the quarter-master and one keeping an eye on the duty engineer. Most of the rest of my men are asleep in the fo'c'sle —and heaven knows they need all the sleep they can get. I've got four of them asleep in the midships cabin—very handy in emergency."

" Good, good." Farnholme nodded his head in approval. " And the two Chinese nurses and the elderly Malayan one?"

" Also in one of the midships cabins. They're pretty sick and dazed, all three of them."

" And Van Effen?"

" Asleep on deck, under a boat. Just outside the wheel-house, not ten feet from the captain." Parker grinned. " He's no longer mad at you, but his knife is still pretty deep in Siran. It seemed a good place to have Van Effen sleep. A reliable sort of chap."

" He's all of that. How about food?"

" Lousy, but plenty of it. Enough for a week or ten days."

" I hope we get the chance to eat it all," Farnholme said grimly. " One more thing. Have you impressed on everyone, especially Siran, that I'm now pretty small beer around these parts and that there's only one man that matters—yourself?"

" I don't think you're as well thought of as you were previously," Parker said modestly.

" Excellent." Unconsciously, almost, Farnholme touched the belt under his shirt. " But don't overdo it—just ignore me whenever possible. By the way, there's something you can do for me on your way for'ard. You know the radio shack?"

" Behind the wheelhouse? Yes, I've seen it."

" The operator, Willie Loon or something like that, sleeps in it. I think he's a pretty decent sort of lad—God knows what he's doing aboard this floating coffin—but I don't want to approach him myself. Find out from him what his set's transmitting radius is and let me know before dawn. I'll probably have a call to make round about that time."

" Yes, sir." Parker hesitated, made to speak, then changed his mind about the question he had been going to ask. " No time like the present. I'll go and find out now. Good night."

Nicolson lifted his shoulders in a half-shrug and smiled: but his face was dark with worry. " You, too, Bo'sun? Maybe my judgment was wrong. I'm sure that Siran will never stand trial. But I can't kill him, not yet."

" He's just waiting his chance, sir." McKinnon was as worried as Nicolson. " A killer. You heard the Brigadier's story."

" That's the trouble. I did hear his story." Nicolson nodded heavily, looked at Farnholme, glanced at McKinnon and then stared down at his hands. " I didn't believe a damn' single word he said. He was lying all the way."

* * *

The sun wheeled like a great burning ball above the eastern horizon. Inside an hour nearly all talk was stopped and people were crawling back into their shells of remote indifference, each alone with his own private hell of thirst and pain. Hour succeeded interminable hour, the sun climbed higher and higher into the empty washed-out blue of the windless sky, and the lifeboat remained as she had been for days on end now, motionless on the water. That they had moved many miles south in those days Nicolson was well aware, for the current set due south from Straat Banka to the Sunda Strait eleven months out of twelve: but there was no movement relative to the water surrounding them, nothing that the human eye could see.

Nobody moved aboard the boat any more than the boat moved on the surface of the sea. With the sun swinging high towards the zenith, the slightest effort brought exhaustion in its wake, a panting of breath that whistled shrilly through a bone-dry mouth and cracked and blistered lips. Now and again the little boy moved about and talked to himself in his own private language, but as the day lengthened and the hot and humid air became more and more oppressive and suffocating, his activities and his talk lessened and lessened until finally he was content to lie still on Gudrun's lap, gazing up thoughtfully into the clear blue eyes: but by and by his eyelids grew heavy and dropped, and he fell asleep. Arms outstretched in dumb show Nicolson offered to take him and give her a rest, but she just smiled and shook her head. It suddenly came home to Nicolson, with a sense of something like wonder, that she nearly always smiled when she spoke: not always, but he'd yet to hear his first complaint from her or see the first expression of discontent. He saw the girl looking at him, strangely, and he forced a smile on his face, then looked away.

Now and again a murmur of voices came from the side benches on the starboard side. What the brigadier and Miss Plenderleith found to talk about Nicolson couldn't even begin to guess, but find it they did, and plenty of it. In the gaps in their conversation they just sat and looked into one another's eyes, and the brigadier held her thin wasted hand in his all the time. Two or three days ago it had struck Nicolson as mildly humorous, and he had had visions of the brigadier in a bygone and gentler age, immaculately dressed in white tie and tails and carnation in his buttonhole, hair and moustache as jet black as they were now snowy white, his hansom cab ready while he himself stood at the stage door entrance, waiting. But he couldn't see anything funny in it, not any longer. It was all rather quiet and pathetic, a Darby and Joan waiting patiently for the end, but not at all afraid.

Slowly Nicolson's gaze travelled round the boat. There wasn't much change from yesterday that he could see, except that everybody seemed just that much weaker, that much more exhausted than they had been, with hardly the strength left to move into the few solitary scraps of shade that remained. They were very low. It didn't need any expert medical eye to see that the distance from listlessness to lifelessness was only a very short step indeed. Some were now so far through that it was only by a conscious effort that they could rouse themselves to accept their midday ration of water, and even then one or two found the greatest difficulty in swallowing. Forty-eight hours and most of them would be dead. Nicolson knew where they were, near enough, since he still had his sextant with him: in the vicinity of the Noordwachter light, perhaps fifty miles due east of the coast of Sumatra. If neither wind nor rain came within the next twenty-four hours, then it wouldn't matter after that whether it came or not.

On the credit side, the only cheering item was that of the captain's health. He had come out of his coma just after dawn and now, sitting on a cross seat and wedged between a thwart and bench, he seemed determined not to lose consciousness again. He could speak normally now—as normally as any of them could speak with thirst choking in their throats—and he no longer coughed blood, not at any time. He had lost a great deal of weight in the past week, but in spite of that looked stronger than he had done for days. For a man with a bullet lodged either in his lung or the chest wall to survive

172

the rigours of the previous week, and at the same time be denied all medical attention or medicines was something Nicolson would have refused to believe unless he had seen it. Even now, he found Findhorn's recuperative powers—Findhorn was almost at his retiring age—difficult to credit. He knew, too, that Findhorn had really nothing to live for, no wife, no family, just nothing, which made his courage and recovery all the more astonishing. And all the more bitter for, with all the guts in the world, he was still a very sick man, and the end could not be very far away. Maybe it was just his sense of responsibility, but perhaps not. It was difficult to say, impossible to say. Nicolson realised that he himself was too tired, too uncaring to worry about it longer. It didn't matter, nothing mattered. He closed his eyes to rest them from the harsh, shimmering glare of the sea, and quietly dropped off to sleep in the noonday sun.

He awoke to the sound of someone drinking water, not the sound of a person drinking the tiny little rations of hot, brackish liquid that McKinnon doled out three times a day, but great, gasping mouthfuls at a time, gurgling and splashing as if he had a bucket to his head. At first Nicolson thought that someone must have broached the remaining supplies, but he saw immediately that it wasn't that. Sitting on a thwart up near the mast, Sinclair, the young soldier, had the baler to his head. It was an eight-inch baler, and it held a lot of water. His head was tilted right back, and he was just draining the last few drops from it.

Nicolson rose stiffly to his feet, carefully picked his way for'ard through the bodies sprawled over seats and benches and took the can from the boy's unresisting hand. He lifted the baler and let a couple of drops trickle slowly into his mouth. He grimaced at the prickly saltiness of the taste. Seawater. Not that there had really been any doubt about it. The boy was staring up at him, his eyes wide and mad, pitiful defiance in his face. There were perhaps half a dozen men watching them, looking at them with a kind of listless indifference. They didn't care. Some of them at least must have seen Sinclair dipping the baler in the sea and then drink from it, but they hadn't bothered to stop him. They hadn't even bothered to call out. Maybe they even thought it was a good idea. Nicolson shook his head and looked down at the soldier.

"That was sea-water, wasn't it, Sinclair?"

The soldier said nothing. His mouth was twitching, as if he were forming words, but no sound came out. The insane

173

eyes, wide and flat and empty, were fixed on Nicolson, and the lids didn't blink, not once.

"Did you drink all of it?" Nicolson persisted, and this time the boy did answer, a long, monotonous string of oaths in a high, cracked voice. For a few seconds Nicolson stared down at him without speaking, then shrugged his shoulders tiredly and turned away. Sinclair half rose from his thwart, clawed fingers reaching for the baler, but Nicolson easily pushed him away, and he sank back heavily on his seat, bent forward, cradled his face in his hands and shook his head slowly from side to side. Nicolson hesitated for a moment, then made his way back to the sternsheets.

Midday came and went, the sun crossed over its zenith and the heat grew even more intense. The boat now was as soundless as it was lifeless and even Farnholme's and Miss Plenderleith's murmurings had ceased and they had dropped off into an uneasy sleep. And then, just after three o'clock in the afternoon, when even to the most resolute it must have seemed that they were lost in an endless purgatory, came the sudden change.

Little enough in itself, the change was as dramatic as it was abrupt, but a change so slight that at first it failed to register or have its significance encompassed by exhausted minds. It was McKinnon who noticed it first, noticed it and knew what it meant, and he sat bolt upright in the sternsheets, blinking at first in the sea-mirrored glare of the sun, then searching the horizon from north to east. Seconds later he dug his fingers into Nicolson's arm and shook him awake.

"What is it, Bo'sun?" Nicolson asked quickly. "What's happened?" But McKinnon said nothing, just sat there looking at him, cracked, painful lips drawn back in a grin of sheer happiness. For a moment Nicolson stared at him, blankly incomprehending, thinking only that at last McKinnon, too, had gone over the edge, then all at once he had it.

"Wind!" His voice was only a faint, cracked whisper, but his face, a face that could feel the first tentative stirrings of a breeze degrees cooler than the suffocating heat of only minutes previously, showed how he felt. Almost at once, exactly as McKinnon had done, he too stared away to the north and east and then, for the first and only time in his life, he thumped the grinning bo'sun on the back. "Wind, McKinnon! And cloud! Can you see it?" His pointing arm stretched away to the north-east: away in the far distance a bluish purple bar of cloud was just beginning to lift over the horizon.

" I can see it, sir. No doubt about it at all. Coming our way, all right."

" And that wind's strengthening all the time. Feel it?" He shook the sleeping nurse by the shoulder. " Gudrun! Wake up! Wake up!"

She stirred, opened her eyes and looked up at him. " What is it, Johnny?"

" Mr. Nicolson to you." He spoke with mock severity, but he was grinning with delight. " Want to see the most wonderful sight anyone ever saw?" He saw the shadow of distress cross the clear blue of her eyes, knew what she must be thinking, and smiled again. " A raincloud, you chump! A wonderful, wonderful rain-cloud. Give the captain a shake, will you?"

The effect on the entire boat's company was astonishing, the transformation almost beyond belief. Within two minutes everybody was wide awake, twisted round and staring eagerly towards the north-east, chattering excitedly to one another. Or not quite everybody—Sinclair, the young soldier, paid no heed at all, just sat staring down at the bottom of the boat, lost in a vast indifference. But he was the solitary exception. For the rest, they might have been condemned men granted the right to live again, and that was almost literally true. Findhorn had ordered an extra ration of water all round. The long bar of clouds was perceptibly nearer. The wind was stronger and cool on their faces. Hope was with them again and life once more worth the living. Nicolson was dimly aware that this excitement, this physical activity, was purely nervous and psychological in origin, that, unknown to them, it must be draining their last reserves of strength, and that any disappointment, any reversal of this sudden fortune, would be the equivalent of a death penalty. But it didn't seem likely.

" How long, do you think, my boy?" It was Farnholme talking.

" Hard to say." Nicolson stared off to the north-east. " Hour and a half, perhaps, maybe less if the wind freshens." He looked at the captain. " What do you think, sir?"

" Less," Findhorn nodded. " Wind's definitely strengthening, I think."

" ' I bring fresh showers for thirsting flowers '," the second engineer quoted solemnly. He rubbed his hands together. " For flowers substitute Willoughby. Rain, rain, glorious rain!"

"A bit early to start counting your chickens yet, Willy," Nicolson said warningly.

"What do you mean?" It was Farnholme who replied, his voice sharp.

"Just that rain-clouds don't necessarily mean rain, that's all." Nicolson spoke as soothingly as he could. "Not at first, that is."

"Do you mean to tell me, young man, that we'll be no better off than we were before?" There was only one person on the boat who addressed Nicolson as ' young man.'

"Of course not, Miss Plenderleith. These clouds look thick and heavy, and it'll mean shelter from the sun, for one thing. But what the captain and I are really interested in is the wind. If it picks up and holds we can reach the Sunda Straits sometime during the night."

"Then why haven't you the sails up?" Farnholme demanded.

"Because I think the chances are that we *will* have rain," Nicolson said patiently. "We've got to have something to funnel the water into cups or baler or whatever we use. And there's not enough wind yet to move us a couple of feet a minute."

For the better part of an hour after that nobody spoke. With the realisation that salvation wasn't as immediate as they had thought, some of the earlier listlessness had returned. But only some. The hope was there, and none of them had any intention of letting it go. No one closed his eyes or went to sleep again. The cloud was still there, off the starboard beam, getting bigger and darker all the time, and it had all their attention. Their gaze was on that and on nothing else and maybe that was why they didn't see Sinclair until it was too late.

It was Gudrun Drachmann who saw him first, and what she saw made her rise as quickly as she could and stumble for'ard towards the boy. His eyes upturned in his head so that his pupils had vanished and only the whites were visible, he was jerking convulsively in his seat, his teeth chattering violently like a man in an ague and his face was the colour of stone. Even as the girl reached him, calling his name softly, beseechingly, he pushed himself to his feet, struck at her so that she stumbled and fell against the brigadier, and then, before anyone had time to recover and do anything, tore off his shirt, flung it at the advancing Nicolson and jumped overboard,

176

" Good night, Lieutenant." Farnholme remained leaning over the taffrail for a few more minutes, listening to the asthmatic clanking of the *Kerry Dancer's* superannuated engine as she throbbed her way steadily east-south-east through the calm and oily sea. By and by he straightened up with a sigh, turned and went below. The whisky bottles were in one of his bags in the aftercastle and he had his reputation to sustain.

*　　　*　　　*

Most men would have objected strongly to being waked at half-past three in the morning and asked a purely technical question about their work, but not Willie Loon. He merely sat up in his bunk, smiled at Lieutenant Parker, told him that the effective range of his transmitter was barely five hundred miles and smiled again. The smile on his round pleasant face was the essence of good will and cheerfulness, and Parker had no doubt but that Farnholme had been a hundred per cent correct in his assessment of Willie Loon's character. He didn't belong here.

Parker thanked him, and turned to go. On his way out he noticed on the transmitting table something he had never expected to see on a ship such as the *Kerry Dancer*—a round, iced cake, not too expertly made, it's top liberally beskewered with tiny candles. Parker blinked, then looked at Willie Loon.

" What on earth is this for?"

" A birthday cake." Willie Loon beamed proudly at him. " My wife—that's her picture there—made it. Two months ago, now, to be sure I would have it. It is very pretty, is it not?"

" It's beautiful," Lieutenant Parker said carefully. He looked at the picture again. " Beautiful as the girl who made it. You must be a very lucky man."

" I am." Again he smiled, blissfully. " I am very lucky indeed, sir."

" And when's the birthday?"

" To-day. That is why the cake is out. I am twenty-four years old to-day."

" To-day!" Parker shook his head. " You've certainly picked a wonderful day to have a birthday on, by all the signs. But it's got to be some time, I suppose. Good luck, and many happy returns of the day."

He turned, stepped over the storm combing, and closed the door softly behind him.

CHAPTER THREE

WILLIE LOON died when he was twenty-four years of age. He died on his twenty-fourth birthday, at the high noon of day, with the harsh glare of the equatorial sunlight striking savagely through the barred skylight above his head. A white light, a bright merciless light that mocked the smoking flame from the solitary candle still burning on the birthday cake, a yellow flame that bloomed and faded, bloomed and faded, regularly, monotonously, as the ship rolled and the black bar of shadow from the skylight passed and repassed across it—across the candle, across the cake and across the picture of Anna May, the shy-smiling Batavian girl who had baked it.

But Willie Loon could not see the candle or the cake or the picture of his young wife, for he was blind. He could not understand why this should be so, for the last of these hammer-blows of just ten seconds ago had struck the back of his head, not the front. He could not even see his radio transmitting key, but that did not matter, for Mr. Johnson of the Marconi school had always insisted that no one could be a real Marconi man until he was as good in pitch darkness as he was in the light of day. And Mr. Johnson had also said that the Marconi man should be the last to leave his post, that he should leave the ship together with his captain. And so Willie Loon's hand moved up and down, up and down, in the staccato, off-beat rhythm of the trained operator, triggering off the key, sending the same call over and over again: S.O.S., enemy air attack, 0.45 N, 104.24 E, on fire: S.O.S., enemy air attack, 0.45 N, 104.24 E, on fire: S.O.S. . . .

His back hurt, hurt abominably. Machine-gun bullets, he did not know how many, but they hurt, badly. But better that, he thought tiredly, than the transmitter. If his back hadn't been there the transmitter would have been smashed, there would have been no distress signal, no hope at all. A fine Marconi man he would have been with the most important message of his life to send and no way of sending it . . . But he was sending that message, the most important message of his life, although already his hand was becoming terribly heavy and the transmitting key was starting to jump around from side to side, eluding the fumbling, sightless fingers.

There was a strange, muted thunder in his ears. He wondered vaguely, if it was the sound of aero engines, or if the flames that enveloped the foredeck were bearing down on him, or if it was just the roaring of his own blood in his head. Most likely it was his own blood, for the bombers should have gone by now, their work done, and there was no wind to fan the flames. It didn't matter. Nothing really mattered except that his hand should keep bearing down on that transmitting key, keep sending out the message. And the message went out, time and time again, but it was now only a jumbled, meaningless blur of dots and dashes.

Willie Loon did not know this. Nothing was very clear to him any longer. Everything was dark and confused and he seemed to be falling, but he could feel the edge of his chair catching him behind the knees and he knew he was still there, still sitting at his transmitter and he smiled at his own foolishness. He thought again of Mr. Johnson and he thought that perhaps Mr. Johnson would not be ashamed of him if he could see him then. He thought of his dark and gentle Anna May, and smiled again, without bitterness. And then there was the cake. Such a lovely cake, made as only she could make it, and he hadn't even tasted it. He shook his head sadly, cried out once as the sharp scalpel of agony sliced through his shattered head and reached the unseeing eyes.

For a moment, just for a moment, consciousness returned. His right hand had slipped off the transmitting key. He knew it was desperately urgent that he should move his hand back, but all the power seemed to have gone from his right arm. He moved his left hand across, caught his right wrist and tried to lift it, but it was far too heavy, it might have been nailed to the table. He thought again, dimly, briefly, of Mr. Johnson, and he hoped he had done his best. Then silently, without even a sigh, he slid forward wearily on to the table, his head cradling on his crossed hands, his left elbow crushing down on the cake until the candle leaned over horizontally, the dripping wax pooling on the polished table, the smoke, thick now and very black, spiralling lazily upwards until it flattened against the deckhead, and spread across the tiny cabin. A dark, oily smoke, but it could do nothing to soften the cruel shafts of sunshine or hide the three little neat, red-ringed holes in the back of Willie Loon's shirt as he lay sprawled tiredly across

the table. By and by the candle flickered feebly, flared up once
and died.

*   *   *

Captain Francis Findhorn, O.B.E., Commodore of the
British-Arabian Tanker Company and master of the 12,000
ton motor-ship *Viroma,* gave the barometer a last two taps
with his fingernail, looked at it without expression for a
moment then walked back quietly to his seat in the port corner
of the wheelhouse. Unthinkingly, he reached up to direct the
overhead ventilation louver on to his face, winced as the
blast of hot, humid air struck at him, then pushed it away
again, quickly but without haste. Captain Findhorn never did
anything with haste. Even the next simple gesture of taking
off his gold-braided white cap and rubbing the dark, thinning
hair with his handkerchief was made with an unhurried speed,
with so complete a lack of unnecessary and wasted movement
that one instinctively knew this calm deliberation, this un-
studied economy of motion, to be an inseparable part of the
man's nature.

There was a soft padding behind him, footsteps crossing the
iron-hard teak deck. Captain Findhorn replaced his cap,
slewed round in his chair and looked at his chief officer who
was standing where he himself had been seconds before,
gazing thoughtfully at the barometer. For a few moments
Captain Findhorn studied him in silence, thought that his
chief officer was a classic refutation of the widely-held belief
that light-haired, light-skinned people cannot sunburn well:
between the white shirt and the fair flaxen hair, sun-bleached
almost to a platinum blond, the back of the neck was a strip
of old, dark oak. Then the chief officer had turned round and
caught his eye, and Findhorn smiled, briefly.

"Well, Mr. Nicolson, what do you make of it?" The
quartermaster was only feet away: with members of the crew
within earshot, the captain was always punctiliousness itself
towards his senior officers.

Nicolson shrugged his shoulders and walked across to the
screen door. He had a peculiarly soft-footed, almost catlike
gait, as if he were stepping on old, dry sticks and feared he
might break them. He looked at the brassy oven of the sky,
at the oily copper sheen of the water, at the far horizon to the
east where the two met in a shimmer of metallic blue, and
finally at the glassy swell that was building up to the north-
east, pushing up on their port quarter. He shrugged again,

36

turned and looked at the captain, and for the hundredth time Findhorn found himself marvelling at the clear, ice-blue of his officer's eyes, doubly striking in the sunburnt darkness of the face. He had never seen eyes like them, remotely like them, anywhere. They always reminded Captain Findhorn of Alpine lakes, and this irritated the captain, for he had a precise, logical mind, and he had never been in the Alps in his life.

"Not much doubt about it, sir, is there?" The voice was soft, controlled, effortless—the perfect complement to the way he walked and carried himself: but it had a deep, resonant quality that enabled him to be heard through a roomful of talking people or in a high wind with an abnormal ease and clarity. He gestured through the open screen door. "All the signs. The glass is only 28.5, but it was .75 hardly an hour ago. It's falling like a stone. The wrong time of the year, and I've never heard of a tropical storm in these latitudes, but we're in for a bit of a blow, I'm afraid."

"You have a genius for understatement, Mr. Nicolson," Findhorn said dryly. "And don't refer disrespectfully to a typhoon as 'a bit of a blow'. It might hear you." He paused a moment, smiled and went on softly. "I hope it does, Mr. Nicolson. It's a Godsend."

"It would be all of that," Nicolson murmured. "And rain. There'll be plenty of rain?"

"Buckets of it," Captain Findhorn said with satisfaction. "Rain, high seas and a ten or eleven wind and there's nary a son in the Nipponese army or navy will see us this night. What's our course, Mr. Nicolson?"

"One-thirty, sir."

"We'll keep it there. The Carimata Straits for us by noon to-morrow, and then there's always a chance. We'll turn aside only for their Grand Fleet and we'll turn back for nothing." Captain Findhorn's eyes were calm, untroubled. "Think there'll be anyone out looking for us, Mr. Nicolson?"

"Apart from a couple of hundred aircraft pilots and every ship in the China Sea, no." Nicolson smiled briefly, and the smile touched and whitened the wrinkles at his eyes and was gone. "I doubt if there's any of our little yellow pals within 500 miles who *doesn't* know that we broke out of Singapore last night. We must be the juiciest tit-bit since the *Prince of Wales* went down, and the size of the flap will be corresponding. They'll have combed every exit—Macassar, Singapore, Durian and Rhio—and the High Command will be throwing blue fits and chucking themselves on to their swords by the dozen."

"But they never thought to check the Tjombol Straits and Temiang?"

"I suppose they're reasonably sane and do us the compliment of thinking we are also," Nicolson said thoughtfully. "No sane man would take a big tanker through these waters at night, not with the draught we've got, and not a light in sight."

Captain Findhorn inclined his head, half-nod, half-bow. "You have rather a pretty line in compliments yourself, Mr. Nicolson."

Nicolson said nothing. He turned away and walked to the other side of the bridge, past the quartermaster and Vannier, the fourth officer. His feet on the deck made no more sound, almost, than the whisper of falling leaves. At the far end of the bridge he stopped, looked through the starboard wheelhouse door at the haze-blurred silhouette of Linga Island melting softly into the purple distance, then turned back again. Vannier and the quartermaster watched him silently, tired speculation in tired eyes.

From above their heads came the occasional murmur of voices, or the shuffling of aimless, wandering feet. Up there were the gunners who manned the two wheelhouse top Hotchkisses, .5's well spaced on each side of the starboard compass platform teak screen. Old guns these, very old and feeble and inaccurate, good only for boosting the morale of those who had never had to use them against an enemy. The suicide seats, these two gun positions were called: the exposed wheelhouse top, highest point of the bridge superstructure, always held priority for strafing attacks on tankers. The gunners knew this, and they were only human: they had been unhappy, increasingly restless, for days now.

But the fidgety unease of the gunners, the quartermaster's hands moving gently on the spokes of the wheel—these were only small, insignificant sounds that punctuated the strange, hushed silence that lay over the *Viroma*, an enveloping, encompassing silence, thick, cocoon-like, almost tangible. And the little sounds came and went and left the silence deeper, more oppressive than before.

It was the silence that comes with great heat and the climbing humidity that spills out sweat over a man's arms and body with every mouthful of liquid he drinks. It was the dead, flat silence that lies over the China Sea while the gathering storm

landing flat-faced with a splash that sent water spattering all over the boat.

For a few seconds no one moved. It had been all so swift and unexpected that they could have imagined it. But there was no imagination about the empty thwart in the boat, the spreading ripples on the glassy surface of the sea. Nicolson stood motionless, arrested in mid-step, the ragged shirt caught in one hand. The girl was still leaning against Farnholme, saying 'Alex', 'Alex', over and over again, meaninglessly. And then there came another splash from right aft, not so loud this time. The bo'sun had gone after him.

The second splash brought Nicolson back to life and action with a perceptible jerk. Stooping quickly, he caught hold of the boat-hook and turned quickly to the side of the boat, kneeling on the bench. Almost without thinking he had dragged his pistol from his belt and was holding it in his free hand. The boat-hook was for McKinnon, the pistol for the young soldier. The panic-stricken grip of a drowning man was bad enough: God only knew what that of a drowning madman might be like.

Sinclair was thrashing about the water about twenty feet from the boat and McKinnon, just surfaced, was splashing determinedly towards him—like nearly all Islanders, swimming was not one of his better accomplishments—when Nicolson caught sight of something that struck at him like an ice-cold chill. He swung the boat-hook in a wide curving arc that brought it crashing into the water only inches from McKinnon's shoulder. Instinctively the bo-sun caught hold of it and twisted round, his dark face a mass of startled incomprehension.

" Back, man, back!" Nicolson shouted. Even in that moment of near-panic he could hear that his voice was hoarse and cracked. " For God's sake, hurry up!"

McKinnon started to move slowly towards the boat, but not of his own volition: he still held on to the boat-hook, and Nicolson was drawing it quickly inboard. McKinnon's face still had its almost comical expression of bewilderment. He looked over his shoulder to where Sinclair was still splashing aimlessly around, more than thirty feet away now, looked back again towards the boat, opened his mouth to speak and then shouted aloud with pain. A split second passed, he shouted again, and then, mysteriously galvanised into furious activity, splashed his way madly towards the boat. Five fran-

tic strokes and he was alongside, half-a-dozen hands dragging
him head-first into the boat. He landed face down on a cross
seat, and, just as his legs came inboard, a greyish, reptilian
shape released its grip on his calf and slid back soundlessly into
the water.

"What—what on earth was that?" Gudrun had caught a
glimpse of the vicious teeth, the evil snake's body. Her voice
was shaking.

"Barracuda," Nicolson said tonelessly. He carefully avoided
looking at her face.

"Barracuda!" The shocked whisper left no doubt but that
she had heard all about them, the most voracious killers in the
sea. "But Alex! Alex! He's out there! We must help him
quickly!"

"There's nothing we can do." He hadn't meant to speak so
harshly, but the knowledge of his utter powerlessness affected
him more than he knew. "There's nothing anyone can do for
him now."

Even as he was speaking, Sinclair's agonised scream came at
them across the water. It was a frightening sound, half
human, half-animal, and it came again and again, strident
with some nameless terror, as he flung himself convulsively
about, at times rising half-clear of the sea and arching so far
back that his hair almost touched the water, his hands churn-
ing foam as he beat insanely at some invisible enemies. The
Colt in Nicolson's hand crashed six times in rapid succession,
kicking up gouts of flying water and spray around the soldier,
quick, unsighted shots that could never have hoped to accom-
plish anything. Careless, almost, one might have called them
all except the first: there had been nothing careless about that
shot, it had taken Sinclair cleanly through the head. Long
before the smell of cordite and blue wisps of smoke had drifted
away to the south, the water was calm again and Sinclair had
vanished, lost to sight beneath the steel-blue mirror of the
sea.

Twenty minutes later that sea was no longer blue but
churned to a milky, frothing white as the sheets of driving
torrential rain swept across it from horizon to horizon.

*   *   *

Close on three hours had passed, and it was about the time
of sundown. It was impossible to see the sun, to know where
it was, for the rain-squalls still marched successively south and
in the failing light the sky was the same leaden grey at all
178

points of the compass. The rain still fell, still swept across the unprotected boat, but nobody cared. Drenched to the skin, shivering often in the cold rain that moulded and plastered thin cottons to arms and bodies and legs, they were happy. In spite of the sudden, numbing shock the death of Sinclair had given them, in spite of the realisation of the tragic futility of his death with the life-giving rain so near at hand, in spite of these things they were happy. They were happy because the law of self-preservation still yielded place to none. They were happy because they had slaked their terrible thirsts and drunk their fill, and more than their fill, because the cold rain cooled down their burns and blistered skins, because they had managed to funnel over four gallons of fresh rain-water into one of the tanks. They were happy because the lifeboat, driven by the spanking breeze, had already covered many of the miles that stretched between where they had lain becalmed and the now steadily nearing coast of Western Java. And they were deliriously happy, happier than they had dreamed that they could ever be again, because salvation was at hand, because miracles still happened and their troubles were over at last.

It was, as ever, McKinnon that had seen it first, a long, low shape through a distant gap in the rain-squalls, just over two miles away. They had no reason to fear anything but the worst, the inevitable worst, and it had taken only seconds to lower the tattered lug and jib, knock the pin from the mast clamp, unship the mast itself and cower down in the bottom of the boat, so that it had become, even from a short distance, no more than an empty, drifting lifeboat, difficult to see in the mists of driving rain, possibly not worth investigating even if it had been seen. But they had been seen, the long grey shape had altered course to intercept their line of drift, and now they could only thank God that it had altered its course, bless the sharp-eyed lookouts who had impossibly picked out their little grey boat against its vast grey background.

It was Nicolson who had at first incredulously identified it, then Findhorn, McKinnon, Vannier, Evans and Walters had all recognised it too. This was not the first time they had seen one of them, and there could be no possible doubt about it. It was a U.S. Navy Torpedo Boat, and their torpedo boats couldn't be confused with anything afloat. The long, sweeping flare of the bows, the seventy-foot plywood shell driven by its three high-speed marine motors, its quadruple torpedo tubes and .50 calibre machine-guns were quite unmistakable. It was flying no flag at all, but, almost as if to remove any last doubts they might have about its nationality, a seaman aboard the torpedo boat broke out a large flag that streamed out stiffly in the wind of its passing: it was approaching at a speed of something better than thirty knots—nowhere near its maximum—and the white water was piled high at its bows. Even in the gathering gloom there was no more mistaking the flag than there was the torpedo boat: the Stars and Stripes is probably the most easily identifiable flag of all.

They were all sitting up in the lifeboat now, and one or two were standing, waving at the M.T.B. A couple of men on the M.T.B. waved back, one from the wheelhouse, the other standing by one of the for'ard turrets. Aboard the lifeboat, people were gathering their few pitiful possessions together, preparatory to boarding the American vessel, and Miss Plenderleith was in the act of skewering her hat more firmly on to her head when the M.T.B. abruptly slowed down her big Packard motors, jammed them into reverse and came sliding smoothly alongside, only feet away, dwarfing the little lifeboat. Even before she stopped completely, a couple of heaving lines came sailing across the gap of water and smacked accurately fore and aft into the lifeboat. The co-ordinated precision, the handling of the boat clearly bespoke a highly-trained crew. And then both boats were rubbing alongside, Nicolson had his hand on the M.T.B.'s side, the other raised in greeting to the short, rather stocky figure that had just appeared from behind the wheelhouse.

" Hallo there!" Nicolson grinned widely, and stretched out a hand in greeting. " Brother, are we glad to see you!"

" Not half as glad as we are to see you." There was a gleam of white teeth in a sunburnt face, an almost imperceptible movement of the left hand, and the three sailors on deck were no longer interested bystanders but very alert, very attentive guards, with suddenly produced sub-machine-guns rock-steady in their hands. A pistol, too, had appeared in the speaker's right hand. " I fear, however, that your rejoicing may prove to be rather shorter-lived than ours. Please to keep very still indeed."

Nicolson felt as if he had been kicked in the stomach. With a queer sort of detachment he saw that his hand was no longer resting loosely against the ship's side but was bar-taut, each separate tendon standing out rigidly from the back of his hand. In spite of all the water he had drunk, his mouth felt uddenly as dry as a kiln. But he managed to keep his voice teady enough.

"What kind of bad joke is this?"

"I agree." The other bowed slightly, and for the first time Nicolson could see the unmistakable slant, the tight-stretched kin at the corner of the eyes. "For you it is not funny at all. Look." He gestured with his free hand, and Nicolson looked. The Stars and Stripes was already gone and, even as he watched, the Rising Sun of Japan fluttered up and took its place.

"A regrettable stratagem, is it not?" the man continued. He seemed to be enjoying himself thoroughly. "As is also the boat and, alas, the passably Anglo-Saxon appearance of my men and myself. Though specially chosen on account of this ast, I can assure you we are not especially proud of it. All hat, however, is by the way." His English was perfect, with a pronounced American accent, and he obviously took pleasure in airing it. "There has been much sunshine and storm in he past week. It is most considerate of you to have survived t all. We have been waiting a long time for you. You are very welcome."

He stopped suddenly, teeth bared, and lined up his pistol on the brigadier, who had sprung to his feet with a speed astonishing in a man of his years, an empty whisky bottle swinging n his hands. The Japanese officer's finger tightened involuntarily on the trigger, then slowly relaxed when he saw that the bottle had been intended not for him but for Van Effen, who had half-turned as he had sensed the approaching blow, but raised his arm too late. The heavy bottle caught him just above the ear and he collapsed over his thwart as if he had been shot. The Japanese officer stared at Farnholme.

"One more such move and you will die, old man. Are you mad?"

"No, but this man was, and we would all have died. He was reaching for a gun." Farnholme stared down angrily at the fallen man. "I have come too far to die like this, with three machine-guns lined on me."

"You are a wise old man," the officer purred. "Indeed, there is nothing you can do."

There was nothing they could do, Nicolson realised helplessly, nothing whatsoever. He was conscious of an overwhelming bitterness, a bitterness that he could taste in his mouth. That they should have come so far, that they should have overcome

so much, overcome it impossibly and at the expense of fiv
lives, and then that it should all come to this. He heard th
murmur of Peter's voice behind him and when he turned roun
the little boy was standing up in the sternsheets, looking at th
Japanese officer through the lattice screen of his crosse
fingers, not particularly afraid, just shy and wondering, an
again Nicolson felt the bitterness and the angry despair floo
over him almost like a physical tide. Defeat one could accep
but Peter's presence made defeat intolerable.

The two nurses were sitting one on either side of him, Lena
dark, sooty eyes wide with terror, Gudrun's blue ones with
sadness and despair that all too accurately reflected his ow
feelings. He could see no fear in her face, but high on th
temple, where the scar ran into the hairline, he could see
pulse beating very quickly. Slowly, involuntarily, Nicolson'
gaze travelled all round the boat, and everywhere the expres
sions were the same, the fear, the despair, the stunned an
heart-sickening defeat. Not quite everywhere. Siran's face wa
expressionless as ever. McKinnon's eyes were flickering from
side to side as he looked swiftly over the lifeboat, up at th
M.T.B. and then down into the lifeboat again—gauging
Nicolson guessed, their suicidal chances of resistance. An
the brigadier seemed almost unnaturally unconcerned: his arm
round Miss Plenderleith's thin shoulders, he was whispering
something in her ear.

" A touching and pathetic scene, is it not?" The Japanese
officer shook his head in mock sorrow. " Alas, gentlemen
alas for the frailty of human hopes. I look upon you and
am almost overcome myself. Almost, I said, but not quite
Further, it is about to rain, and rain heavily." He looked a
the heavy bank of cloud bearing down from the north-east, a
the thick curtain of rain, now less than half a mile away
sweeping across the darkening sea. " I have a rooted objection
to being soaked by rain, especially when it is quite unneces
sary. I suggest, therefore——"

" Any more suggestions are superfluous. Do you expect me
to remain in this damned boat all night?" Nicolson swung
round as the deep, irate voice boomed out behind him. He
swung round to see Farnholme standing upright, one hand
grasping the handle of the heavy Gladstone bag.

" What—what are you doing?" Nicolson demanded.

Farnholme looked at him, but said nothing. Instead he
smiled, the curve of the upper lip below the white moustache a

masterpiece of slow contempt, looked up at the officer standing above them and jerked a thumb in Nicolson's direction.

"If this fool attempts to do anything silly or restrain me in any way, shoot him down."

Nicolson stared at him in sheer incredulity, then glanced up at the Japanese officer. No incredulity there, no surprise even, just a grin of satisfaction. He started to speak rapidly in some language quite unintelligible to Nicolson, and Farnholme answered him, readily and fluently, in the same tongue. And then, before Nicolson had quite realised what was happening, Farnholme had thrust a hand into his bag, brought out a gun and was making for the side of the boat, bag in one hand, gun in the other.

"This gentleman said we were welcome." Farnholme smiled down at Nicolson. "I fear that he referred only to myself. A welcome and, as you can see, honoured guest." He turned to the Japanese. "You have done splendidly. Your reward shall be great." Then he broke once more into the foreign language —Japanese, it must be, Nicolson was sure—and the conversation lasted for almost two minutes. Once more he looked down at Nicolson. The first heavy drops of the next rain-squall were beginning to patter on the decks of the M.T.B.

"My friend here suggests that you come aboard as prisoners. However, I have convinced him that you are too dangerous and that you should be shot out of hand. We are going below to consider in comfort the exact methods of your disposal." He turned to the Japanese. "Tie their boat aft. They are desperate men—it is most inadvisable to have them alongside. Come, my friend, let us go below. But one moment—I forget my manners. The departing guest must thank his hosts." He bowed ironically. "Captain Findhorn, Mr. Nicolson, my compliments. Thank you for the lift. Thank you for your courtesy and skill in rendezvousing so accurately with my very good friends."

"You damned traitor!" Nicolson spoke with slow savagery.

"There speaks the youthful voice of unthinking nationalism." Farnholme shook his head sadly. "It's a harsh and cruel world, my boy. One has to earn a living somehow." He waved a negligent, mocking hand. "Au revoir. It's been very pleasant."

A moment later he was lost to sight and the rain swept down in blinding sheets.

CHAPTER TWELVE

FOR WHAT seemed a long time no one in the lifeboat spoke o moved, except to ride with the slight rolling of the boat oblivious of the cold driving rain they just stared blankly stupidly, at the spot where Farnholme had been standing before he had disappeared.

It probably wasn't a long time, it just seemed that way, i was probably only a matter of seconds before Nicolson hear Miss Plenderleith call him by name and say something. Bu in the swish of the heavy rain in the sea and frenetic drum ming on the torpedo boat's deck, her voice was only a mean ingless murmur. He turned and stooped, the better to hear, an even in that moment of shock her appearance caught and hel his attention. She was sitting on the port side bench, her bac as straight as a wand, her hands clasped primly in her lap, he face quiet and composed. She might have been sitting in he drawing-room at home, but for one thing: her eyes wer flooded with tears and, even as he watched, two large drop trickled slowly down the lined cheeks and fell on to her hands

"What's the matter, Miss Plenderleith?" Nicolson aske gently. "What is it?"

"Take the boat farther back," she said. Her eyes stare sightlessly ahead, and she gave no signs of seeing him. "H told you. Farther back, at once."

"I don't understand." Nicolson shook his head. "Why d you want us——"

He broke off abruptly as something hard and cold struc painfully at the back of his neck. He whirled round and stare up at the Japanese who had just prodded him with the barre of his machine-gun, at the smooth, yellow face shining in th rain.

"No speaking, Englishman." His English was far poore than his officer's. He looked dangerous, the kind of man wh might welcome the opportunity to use the gently waving gu in his hand. "No speaking, anyone. I do not trust you. I wi kill."

"You heard what I said." Miss Plenderleith's voice wa firm and clear, without the vestige of a tremor. "Please."

The sailor moved his gun till it was lined up on Mis

Plenderleith's head, and dozen pairs of eyes watched as the knuckles of his right index finger whitened under the pull. His lips were drawn back in an evil smile and Nicolson knew that the Japanese—many of them, at least—required far less provocation to kill. But Miss Plenderleith just stared up at him with an expressionless face—almost certainly she wasn't seeing him anyway—and he suddenly lowered the gun with some angry exclamation and took a pace backwards. He jerked his head at the other armed sailor—the officer had taken the third with him when he had gone below—and gestured that the rope made fast to the lifeboat's bow should be brought farther aft. Nicolson and McKinnon paid the lifeboat along the torpedo boat's side, and very soon they were streaming off its stern at the end of a couple of fathoms of rope. The two sailors stood side by side on the poop of the torpedo boat, side by side, cocked carbines ready in their hands. Their eyes searched the lifeboat hungrily, searched for the slightest movement, for anything at all that would give them an excuse to use their guns.

The torpedo boat was moving again, engines throttled back to dead slow but still enough to send it cutting through the water at three or four knots. It headed north-east, into the sea and the heavy rain, rain so heavy that, from the lifeboat, the bows of the torpedo boat were almost lost in the mirk and the gloom. The lifeboat itself was beginning to pitch at the end of the tautened rope, but not heavily.

Miss Plenderleith had her back to the rain and the guards. Perhaps there were still tears on her cheeks, it was difficult to say—the heavy rain was soaking through the straw brim of her hat, and all her face was wet. But her eyes were clearer now, and they were looking straight at Nicolson. He caught her glance, saw her drop it to the carbine lying by her side where Farnholme had left it, saw her raise her eyes to his again.

"Don't look at me," she murmured. "Pay no attention to me. Can they hear me?"

Nicolson stared ahead at the guards, his face bleak. The tiny shake of his head must have been imperceptible to them.

"Can you see the gun? Behind my bag?"

Nicolson looked idly at the bench where Miss Plenderleith was sitting and looked away again. Behind the canvas and leather bag where Miss Plenderleith kept her knitting and all her worldly possessions he could see the heel of the butt of the carbine. Farnholme's gun, the carbine he had used so effect-ively against—— Suddenly there flooded into Nicolson's mind the recollection of all the times the brigadier had used that gun, of the damage he'd done with it, how he'd blown up the big gun on the submarine, how he'd beaten off the attack by the Zero that had attacked the lifeboat, how he'd saved his Nicolson's life on the beach of that little island, and all at once he knew that there was something fantastically wrong with this desertion and betrayal, that no man could so wholly alter——

"Can you see it?" Miss Plenderleith repeated urgently. Nicolson was startled, but didn't show it. He nodded slowly, carefully. The butt of the carbine was less than a foot from his hand.

"It's cocked," Miss Plenderleith said quietly. "It's ready to fire. Foster said it was ready to fire."

This time Nicolson did look at her, slow astonishment and wonder in his face, his eyes blinking in the driving rain as he tried to read her expression. And then he had forgotten all about Miss Plenderleith, and he was half out of his seat, staring intently for'ard, his head automatically reaching for the carbine.

Even at that distance of forty or fifty feet the sound of the explosion was deafening and the sheer physical shock of the pressure wave like an invisible blow in their faces. Smoke and flames belched out through a great hole blown in the starboard side and almost at once the torpedo boat was heavily on fire amidships. The guards, their charge completely forgotten, had swung round to face for'ard, but one of them, caught off-balance by the force of the explosion, stumbled, flung away his machine-gun in a clawing, desperate attempt to regain balance and save himself, failed and fell backwards over the stern into the sea: the other had only taken a couple of running paces forward when the blast of the carbine in Nicolson's hand pitched him forward on his face, dead. Even as he was falling, McKinnon was plunging towards the bows, an axe in his hand, and one vicious blow on the tow-rope taut-stretched across the gunwale severed it completely. Immediately, Nicolson pushed the tiller hard over to starboard, and the lifeboat slewed away heavily to the west. The torpedo boat still throbbed north-east on unaltered course, and within half a minute all signs of it, even the flames that twisted high above the bridge, were completely lost in the rain-squalls and the rapidly falling darkness.

Swiftly, and in a strange unanimity of silence, they stepped the mast, hoisted the lug and jib, and bore off into the rain and the gloom with as much speed as they could command from their tattered sails. With the port gunwale dipping perilously low, Nicolson steered a point north of west: when the torpedo boat recovered from the shock and the fire—and it was probably too large a craft to be permanently crippled by an explosion even of that magnitude—it would come looking for them, but it would almost certainly go looking towards the south-west, in the direction the wind was blowing, in the direction of the Sunda Strait and freedom.

Fifteen minutes passed slowly by, fifteen minutes in which there was only the swift slap of the waves against the hull, the flapping of shredded sails, the creaking of blocks and the tap-tapping of the yard against the mast. Now and again someone would be about to speak, to seek out the reason for the explosion aboard the torpedo boat, then he would catch sight of that stiff-backed little figure with the ridiculous straw hat skewered on the grey bun of hair, and change his mind. There was something about the atmosphere, there was something about that little figure, about the upright carriage, about the indifference to the cold and the rain, about its fierce pride and complete helplessness that precluded easy conversation, that precluded any conversation at all.

It was Gudrun Drachmann who had the courage to make the first move, the delicacy to make it without blundering. She rose carefully to her feet, the blanketed form of the little boy in her arm, and moved across the canted bottom-boards towards the empty seat beside Miss Plenderleith—the seat where the brigadier had been sitting. Nicolson watched her go, unconsciously holding his breath. Far better if she hadn't gone. So easy to make a mistake, so almost impossible not to make a mistake. But Gudrun Drachmann made no mistake.

For a minute or two they sat together, the young and the old, sat without moving, sat without speaking. Then the little boy, half-asleep in his wet blanket, stretched out a chubby hand and touched Miss Plenderleith on her wet cheek. She started, half turned in her seat, then smiled at the boy and caught her hand in his, and then, almost without thinking, she had the little boy on her lap and was hugging him in her thin arms. She hugged him tightly, but it was as if the child knew that there was something far amiss, he just stirred sleepily and looked at her gravely under heavy eyelids. Then, just as

187

gravely, he smiled at her, and the old lady hugged him again, even more tightly, and smiled back down at him, smiled as if her heart was breaking. But she smiled.

"Why did you come and sit here?" she asked the girl. "You and the little one—why did you come?" Her voice was very low.

"I don't know." Gudrun shook her head, almost as if the thought were occurring to her for the first time. "I'm afraid I just don't know."

"It's all right. I know." Miss Plenderleith took her hand and smiled at her. "It's very curious, it is really very curious. That you should come, I mean. He did it for you, he did it all for you—for you and the little one."

"You mean——"

"Fearless Foster." The words were ridiculous, but not the way Miss Plenderleith said them. She said them as if she were saying a prayer. "Fearless Foster Farnholme. That was what we used to call him, when we were in school. He was afraid of nothing that walked on earth."

"You have known him so long, Miss Plenderleith?"

"He said you were the best of us all." Miss Plenderleith hadn't even heard the question. She shook her head musingly, her eyes soft with remembrance. "He teased me about you this afternoon. He said he didn't know what the young men of the present generation were coming to and, by heaven, if he was thirty years younger, he'd have had you to the altar years ago."

"He was very kind." Gudrun smiled without any embarrassment. "I'm afraid he didn't know me very well."

"That's what he said, that's exactly what he said." Miss Plenderleith gently removed the child's thumb from his mouth: he was almost asleep. "Foster always said that education was very important, but that it didn't really matter, because intelligence was more important than that, and that even intelligence didn't count for so much, that wisdom was far more important still. He said he had no idea in the world whether you had education or intelligence or wisdom and that it couldn't matter less, a blind man could see that you had a good heart, and the good heart was all that mattered in this world." Miss Plenderleith smiled, her grief momentarily lost in nostalgic remembrance. "Foster used to complain that there were very few good-hearted people like himself left."

"Brigadier Farnholme was very kind," Gudrun murmured.

"Brigadier Farnholme was a very clever man," Miss

Plenderleith said in gentle reproof. "He was clever enough to —well, never mind. You and the little boy. He was very fond of the little boy."

"Trailing clouds of glory do we come," Willoughby murmured.

"What's that?" Miss Plenderleith looked at him in surprise. "What did you say?"

"Nothing. Just a passing thought, Miss Plenderleith."

Miss Plenderleith smiled at him, then sat gazing down at the little boy. Silence again, but a comfortable silence now. It was Captain Findhorn, speaking for the first time, who broke it, who asked the question they all wanted answered.

"If we come home again, we will owe it all to Brigadier Farnholme. I do not think any of us will ever forget that. You have told us why he did it. You seem to have known him far better than any of us, Miss Plenderleith. Can you tell me how he did it."

Miss Plenderleith nodded. "I'll tell you. It was very simple, because Foster was a very simple and direct man. You all noticed that big Gladstone bag he carried?"

"We did." Findhorn smiled. "The one he carried his—ah —supplies in."

"That's right, whisky. Incidentally, he hated the stuff— used it only for local colour. Anyway, he left all the bottles and all the other contents of his bag behind on the island, in a hole in the rocks, I believe. Then he——"

"What? What did you say?" It was Van Effen speaking, still groggy from Farnholme's blow on the head, leaning so far forward on his seat that he winced with the pain of his injured leg. "He—he left all his stuff behind?"

"That's what I said. Why should you find that so surprising, Mr. Van Effen?"

"No reason at all, I suppose." Van Effen leaned back and smiled at her. "Please continue."

"That's all, really. He'd found lots of Japanese grenades on the beach that night and he'd stuffed fourteen or fifteen into his Gladstone bag."

"Into his bag?" Nicolson patted the seat beside him. "But they're under here, Miss Plenderleith."

"He found more than he told you." Miss Plenderleith's voice was very low. "He took them all aboard with him, he spoke Japanese fluently and he had no difficulty in persuading them that he was carrying Jan Bekker's plans with him. When he got below he was going to show them the plans, put his

hand inside the bag, press a grenade release catch and leave
his hand there. He said it would only take four seconds."

*   *   *

There was no moon that night, and no stars, only the dark
scudding cloud-wrack overhead, and Nicolson drove the lifeboat on, for hour after hour, by guess and by God. The glass
of the compass bowl had cracked, nearly all the spirit had
escaped and the card was gyrating so uncontrollably that
trying to read it in the feeble light of a failing torch was quite
impossible. He steered instead by the wind, trying to keep it on
the port quarter all the time, gambling that the trades would
hold steady, and neither back nor veer to any appreciable
degree. Even with the wind steady, handling the boat was
difficult enough: more and more water was pouring in
through the ruptured planks aft and she was sitting heavily by
the stern, falling away to the south time after time.

As the night passed his anxiety and tension increased, a
tension that communicated itself to most of the others in the
boat, few of whom slept that night. Shortly after midnight,
even with the roughest dead reckoning, Nicolson knew that
he must be within ten or twelve miles of the Sunda Straits.
Not more, probably even a good deal less, perhaps only five
miles. And he had reason to be anxious. Their chart of the
Eastern Archipelago was now salt-stained, rotted and useless,
but he remembered all too clearly the rocks, the reefs and the
shoals that lay off the south-east coast of Sumatra. But he
couldn't remember where they were, and he didn't know where
the lifeboat was, perhaps even his latitude reckonings were so
far out that they would miss the Straits altogether. Their
chances of tearing the bottom out on some off-shore reef
seemed as good as their chances of missing it: and the passengers were so sick, so tired and so hurt that were they to pile
up not more than half a mile from land not half of them had
a hope of survival. And, even if they missed all the waiting
perils, they would still have to beach the boat through heavy
surf.

Shortly after two o'clock in the morning Nicolson sent the
bo'sun and Vannier up to the bows to keep a lookout ahead.
Half a dozen others volunteered to stand up and keep watch
also, but Nicolson curtly ordered them to remain where they
were, to lie as low as possible in the bottom of the boat and
give maximum stability. He might have added, but he didn't,

190

that McKinnon's eyes were probably better than all the others put together.

Half an hour more passed, and suddenly Nicolson became aware that some subtle change was taking place. The change itself wasn't sudden, it was the realisation of the change that struck at him almost like a blow and made him peer desperately ahead into the darkness. The long, low swell from the north-west was changing, it was becoming shorter and steeper with every minute that passed, but he was so tired, so physically exhausted with steering blindly all night long that he'd almost missed the change. And the wind was still the same, no stronger, no weaker than it had been for hours past.

"McKinnon!" Nicolson's hoarse shout had half a dozen dozing people struggling up to a sitting position. "We're running into shallows!"

"Aye, I think you're right, sir." The bo'sun's voice, not particularly perturbed, carried clearly against the wind. He was standing upright on the mast thwart, on the port side, one hand gripping the mast, the other shading his eyes as he stared ahead into the night.

"Can you see anything?"

"Damn the thing I see," McKinnon called back. "It's a bloody black night, sir."

"Keep looking. Vannier?"

"Sir?" The voice was excited, but steady enough for all that. On the brink of breakdown less than twelve hours ago, Vannier had made a remarkable recovery and seemed to have regained more life and energy than any of them.

"Get the lug down! Fast as you can. Don't furl it—no time. Van Effen, Gordon, give him a hand." The lifeboat was beginning to pitch quite violently in the rapidly shortening seas. "See anything yet, Bo'sun?"

"Nothing at all, sir."

"Cut Siran loose. And his two men. Send them back amidships." He waited for half a minute until the three men came stumbling aft. "Siran, you and your men get a crutch apiece. Gordon, you get another. When I give the words you will ship oars and start pulling."

"Not to-night, Mr. Nicolson."

"You said?"

"You heard what I said. I said 'not to-night'." The tone was cool and insolent. "My hands are numb. And I'm afraid I don't just feel like co-operating."

"Don't be a bloody fool, Siran. Lives depend on this."

"Not mine." Nicolson could see the white gleam of teeth in the darkness. "I am an excellent swimmer, Mr. Nicolson."

"You left forty people to die, didn't you, Siran?" Nicolson asked obliquely. The safety-catch of his Colt clicked, unnaturally loud in the sudden silence. A second passed, two, three, then Siran slammed a crutch home into its socket, reached for an oar and muttered orders to his two men.

"Thank you," Nicolson murmured. He raised his voice. "Listen, all of you. I think we're nearing shore. The chances are that there will be rocks or reefs off the beach, or a heavy surf running. The boat may founder or capsize—not likely, but it may." It'll be a ruddy miracle if it doesn't, he thought bleakly. "If you find yourselves in the water, stick together. Hang on to the boat, the oars, lifebelts or anything that will float. And whatever happens, hang on to each other. Do you all understand?"

There was a low murmur of assent. Nicolson flashed his torch round the inside of the boat. From what he could see in the sickly yellow light everybody was awake. Even their sodden, shapeless clothes couldn't disguise the peculiar tenseness of their attitudes. Quickly he switched off the light. Weak though the beam was, his pupils were narrowing enough to affect his night vision and he knew it.

"Still nothing, Bo'sun?" he called out.

"Nothing at all, sir. It's as black as a—wait a minute!" He stood there immobile, one hand on the mast, head cocked sideways, saying nothing.

"What is it, man?" Nicolson shouted. "What can you see?"

"Breakers!" McKinnon called. "Breakers or surf. I can hear it."

"Where? Where are they?"

"Ahead. Can't see them yet." A pause. "Starboard bow, I think."

"Cut the jib!" Nicolson ordered. "Mast down, Vannier." He leaned far over on the tiller, bringing the lifeboat round to face wind and sea. She answered the helm slowly, soggily; there were at least fifty gallons of sea-water swishing about the after end of the boat, but she came round eventually: even water-logged and in a running sea, she'd still carried enough way from the thrust of the jib.

"I can see it now." It was McKinnon shouting from the bows. "Starboard quarter, sir."

Nicolson twisted in his seat, looked quickly over his shoulder. For a moment or two he could see nothing, he couldn't even hear anything, and then he could both hear and see it, a thin white line in the darkness, a long continuous line that vanished and appeared again, closer than it had been when it faded. Surf, it must be surf, no breakers ever looked like that in the darkness. Thank God for so much anyway. Nicolson faced for'ard again.

" Right, Bo'sun, let it go."

McKinnon had been waiting the word, the iron-hooped mouth of the sea-anchor in his hands. Now he flung it as far for'ard into the sea as he could, paying out the warp as the sea-anchor filled and started dragging.

" Get those oars out!" Nicolson had already unshipped the rudder and drawn the shaft of the steering oar up through the grummet, sculling furiously to keep the lifeboat head on to sea until the sea-anchor took hold: no easy work when he couldn't make out the set of the waves in the darkness, when he'd nothing to guide him but the wind in his face and the water-logged movement of the boat. He could hear the scraping and muffled oaths as men tried to free trapped oars, then the metallic clunks as they dropped into the crutches. " Give way together," he called. " Easy, now, easy!"

He had no hope that they would pull together in the darkness, and he didn't expect it. Just so long as they pulled, he could correct any excesses with his steering oar. He glanced quickly over his shoulder. The line of surf was almost directly astern now, and its low sullen booming carried clearly to his ears, even against the wind. It could have been fifty yards away, it could have been two hundred and fifty yards away. It was impossible to tell in the darkness.

He faced round again, tried to peer for'ard, but the wind whipped the rain and the salt spray into his eyes, and he could see nothing. The wind appeared to be strengthening. He cupped his hands to his mouth and shouted. " How's it taking, McKinnon?"

" Och, it's just fine, sir. Taking grand." Several fathoms of the sea-anchor were already stretched out tautly over the bow, and the bo'sun had just finished stabbing the attached oil-bag with his gully knife. He'd made a thorough job of the stabbing, the oil wouldn't have to last for long, and the more they had over the surface of the sea the easier would be their passage through the surf. He passed the oil-bag over the bows, let some more of the warp pass through his hands, then tied it securely to the mast thwart.

They hadn't taken all the beaching precautions a moment too soon. The surf had been much nearer fifty than two hundred and fifty yards, and already they were almost on it. Carefully, expertly, making the fullest possible use of the oars, steering oar and sea anchor, Nicolson slowly backed the lifeboat on to the beginning of the smooth convexity of the swell of the surf. Almost immediately the boat picked up speed, rose and rode in swiftly with the giant wave as the oars came out of the water and McKinnon pulled the tripping line of the sea-anchor, sped along smoothly and soundlessly as the surf curved its way into seething white destruction, checked suddenly as oars dipped and the tripping line was released at Nicolson's sharp command, then plunged over the breaking crest of the surf and raced in to the shelving beach in a phosphorescent smother of foam and spray—there had been no time for the sea to carry the oil so far ahead—with the bar-taut anchor warp holding the stern pointing straight in to the shore, and the white water passing them by, out-distancing them in the race for the shore. It was then and only then, when the worst was safely by, that Nicolson, peering intently astern, saw something that shouldn't have been there. His hoarse shout of warning came almost on the instant of recognition, but it came too late.

The jagged rock—or maybe it was a knife-edge of coral—sliced the bottom out of the rushing boat, from the stern clear back to the bows. The jarring, braking shock jerked people free from their clutching handholds, flung them in headlong confusion, all arms and bodies and legs, towards the stern, and hurled two or three over the side into the water. A second later the wrecked boat slewed violently to the side and overturned, catapulting everyone into the seething afterwash of the surf.

Of the seconds that followed no one had afterwards any more than a confused, inchoate recollection, a recollection of being rolled over and over by the surging sea, of swallowing sea-water and scrambling to their feet on the shingly, shelving beach only to be knocked down and buffeted by the inverted lifeboat, scrambling to their feet again to have their legs sucked from under them by the retreating seas, struggling upright again and wading, staggering ashore to fling themselves down on the beach in gasping, heart-pounding exhaustion.

Nicolson made three trips to the beach altogether. The

first was with Miss Plenderleith. The shock of the collision had flung her hard against him even as they went over the stern, and he had instinctively tightened his arm round her as they had gone to the bottom together. She had been almost twice the weight he had expected, she had both her forearms locked through the handles of her heavy canvas travelling bag, and resisted Nicolson's efforts to tear it away with what he could only imagine to be a strength—an unreasoning suicidal strength—born of fear and panic. But he had got her ashore somehow, still grimly clutching her bag, waited his chance for the receding surf, then plunged back into the sea to help Vannier carry the captain ashore. Findhorn hadn't wanted assistance, he kept on repeating that he didn't want assistance, but his legs and his strength had gone as a result of his wound and the suffering of the past week, and he would have drowned where he had lain, in a couple of feet of water. Slipping, stumbling, falling and getting up again, they had carried him ashore bodily and dumped him on the shingle beyond the reach of the waves.

By now there were almost a dozen of them clustered in a tight knot on the beach, some lying, some sitting, some standing, indistinct blurs in the darkness who gasped for breath or moaned or retched sea-water in convulsive agony. Chest heaving and gasping for breath himself, Nicolson started to take a quick roll-call of those present. But he didn't even get beyond the first name.

"Gudrun. Miss Drachmann!" There was no reply, just the moaning and the painful retching. "Miss Drachmann! Has anyone seen Miss Drachmann? Has anyone got Peter?" There was only silence. "For God's sake, somebody answer! Has anyone seen Peter? The little boy? Has anyone seen him?" But there was only the sullen boom of the surf, the rustling shirr of the retreating sea dragging the shingle down the beach.

Nicolson dropped to his knees, felt the forms and faces of those who were lying on the beach. No Peter there, no Gudrun Drachmann. He jumped to his feet, knocked staggering someone who was standing in his way and rushed madly down into the sea, plunged out into the water and was knocked off his feet by the surge of the incoming surf. He was on his feet again like a cat, all his exhaustion gone as if it had never existed. He was vaguely conscious of someone plunging into the sea behind him but paid no attention.

Six running, splashing steps at the full stretch of his legs and something struck him with cruel, numbing force against the knee-caps. The boat, drifting upside down. He somersaulted in mid-air, struck his shoulder against the keel, landed flat on his back on the water on the other side with an explosive smack that drove all the breath out of his body, then was on his way again, propelled by a fear and a nameless anger such as he had never known before. The pain in his chest and his legs was another turn of the rack for every step he took, but he drove himself on remorselessly as if the fire in his legs and his body's gasping demands for air simply did not exist. Another two steps and he had crashed into something soft and yielding and knocked it backwards into the next incoming rush of water. He stooped, grabbed hold of a shirt and lifted, bracing the two of them against the surge of the sea.

" Gudrun?"

" Johnny! Oh, Johnny!" She clung to him and he could feel her trembling.

" Peter! Where's Peter?" he demanded urgently.

" Oh, Johnny!" The habitual cool self-possession was gone, and her voice was almost a wail. " The boat struck and—and——"

" Where is Peter?" His fingers digging deeply into her shoulders, he was shaking her violently, his voice a savage shout.

" I don't know, I don't know! I—I can't find him." She broke away, dived sideways into the water that was boiling waist-high by them. He caught her, jerked her to her feet and whirled round. It was Vannier who had followed him into the surf, and he was right behind him. He thrust the girl at him.

" Take her ashore, Vannier."

" I won't go! I won't!" She was struggling in Vannier's arms, but she hadn't the strength left to struggle very much. " I lost him! I lost him!"

" You heard me, Vannier?" Nicolson's voice as he turned away was a cutting whip. Vannier mumbled " Yes, sir " to the retreating back and started to drag the half-hysterical girl through the surf.

Again and again Nicolson plunged into the white water, his hands scrabbling desperately along the shingled bed of the sea: again and again he came up empty-handed. Once he thought he had found him, but it was only an empty bag; he threw it away like a man demented and flung himself yet farther out into the surf, near the coral that had sunk them. He was up almost shoulder high in the water now, being swept

196

off his feet with monotonous regularity, swallowing great mouthfuls of sea, shouting the name of the boy over and over again like some crazy litany, driving his exhausted body to incredible, inhuman efforts, driven by a horrifying fear, a dreadful anxiety that left him no longer sane, and anxiety such as he had not known could exist in the heart of any man. Two minutes, perhaps three, had elapsed since the boat had struck, and even in his madness he knew that the little boy could not have lived so long in these waters. What little reason he had left told him so, but he ignored it, dived once more through the creaming surf to the shingled floor of the sea. But again nothing, below the water or on the surface, only the wind, the rain, the darkness and the deep-throated booming of the surf. And then, high and clear above the wind and the sea, he heard it.

The child's thin, terrified cry came from his right, along the beach, about thirty yards away. Nicolson whirled and plunged in that direction, cursing the deep waters that reduced his stumbling run to grotesque slow-motion. Again the child cried, not a dozen feet away this time. Nicolson shouted, heard a man's answering call, and then all at once he was upon them, the looming bulk of a man as tall as himself, with the child high up in his arms.

"I am very glad to see you, Mr. Nicolson." Van Effen's voice was very faint and far away. "The little one is not harmed. Please to take him from me." Nicolson had barely time to snatch him in his arm before the Dutchman swayed on his feet, just once, then toppled and fell his length, face down in the foaming water.

CHAPTER THIRTEEN

THE JUNGLE, dank, dripping and steaming hot, was all around them. High above, through tiny gaps in the interwoven branches of heavily lianad trees, they could catch glimpses of the grey sullen sky, the same sky that had completely obscured the sunrise, just over two hours previously. The light that filtered down from these tree-tops had a strangely unreal quality, sinister and foreboding, but a quality that accorded well with the claustrophobic green walls of the jungle and the scummed, miasmal swamps that bounded both sides of the jungle path.

Even as a jungle path it was almost a failure. As far as the jungle was concerned, it offered a fairly free passage, and axe or machetes had evidently been busy, fairly recently, on either side. But as a path it was treacherous to a degree, one moment hard-packed and worn smooth by constant use, the next vanishing abruptly and mysteriously as it rounded a giant tree-trunk and dipped into the waiting swamps ahead then reappearing a few yards ahead, smooth and firm again.

Nicolson and Vannier, already covered to the waists in the rotting, evil-smelling slime, were beginning to discover the techniques for dealing with these sudden breaches in the path. Invariably, they were beginning to find, there was an alternative route round these swamp patches and if they cast around long enough they usually found it. But it took too long to seek out these bypasses and, more than once, they had wandered so far from the track that they had regained it only by chance, so that now, unless the bypass was almost immediately obvious, they plunged through the swamps and regained firm land on the other side, pausing every time to wipe off as much of the slime as possible and the ugly grey leeches that fastened to their legs. Then they would hurry on again, following the tortuous path round the massive trees as best they could in the weird, dim half-light of the tropical forest, trying their best to ignore the strange stirrings and rustlings that paralleled their progress on either side.

Nicolson was a seaman, first, last and all the time. He was little at home on land, still less so in the jungle, and this was not a journey that he would ever have made, would ever have contemplated making, had there been any option. But there had been no option, none whatsoever, a fact that had become cruelly evident soon after the first grey stirrings of dawn had let him look around to assess their position and the condition of the boat's company. Both had been very far from reassuring.

They had landed somewhere on the Java shore of the Sunda Straits, in a deep bay, two miles wide across the horns with a narrow shingled beach and a jungle that crowded down almost to the water's edge, a dense, impenetrable looking jungle that ran back into the high rain-forests that covered the slopes of the low hills to the south. The shores of the bay itself were completely empty of any life, animal or human, or any signs of life: there was only their own little company, huddled for what pitiful shelter they could under a cluster of palms, and, about a hundred yards along the beach, the up-turned lifeboat.

The lifeboat was in bad shape. A great hole, almost fifteen feet in length, had been ripped out between the keel and the bilge grab-rail, and the keel itself had been broken and wrenched away from its hog piece. The lifeboat was beyond repair, a total loss. There was only the jungle left for them, and they were in no condition to face that.

Captain Findhorn, for all his courage, was still a very sick man, unable to walk a dozen steps. Van Effen was weak too, and in considerable pain, violently sick at regular intervals: before Nicolson and McKinnon had succeeded in freeing his badly mangled leg from the clam that had seized it while he had been bringing the child ashore, he had almost drowned in the shallow water, and this, coupled with the shrapnel wound in the thigh received some days previously and the crack on the skull lately given him by Farnholme had dangerously lowered his resistance and powers of recuperation. Both Walters and Evans had swollen arms from infected wounds, and they, too, suffered constantly, while McKinnon, though in no great pain, limped on a badly stiffened leg. Willoughby was weak, Gordon shiftless and worse than useless and Siran and his men obviously intended to be of help to no one but themselves.

That left only Nicolson and the fourth officer, and Nicolson knew that there was nothing they could do for the others, not directly. To try to repair the lifeboat was out of the question, and to think of building any kind of boat or raft with the few tools they had left was just ridiculous. On land they were, and on land they would have to remain. But they couldn't remain on that beach indefinitely. If they did, they would starve. Nicolson had no illusions about their ability to survive for any time at all on the food they could scrape from trees, bushes, on and under the ground. An experienced jungle man might get enough for survival, but the chances were that they would poison themselves in the very first meal they took. Even if they didn't, bark and berries wouldn't keep seriously ill men alive for long, and without medicines and fresh bandages for infected and suppurating wounds, the outlook was bleak indeed.

Food, shelter, bandages and medicine—these were the essentials and wouldn't just come to them. They would have to go to look for them, to seek for help. How far distant help might be, and in what direction it would lie, was anybody's guess. The north-west corner of Java, Nicolson knew, had a fair population, and there were, he remembered, one or two largish towns some way inland. Too far inland—their best chances lay with the coastal fishing villages. They might encounter hostility instead of help, they might possibly encounter Japanese—in a mountainous land of forest and jungle like Java, they would almost certainly confine their activities to the coastal areas. But these possibilities, Nicolson realised, weren't even worth considering: they had to do this, and the incidental risks, no matter how severe, had to be ignored. Less than an hour after dawn he had taken a Colt .455—the only other salvaged weapon, the brigadier's machine-carbine he had left with McKinnon—and moved off into the jungle, Vannier close behind him.

Less than twenty yards inland, just before they had reached the belt of forest, they had struck a well-defined path, running north-east and south-west between the woods and the sea. Automatically, without even looking at one another, they had turned south-west: it wasn't until they had gone some distance that Nicolson realised why they had done it: in the long run, the south represented ultimate escape and freedom. Less than half a mile from where they had left the others, the beach to their left curved away to the west and north-west, following the lower horn of the bay: but the path had carried straight on across the base of the promontory, leaving the scrub and bushes and penetrating deep into the rain-forest itself.

Ninety minutes and three miles after leaving the beach Nicolson called a halt. They had just struggled through a thirty-yard patch of watery swamp that had taken them almost up to the armpits, and both men were exhausted. The effort, the sheer labour involved in their grotesquely slow-motion wading through these swamps was energy-sapping enough for men who had had little to drink and almost nothing to eat for a week: but even worse was the steaming jungle, the oppressive heat, the enervating humidity that stung and blinded their eyes with sweat.

Safe on a patch of firm ground, Nicolson sat and leaned his back against a thick tree-trunk. He wiped some mud off his forehead with the back of his left hand—the right still clutched the gun—and looked at Vannier, who had slid down almost full length on the ground, a forearm across his eyes, his chest rising and falling, deeply, quickly.

"Enjoying yourself, Fourth? I bet you never thought your

econd Mate's ticket was a licence for traipsing through the
adonesian jungles?" Unconsciously, almost, he kept his voice
own to a gentle murmur: the jungle, and everything about it,
reathed hostility.

"Bloody awful, isn't it, sir?" Vannier stirred, groaned
oftly as some aching muscle rebelled, then tried to smile.
These tree-swinging Tarzans you see in films give you a
uite erroneous idea of how progress is made through the
ungle. Me, I think this damn' path here just goes on for ever
nd ever. You don't think we're travelling in circles, do you,
r?"

"Possible enough," Nicolson admitted. "Haven't seen the
un all day, and it's so blasted thick overhead that you can't
ven see lightness in the sky. We *could* be going north, south,
r west, but I don't think so. I think this path will come out
gain to the sea."

"I hope you're right." Vannier was gloomy, but not depres-
ed. Looking at the thin, sun-darkened face, with the now too-
rominent cheekbones and the blistered, resolute mouth,
Nicolson thought that, in the past few days, the furnace of
rivation and experience had cast Vannier in a completely
lifferent mould, changing him from an irresolute, uncertain
oy to a toughened, determined man, a man aware of new-
ound resources and unsuspected capacities, a man well worth
aving by his side.

A minute, perhaps two, passed in silence, a silence marred
nly by the diminishing sound of their breathing and the
odden dripping of water in the leaves of the trees. Then,
bruptly, Nicolson stiffened, his left hand reaching out to
ouch Vannier warningly on the shoulder. But the warning
vas unheeded. Vannier, too, had heard it, was drawing his legs
inder him and rising steadily, noiselessly to his feet. Seconds
ater both men were standing behind the trunk of the tree,
vaiting.

The murmur of voices and the soft pad of footsteps on the
natted jungle floor came steadily nearer, the owners of the
voices still hidden by the curve in the trail, less than ten yards
away. They would have to wait till the last moment before
dentifying the approaching men, but it couldn't be helped.
Nicolson looked swiftly round for a better place of hiding
out there was none. The tree-trunk would have to do, and
pehind the tree-trunk they would wait. The approaching men
—it sounded as if there were only two of them—might be
Japanese. Even muffled by his shirt-front, the click of the

Colt's safety-catch sliding off sounded unnaturally loud:
month ago he would have shrunk from the thought of shoot
ing unsuspecting men from ambush; a month ago . . .

Suddenly the approaching men had rounded the bend in th
trail and were in full view. Three men, not two, and certainl
not Japanese, Nicolson realised with quick relief. Relief and
vague surprise: subconsciously he had expected, if no
Japanese, Sumatran natives dressed in the scanty minimun
the climate demanded and carrying spears or blow-pipes: tw
of the newcomers were dressed in denims and faded blu
shirts. Even more upsetting to preconceived notions was th
rifle the eldest of the three carried. But it didn't upset th
steadiness of the Colt in his hand. Nicolson waited until the
were only ten feet away then stepped out into the middle o
the path, the pistol barrel lined up motionless on the chest o
the man with the rifle.

The man with the rifle was quick. A break in mid-stride,
flicker of the seamed brown eyes under the straw hat and th
long snout of the rifle was swinging up as the left hand reache
down for the barrel. But the young man by his side was eve
quicker. His sinewy hand darted out and clamped down on th
barrel of the other's rifle, checking its upward sweep, and h
answered the surprise and anger in the other's face with quick
sharp words. The elder man nodded heavily, looked away an
let the gun droop till its muzzle almost touched the ground
Then he muttered something to the young man, who nodde
and looked at Nicolson, eyes hostile in a calm, smooth face

"*Begrijp U Nederlands?*"

"Dutch? Sorry, I don't understand." Nicholson lifted hi
shoulders in incomprehension, then looked briefly at Vannier
"Take his gun, Fourth. From the side."

"English? You speak English?" The young man's tongu
was slow and halting. He was peering at Nicholson with eyes
suspicious but no longer hostile, then his glance lifted an inch
or two above Nicolson's eyes and he suddenly smiled. He
turned and spoke rapidly to the man by his side, then looke
at Nicolson. "I tell my father you are English. I know you
hat. Of course you are English."

"This?" Nicolson touched the badge on his uniform cap.

"Yes. I live in Singapore"—he waved his hand vaguely
towards the north—"for almost two years. Often I see English
officers from ships. Why are you here?"

"We need help," Nicolson said bluntly. His first instinct
had been to temporise, make sure of his ground, but something

about the quiet dark eyes of the young man changed his mind: not he realised wryly, that he was in any position to temporise anyway. " Our ship has been sunk. We have many sick, many hurt. We need shelter, food, medicines."

" Give us back the gun," the young man said abruptly.

Nicolson didn't hesitate. " Give them back the gun, Fourth."

" The gun?" Vannier was apprehensive, and looked it. ' But how do you know——"

" I don't. Give them the gun." Nicolson thrust the Colt into his belt.

Reluctantly, Vannier handed the rifle back to the man in the straw hat. The man snatched it, folded his arms over his gun and stared off into the forest. The young man looked at him in exasperation, then smiled apologetically to Nicolson.

" You must excuse my father," he said haltingly. " You have hurt his feelings. Men do not take guns from him."

" Why?"

" Because Trikah is Trikah, and nobody dare." The young man's voice held a blend of affection and pride and amusement. " He is the headman of our village."

" He is your chief?" Nicolson looked at Trikah with new interest. On this man, on his capacity to make decisions, to lend or refuse aid, all their lives might depend. Now that he looked closely, Nicolson could see in the lined brown face, grave and unsmiling, the authority, the repose one would associate with the ruler of a tribe or village. Trikah, in appearance, was very like his son and the boy who stood some distance behind them—a younger son, Nicolson guessed. All three shared the low, wide forehead, intelligent eyes, finely chiselled lips and thin, almost aquiline nose: they had no negroid characteristics whatsoever, were almost certainly of unmixed Arabian descent. A good man to help you, Nicolson thought—if he would help you.

" He is our chief," the young man nodded. " I am Telak, his eldest son."

" My name is Nicolson. Tell your father I have many sick English men and women on the beach, three miles to the north. We must have help. Ask him if he will help us."

Telak turned to his father, spoke rapidly in a harsh staccato tongue for a minute, listened to his father, then spoke again. " How many are sick?"

" Five men—at least five men. There are also three women

203

—I do not think they could walk far. How many miles is it t
your village?"

"Miles?" Telak smiled. "A man can walk there in te
minutes." He spoke again to his father, who nodded severa
times as he listened, then turned and spoke briefly to the youn
boy by his side. The boy listened intently, appeared to repea
instructions, flashed his white teeth in a smile at Nicolson an
Vannier, turned quickly and ran off in the direction he ha
come.

"We will help you," Telak said. "My young brother ha
gone to the village—he will bring strong men and litters fo
the sick. Come, let us go to your friends."

He turned, led the way into an apparently impenetrabl
patch of forest and undergrowth, skirted the swamp throug
which Nicolson and Vannier had so lately waded, and le
them back on to the path again, all inside a minute. Vannie
caught Nicolson's eye and grinned.

"Makes you feel stupid, doesn't it? Easy enough when yo
know how."

"What does your friend say?" Telak asked.

"Just that he wishes we had had you with us earlier on,"
Nicolson explained. "We spent most of our time wading up to
the waists in swamps."

Trikah grunted an inquiry, listend to Telak, then muttered to
himself. Telak grinned.

"My father says only fools and very little children get their
feet wet in the forest. He forgets that one must be used to
it." He grinned again. "He forgets the time—the only time—
he was ever in a car. When it moved off he jumped over the
side and hurt his leg badly."

Telak talked freely as they walked along through the filtered
green light of the jungle. He made it quite obvious that he and
his father were in no way pro-British. Nor were they pro-
Dutch nor pro-Japanese. They were just pro-Indonesian, he
explained, and wanted their country for themselves. But, once
the war was over, if they had to negotiate with anyone for the
freedom of their country, they would rather do it with the
British or the Dutch. The Japanese made great protestations
of friendship, but once the Japanese moved in on a country,
they never moved out again. They asked for what they called
co-operation, Telak said, and already they were showing that
if they didn't get it one way, willingly, they would get it another—with the bayonet and the tommy-gun.

Nicolson looked at him in quick surprise and sudden dismay.

"There are Japanese near here? They have landed, then?"

"Already they are here," Telak said gravely. He gestured to the east. "The British and Americans still fight, but they cannot last long. Already the Japanese have taken over a dozen towns and villages within a hundred miles of here. They have—what do you call it—a garrison, they have a garrison at Bantuk. A big garrison, with a colonel in charge. Colonel Kiseki." Telak shook his head like a man shivering with cold. "Colonel Kiseki is not human. He is an animal, a jungle animal. But the jungle animals kill only when they have to. Kiseki would tear the arm off a man—or a little child—as a thoughtless child would pull the wings off a fly."

"How far away from your village is this town?" Nicolson asked slowly.

"Bantuk?"

"Where the garrison is. Yes."

"Four miles. No more."

"Four miles! You would shelter us—you would shelter so many within four miles of the Japanese! But what will happen if——"

"I am afraid that you cannot stay long with us," Telak interrupted gravely. "My father, Trikah, says it will not be safe. It will not be safe for you or for us. There are spies, there are those who carry information for reward, even among our own people. The Japanese would capture you and take my father, my mother, my brothers and myself to Bantuk."

"As hostages?"

"That is what they would call it." Telak smiled sadly. "The hostages of the Japanese never return to their villages. They are a cruel people. That is why we help you."

"How long can we stay?"

Telak consulted briefly with his father, then turned to Nicolson. "As long as it is safe. We will feed you, give you a hut for sleeping and the old women of our village can heal any wounds. Perhaps you can stay three days, but no more."

"And then?"

Telak shrugged his shoulders and led the way through the jungle in silence.

They were met by McKinnon less than a hundred yards from where the boat had beached the previous night. He was running, staggering from side to side, and not because of his stiffened leg: blood was trickling down into his eyes from a

205

bruised cut in the middle of his forehead, and Nicolson knew without being told who must have been responsible.

Furious, mortified and blaming only himself, McKinnon was very bitter, but no fault could really be attached to him The first he had known of the heavy hurtling stone that had knocked him unconscious was when he had recovered his senses and found it lying by his side, and no man can watch three others, indefinitely and simultaneously. The others had been powerless, for the concerted attack had been carefully planned and the only carbine in the company snatched by Siran from McKinnon even as he fell. Siran and his men, Findhorn said, had made off towards the north-east.

McKinnon was all for pursuing the men, and Nicolson, who knew that Siran, alive and free, was a potential danger no matter where he was, agreed. But Telak vetoed the idea. Impossible to find them in the jungle in the first place, he said: and searching for a man with a machine-gun who could pick his place of ambush and then lie still was a very quick way of committing suicide. Nicolson acknowledged the verdict of an expert and led them down to the beach.

Just over two hours later the last of the litter-bearers entered Trikah's *kampong*—the village clearing in the jungle. Small thin men but amazingly tough and enduring, most of the bearers had made the journey without being relieved of their loads or once stopping.

Trikah, the chief was as good as his promise. Old women washed and cleaned suppurating wounds, covered them with cool, soothing pastes, covered these in turn with large leaves and bound the whole with strips of cotton. After that, all were fed, and fed magnificently. More correctly, they were given a splendid selection of food to eat—chicken, turtle eggs, warmed rice, durians, crushed prawns, yams, sweet boiled roots and dried fish: but hunger had long since died, they had lived too long with starvation to do anything but token justice to the spread before them. Besides, the paramount need was not for food, but for sleep, and sleep they soon had. No beds, no hammocks, no couch of twigs or grass: just cocoa-nut matting on the swept earthen floor of a hut, and that was enough, more than enough, it was paradise for those who had been without a night's sleep for longer than their weary minds could remember. They slept like the dead, lost beyond call in the bottomless pit of exhaustion.

*　　　*　　　*

When Nicolson awoke, the sun had long gone and night had fallen over the jungle. A still, hushed night, and a still, hushed jungle. No chatter of monkeys, no cries of night birds, no sounds of any life at all. Just the hush and the stillness and the dark. Inside the hut it was hushed, too, and still, but not dark: two smoking oil lamps hung from poles near the entrance.

Nicolson had been deep sunk in drugged, uncaring sleep. He might have slept for hours longer, and would have, given the opportunity. But he did not awake naturally. He awoke because of a sharp stab of pain that reached down even through the mists of sleep, a strange unknown pain that pierced his skin, cold and sharp and heavy. He awoke with a Japanese bayonet at his throat.

The bayonet was long and sharp and ugly, its oiled surface gleaming evilly in the flickering light. Down its length ran the notched runnel for blood. At a distance of a few inches, it looked like a huge metallic ditch, and into Nicolson's uncomprehending, half-waking mind flickered evil visions of slaughter and mass burials. And then the film was away from his eyes, and his gaze travelled with sick fascination up the shining length of the bayonet, up to the barrel of the rifle and the bronzed brown hand that held it half-way down, beyond the bolt and magazine to the wooden stock and the other bronzed hand, beyond that again to the belted grey-green uniform and the face beneath the visored cap, a face with the lips drawn far back in a smile that was no smile at all, but an animal snarl of hate and expectancy, a sneering malignancy well matched by the blood lust in the porcine little eyes. Even as Nicolson watched, the lips drew still further back over the long, canine teeth, and the man leaned again on the stock of his rifle. The point of the bayonet went right through the skin at the base of the throat. Nicolson felt the waves of nausea flood over him, almost like the waves of the sea. The lights in the hut seemed to flicker and grow dim.

Seconds passed and his vision gradually returned. The man above him—an officer, Nicolson could see now, he had a sword by his side—had not moved, the bayonet still rested on his throat. Slowly, painfully, as best he could without moving head or neck even a millimetre, Nicolson let his eyes wander slowly round the hut, and the sickness came back to him again. Not from the bayonet, this time, but from the bitterness, the hopelessness that welled up in his throat in an almost physical tide of despair. His guard was not the only one in the hut. There must have been at least a dozen of them, all armed with rifles and bayonets, all with rifles and bayonets pointing down at the sleeping men and women. There was something weird and ominous about their silence and stealth and unmoving concentration. Nicolson wondered dimly whether they were all to be murdered in their sleep, and had no sooner done so when the man above him shattered the idea and the brooding silence.

"Is this the swine you spoke of?" He spoke in English, with the precise, grammatical fluency of an educated man who has not learned the language among the people who spoke it. "Is this their leader?"

"That is the man Nicolson." It was Telak who spoke, shadowed just beyond the doorway. He sounded remote, indifferent. "He is in charge of the party."

"Is that the case? Speak up, you English pig!" The officer emphasised his request with another jab at Nicolson's throat. Nicolson could feel the blood trickling slowly, warmly, on to the collar of his shirt. For a moment he thought to deny it, to tell the man that Captain Findhorn was his commanding officer, but instinct immediately told him that things would go very hard with the man whom the Japanese recognised as the leader. Captain Findhorn was in no condition to take any further punishment. Even a blow, now, could easily be enough to kill him.

"Yes, I am in charge." Even to himself, his voice sounded weak and husky. He looked at the bayonet, tried to gauge his chances of knocking it aside, recognised that it was hopeless. Even if he did, there were another dozen waiting men ready to shoot him down. "Take that damned thing away from my neck."

"Ah, of course! How forgetful of me." The officer removed his bayonet, stepped back a pace and then kicked Nicolson viciously in the side, just above the kidney. "Captain Yamata, at your service," he murmured silkily. "An officer in His Imperial Majesty's Nipponese Army. Be careful how you speak to a Japanese officer in future. On your feet, you swine." He raised his voice to a shout. "All of you, on your feet!"

Slowly, shakily, grey-faced beneath his dark tan and almost retching with the agony in his side, Nicolson rose to his feet. All around the hut others, too, were shaking off the dark fog of sleep and pushing up dazedly off the floor, and those who were too slow, too sick or too badly hurt were jerked cruelly upright regardless of their moans and cries and hustled out towards the door. Gudrun Drachmann, Nicolson saw, was one of those who were roughly handled; she had bent over to roll a still sleeping Peter in a blanket and gather him in her arms, and the guard had jerked them both up with a violence that must nearly have dislocated the girl's arm: the sharp cry of pain was hardly uttered before she had bitten it off in tight-lipped silence. Even in his pain and despair Nicolson found himself looking at her, looking and wondering, wondering at her patience and courage and the selfless unceasing devotion with which she had looked after the child for so many long days and endless nights, and as he looked and wondered he was conscious of a sudden and almost overwhelming sense of pity, conscious that he would have done anything to save this girl from further harm and hurt degradation, a feeling, he had to confess to himself with slow surprise, that he could never remember having had for any other than Caroline. He had known this girl for only ten days, and he knew her better than he would have known most in a dozen lifetimes: the quality and the intensity of their experiences and suffering in the past ten days had had the peculiar power and effect of selecting, highlighting and magnifying with a brutal and revealing clarity faults and merits, vices and virtues that might otherwise have remained concealed or dormant for years. But adversity and privation had been a catalyst that had brought the best and the worst into unmistakable view and, like Lachie McKinnon, Gudrun Drachmann had emerged shining and untarnished out of the furnace of pain and suffering and the extremest hardships. For a moment and incredibly, Nicolson forgot where he was, forgot the bitter past and empty future and looked again at the girl and he knew for the first time that he was deceiving himself, and doing it deliberately. It wasn't pity, it wasn't just compassion he felt for this slow-smiling scarred girl with a skin like a rose at dusk and the blue eyes of northern seas: or if it had been, it would never be again. Never again. Nicolson shook his head slowly and smiled to himself, then grunted with pain as Yamata drove the heel of his rifle between his shoulder blades and sent him staggering towards the door.

It was almost pitch dark outside, but light enough for Nicolson to see where the soldiers were taking them—towards the brightly-lit elders' meeting-place, the big square council house where they had eaten earlier, on the other side of the *kampong*. It was also light enough for Nicolson to see something else—the faint outline of Telak, motionless in the gloom. Ignoring the officer behind him, ignoring the certainty of another teeth-rattling blow, Nicolson stopped, less than a foot away from him. Telak might have been a man carved from stone. He made no movement, no gesture at all, just stood still in the darkness, like a man far lost in thought.

"How much did they pay you, Telak?" Nicolson's voice was hardly more than a whisper.

Seconds passed and Telak did not speak. Nicolson tensed himself for another blow on the back, but no blow came. Then Telak spoke, his words so faraway a murmur that Nicolson had to bend forward, involuntarily, to hear him.

"They paid me well, Mr. Nicolson." He took a pace forward and half-turned, so that his side and profile were suddenly caught in the light streaming from the door of the hut. His left cheek, neck, arm and upper chest were a ghastly mass of sword or bayonet cuts, it was impossible to tell where one began and the other ended; the blood seemed to mask the whole side of his body and, even as Nicolson watched, he could see it drip soundlessly on to the hard-beaten earth of the *kampong*. "They paid me well," Telak repeated tonelessly. "My father is dead, Trikah is dead. Many of our men are dead. We were betrayed and they took us by surprise."

Nicolson stared at him without speaking, all thought temporarily blocked by the sight of Telak—a Telak, he could see now, with another Japanese bayonet only inches from his back. Not one bayonet, but two: Telak would have fought well before they struck him down. And then thought did come, pity and shock that this should have happened, and so soon, to men who had so selflessly befriended them, then, swift on the heels of that thought, bitter regret for the words that he himself had just uttered, for the horribly unjust accusation that must have been the last few grains of salt in the wounds of Telak's sorrow and suffering. Nicolson opened his mouth to speak, but no words came out, only a gasp of pain as a rifle butt again thudded into his back, a gasp synchronised with Yamata's low, evil laugh in the darkness.

Rifle now reversed, the Japanese officer drove Nicolson across the *kampong* at the jabbing point of his bayonet. Ahead of him, Nicolson could see the others being herded through the sharply-limned rectangle of light that was the entrance to the council house. Some were already inside. Miss Plenderleith was just passing through, with Lena at her back, then Gudrun with Peter, followed closely by the bo'sun and Van Effen. Then Gudrun, approaching the door, stumbled over something on the ground, overbalanced with the weight of the little boy in her arms, and almost fell. Her guard caught her savagely by the shoulder and pushed. Perhaps he meant to push her through the door, but if he did his direction was bad, for girl and child together crashed heavily into the lintel of the doorway. Almost twenty feet away Nicolson could hear the thud of a head or heads against unyielding wood, the girl's exclamation of pain and young Peter's shrill, high-pitched cry of fear and hurt. McKinnon, only a few feet behind the girl shouted something unintelligible—his native Gaelic, Nicolson guessed—took two quick steps forward and leapt for the back of the guard who had pushed the girl: but the swinging rifle butt of the soldier behind was even faster and the bo'sun never saw it coming. . . .

*　　　*　　　*

The council house, brightly lit now with half a dozen oil-lamps, was a large, lofty room, twenty feet in width by thirty in length, with the entrance door in the middle of one of the longer sides. To the right hand side of the door, taking up nearly all the width of the room, was the elder's platform, with another door behind it leading out to the *kampong*. All the rest of the big wooden house, facing the door and to the left of it, was completely bare, hard-packed earth and nothing else. On this bare earth the prisoners sat in a small, tight semi-circle. All except McKinnon—Nicolson could just see him from where he sat, the shoulders, the lifeless, outflung arms and the back of the dark, curly head cruelly illuminated by the harsh bar of light streaming out from the doorway of the council house, the rest of his body shadowed in the darkness.

But Nicolson had only an occasional glance to spare for the bo'sun, none at all for the watchful guards who lounged behind them or with their backs to the doorway. He had eyes at the moment only for the platform, for the men on the platform, thoughts only for his own stupidity and folly and squeamishness, for the carelessness that had led them all, Gudrun and Peter and Findhorn and all the rest of them, to this dark end.

Captain Yamata was sitting on the platform, on a low bench, and next to him was Siran. A grinning, triumphant Siran who no longer bothered to conceal his emotions with an expressionless face, a Siran obviously on the best of terms with the broadly smiling Yamata, a Siran who from time to time removed a long black cheroot from his gleaming teeth and blew a contemptuous cloud of smoke in the direction of Nicolson. Nicolson stared back with bleak unwavering eyes, his face drained of all expression. There was murder in his heart.

It was all too painfully obvious what had happened. Siran had pretended to go north from the beach where they had land—a subterfuge, Nicolson thought savagely, that any child should have expected. He must have gone some little way to the north, hidden, waited until the litter-bearers had moved off, followed them, bypassed the village, moved on to Bantuk and warned the garrison there. It had all been so inevitable, so clearly what Siran had been almost bound to do that any fool should have foreseen it and taken precautions against it. The precautions consisting of killing Siran. But he, Nicolson, had criminally failed to take these precautions. He knew now that if he ever again had the chance he would shoot Siran with as little emotion as he would a snake or an old tin can. He knew also that he would never have the chance again.

Slowly, with as much difficulty as if he were fighting against the power of magnetism, Nicolson dragged his gaze away from Siran's face and looked round the others sitting on the floor beside him. Gudrun, Peter, Miss Plenderleith, Findhorn, Willoughby, Vannier—they were all there, all tired and sick and suffering, nearly all quiet and resigned and unafraid. His bitterness was almost intolerable. They had all trusted him, trusted him completely, implicitly depended upon him to do all in his power to bring them all safely home again. They had trusted him, and now no one of them would ever see home again . . . He looked away towards the platform. Captain Yamata was on his feet, one hand hooked in his belt, the other resting on the hilt of his sword.

"I shall not delay you long." His voice was calm and precise. "We leave for Bantuk in ten minutes. We leave to see my commanding officer, Colonel Kiseki, who is very anxious to see you all: Colonel Kiseki had a son who commanded the captured American torpedo boat sent to meet you." He was aware of the sudden quick looks between the prisoners, the sharp indrawing of breath and he smiled faintly. "Denial will serve you nothing. Captain Siran here will make an excellent witness. Colonel Kiseki is mad with grief. It would have been better for you—for all of you, each last one of you—had you never been born.

"Ten minutes," he went on smoothly. "Not more. There is something we must have first, it will not take long, and then e will go." He smiled again, looked slowly round the prisoners squatting on the floor beneath him. "And while we wait, I am sure you would all care to meet someone whom you think you know but do not know at all. Someone who is a very good friend of our glorious Empire, someone who, I feel sure, our glorious Emperor will wish to thank in person. Concealment is no longer necessary, sir."

There was a sudden movement among the prisoners, then one of them was on his feet, advancing towards the platform, speaking fluently in Japanese and shaking the bowing Captain Yamata by the hand. Nicolson struggled half-way to his feet, consternation and disbelief in every line of his face, then fell heavily to the ground as a rifle butt caught him across the shoulder. For a moment his neck and arm seemed as if they were on fire, but he barely noticed it.

"Van Effen! What the devil do you think——"

"Not Van Effen, my dear Mr. Nicolson," Van Effen protested. "Not 'Van' but 'von'. I'm sick and tired of masquerading as a damned Hollander." He smiled faintly and bowed. "I am at your service, Mr. Nicolson. Lieutenant-Colonel Alexis von Effen, German counter-espionage."

Nicolson stared at him, stared without speaking, nor was he alone in his shocked astonishment. Every eye in the council house was on Van Effen, eyes held there involuntarily while stunned minds fought to orientate themselves, to grasp the situation as it was, and memories and incidents of the past ten days slowly coalesced into comprehension and the tentative beginnings of understanding. The seconds dragged interminably by and formed themselves into a minute, and then almost another minute, and there were no more tentative wonderings and deepening suspicions. There was only certainty, stone cold certainty that Colonel Alexis von Effen was really who he claimed to be. There could be no doubt at all.

It was Van Effen who finally broke the silence. He turned his head slightly and looked out the door, then glanced again at his late comrades in distress. There was a smile on his face, but there was no triumph in it, no rejoicing, no signs of pleasure at all. If anything, the smile was sad.

"And here, gentlemen, comes the reason for all our trials and suffering of the past days, of why the Japanese—my people's allies, I would remind you—have pursued and harried us without ceasing. Many of you wondered why we were so important to the Japanese, our tiny group of survivors. Now you will know."

213

A Japanese soldier walked past the men and women on th
floor and dumped a heavy bag between Van Effen an
Yamata. They all stared at it, then stared at Miss Plenderleitl
It was her bag, and her lips and knuckles were pale as ivory
her eyes half-shut as if in pain. But she made no move an
said nothing at all.

At a sign from Van Effen the Japanese soldier took on
handle of the bag, while Van Effen took the other. Betweer
them they raised it to shoulder height, then inverted it. No
thing fell to the ground, but the heavily weighted lining drop
ped through the inverted mouth of the canvas and leather ba
and hung down below it as it were filled with lead. Van
Effen looked at the Japanese officer. " Captain Yamata?"

" My pleasure, Colonel." Yamata stepped forward, th
sword hissing from its sheath. It gleamed once in the brigh
yellow light from the oil-lamps, then its razored edge slice
cleanly through the tough canvas lining as if it had been s
much paper. And then the gleam of the sword was lost
buried, extinguished in the dazzling, scintillating stream o
fire that poured from the bag and pooled on the earth beneatl
in a deep, lambent cone of coruscating brilliance.

" Miss Plenderleith has quite a taste in gee-gaws and
trinkets." Van Effen smiled pleasantly and touched the spark
ling radiance at his feet with a casual toe. " Diamonds, Mr
Nicolson. The largest collection, I believe, ever seen outside
the Union of South Africa. These are valued at just under two
million pounds."

CHAPTER FOURTEEN

THE SOFT murmur of Van Effen's voice faded away and the
silence in the council house was heavy and deep. For each
man and woman there the others might not have existed
The great heap of diamonds at their feet, sparkling and flaming
with a barbaric magnificence in the light of the flickering oil
lamps, had a weirdly hypnotic quality, held every eye in
thrall. But by and by Nicolson stirred and looked up at Van
Effen. Strangely enough, he could feel no bitterness, no hostility towards this man : they had come through too much together, and Van Effen had come through it better than most, un-

214

selfish, enduring and helpful all the way. The memory of that was much too recent to be washed away.

" Borneo stones, of course," he murmured. " From Banjermasin by the *Kerry Dancer*—couldn't have been any other way. Uncut, I suppose—and you say they're worth two million?"

" Rough cut and uncut," Van Effen nodded. " And their market value is at least that—a hundred fighter planes, a couple of destroyers, I don't know. In wartime they're worth infinitely more to any side that gets its hands on them." He smiled faintly. " None of these stones will ever grace milady's fingers. Industrial use only—diamond-tipped cutting tools. A great pity, is it not?"

No one spoke, no one as much as glanced at the speaker. They heard the words, but the words failed to register, for that moment they all lived in their eyes alone. And then Van Effen had stepped quickly forward, his foot swinging, and the great pile of diamonds were tumbling over the earthen floor in a glittering cascade.

" Trash! Baubles!" His voice was harsh, contemptuous. " What matter all the diamonds, all the precious stones that ever were when the great nations of the world are at each other's throats and men are dying in their thousands and their hundreds of thousands? I wouldn't sacrifice a life, not even the life of an enemy, for all the diamonds in the Indies. But I have sacrificed many lives, and put many more I'm afraid, in deadly danger to secure another treasure, an infinitely more valuable treasure than these few paltry stones at our feet. What do a few lives matter, if losing them enables a man to save a thousand times more?"

" We can all see how fine and noble you are," Nicolson said bitterly. " Spare us the rest and get to the point."

" I have already arrived," Van Effen said equably. " That treasure is in this room, with us, now. I have no wish to prolong this unduly or seek after dramatic effect." He stretched out his hand. " Miss Plenderleith, if you please."

She stared at him, her eyes uncomprehending.

" Oh, now, come, come." He snapped his fingers and smiled at her. " I admire your performance, but I really can't wait all night."

" I don't know what you mean," she said blankly.

" Perhaps it may help you if I tell you that I know everything." There was neither gloating nor triumph in Van Effen's voice, only certainty and a curious overtone of weariness.

"Everything, Miss Plenderleith, even to that simple little ceremony in a Sussex village on 18th February, 1902."

"What the devil are you talking about?" Nicolson demanded.

"Miss Plenderleith knows, don't you, Miss Plenderleith?" There was almost compassion in Van Effen's voice: for the first time the life had faded from her lined old face and her shoulders were sagging wearily.

"I know." She nodded in defeat and looked at Nicolson. "He is referring to the date of my marriage—my marriage to Brigadier-General Farnholme. We celebrated our fortieth wedding anniversary aboard the lifeboat." She tried to smile, but failed.

Nicolson stared at her, at the tired little face and empty eyes, and all at once he was convinced of the truth of it. Even as he looked at her, not really seeing her, memories came flooding in on him and many things that had baffled him gradually began to become clear . . . But Van Effen was speaking again.

"18th February, 1902. If I know that, Miss Plenderleith, I know everything."

"Yes, you know everything." Her voice was a distant murmur.

"Please." His hand was still outstretched. "You would not care for Captain Yamata's men to search you."

"No." She fumbled under her salt-stained, bleached jacket, undid a belt and handed it to Van Effen. "I think this is what you want."

"Thank you." For a man who had secured what he had spoken of as a priceless treasure, Van Effen's face was strangely empty of all triumph and satisfaction. "This is indeed what I want."

He undid the pouches of the belt, lifted out the photostats and films that had lain inside and held them up to the light of the flickering oil-lamps. Almost a minute passed while he examined them in complete silence, then he nodded his head in satisfaction and returned papers and films to the belt.

"All intact," he murmured. "A long time and a long way —but all intact."

"What the devil are you talking about?" Nicolson demanded irritably. "What is that?"

"This?" Van Effen glanced down at the belt he was buckling round his waist. "This, Mr. Nicolson, is what makes everything worth while. This is the reason for all the action nd suffering of the past days, the reason why the *Kerry Dancer* and the *Viroma* were sunk, why so many people have died, why my allies were prepared to go to any length to prevent your escape into the Timor Sea. This is why Captain Yamata is here now, although I doubt whether even he knows that—but his commanding officer will. This is——"

"Get to the point!" Nicolson snapped.

"Sorry." Van Effen tapped the belt. "This contains the complete, fully detailed plans, in code, of Japan's projected invasion of Northern Australia. Japanese codes are almost impossible to break, but our people know that there is one man in London who could do it. If anyone could have escaped with these and got them to London, it would have been worth a fortune to the allies."

"My God!" Nicolson felt dazed. "Where—where did they come from?"

"I don't know." Van Effen shook his head. "If we had known that they would never have got into the wrong hands in the first place . . . The full-scale invasion plans, Mr. Nicolson —forces employed, times, dates, places—everything. In British or American hands, these would have meant three months' setback to the Japanese, perhaps even six. At this early stage of the war, such a delay could have been fatal to the Japanese: you can understand their anxiety to recover these. What's a fortune in diamonds compared to these, Mr. Nicolson?"

"What, indeed," Nicolson muttered. He spoke automatically, a man with his mind far away.

"But now we have both—the plans and the diamonds." There was still that strange, complete lack of any inflection of triumph in Van Effen's voice. He reached out a toe and touched the pile of diamonds. "Perhaps I was over hasty in expressing my contempt of these. They have their own beauty."

"Yes." The bitterness of defeat was sharp in Nicolson's mouth, but his face was impassive. "A fantastic sight, Van Effen."

"Admire them while you may, Mr. Nicolson." Captain Yamata's voice, cold and harsh, cut through the spell, brought them all tumbling back to reality. He touched the tip of the cone of diamonds with his sword-point and the white fire glittered and blazed as the stones spilled over on to the ground. "They *are* beautiful, but man must have eyes to see."

"What's that supposed to mean?" Nicolson demanded.

"Just that Colonel Kiseki has had orders only to recover the diamonds and deliver them intact to Japan. Nothing was said about prisoners. You killed his son. You will see what I mean."

"I can guess." Nicolson looked at him with contempt. "A shovel, a six by two hole and a shot in the back when I've finished digging. Oriental culture. We've heard all about it."

Yamata smiled emptily. "Nothing so quick and clean and easy, I assure you. We have, as you say, culture. Such crudities are not for us."

"Captain Yamata." Van Effen was looking at the Japanese officer, fractionally narrowed eyes the only sign of emotion in an expressionless face.

"Yes, Colonel?"

"You—you can't do that. This man is not a spy, to be shot without trial. He's not even a member of the armed forces. Technically, he's a non-combatant."

"Of course, of course." Yamata was heavily ironic. "To date he has only been responsible for the deaths of fourteen of our sailors and an airman. I shudder to think of the carnage if he ever became a combatant. And he killed Kiseki's son."

"He didn't. Siran will bear that out."

"Let him explain that to the colonel," Yamata said indifferently. He sheathed his sword. "We quibble, and uselessly. Come, let us go. Our truck should be here shortly."

"Truck?" Van Effen queried.

"We left it almost a mile away." Yamata grinned. "We did not wish to disturb your sleep. What's the matter, Mr. Nicolson?" he finished sharply.

"Nothing," Nicolson answered shortly. He had been staring out through the open doorway and in spite of himself a flicker of excitement had crossed his face, but he knew that his eyes had been safely away before Yamata had caught his expression. "The truck isn't here yet. I would like to ask Van Effen one or two questions." He hoped his voice sounded casual.

"We have a minute or two," Yamata nodded. "It might amuse me. But be quick."

"Thank you." He looked at Van Effen. "As a matter of interest, who gave Miss Plenderleith the diamonds—and the plans?"

"What does it matter now?" Van Effen's voice was heavy, remote. "It's all past and done with now."

"Please," Nicolson persisted. It had suddenly become essential to stall for time. "I really would like to know."

218

" Very well." Van Effen looked at him curiously. " I'll tell you. Farnholme had them both—and he had them nearly all the time. That should have been obvious to you from the fact that Miss Plenderleith had them. Where the plans came from I've told you I don't know: the diamonds were given him by the Dutch authorities in Borneo."

" They must have had a great deal of faith in him," Nicolson said dryly.

" They had. They had every reason to. Farnholme was utterly reliable. He was an infinitely resourceful and clever man, and knew the East—especially the islands—as well as any man alive. We know for a fact that he spoke at least fourteen Asiatic languages."

" You seem to have known a great deal about him."

" We did. It was our business—and very much to our interest—to find out all we could. Farnholme was one of our arch-enemies. To the best of our knowledge he had been a member of your Secret Service for just over thirty years."

There were one or two stifled gasps of surprise and the sudden low murmur of voices. Even Yamata had sat down again and was leaning forward, elbows on his knees, his keen dark face alight with interest.

" Secret Service!" Nicolson let his breath go in a long, soundless whistle of surprise, rubbed a hand across his forehead in a gesture of disbelief and wonderment. He had guessed as much five minutes ago. Under the protective cover of his hand his eyes flickered sideways for a split second, glanced through the open door of the council house, then looked at Van Effen. " But—but Miss Plenderleith said he commanded a regiment in Malaya, some years ago."

" That's right, he did." Van Effen smiled. " At least, he appeared to."

" Go on, go on." It was Captain Findhorn who urged him.

" Not much to go on with. The Japanese and myself knew of the missing plans, within hours of their being stolen. I was after them with official Japanese backing. We hadn't reckoned on Farnholme having made arrangements to take the diamonds with him also—a stroke of genius on Farnholme's part. It served a double purpose. If anyone penetrated his disguise as an alcoholic beachcomber on the run, he could buy his way out of trouble. Or if anyone were still suspicious of him and discovered the diamonds they would be sure to think that that accounted for his disguise and odd behaviour and let it go at that. And, in the last resort, if the Japanese discovered on what ship he was, he hoped that cupidity or their natural desire to recover such a valuable wartime merchandise would make them think twice about sinking the ship, in the hope that they might get the plans and so recover the diamonds another way, killing two birds with one stone. I tell you, Farnholme was brilliant. He had the most diabolically ill luck."

"It didn't work out that way," Findhorn objected. "Why did they sink the *Kerry Dancer*?"

"The Japanese didn't know he was aboard at the time," Van Effen explained. "But Siran did—he always did. He was after the diamonds, I suspect, because some renegade Dutch official double-crossed his own people and gave Siran the information in return for a promised share of the profits when Siran laid hands on the stones. He would never have seen a single guilder or stone. Neither would the Japanese."

"A clever attempt to discredit me." It was Siran speaking for the first time, his voice smooth and controlled. "The stones would have gone to our good friends and allies, the Japanese. That was our intention. My two men here will bear me out."

"It will be difficult to prove otherwise," Van Effen said indifferently. "Your betrayal this night is worth something. No doubt your masters will throw the jackal a bone." He paused, then went on: "Farnholme never suspected who I was—not, at least, until after we had been several days in the lifeboat. But I had known him all along, cultivated him, drunk with him. Siran here saw us together several times and must have thought that Farnholme and I were more than friends, a mistake anyone might make. That, I think, is why he rescued me—or rather didn't chuck me overboard when the *Kerry Dancer* went down. He thought I either knew where the diamonds were or would find out from Farnholme."

"Another mistake," Siran admitted coldly. "I should have let you drown."

"You should. Then you might have got the whole two million to yourself." Van Effen paused for a moment's recollection, then looked at the Japanese officer. "Tell me, Captain Yamata, has there been any unusual British naval activity in the neighbourhood recently?"

Captain Yamata looked at him in quick surprise. "How do you know?"

"Destroyers, possibly?" Van Effen had ignored the question. "Moving in close at night?"

220

" Exactly." Yamata was astonished. " They come close in
Java Head each night, not eighty miles from here, then re-
re before dawn, before our planes can come near. But
ow——"

" It is easily explained. On the dawn of the day the *Kerry
Dancer* was sunk, Farnholme spent over an hour in the radio
oom. Almost certainly he told them of his escape hopes—
outh from the Java Sea. No allied ship dare move north of
ndonesia—it would be a quick form of suicide. So they're
atrolling the south, moving close in at nights. My guess is
hat they'll have another vessel patrolling near Bali. You have
nade no effort to deal with this intruder, Captain Yamata?"

" Hardly." Yamata's tone was dry. " The only vessel we
ave here is our commander's, Colonel Kiseki's. It is fast
nough, but too small—just a launch, really only a mobile
adio station. Communications are very difficult in these
arts."

" I see." Van Effen looked at Nicolson. " The rest is ob-
ious. Farnholme came to the conclusion that it was no longer
afe for him to carry the diamonds round with him any longer
—nor the plans. The plans, I think, he gave to Miss Plender-
eith aboard the *Viroma*, the diamonds on the island—he
mptied his own bag and filled it with grenades . . . I have
ever known a braver man."

Van Effen was silent for a few moments, then continued.
The poor renegade Muslim priest was just that and no more:
Farnholme's story, told on the spur of the moment, was com-
letely untrue, but typical of the audacity of the man—to
ccuse someone else of what he was doing himself . . . And
ust one final thing—my apologies to Mr. Walters here." Van
Effen smiled faintly. " Farnholme wasn't the only one who
was wandering into strange cabins that night. I spent over an
our in Mr. Walters's radio room. Mr. Walters slept well. I
arry things with me that ensure that people will sleep well."

Walters stared at him, then glanced at Nicolson, remember-
ng how he had felt that next morning, and Nicolson remembered how the radio operator had looked, white, strained and
ick. Van Effen caught Walters's slow nod of understanding.

" I apologise, Mr. Walters. But I had to do it, I had to send
ut a message. I am a skilled operator, but it took me a long
ime. Each time I heard footsteps in the passage outside, I
died a thousand deaths. But I got my message through."

" Course, speed and position, eh?" Nicolson said grimly.

221

" Plus a request not to bomb the oil cargo tanks. You ju
wanted the ship stopped, isn't that it?"

" More or less," Van Effen admitted. " I didn't expect the
to make quite so thorough a job of stopping the ship, thoug
On the other hand, don't forget that if I hadn't sent th
message, telling them the diamonds were on board, they woul
probably have blown the ship sky-high."

" So we all owe our lives to you," Nicolson said bitterly
" Thank you very much." He looked at him bleakly for
long, tense moment, then swung his gaze away, his eyes s
obviously unseeing that no one thought to follow his gaz
But his eyes were very far indeed from unseeing, and ther
could be no doubt about it now. McKinnon had moved, an
moved six inches, perhaps nearer nine, in the past few minute
not in the uncontrolled, jerky twitchings of an unconsciou
man in deep-reaching pain, but in the stealthy, smoothly co
ordinated movements of a fully conscious person concentra
ting on inching silently across the ground, so silently, s
soundlessly, with such imperceptible speed that only a ma
with his nerves strung up to a pitch of hyper-sensitivity coul
have seen it at all. But Nicolson saw it, knew there could b
no mistake at all. Where originally there had been head
shoulders and arms lying in the bar of light that streamed ou
through the door, now there was only the back of the blac
head and one tanned forearm. Slowly, unconcernedly, his fac
an empty, expressionless mask, Nicolson let his gaze wande
back to the company. Van Effen was speaking again, watchin
him with speculative curiosity.

" As you will have guessed by now, Mr. Nicolson, Farn
holme remained safely in the pantry during the fight becaus
he was sitting with two million pounds in his lap and wasn'
going to risk any of it for any old-fashioned virtue of courag
and honour and decency. I remained in the dining-saloon
because I wasn't going to fire on my allies—and you will recal
that the only time I did—at the sailor in the conning-tower o
the submarine—I missed. A very convincing miss, I've alway
thought. After the initial attack no Japanese 'plane attacke
us on the *Viroma*, when we were clearing the boat—or after
wards: I had signalled with a torch from the top of th
wheelhouse.

" Similarly the submarine did not sink us—the captair
wouldn't have been very popular had he returned to base an
reported that he had sent two million pounds worth of dia
monds to the bottom of the South China Sea." He smiled

222

again without mirth. "You may remember that I wished to surrender to that submarine—you adopted a rather hostile view-point about that."

"Then why did that 'plane attack us?"

"Who knows?" Van Effen shrugged his shoulders. "Getting desperate, I suppose. And don't forget that it had a sea-plane in attendance—it could have picked up one or two selected survivors."

"Such as yourself?"

"Such as myself," Van Effen admitted. "Shortly after this Siran found out that I hadn't the diamonds—he searched my bag during one of the nights we were becalmed: I saw him do it and I let him do it, and there was nothing in it anyway. And it always lessened my chances of being stabbed in the back—which happened to his next suspect, the unfortunate Ahmed. Again he chose wrongly." He looked at Siran with unconcealed distaste. "I suppose Ahmed woke up while you were rifling his bag?"

"An unfortunate accident." Siran waved an airy hand. "My knife slipped."

"You have very little time to live, Siran." There was something curiously prophetic about the tone of Van Effen's voice, and the contemptuous smile drained slowly from Siran's face. "You are too evil to live."

"Superstitious nonsense!" The smile was back, the upper lip curled over the even white teeth.

"We shall see, we shall see." Van Effen transferred his gaze to Nicolson. "That's all, Mr. Nicolson. You'll have guessed why Farnholme hit me over the head when the torpedo boat came alongside. He had to, if he was to save your lives. A very, very gallant man—and a fast thinker." He turned and looked at Miss Plenderleith. "And you gave me quite a fright, too, when you said Farnholme had left all his stuff on the island. Then I realised right away that he couldn't have done that, because he'd never have a chance of going back there again. So I knew you must have it." He looked at her compassionately. "You are a very courageous lady, Miss Plenderleith. You deserved better than this."

He finished speaking, and again the deep, heavy silence fell over the council house. Now and again the little boy whimpered in his uneasy sleep, a small frightened sound, but Gudrun rocked and soothed him in her arms and by and by he lay still. Yamata was staring down at the stones, the thin aquiline face dark and brooding, seemingly in no hurry to move off. The prisoners were almost all looking at Van Effen their expressions ranging from astonishment to blank incredulity. Behind them stood the guards, ten or twelve in all, alert and watchful and their guns ready in their hands. Nicolson risked a last quick look out through the lighted doorway, felt the breath checking in his throat and the almost unconscious tightening of his fists. The doorway and the lighted oblong beyond it were completely empty. McKinnon had gone. Slowly, carelessly, easing out his pent-up breath in a long soundless sigh, Nicolson looked away—and found Van Effen's speculative eyes full upon him. Speculative—and understanding. Even as Nicolson watched, Van Effen looked sideways through the door for a long, meaningful moment, looked back at Nicolson again. Nicolson felt the chill wave of defeat wash through his mind, wondered if he could get to Van Effen's throat before he spoke. But that would do no good, it would only postpone the inevitable. Even if he killed him—but Nicolson knew he was fooling himself, he hadn't a chance, and even if he had, even to save themselves, he could do Van Effen no harm. He owed Van Effen a life—Peter's. Van Effen could have freed himself very easily that morning—the clam hadn't been all that large. He could have let Peter go and released himself by the use of both his hands: but he had elected, instead, to stand there in agony with the child in his arms and have his leg badly mauled and cut . . . Van Effen was smiling at him, and Nicolson knew it was too late to stop him from speaking.

" Beautifully done, wasn't it, Mr. Nicolson?"

Nicolson said nothing. Captain Yamata lifted his head and looked puzzled. " What was beautifully done, Colonel?"

" Oh, just the whole operation." Van Effen waved his hand. " From beginning to end." He smiled deprecatingly, and Nicolson could feel the blood pounding in his pulse.

" I don't know what you're talking about," Yamata growled. He rose to his feet. " Time we were going. I can hear the truck coming."

" Very well." Van Effen flexed his wounded leg stiffly: with the clam bite and the shrapnel wound in his thigh it was almost useless to him. " To see your colonel? To-night?"

" Inside the hour," Yamata said briefly. " To-night Colonel Kiseki entertains important headmen and chiefs in his villa. His son lies dead, but duty crushes grief. Crushes it, I say, not kills it. But the sight of all these prisoners will lighten his saddened heart."

Nicolson shivered. Someone, he thought wryly, walking over his grave. Even without the almost sadistic anticipation in Yamata's voice, he had no illusions as to what lay in store for himself. For a moment he thought of all the stories he had heard of Japanese atrocities in China, then resolutely pushed the thought away. An empty mind on a razor edge was his only hope, he knew, and that no hope at all. Not even with McKinnon out there, for what could McKinnon do except get himself killed. The thought that the bo'sun might try to make good his own escape never crossed Nicolson's mind. McKinnon just wasn't made that way . . . Van Effen was speaking again.

"And afterwards? When the colonel has seen the prisoners? You have quarters for them?"

"They won't need quarters," Yamata said brutally. "A burial party will be all that's required."

"I'm not joking, Captain Yamata," Van Effen said stiffly.

"Neither am I, Colonel." Yamata smiled, said no more. In the sudden silence they could hear the squeal of brakes and the blipping of an accelerator as the truck drew up in the middle of the *kampong*. Then Captain Findhorn cleared his throat.

"I am in charge of our party, Captain Yamata. Let me remind you of international wartime conventions." His voice was low and husky, but steady for all that. "As a captain in the British Mercantile Marine, I demand——"

"Be quiet!" Yamata's voice was almost a shout, and his face was twisted in ugliness. He lowered his voice until it was almost a whisper, a caressing murmur more terrifying by far than a roar of anger. "You demand nothing, Captain. You are in no position to demand anything. International conventions! Bah! I spit at international conventions. These are for the weak, for simpletons and for children. The strong have no need for them. Colonel Kiseki has never heard of them. All Colonel Kiseki knows is that you have killed his son." Yamata shivered elaborately. "I fear no man on earth, but I fear Colonel Kiseki. Everyone fears Colonel Kiseki. At any time he is a terrible man. Ask your friend there. He has heard of him." He pointed at Telak, standing in the background between two armed guards.

"He is not a man." All Telak's left side was ridged and lumped in long streaks of coagulated blood. "He is a fiend. God will punish Colonel Kiseki."

"Ah, so?" Yamata said something quickly in Japanese, and

Telak staggered back as a rifle butt jabbed cruelly into his face. "Our allies," Yamata purred apologetically, "but they have to be educated. In particular, they must not speak ill of our senior army officers . . . At any time, I said, Colonel Kiseki is a terrible man. But now that his only son has been killed . . ." He allowed his voice to trail off into silence.

"What will Colonel Kiseki do?" There was no trace of emotion, of any feeling in Van Effen's voice. "Surely the women and children——"

"They will be the first to go—and they will take a long time going." Captain Yamata might have been discussing arrangements for a garden party. "Colonel Kiseki is a connoisseur, an artist in this sort of thing—it is an education for lesser men such as myself to watch him. He thinks mental suffering is no less important than physical pain." Yamata was warming to his subject, and finding it more than pleasant. "For instance, his main attention will be directed towards Mr. Nicolson here."

"Inevitably," Van Effen murmured.

"Inevitably. So he will ignore Mr. Nicolson—at first, that is. He will concentrate instead on the child. But he may spare the boy, I don't know, he has a strange weakness for very small children." Yamata frowned, then his face cleared. "So he will pass on to the girl here—the one with the scarred face. Siran tells me she and Nicolson are very friendly, to say the least." He looked at Gudrun for a long moment of time, and the expression on his face woke murder in Nicolson's heart. "Colonel Kiseki has rather a special way with the ladies— especially the young one: a rather ingenious combination of the green bamboo bed and the water treatment. You have heard of them, perhaps, Colonel?"

"I have heard of them." For the first time that evening Van Effen smiled. It wasn't a pleasant smile, and Nicolson felt fear for the first time, the overwhelming certainty of ultimate defeat. Van Effen was toying with him, the cat with the mouse, sadistically lending false encouragement while waiting for the moment to pounce. "Yes, indeed I have heard of them. It should be a most interesting performance. I presume I shall be permitted to watch the—ah—festivities?"

"You shall be our guest of honour, my dear Colonel," Yamata purred.

"Excellent, excellent. As you say, it should be most educative." Van Effen looked at him quizzically, waved a lacka-daisical hand towards the prisoners. "You think it likely that

Colonel Kiseki will—ah—interview them all? Even the wounded?"

"They murdered his son," Yamata answered flatly.

"Quite so. They murdered his son." Van Effen looked again at the prisoners, and his eyes were bleak and cold. "But one of them also tried to murder me. I don't think Colonel Kiseki would miss just one of them, would he?"

Yamata raised his eyebrows. "I'm not quite certain that I——"

"One of them tried to kill me," Van Effen said harshly. "I have a personal score to settle. I would take it as a great favour, Captain Yamata, to be able to settle that score now."

Yamata looked away from the soldier who was pouring the diamonds back into the torn bag and stroked his chin. Nicolson could once more feel the blood pounding in his pulse, forced himself to breathe quietly, normally. He doubted if anyone else knew what was going on.

"I suppose it is the least you are entitled to—we owe you a very great deal. But the colonel——" Suddenly the doubt and uncertainty cleared from Yamata's face, and he smiled. "But of course! You are a senior allied officer. An order from you——"

"Thank you, Captain Yamata," Van Effen interrupted. "Consider it given." He whirled round, limped quickly into the middle of the prisoners, bent down, twisted his hand in Gordon's shirt-front and jerked him viciously to his feet. "I've been waiting a long time for this, you little rat. Get across there." He ignored Gordon's struggles, his fear-maddened face and incoherent protestations of innocence, marched him across to an empty space at the back of the council house, at a point directly opposite the door, and flung him into a huddled heap, sprawled almost his length against the back wall of the hut, one arm raised in pathetic defence, unreasoning panic limned in every line of his unlovely face.

Van Effen ignored the panic, the protestations and the man, turned quickly round and limped across towards the elders' platform, towards the Japanese soldier who stood with his own rifle under one arm and Farnholme's machine-carbine under the other. With the careless assurance of a man who expects neither question nor resistance, Van Effen firmly relieved the soldier of the machine-carbine, checked that it was fully loaded, slipped the catch to automatic and hobbled back again towards Gordon who still lay where he had left him, eyes unnaturally wide and staring, moaning softly, long, quivering indrawn breaths were the only sound in the room. Every eye in the room was on Van Effen and Gordon, eyes that reflected various states of pity or anger or anticipation or just blank incomprehension. Nicolson's face was quite expressionless, Yamata's almost so, but the tongue running slowly over his lips gave him away. But no one spoke, no one moved, no one thought to speak or move. A man was about to be killed, to be murdered, but some indefinable factor in that electric atmosphere prevented any protest, any interruption, from anyone inside that house. And when the interruption did come, a sudden, jarring shock that shattered the spell as a stone might shatter a delicate crystal, it came from the *kampong* outside.

The high-pitched yell in Japanese jerked every head towards the door. Immediately afterwards came the sound of a short, sharp scuffle, a cry, a revolting, hollow sound like a giant cleaver splitting a water-melon, a momentary, weirdly ominous silence, then a roar and a rush of smoke and flame and the doorway and most of the wall were engulfed, with incredible speed, in a leaping, crackling wall of flame.

Captain Yamata took two steps towards the doorway, opened his mouth to shout an order and died with his mouth still open, the slugs from Van Effen's carbine tearing half his chest away. The staccato hammering of the machine-gun inside the room was almost deafening, completely blotting out the roar of the flames. The sergeant still on the platform died next, then a soldier beside him, then a great red flower spread outwards from the centre of Siran's face, and still Van Effen crouched low over the slowly swinging barrel of his carbine, his hand locked on the trigger, his face that of a man carved from stone. He staggered when the first Japanese rifle bullet caught him high up on the shoulder, stumbled and fell to one knee as a second bullet smashed into his side with the force of a battering ram, but still no flicker of expression crossed his face and the ivory-knuckled trigger finger only tightened the more. That much and that only Nicolson saw before he catapulted himself backwards and crashed into the legs of a soldier lining his tommy-gun on the man by the far wall. They went down together in a writhing, twisting, furiously struggling heap, then Nicolson was smashing the butt of the tommy-gun again and again into the dark blur of the face before him and was on his feet once more, knocking aside a gleaming bayonet blade and kicking viciously for an unprotected groin.

Even as he closed with the man, hooked fingers locking

228

ound a scrawny throat, he was conscious that Walters and Evans and Willoughby were on their feet also, fighting like madmen in the weird half-light compounded of the red glare of the flames and the choking acrid smoke that filled the room. He was conscious, too, that Van Effen's machine-carbine had fallen silent, that another machine-gun, with a different cyclic rate, was firing through the licking, resinous flames that all but curtained off the doorway. And then he had forgotten all about these things, another man had seized him from behind and locked an elbow round his throat, strangling him in a grim and savage silence. There was a red mist, a mist shot through with sparks and flame, swimming before his eyes, and he knew it was his own blood pounding in his head and not the furiously burning walls of the council house. His strength was going, he was just sliding away into the darkness, when he vaguely heard the man behind him cry out in agony, and then McKinnon had him by the arm, leading him at a stumbling run out through the blazing doorway. But they were too late— too late at least for Nicolson. The blazing overhead beam falling from the roof caught him only a glancing blow on head and shoulder, but it was enough, in his weakened state more than enough, and the darkness closed over him.

He came to almost a minute later, lying huddled against the wall of the nearest upwind hut from the council house. He was dimly aware of men standing and moving around him, of Miss Plenderleith wiping blood and soot from his face, of the great tongue of flame licking thirty or forty feet vertically upwards into a dark and starless sky as the coucil house, a wall and most of the roof already gone, burnt torch-like to destruction.

Consciousness returned. He staggered to his feet, pushing Miss Plenderleith ungently to one side. All firing had stopped now, he realised, and he could hear the distant sound of a truck engine revving and fading, revving and fading as it slammed through the gears—the Japanese, or what few of them were left, leaving in a panic-stricken hurry.

" McKinnon!" He had to raise his voice above the crackling roar of the flames. " McKinnon! Where are you?"

" He's round the other side of that house, somewhere." It was Willoughby speaking, and he was pointing to the burning council house. " He's all right, Johnny."

" Everybody out?" Nicolson demanded. " Anybody left inside that thing. For God's sake tell me!"

" They're all out, I think, sir." Walters was at his side, his voice hesitant. "Nobody left where we were all sitting, I know that."

"Thank God, thank God!" He stopped abruptly. "Is Van Effen out?"

No one said anything.

"You heard what I said," Nicolson shouted. "Is Van Effen out?" He caught sight of Gordon, reached him in two steps and caught him by the shoulder. "Is Van Effen still in there? You were nearest him."

Gordon stared at him blankly, his eyes still wide with fear. His mouth was working, the lips jerking and twisting in uncontrollable fashion, but no words came out. Nicolson released his grip on the shoulder, struck him twice, savagely, across the face, open-handed and back-handed, caught him again before he could fall.

"Answer me or I'll kill you, Gordon. Did you leave Van Effen in there?"

Gordon nodded his head jerkily, his fear-whitened face wealing red from the imprint of Nicolson's fingers.

"You left him in there?" Nicolson demanded incredulously. "You left him to die in that inferno?"

"He was going to murder me!" Gordon whined. "He was going to kill me."

"You bloody fool! He saved your life. He saved all our lives." He sent Gordon staggering with a savage shove, brushed off a couple of restraining hands and had covered the ten paces to the council house and leapt through the sheeted flame of the doorway before he had properly realised what he was doing.

The heat inside struck at him with the physical impact of a violent blow, he could feel it engulf him, wash over him in a great wave of burning pain. The superheated air, starved now of its life-giving oxygen, seared down into his lungs like fire itself. He could smell his hair singeing almost immediately, and the tears flooded into his eyes and threatened to blind him, and had it been any darker inside he would have been blinded: but in the savage red glare of the flames it was as bright, almost, as the noon-day sun.

There was no difficulty in seeing Van Effen. He was huddled against the still intact far wall, sitting on the ground, propped up on one arm. His khaki shirt and drill trousers were saturated with blood, and his face was ashen. Gasping, choking, his heaving lungs fighting for air and getting none, Nicolson stumbled as fast as he could across to the far wall of the council house. He had to hurry, he knew, he could last only moments in this atmosphere, half a minute at the most. His clothes were already smouldering, torn edges smoking and burning irregularly red, his tortured lungs couldn't find the oxygen for his rapidly weakening body and the heat on his face and body was like a blast furnace.

Van Effen looked at him vaguely, without either expression or comment. Probably half dead already, Nicolson thought, God only knew how the man had survived even that long. He stooped, tried to pry Van Effen's fingers free from the guard and trigger of the machine-carbine, but it was hopeless, the hand was locked across the metal like a band of iron. There was no time to lose, perhaps it was already too late. Gasping, struggling, the sweat running off his overheated body in streams, Nicolson put out the last of his fading strength in one despairing effort and raised the wounded man up in his arms.

He had covered half the return journey when a crackling, rending noise, loud even above the roar of the flames, made him break step and halt just in time as several blazing, smoking timbers from the roof crashed to the ground in a pyrotechnic eruption of flying sparks and red-hot embers not three feet from where he stood. The doorway was completely blocked off. Nicolson jerked back his head, stared upwards through smarting, sweat-filmed eyes, gathered a hasty blurred impression of a crumbling, caving roof already falling in upon him, and waited no longer. Four stumbling, plunging steps it took him to cross the blazing beams that lay between them and the doorway, and four steps were eternity. The now tindery dry khaki drills caught fire immediately and the writhing cocoons of flame ran up his legs so fast and so far that he could feel their hungry tips licking agonisingly at the bare forearms that supported the dead weight of Van Effen. Red-hot swords of fire pierced the soles of his feet in merciless excoriation and his nostrils were full of the sickening stench of scorching flesh. His mind was going, his strength was gone, and no sense of time or purpose or direction was left him when he felt urgent hands catching him by the arms and shoulders and pulling him out into the cool, sweet, life-giving air of the evening.

It would have been the easiest thing in the world to hand Van Effen over to outstretched arms, to collapse himself on the ground and let the waiting wave of unconsciousness wash over him and carry him off to merciful oblivion, and the temptation to do both was almost irresistible. But he did neither, just stood instead with wide-planted feet, sucking giant

draughts of air into a body that seemed able to accommodat
only a fraction of what it needed. Seconds passed and hi
mind began to clear, the trembling in his legs eased, and h
could see Walters and Evans and Willoughby crowding roun
him, but he ignored them, brushed through and carried Var
Effen to the shelter of the nearest up-wind hut in the *kam
pong*.

Slowly, with an infinite gentleness, he lowered the woundec
man to the ground, and started to unbutton the holed anc
blood-stained shirt. Van Effen caught his wrists with feeble
hands.

"You are wasting your time, Mr. Nicolson." His voice was
only a feeble murmur with blood in it, barely audible above
the crackling roar of the flames.

Nicolson ignored him, ripped the sides of the shirt apart
and winced in shock at the sight that lay below. If Van Effen
were to live, he would have to be strapped up, and at once.
He tore off his own charred and shredded shirt, ripped it and
padded the wounds as his eyes travelled up to the German's
white, pinched face. Van Effen's lips twisted in some kind of a
smile, it might have been a sardonic smile, but it was difficult
to tell without reading the expression in his eyes, and it was
no longer possible to read anything in Van Effen's eyes for
they were already misted over with the glaze of approaching
unconsciousness.

"I told you—don't waste time," he murmured. "The
launch—Kiseki's launch. Get it. It has a radio, probably a
big transmitter—you heard what Yamata said ... Walters can
send a message." His voice was an urgent whisper. "At once,
Mr. Nicolson, at once." His hands dropped away from Nicolson's wrists and fell limply by his side, palm upwards on the
hard-packed earth of the *kampong*.

"Why did you do it, Van Effen?" Nicolson stared down at
the sick man and shook his head, slowly, wonderingly, from
side to side. "Why in the name of heaven did you do it?"

"God only knows. Or maybe I know also." He was breathing very rapidly, very shallowly, now, with only a few gasping
words to every breath. "Total war is total war, Mr. Nicolson,
but this is work for barbarians." He gestured weakly at the
blazing hut. "If any one of my countrymen could have
been with me to-night, he would have done what I have done.
We're people, Mr. Nicolson, we're just people." He reached up
one flaccid hand, pulled the opened shirt to one side, and
smiled. "If you cut us, do we not bleed?" He burst into a
232

paroxysm of bubbling, whooping coughs that contracted torn stomach muscles and lifted head and shoulders clear of the ground, then sank back again, so quiet, so still, that Nicolson stooped quickly forward, in sudden surety that the man was gone. But Van Effen lifted his eyelids again, with the slowness and infinite effort of a man raising a massive weight and smiled at Nicolson through filmed and misted eyes.

"We Germans do not go easily. This is not the end of van Effen." He paused for a long moment, went on in a whisper: "Winning a war costs a great deal. It always costs a great deal. But sometimes the cost is too high, and it is not worth the price. To-night the cost, the price asked, was far too high. I—I could not pay the price." A great gout of flame shot up from the roof of the council house, bathing his face in its red and savage glare, then it died down again and his face was white and still and he was murmuring something about Kiseki.

"What is it?" Nicolson was so low over him now that their faces were almost touching. "What did you say?"

"Colonel Kiseki." Van Effen's voice was very far away. He tried to smile again, but it was only a pathetic twitch of his lower lip. "Perhaps we have something in common. I think——" Here his voice faded into nothingness, then came again, strongly. "I think we both have a weakness for very little children."

Nicolson stared down at him, then twisted round as a loud, rending crash echoed across the *kampong* and a sheet of flame leapt up, a flame that illumined every remotest corner of the little village. The council house, its last supports burnt out, had collapsed in on itself and was burning more furiously than ever. But only for a moment. Even as Nicolson watched the licking tongues of flame shrank back down towards the earth and the dark gloomy shadows crept forward from every side. Nicolson looked away and bent down to talk again to Van Effen, but Van Effen was unconscious.

Slowly, wearily, Nicolson straightened himself, but remained sunk on his knees, staring down at the grievously wounded man. All at once the exhaustion, the despair, and the sharp, fiery agony of his legs and feet and arms flooded in on him and the temptation to let himself go, to slip into the friendly, embracing darkness that hovered round the woolly, shadowed edges of his mind was almost overpowering. He was actually swaying backwards and forwards on his knees, eyes all but closed and his arms swinging limply from his shoulders, when he heard a voice shouting, the sound of feet thudding across the *kampong* at a dead run and felt the hard urgent fingers biting cruelly through the red charred skin of his upper arm.

"Come on, sir, come on! For God's sake get to your feet!" There was a fierceness, a burning desperation in McKinnon's voice that Nicolson had never heard before. "They've got them, sir. Those yellow devils have taken them away!"

"What? What?" Nicolson shook his aching fuzzy head from side to side. "They've taken what away? The plans, the diamonds? They're welcome to all——"

"I hope the diamonds go to hell and roast there with every little yellow bastard in the East." McKinnon was half-sobbing, half-shouting at the top of his voice in a voice Nicolson had never heard before, his eyes were flooded with tears, his great fists white-knuckled by his side, and he was quite mad, insane with rage. "It's not only the diamonds they've taken, sir, I wish to God it was. The inhuman devils have taken hostages with them, I saw them throw them into their truck. The captain, Miss Drachmann and that poor wee boy!"

CHAPTER FIFTEEN

BEYOND ANGER lies fury, the heedless, ungovernable rage of the berserker, and beyond that again, a long, long step beyond the boundary of madness, lies the region of cold and utterly uncaring indifference. When a man enters that region, as few ever do, he is no longer himself, he is a man beside himself, a man outwith all his normal codes and standards of feeling and thought and emotions, a man for whom words like fear and danger and suffering and exhaustion are words that belong to another world and whose meaning he can no longer comprehend. It is a state characterised by an abnormally heightened clarity of mind, by a hyper-sensitive perception of where danger lies, by a total and unhuman disregard for that danger. It is, above all, a state characterised by an utter implacability. It was in such a state that Nicolson found himself at half-past eight on the evening of that day in late February, seconds only after McKinnon had told him that Gudrun and Peter were gone.

His mind was clear, unnaturally so, swiftly weighing up the

234

situation as far as he knew it, balancing the possibilities and the probabilities, racing ahead and formulating the only plan that could offer any hope at all of success. His weariness, the sheer physical exhaustion, had dropped from him like a falling cloak: he knew the change was psychological, not physiological, that he would pay heavily for it later, but it didn't matter, he was oddly certain that no matter what the source of his energy, it would carry him through. He was still aware, remotely, of the severe burns on his legs and arms, of the pain in his throat where the Japanese bayonet had bitten in so deeply, but his awareness was no more than an intellectual acknowledgment of these burns and wounds, they might well have belonged to another man.

His plan was simple, suicidally simple, and the chances of failure so high that they seemed inevitable, but the thought of failure never entered his mind. Half a dozen questions fired at Telak, the same at McKinnon and he knew what he must do, what everyone must do if there was to be any hope at all. It was McKinnon's story that settled the problem for him.

The council house had blazed so fiercely, had gone up with such incredible speed, for one reason only—McKinnon had saturated the whole windward wall with the contents of a four-gallon can of petrol. He had stolen this from the Japanese truck within a couple of minutes of its arrival—the driver had kept careless watch and was now lying on the ground, less than ten feet away—and he had been just on the point of setting fire to it when a patrolling sentry had almost literally stumbled across him. But he had done more than steal the petrol, he had tried to immobilise the truck. He had searched for the distributor, failed to find it in the darkness, but had located the carburettor intake fuel line, and the soft copper had bent like putty in his hands. It seemed unlikely, impossible rather, that the truck could get much more than a mile on the cupful of fuel that remained—and it was four miles to the town of Bantuk.

Quickly, Nicolson asked Telak for co-operation, and got it at once. With his father and several of his tribesmen dead, neutrality no longer existed for Telak. He said little, but what little he did say was bitter and savage and concerned with nothing but vengeance. He nodded immediate compliance to Nicolson's request that he provide a guide to lead the main party—only seven now, all told, under the leadership of Vannier—via the main road to Bantuk, where they were to seize and board the launch, if this could be done in absolute silence, and rapidly translated to one of his tribesmen, giving him the rendezvous. He then ordered half a dozen of his men to search the dead Japanese soldiers lying around the *kampong* and to bring all their weapons and ammunition to a central spot. A tommy-gun, two automatic rifles and a strange automatic pistol proved to be still serviceable. Telak himself disappeared into a nearby hut and emerged with two Sumatran parangs, honed to razor-sharp edges, and a couple of curious, elaborately-chased daggers, ten inches long and shaped like a flame, which he stuck in his own belt. Within five minutes of the destruction of the council house, Nicolson, McKinnon and Telak were on their way.

The road to Bantuk—no road, really, but a graded jungle path barely six feet wide—wound tortuously in and out among palm-oil plantations, tobacco plantations and evil-smelling swamps, waist deep and infinitely treacherous in the darkness. But the way Telak led them that night skirted the road only once, crossed it twice, penetrated straight through swamps and paddy fields and plantations, arrow-straight for the heart of Bantuk. All three men were hurt, and badly: all of them had lost blood, Telak most of all, and no competent doctor would have hesitated to immobilise any of the three in hospital: but they ran all the way to Bantuk, across impossible, energy-sapping, heart-breaking terrain, never once breaking down into a walk. They ran with their hearts pounding madly under the inhuman strain, leaden legs fiery with the pain of muscles taxed far beyond endurance, chests rising and falling, rising and falling as starving lungs gasped for more and still more air, the sweat running off their bodies in streams. They ran and they kept on running, Telak because this was his element and his father lay dead in the village with a Japanese bayonet through his chest, McKinnon because he was still mad with rage and his heart would keep him going until he dropped, Nicolson because he was a man beside himself and all the pain and labour and suffering was happening to someone else.

The second time they crossed the road they saw the Japanese truck, not five yards away in the darkness. They didn't even break stride, there could be no doubt that it was abandoned, that the Japanese had taken their prisoners with them and hurried on on foot towards the town. And the truck had managed to travel much farther than they had expected before it had broken down, at least half-way towards Bantuk, and they had no means of knowing how long ago the Japanese had left it. Nicolson was coldly aware that their chances now were all the poorer, very slender indeed. All of them knew it, but not one of them expressed the thought, suggested that they might ease their killing pace, even if only a fraction. If anything they lengthened their strides and pounded on even more desperately through the darkness.

More than once, after the sight of that truck, pictures flashed into Nicolson's mind of how the Japanese soldiers must be treating their prisoners as they hurried them on fearfully along the jungle path. He had visions of rifle butts, maybe even bayonets, prodding viciously into the sick old captain, stumbling in sheer weakness and weariness, and into Gudrun as she, too, stumbled along in the darkness, cruelly handicapped by the crippling weight of the little boy in her arms— even after half a mile, a two-year old can become an intolerable weight. Or maybe she had dropped young Peter, maybe they had abandoned the little boy in their haste, left him by the side of the jungle, left him surely to die. But the mentor watching over Nicolson's mind that night never let these thoughts stay with him long. They stayed long enough only to spur him on to even greater efforts, never long enough for obsession and ultimate weakness. Throughout all that interminable lurching, gasping run in the darkness, Nicolson's mind remained strangely cold and remote.

It had turned cold, the stars had gone and it was beginning to rain when at last they reached the outskirts of Bantuk. Bantuk was a typical Javanese coastal town, not too big, not too little, a curious intermingling of the old and the new, a blend of Indonesia of a hundred years ago and of Holland ten thousand miles away. On the shore, following the curve of the bay, were the crazy, ramshackle huts erected on long bamboo poles below the highwater mark, with their suspended nets to trap the tidal catch of fish, and half-way along the beach a curved breakwater hooked far out into the bay, sheltering launches and fishing vessels, the tented prahus and the double outrigger canoes too large to be dragged up past the fishing-huts. Paralleling the beach, behind the huts, stretched two or three straggling, haphazard rows of straw-roofed wooden huts as found in the villages in the interior, and behind that again was the shopping and business centre of the community, which led in turn to the houses that stretched back into the gentle valley behind. A typical Dutch suburb, this last, not perhaps with the wide, lined boulevards of Batavia or Medan, but with trim little bungalows and the odd colonial mansion, every one of them with its beautifully kept garden.

It was towards this last section of the town that Telak now led his two companions. They raced through the darkened streets in the middle of the town, making no attempt at concealment, for the time for concealment was past. Few people saw them, for there were few abroad in the rain-washed streets. At first Nicolson thought that the Japanese must have declared a curfew, but soon saw that this was not the case, for a few coffee shops here and there were still open, their smocked Chinese proprietors standing under the awnings at the doorways, watching their passing in an impassive silence.

Half a mile inland from the bay, Telak slowed down to a walk and gestured Nicolson and McKinnon into the sheltered gloom of a high hedge. Ahead of them, not more than fifty yards away, the metalled road they were now standing on ended in a cul-de-sac. The bounding wall was high, arched in the middle, and the archway beneath was illuminated by a pair of electric lanterns. Below the archway itself two men were standing, talking and smoking, each leaning a shoulder against the curving walls. Even at that distance there was no mistaking the grey-green uniforms and hooked caps of the Japanese army, for the light was strong. Behind the archway they could see a drive-way stretching back up the hill, illuminated by lamps every few yards. And beyond that again was a high, white-walled mansion. Little of it was visible through the archway, just a pillared stoop and a couple of big bay windows to one side, both of them brightly lit. Nicolson turned to the gasping man by his side.

" This is it, Telak?" They were the first words spoken since they had left the *kampong*.

" This is the house." Telak's words, like Nicolson's, came in short, jerky gasps. " The biggest in Bantuk."

" Naturally." Nicolson paused to wipe the sweat off his face and chest and arms. Very particularly he dried the palms of his hands. " This is the way they would come?"

" No other way. They are sure to come up this road. Unless they have already come."

" Unless they have already come," Nicolson echoed. For the first time the fear and anxiety swept through his mind like a wave, a fear that would have panicked his mind and an anxiety that would have wrecked his plans but he thrust them ruthlessly aside. " If they've come, it's already too late. If not, we still have time in hand. We may as well get our breath back for a minute or two—we can't go into this more dead than alive. How do you feel, Bo'sun?"

"My hands are itching, sir," McKinnon said softly. "Let's go in now."

"We won't be long," Nicolson promised. He turned to Telak. "Do I see spikes above the walls?"

"You do." Telak's voice was grim. "The spikes are nothing. But they're electrified all the way."

"So this is the only way in?" Nicolson asked softly.

"And the only way out."

"I see. I see indeed." No words were spoken for the next two minutes, there was only the sound of their breathing becoming shallower and more even, the intervals between breaths lengthening all the time. Nicolson waited with an almost inhuman patience, carefully gauging the moment when recovery would be at its maximum but the inevitable reaction not yet set in. Finally he stirred and straightened, rubbing his palms up and down the charred remnants of his khaki drills to remove the last drop of excess moisture, and turned again to Telak.

"We passed a high wall on this side about twenty paces back?"

"We did," Telak nodded.

"With trees growing up behind it, close to the wall?"

"I noticed that also," Telak nodded.

"Let's get back there." Nicolson turned and padded softly along in the shelter of the hedge.

It was all over inside two minutes, and no one more than thirty or forty yards away could have heard the slightest whisper of sound. Nicolson lay on the ground at the foot of the high wall and moaned softly, then more loudly, more pitifully still as his first groans had attracted no attention at all. Within seconds, however, one of the guards started, straightened up and peered anxiously down the road, and a moment later the second guard, his attention caught by an especially anguished moan, did the same. The two men looked at one another, held a hurried consultation, hesitated, then came running down the road, one of them switching on a torch as he came. Nicolson moaned even more loudly, twisted in apparent agony so that his back was to them and so that he could not be so quickly identified as a Westerner. He could see the flickering gleam of bayonets in the swinging light of the torch, and an edgy guard would be just that little bit liable to prefer investigating a corpse to a living enemy, no matter how seriously hurt he might appear to be.

Heavy boots clattering on the metalled road, the two men slithered to a stop, stooped low over the fallen man and died while they were still stooping, the one with a flame-shaped dagger buried to the hilt in his back as Telak dropped off the high wall above, the other as McKinnon's sinewy hands found his neck a bare second after Nicolson had kicked the rifle out of his unsuspecting hand.

Nicolson twisted swiftly to his feet, stared down at the two dead men. Too small, he thought bitterly, far too damned small. He'd hoped for uniforms, for disguise, but neither of these two uniforms would have looked at any of the three of them. There was no time to waste. Telak and himself at wrists and ankles, one swing, two, a powerful boost from McKinnon in the middle and the first of the guards was over the high wall and safely out of sight, five seconds more and the other had joined him. Moments later all three men were inside the grounds of the mansion.

The well-lighted pathway was flanked on both sides by either high bushes or trimmed trees. On the right-hand side, behind the trees, was only the high wall with the electric fence on top: on the other side of the drive-way was a wide, sloping lawn, bare in patches but well-kept and smooth, dotted with small trees irregularly planted in circular plots of earth. Light reached the lawn from the drive-way and the front of the house, but not much. The three men flitted soundlessly across the grass, from the shadowed shelter of one tree to the next until they reached a clump of bushes that bordered the gravel in front of the portico of the house. Nicolson leaned forward and put his mouth to Telak's ear.

" Ever been here before?"

" Never." Telak's murmur was as soft as his own.

" Don't know about any other doors? Never heard if the windows are barred or live-wired or fitted with intruder alarms?"

Telak shook his head in the darkness.

" That settles it," Nicolson whispered. " The front door. They won't be expecting visitors, especially visitors like us, through the front door." He groped at his belt, unhooked the parang Telak had given him and began to straighten up from his kneeling position. " No noise, no noise at all. Quick and clean and quiet. We mustn't disturb our hosts."

He took half a pace forward, choked a muffled exclamation and sank back to his knees again. He had little option. McKinnon, for all his medium height, weighed almost two hundred pounds and was phenomenally strong.

"What is it," Nicolson whispered. He rubbed his burnt forearm in silent agony, certain that McKinnon's digging forefingers had torn off some of the skin.

"Someone coming," McKinnon breathed in his ear. "Must have guards outside."

Nicolson listened a second, then shook his head in the gloom to show that he could hear nothing. For all that he believed the bo'sun—his hearing was on a par with his remarkable eyesight.

"On the verge, not the gravel," McKinnon murmured. "Coming this way. I can take him."

"Leave him alone." Nicolson shook his head strongly. "Too much noise."

"He'll hear us crossing the gravel." McKinnon's voice sank even lower, and Nicolson could hear the man coming now, could hear the soft swish of feet in the wet grass. "There'll be no noise. I promise it."

This time Nicolson nodded and gripped his arm in token of consent. The man was almost opposite them now, and in spite of himself Nicolson shivered. To his certain knowledge this would be the soft-spoken Highland bo'sun's fourth victim that night, and only one of them, so far, had managed to get even a breath of sound past his lips. How long one could live with a man—three years in this case—and not really get to know him . . .

The man was just a foot past them, head turned away as he looked towards the two lighted windows and the far-off murmur of voices from behind them, when McKinnon rose to his feet, noiseless as a wraith, hooked hands closing round the man's neck like a steel trap. He was as good as his word. There was no noise at all, not even the faintest whisper of sound.

They left him behind the bushes and crossed the gravel at a steady, unhurried walk, in case there were still some guards in the grounds to hear them, mounted the steps, crossed the portico and walked unchallenged through the wide open double doors.

Beyond lay a wide hall, softly lit from a central chandelier, with a high, arching roof, walls panelled in what looked like oak, and a gleaming parquetry floor, finely tesselated in jarrah and kauri and some light-coloured tropical hardwoods. From either side of the hall, wide, sweeping staircases, a darker-coloured wood than that of the walls, curved up to meet the broad, pillared balcony that ran the full length of both sides and the back. At the foot of either stairway was a set of double doors, closed, and between them, at the back, a third, single door. All the doors were painted white, lending an incongruous note to the dusky satin of the walls. The door at the back of the hall was open.

Nicolson gestured to McKinnon and Telak to take up position one on either side of the double doors to the right, then padded cat-footed across the hall to the open door at the back. He could feel the cool, hard floor under the pads of his feet; that gruelling cross-country run must have torn off most of what charred remains of canvas soles had been left him after he had carried Van Effen out of the burning council house. His mind registered it automatically, but disregarded it, just as it disregarded the pain of the raw, burnt flesh. There would come a time for suffering, but that time was not yet. That feeling of ice-cold indifference coupled with its razor-edged calculation was with him still, more strongly than ever.

He flattened himself against the far wall, cocked his head in listening, his eyes turned towards the open doorway. At first he could hear nothing, then faintly he caught the far-off murmur of voices and the occasional chink of crockery. The kitchens and the servants' quarters, obviously—and if the men behind these double doors were eating, and they might well be, this being about the hour of the late evening meal, servants would be liable to be coming down that long passage and across the hall at any moment. Nicolson slid noiselessly forward and risked a quick glance round the edge of the door. The passage was dimly lit, about twenty feet in length, with two closed doors on either side and one at the far end, open, showing a white rectangle of light. There was no one to be seen. Nicolson stepped into the passage, felt behind the door, found a key, withdrew it, stepped back out into the entrance hall, pulled the door softly shut behind him and locked it.

He recrossed the hall as softly as he had come and rejoined the others at the white-painted double doors. Both men looked at him as he approached—McKinnon still grim and implacable, his surging anger well under control but ready to explode at any moment, Telak a ghastly, blood-smeared sight under the lights, dusky face drawn and grey with fatigue, but revenge would keep him going for a long time yet. Nicolson whispered a few instructions in Telak's ear, made sure he understood and waited until he had slipped away and hidden himself behind the right-hand staircase.

There was a low murmur of voices from behind the double-doors, a murmur punctuated by an occasional guffaw of laughter. For a few moments Nicolson listened with his ear to the crack between the two doors, then tested each in turn with an infinitely gentle pressure of a probing forefinger. Each yielded an almost imperceptible fraction of an inch, and Nicolson straightened, satisfied. He nodded at McKinnon. The two men lined up the guns at their sides, muzzles just touching the white-painted woodwork in front of them, kicking the doors wide open and walked into the room together.

It was a long, low room, wood-panelled and parquet-floored like the hall, with wide bay windows, mosquito-curtained. The far wall of the room had another, smaller window, and the two doors in the left wall had a long, oaken side-board between them, this last the only wall furnishing. Most of the floor space was taken up by a U-shaped banqueting-table and the chairs of the fourteen men who sat around it. Some of the fourteen were still talking, laughing and drinking from the deep glasses in their hands, oblivious of the entrance of the two men, but, one by one, the sudden silence of the others caught the attention of those who still talked, and they too fell silent, staring towards the door and sitting very still indeed.

For a man allegedly mourning the death of his son, Colonel Kiseki was making a magnificent job of dissembling his sorrow. There was no doubt to his identity. He occupied the ornate, high-backed chair of honour at the top of the table, a short, massive man of tremendous girth, with his neck bulging out over his tight uniform collar, tiny, porcine eyes almost hidden in folds of flesh, and very short black hair, grey at the temples, sticking up from the top of his round head like the bristles of a wire brush. His face was flushed with alcohol, empty bottles littered the table in front of him and the white cloth was stained with spilt wine. He had had his head flung back and been roaring with laughter when Nicolson and McKinnon had entered, but now he was sitting hunched forward in his chair, tightly-gripping fists ivory-knuckled on the arms of his chair, the laughter in his puffy face slowly congealing into an expression of frozen incredulity.

No one spoke, no one moved. The silence in the room was intense. Slowly, watchfully, Nicolson and McKinnon advanced one on either side of the table, the soft padding of their feet only intensifying the uncanny silence, Nicolson to the left McKinnon advancing up by the wide bay windows. And still the fourteen men sat motionless in their seats, only their eyes slowly swivelling as they followed the movements of the two men with the guns. Half-way up the left-hand side of the table Nicolson halted, checked that McKinnon had his eye on the whole table, turned and opened the first door on his left, let the door swing slowly open as soon as it had clicked, swung noiselessly round and took a silent step towards the table. As soon as the door had clicked an officer with his back to him, his hand hidden from McKinnon on the other side, had started to slide a revolver from a side holster and already had the muzzle clear when the butt of Nicolson's automatic rifle caught him viciously just above the right ear. The revolver clattered harmlessly on to the parquet floor and the officer slumped forward heavily on to the table. His head knocked over an almost full bottle of wine and it gurgled away in the unnatural silence until it had almost emptied itself. A dozen pairs of eyes, as if mesmerised by the only moving thing in that room, watched the blood-red stain spread farther and farther across the snow-white cloth. And still no one had spoken.

Nicolson turned again to look through the now open door. A long passage, empty. He shut the door, locked it, turned his attention to the next. A cloak-room lay behind this, small, about six feet square and windowless. This door Nicolson left open.

He went back to the table, moved swiftly down one side of it, searching men for weapons while McKinnon kept his tommy-gun gently circling. As soon as he had finished searching he waited until McKinnon had done the same on his side. The total haul was surprisingly small, a few knives and three revolvers, all of the latter taken from army officers. With the one recovered from the floor that made four in all. Two of these Nicolson gave McKinnon, two he stuck in his own belt. For close, concentrated work the automatic rifle was a far deadlier weapon.

Nicolson walked to the head of the table and looked down at the grossly corpulent man sitting in the central chair.

" You are Colonel Kiseki?"

The officer nodded but said nothing. The astonishment had now vanished, and the watchful eyes were the only sign of expression in an otherwise impassive face. He was on balance again, completely under control. A dangerous man, Nicolson thought bleakly, a man whom it would be fatal to underestimate.

"Tell all these men to put their hands on the table, palm upwards, and to keep them there."

"I refuse." Kiseki folded his arms and leaned back negligently in his chair. "Why should I——" He broke off with a gasp of pain as the muzzle of the automatic rifle gouged deeply into the thick folds of flesh round his neck.

"I'll count three," Nicolson said indifferently. He didn't feel indifferent. Kiseki dead was no good to him. "One. Two——"

"Stop!" Kiseki sat forward in his chair, leaning away from the pressure of the rifle, and started to talk rapidly. Immediately hands came into view all round the table, palms upward as Nicolson had directed.

"You know who we are?" Nicolson went on.

"I know who you are." Kiseki's English was slow and laboured, but sufficient. "From the English tanker *Viroma*. Fools, crazy fools! What hope have you? You may as well surrender now. I promise you——"

"Shut up!" Nicolson nodded at the men sitting on either side of Kiseki, an army officer and a heavy-jowled, dark-faced Indonesian with immaculately waved black hair and a well-cut grey suit. "Who are these men?"

"My second in command and the Mayor of Bantuk."

"The Mayor of Bantuk, eh?" Nicolson looked at the mayor with interest. "Collaborating well, I take it?"

"I don't know what you're talking about." Kiseki looked up at Nicolson through narrowed slits of eyes. "The mayor is a founder, a member of our Greater East Asia co-prosperity——"

"For heaven's sake, shut up!" Nicolson glanced round the others sitting at the table—two or three officers, half-a-dozen Chinese, an Arab and some Javanese—then looked back at Kiseki. "You, your second in command and the Mayor remain here. The rest into that cloakroom there."

"Sir!" McKinnon was calling softly from his place by one of the bay windows. "They're coming up the drive now!"

"Hurry up!" Again Nicolson jammed his rifle into Kiseki's neck. "Tell them. Into that cloakroom. At once!"

"In that box? There is no air." Kiseki pretended horror. "They will suffocate in there."

"Or they can die out here. They can take their choice."

245

Nicolson leaned yet more heavily on the rifle and his fore-finger began to whiten on the trigger. "But not until you go first."

Thirty seconds later the room was still and almost empty, three men only sitting at the head of the banqueting-table. Eleven men were jammed into the tiny cloakroom, and the door was locked against them. McKinnon was pressed flat to the wall close by one of the open double doors, and Nicolson was in the open doorway that led into the side passage. He was placed so that he could see the entrance to the double doors through the crack between his own door and the jamb. He was also placed so that the rifle in his hand was lined up on the centre of Colonel Kiseki's chest. And Colonel Kiseki had had his orders. He'd had his orders, and Colonel Kiseki had lived too long, had seen too many desperate and implacable men not to know that Nicolson would shoot him like a dog even on the suspicion, far less the certainty, that he was being double-crossed. Colonel Kiseki's reputation for cruelty was matched only by his courage, but he was no fool. He intended to carry out his orders implicitly.

Nicolson could hear young Peter crying, a tired, dispirited wail, as the soldiers crossed the gravel and mounted the steps to the portico, and his mouth tightened. Kiseki caught his look and his muscles tensed in expectancy, waiting for the numbing crash of the bullet, then saw Nicolson shake his head and visibly, consciously relax. And then the footsteps had crossed the hall, halted at the doorway, then advanced again as Kiseki shouted out an order. A moment later the Japanese escort—there were six of them altogether—were inside the room, pushing their prisoners in front of them.

Captain Findhorn was in the lead. A soldier held him by either arm, his legs were dragging and he was ashen-faced and drawn, breathing quickly, hoarsely and in great pain. As soon as the soldiers halted they released his arms. He swayed once backwards, once forwards, his bloodshot eyes turned up in his head and he crumpled and folded slowly to the floor, fading into the merciful oblivion of unconsciousness. Gudrun Drachmann was directly behind him, Peter still in her arms. Her dark hair was tangled and dishevelled, the once-white shirt ripped half-way down her back. From where he stood, Nicolson couldn't see her back, but he knew the smooth skin would be pock-marked with blood, for the soldier behind had his bayonet pressed into her shoulders. The impulse to step out from behind the door and empty the automatic rifle's

246

magazine into the man with the bayonet was almost overwhelming, but he crushed it down, stood where he was, still and quiet, looking from Kiseki's impassive face to the smudged, scarred face of the girl. She, too, Nicolson could see now, was swaying slightly, her legs trembling with weariness, but she still held her head proudly and high.

Suddenly Colonel Kiseki barked an order. His men stared at him, uncomprehending. He repeated it almost immediately, smashing the flat of his hand down on the table before him, and at once four of the six men dropped the arms they were carrying on to the parquet floor. A fifth frowned in a slow, stupid fashion, as if still unwilling to believe his ears, looked at his companions, saw their arms on the floor, opened his hand reluctantly and let his rifle crash down on the floor beside the weapons of his comrades. Only the sixth, the man with the bayonet in Gudrun's back, realised that something was very far wrong. He dropped lower into a crouch, glanced wildly round then collapsed to the floor like a stricken tree as Telak came up feather-footed from the hall behind him and smashed his rifle down on the unprotected back of the soldier's head.

And then Nicolson and McKinnon and Telak were all in the room, Telak herding the five Japanese soldiers into a corner, McKinnon kicking the double doors shut and keeping a wary eye on the three men at the table, Nicolson unashamedly hugging the girl and the young boy still in her arms, smiling his delight and immense relief and saying nothing, while Gudrun, stiff-backed and straight, stared at him, for a long, long moment in uncomprehending wonder and disbelief, then sagged heavily against him, her face buried in his shoulder, murmuring his name over and over again. McKinnon was looking at them from time to time, grinning hugely, all the savage anger gone from his face. But he didn't look at them for more than a fraction of a second at a time, and the muzzle of his gun never wavered from the three men at the top of the table.

" Johnny, Johnny! " The girl lifted her head and looked at him, the intensely blue eyes now shining and misted, rolling tear-drops cutting through the dark smudges on her cheek. She was shivering now, shivering from reaction and from the cold of her wet rain-soaked clothes, but she was quite oblivious of all that. The happiness in her eyes was something that Nicolson had never seen before. " Oh, Johnny, I thought it was all finished. I thought that Peter and I——" She broke

247

off and smiled at him again. "How in the world did you get here? I—I don't understand. How did you?"

"Private aeroplane." Nicolson waved an airy hand. "It was no trouble. But later, Gudrun. We must hurry. Bo'sun?"

"Sir?" McKinnon carefully removed the smile from his face.

"Tie up our three friends at the head of the table there. Their wrists only. Behind their backs."

"Tie us up!" Kiseki leaned forward, his fists clenched on the table top. "I see no need——"

"Shoot 'em if you have to," Nicolson ordered. "They're no use to us any more." He thought it as well not to add that Kiseki's usefulness was yet to come but feared that the knowledge of his intentions might provoke the man to an act of desperation.

"Consider it done, sir." McKinnon advanced purposefully towards them, tearing down several mosquito curtains as he passed. Twisted, they would make excellent ropes. Nicolson turned away from Gudrun after seeing her and Peter into a chair, and stooped low over the captain. He shook him by the shoulder and Findhorn finally stirred and wearily opened his eyes. Aided by Nicolson he sat up, moving like a very old man and gazed slowly round the room, comprehension slowly dawning on his exhausted mind.

"I don't know how on earth you did it, but well done, my boy." He looked back at Nicolson, inspected him from head to toe, wincing as he saw the cuts and savage burns on his chief officer's legs and forearms. "What a bloody mess! I hope to God you don't feel half as bad as you look."

"Top of the world," sir," Nicolson grinned.

"You're a fluent liar, Mr. Nicolson. You're as much a hospital case as I am. Where do we go from here?"

"Away, and very shortly. A few minutes, sir. Some little things to attend to first."

"Then go by yourselves." Captain Findhorn was half-joking, wholly earnest. "I think I'd rather take my chance as a prisoner of war. Frankly, my boy, I've had it, and I know it. I couldn't walk another step."

"You won't have to, sir. I guarantee it." Nicolson poked an inquiring toe at the bag one of the soldiers had been carrying, stooped and had a look inside. "Even brought the plans and the diamonds right here. But then, where else would they bring them? I hope, Colonel Kiseki, that you hadn't set your heart too much on these?"

248

Kiseki stared at him, his face expressionless. Gudrun Drachmann drew in a quick breath.

"So that's Colonel Kiseki!" She looked at him for a long moment, then shivered. "I can see that Captain Yamata was right enough. Thank God you got here first, Johnny."

"Captain Yamata!" Kiseki's eyes small enough normally in the folds of fat, had almost vanished. "What happened to Captain Yamata?"

"Captain Yamata has joined his ancestors," Nicolson said briefly. "Van Effen shot him almost in half."

"You're lying! Van Effen was our friend, our very good friend."

"'Was' is right," Nicolson agreed. "Ask your men here—later." He nodded to the group still cowering under the menace of Telak's rifle. "Meantime, send one of these men to collect a stretcher, blankets and torches. I needn't warn you what will happen if you try any foolish tricks."

Kiseki looked at him impassively for a moment, then spoke rapidly to one of his men. Nicolson waited until he had gone then turned again to Kiseki.

"You must have a radio in this house. Where is it?"

For the first time Kiseki smiled, displaying a magnificent collection of gold inlays on his front teeth.

"I'm sorry to disappoint you, Mr.—ah——"

"Nicolson. Never mind the formalities. The radio, Colonel Kiseki."

"That is the only one we have." Grinning more broadly still, Kiseki nodded towards the sideboard. He had to nod. McKinnon had already lashed his wrists behind his back.

Nicolson barely glanced at the small receiver.

"Your transmitter, Colonel Kiseki, if you don't mind," Nicolson said softly. "You don't depend on carrier pigeons for communication, do you?"

"English humour. Ha-ha. Very funny indeed." Kiseki was still smiling. "Of course we have a transmitter, Mr.—ah—Nicolson. At the barracks, our soldiers' quarters."

"Where?"

"The other end of the town." Kiseki had the appearance of a man actually enjoying himself. "A mile from here. At least a mile."

"I see." Nicolson looked thoughtful. "Too far—and I very much doubt my ability to march you into your own barracks at the point of a gun, destroy a transmitter and get out again—not without getting myself killed in the process."

"You show signs of wisdom, Mr. Nicolson," Kiseki purred.

"I'm just not suicidally minded." Nicolson rubbed his stubble of beard with a forefinger, then looked up at Kiseki again. "And that's the only transmitter in town, eh?"

"It is. You'll have to take my word for that."

"I'll take your word for it." Nicolson lost interest in the matter, watched McKinnon finish tying up the other officer with an enthusiastic heave that brought a sharp exclamation of pain, then turned as the soldier sent off by the colonel returned with stretcher, blankets and two torches. Then he looked back at the head of the table, first at Kiseki, then at the civilian by his side. The mayor was trying to look indignant and outraged, but only succeeded in looking scared. There was unmistakable fear in his dark eyes, and there was a violent tic at the corner of his mouth. He was sweating freely, and even the beautifully cut grey suit seemed to have become suddenly limp . . . Nicolson switched his glance back to Kiseki.

"The mayor is a good friend of yours, I take it, Colonel?" He could see the look in McKinnon's eyes as he busied himself with the mayor's wrists, the look of a man anxious to be gone and impatient of this talk, but he ignored it.

Kiseki cleared his throat pompously. "In our—what is the word?—capacities as commander of the garrison and the representative of the people we naturally——"

"Spare me the rest," Nicolson interrupted. "I suppose his duties bring him here quite often." He was looking at the mayor now, a deliberately contemptuous speculation in his eyes, and Kiseki fell for it.

"Comes here?" Kiseki laughed. "My dear Nicolson, this *is* the mayor's house. I am only his guest."

"Indeed?" Nicolson looked at the mayor. "You speak a few words of English perhaps, Mr. Mayor."

"I speak it perfectly." Pride momentarily overcame fear.

"Excellent," Nicolson said dryly. "How about speaking some now?" His voice dropped an octave to a calculated theatrically low growl: the mayor didn't look as if he would take much terrifying. "Where does Colonel Kiseki keep his transmitter in this house?"

Kiseki swung round on the mayor, his face suffused with anger at being tricked, started to shout something unintelligible at him, stopped short in mid-torrent as McKinnon cuffed him heavily over the ear.

"Don't be a fool, Colonel," Nicolson said wearily. "And

don't insist on treating me like a fool. Who ever heard of a military commander, especially in a red-hot, troubled area such as this is bound to be, having his communications centre a mile from where he is himself? Obviously the transmitter's here, and just as obviously it would take all night to make you talk. I doubt if the mayor's willing to make such sacrifices for your precious co-prosperity sphere." He turned to the frightened looking civilian again. " I'm in a hurry. Where is it?"

" I will say nothing." The mayor's mouth worked and twisted even when he wasn't speaking. " You can't make me talk."

" You're not even kidding yourself." Nicolson looked at McKinnon. " Just kind of twist his arm, will you, Bo'sun?"

McKinnon twisted. The mayor screamed, more in anticipatory fear than in any real pain. McKinnon slackened his grip.

" Well?"

" I don't know what you were talking about."

This time McKinnon didn't have to be told. He jerked the mayor's right arm high up until the back of his wrist was flat against the shoulder-blade. The mayor shrieked like a pig at the approach of the poleaxe.

" Upstairs." The mayor was sobbing with pain and fear— chiefly fear. " On the roof. My arm—you've broken my arm!"

" You can finish tying him up now, Bo'sun." Nicolson turned away in disgust. " Right, Colonel, you can lead the way."

" My gallant friend here can finish the job." Kiseki spat the words out. His teeth were tightly clenched and the expression on his face boded ill for the mayor should they meet again in different circumstances. " He can show you where it is."

" No doubt. But I would prefer you to come. Some of your men might be wandering about with machine-guns and I'm quite sure they wouldn't hesitate to shoot the mayor and myself full of a lot of little holes. But you're a foolproof life insurance." Nicolson transferred his rifle to his left hand, pulled one of the revolvers from his belt and checked that the safety-catch was off. " I'm in a hurry, Colonel. Come on."

They were back inside five minutes. The transmitter was now a havoc of twisted steel and shattered valves, and they had encountered no one, coming or going. The mayor's screams appeared to have attracted no attention, possibly because of the closed doors, but more probably, Nicolson suspected, because the staff were well accustomed to such sounds emanating from Kiseki's rooms.

McKinnon had not been idle in his absence. Captain Findhorn, covered with blankets and holding a rather fearful Peter Tallon in his arms, was lying comfortably on the stretcher on the floor. A Japanese soldier squatted at each of the four corners of the stretcher, and closer inspection showed that they hadn't much option: the bo'sun had tied their wrists securely to the handles. The mayor and Kiseki's second in command were tied together by a short length of rope linking their right and left elbows respectively. Telak's victim still lay on the floor and Nicolson suspected that he would be there for a long time to come. There was no sign of the sixth man.

"Very nice indeed, Bo'sun." Nicolson looked round approvingly. "Where's our missing friend?"

"He's not really missing, sir. He's in the cloakroom there." Ignoring Kiseki's scowls and protests, McKinnon was busy securing him to the mayor's left elbow. "It was a bit of a job getting the door shut, but I managed it."

"Excellent." Nicolson took a last look round the room. "No point in waiting any longer, then. Let's be on our way."

"Where are we going?" Kiseki had his feet planted wide, his huge head hunched far down into his shoulders. "Where are you taking us?"

"Telak tells me that your personal launch is the finest and fastest for a hundred miles up and down the coast. We'll be through the Sunda Straits and into the Indian Ocean long before the dawn comes."

"What!" Kiseki's face was contorted in fury. "You're taking my launch! You'll never get away with it, Englishman, you'll never get away with it." He paused, another and even more shocking thought occurred to him and he lunged forward across the parquet floor, dragging the other two behind him and kicking out at Nicolson in berserk anger. "You're taking me with you, damn you, you're taking me with you!"

"Of course. What else did you think?" Nicolson said coldly. He stepped back a couple of paces to avoid the flailing feet and jabbed the muzzle of his rifle, none too gently into Kiseki's midriff, just below the breast-bone. Kiseki doubled up in agony. "You're our one guarantee of a safe-conduct. We'd be madmen to leave you behind."

"I won't go," Kiseki gasped. "I won't go. You can kill

me first, but I won't go. Concentration camps! Prisoner-of-war of the English! Never, never, never! You can kill me first!"

"It won't be necessary to kill you." Nicolson pointed out. "We can tie you, gag you, even take you on a stretcher if we have to." He nodded at the cloakroom door. "Plenty of cheap labour in there. But it would only complicate matters. You can come on your feet or you can come on a stretcher with a couple of bullet holes in your legs to quieten you down."

Kiseki looked at the pitiless face and made his choice. He came on his feet.

*   *   *

On their way down to the jetty they met no Japanese soldiers, no one at all. A windless night, but the rain was falling heavily, persistently, and the streets of Bantuk were deserted. At long, long last, luck was turning their way.

Vannier and the others were already aboard the launch. There had been only one man on guard, and Telak and his men had been as silent as the night. Van Effen was already asleep in a bunk below, and Walters was just about to begin transmission. Forty-four feet long and with a fourteen-foot beam, the launch gleamed and shone even in the rain and the darkness and was ready for instant departure.

Willoughby took over the engine-room and almost drooled with sheer joy at the sight of the big, immaculately kept twin diesels. Gordon and Evans loaded another half-dozen drums of fuel oil on to the deck aft. And McKinnon and Vannier were already making a round of the larger vessels behind the breakwater, checking for radio sets, smashing the magneto of the only other launch in the harbour.

They left at exactly ten o'clock at night, purring gently out into a sea as smooth as a mill-pond. Nicolson had begged Telak to accompany them, but he had refused, saying that his place was with his people. He had gone up the long jetty without as much as a backward glance, and Nicolson knew they would never see him again.

As they moved out into the darkness, the four Japanese soldiers, still lashed to the stretchers, ran pell-mell up the vanishing jetty, shouting at the tops of their high-pitched voices. But their cries were abruptly lost, drowned in a sudden clamour of sound as the launch rounded the point of the

253

breakwater, the twin throttles jammed wide open, and headed south-west under maximum power towards Java Head and the Indian Ocean beyond.

They rendezvoused with H.M.A.S. *Kenmore*, a Q-class destroyer, at half-past two in the morning.

THE END

DESMOND BAGLEY

"The fastest-developing writer in the thriller business."
Gavin Lyall

LANDSLIDE

A powerful new story set in the remote fastnesses of
British Columbia. "Very much of the moment . . . as
solid as the clay that starts the landslide is unstable."
Sunday Times

THE GOLDEN KEEL

Peter Halloran is hurtled into a maelstrom of greed and
murder, when he hatches a plot to hi-jack Mussolini's
gold. "Catapults him straight into the Alistair MacLean
bracket." *Sunday Times*

WYATT'S HURRICANE

David Wyatt, civilian weather expert on board a U.S.
Naval aircraft, battles against seemingly impossible
odds when a ferocious hurricane threatens a Caribbean
island. "A tautly written novel of adventure and suspense, packed with exhaustive detail." *Books and
Bookmen*

HIGH CITADEL

High in the peaks of the Andes a passenger plane is hi-
jacked and forced down. "Mr. Bagley at his typewriter
can obviously smell thunder and feel snow underfoot—
and make us feel it too." *Gavin Lyall*

All available in Fontana Books

GEOFFREY JENKINS

A TWIST OF SAND

A compelling story of the sea—and the sinister shores of the Skeleton Coast. "Superb. The best of its genre in a decade." *New York Herald Tribune*

A GRUE OF ICE

Thompson Island holds large deposits of the world's rarest metal—and only one man knows its exact position . . . "Hurtles into a maelstrom of action and suspense. Memorable . . . vivid . . . fantastic." *Ian Fleming*

HUNTER KILLER

A top-secret, missile-launching project; a nuclear submarine; a V.I.P. scientist: some of the ingredients in this riveting thriller, set in the uncharted coral seas of the Indian Ocean. "From the first burial at sea to the final radio message the author keeps the action at hurricane velocity." *New York Times*

THE RIVER OF DIAMONDS

A mining expedition is under way, in search of vast quantities of diamonds on the sea-bed off S.W. Africa. But one man is determined to block the success of the operation. "One of the best adventure stories for a long time." *Sunday Times*

All available in Fontana Books